"I have to get the shop open by the end of April."

If she failed…

No, Mattie couldn't.

She heard Benjamin say, "I'll help." Her dismay must have been visible on her face because he added, "That's why I came over today. Your cousin Mark asked for extra hands to help."

"That's good news," the paramedic said in a chirpy tone. "Let's get you to the hospital and get you x-rayed."

As soon as Mattie sat, the paramedics raised the gurney and began pushing it toward the ambulance.

"Wait a minute!" she cried. "I can't leave my sister."

"I'll watch her," Benjamin said, walking over to the vehicle. "Like I said, I'm helping get this place into shape. Isn't that right, Mattie?"

She wanted to say she didn't need his help, but that would have been a lie. Before the stack of boards had fallen, she'd been praying God would send her help. He had, and she couldn't let her pride get in the way. Benjamin would be there only a short time. She could live with the open wound from her past until the shop opened.

Couldn't she?

Jo Ann Brown loves stories with happily-ever-after endings. A former military officer, she is thrilled to write about finding that forever love all over again with her characters. She and her husband (her real hero, who knows how to fix computer problems quickly when she's on deadline) divide their time between Western Massachusetts and Amish country in Pennsylvania. She loves hearing from readers, so drop her a note at joannbrownbooks.com.

Living on a remote self-sufficient homestead in North Idaho, **Patrice Lewis** is a Christian wife, mother, author, blogger, columnist and speaker. She has practiced and written about rural subjects for almost thirty years. When she isn't writing, Patrice enjoys self-sufficiency projects, such as animal husbandry, small-scale dairy production, gardening, food preservation and canning, and homeschooling. She and her husband have been married since 1990 and have two daughters.

JO ANN BROWN

&

PATRICE LEWIS

An Amish New Beginning

2 Uplifting Stories

Building Her Amish Dream and
The Amish Animal Doctor

LOVE INSPIRED
INSPIRATIONAL ROMANCE

LOVE INSPIRED®
INSPIRATIONAL ROMANCE

Recycling programs
for this product may
not exist in your area.

ISBN-13: 978-1-335-45455-3

An Amish New Beginning

Copyright © 2023 by Harlequin Enterprises ULC

Building Her Amish Dream
First published in 2022. This edition published in 2023.
Copyright © 2022 by Jo Ann Ferguson

The Amish Animal Doctor
First published in 2022. This edition published in 2023.
Copyright © 2022 by Patrice Lewis

For questions and comments about the quality of this book, please contact us at CustomerService@Harlequin.com.

Love Inspired
22 Adelaide St. West, 41st Floor
Toronto, Ontario M5H 4E3, Canada
www.LoveInspired.com

Printed in U.S.A.

CONTENTS

BUILDING HER AMISH DREAM

Jo Ann Brown

For Lisa, Shannon and Jeanine

My nieces who are each superstars
in their own unique way

To every thing there is a season,
and a time to every purpose under the heaven.
—*Ecclesiastes* 3:1

Chapter One

Shushan Bay, Prince Edward Island

He was going to be late.

No, he was already late.

Benjamin Kuhns grimaced as he hurried along the road that edged the narrow beach following Shushan Bay on the southeastern corner of Prince Edward Island. He shouldn't have stopped, though it'd been just for a moment, to admire the soft lapping of the waves on the incredible red sand or to watch birds embroidering their patterns through the sky. Then his eyes had been caught by lovely maple trees along the road. Their bare branches rocked in the wintry March breeze coming off the bay.

Maple was his favorite wood to use in the woodworking shop he'd built among the trees behind the house he shared with his brother in Harmony Creek Hollow. Making clocks was his secret pleasure because his brother would think it was a waste of wood. For the past few months, Benjamin had been wondering if he could make a living selling his creations, but he hadn't done anything about it.

Not yet.

If he tried and it didn't work out, that dream would be gone. He wasn't sure how many more dreams he could watch die.

And he was late. Being late was something he hated, but today it was more important.

"Time is short," his friend James Streicher had said when Benjamin agreed to help James's new neighbor Mark Yutzy from Ontario do repair work on the farm shop he'd bought with his cousins. James had planned to help as well this morning, but a delivery for James's new blacksmith shop had arrived, more than a week late. While James oversaw the setup of his new forge, Benjamin had decided to get out of the way and help the Yutzys.

According to James, the five cousins had to have the shop opened in less than two months. He hadn't explained why, but Benjamin guessed the cousins had sunk all their money into the project. Like James, the cousins had moved to Canada's smallest province in the last few weeks. The new residents were working together to get their businesses up and running so they could attract people to their settlement.

When James had invited Benjamin to travel from northern New York to help establish his smithy, Benjamin had discovered his friend had an ulterior motive. James hoped Benjamin would put down roots in Prince Edward Island, or the Island as locals called it. His friend had already discovered there was a farm for sale about ten miles away. Or sixteen kilometers, he reminded himself, knowing that Canadians used the metric system. The farm was suitable for growing Christmas trees. Since Benjamin had enjoyed selling trees in New York, James had assumed he'd be excited to do the same in Canada.

The truth was that Benjamin hadn't come to the island to see a tree farm, though he'd look at it to placate his friend. He'd come to get away from his brother. Menno believed, as the oldest, he could tell his brother and sister what do to and how to do it. Their sister, Sarah, had stopped listening to him and found the life she wanted with the man she loved. She'd urged Benjamin to follow his heart.

Benjamin was trying. For too long, he'd put off having the adventures he'd craved since he was a kid. He'd tried once, but that had ended in disaster when his heart had led him to a woman who let him believe she shared his values long enough for him to fall in love while she was being courted by another man. She'd used him to make the other guy jealous. Worst, he'd thought her family's welcome was genuine, that they approved of him walking out with Sharrell. How completely they'd fooled him!

His thoughts were interrupted by a shout. "Hey, mister! Help! Hey, mister! Help! Help! Mattie's hurt. Hey, mister! Help!"

The frantic voice came from his left on the opposite side of the road from the bay. A young voice. A scared voice.

He ran toward an opening in the trees that had been planted as a windbreak. In astonishment, he stared at the ruins of a trio of Quonset huts set on a small hill. The two at the rear of the much bigger one were nothing but curved spines. Garbage was piled around them, overgrown by grass and weeds and briars. The bigger one wasn't in much better shape, though it had its metal skin, dulled by sand and wind and salt.

Benjamin saw a teenager rolling a wheelchair toward him. A plain teenager, wearing a *kapp* that bounced on her head as she shoved on the wheels. Her black wool coat was unbuttoned. What was she doing near these ruins?

He put out his hands to keep her from rolling past him, but he needn't have bothered. She brought the chair to a stop with skill he wouldn't have expected for a *kind* with Down syndrome.

"What's wrong?" he asked.

Her panicked eyes searched his face. "The wood fell. She tried to stop it. It fell on my sister. She's not moving. Help!"

"Where?"

She pointed toward the largest Quonset hut.

He groaned. He couldn't help it. From where he stood, the place looked like a tsunami had swept out of the calm bay to propel debris through the double front doors. Why had the kid's sister gone inside?

"Where in the building is she?"

"About halfway in." Without a pause, she added, "My name's Daisy." She picked up the doll on her lap. "This is Boppi Lynn. She's scared for Mattie."

"Your sister is Mattie?"

"*Ja.* Can you help her?"

"Wait here. I'll find her." He edged around her. Over his shoulder, he added, "My name is Benjamin."

He heard wheels and turned to see Daisy right behind him.

"I can help you find her," the girl said.

He had no idea how she'd maneuvered the chair the first time through the hulking stacks of boards and broken pieces of wallboard. A single bump could have collapsed the whole pile. He couldn't let her risk it again. "Stay here. I'll call you if I can't find her."

"Promise?"

He heard distrust in her voice, and he had to wonder how many people had made vows to Daisy and then broken them.

Putting his hands on the arms of her chair, he leaned forward until his eyes were level with hers that were the same deep blue as the bay. "I promise, Daisy. If I need help, I'll call you. In the meantime, stay here and if you see someone passing by, try to get them to stop in case we need more help. Okay?"

"Okay."

Benjamin gave her a grim grin, then ran to the Quonset hut. Half the glass in the two windows on either side of the door was missing. The remaining panes cracked.

The damage was more extensive inside. Though the building was open, the interior reeked of mold and mildew. Shelves had fallen into piles of broken timber. He looked at the half-dozen skylights marching from the front of the building that was large enough to hold two hay wagons pulled by full teams. Only one skylight was intact. Vines were growing from the openings. The floor tiles had been loosened, sitting at odd angles across the space between the front door and a wall of cardboard boxes. Was the destruction as bad beyond the boxes? He couldn't imagine how it could be worse.

What had happened? Was the damage intentional or the result of neglect?

Glass crunched under his work boots. "Mattie?"

No answer came.

He raised his voice and shouted again. Once. Twice.

After the third time, he heard a soft sound. Not an answer. More like a moan.

"Mattie?" he yelled.

"Is she all right?" called Daisy.

He saw her silhouetted in the doorway. "Wait there. You need to be quiet, so I can hear your sister's answer."

"Quiet. I'll be quiet. Quiet. Right."

Under other circumstances, he would have grinned at her chatter to confirm she'd be silent, but that faint moan had unnerved him. How badly was Daisy's sister hurt?

He inched forward, watching out for nails in the boards. His boots were thick enough to protect him from broken glass, but long nails could puncture his foot on one careless step.

Benjamin called Mattie's name again. This time the moan was a bit louder. To his left. Beyond the wall of boxes. Keeping his gaze on the floor, he rounded the end.

His breath caught when he saw who was lying on the other side with boards scattered over her. Not a *kind* as he'd imagined from Daisy's terrified voice. Not a teenager like the girl, but a woman. She was on the cold concrete floor, her eyes closed. She must be a full head shorter than he was. Her hair was the color of spun sunshine. Her white *kapp* was askew, and her black apron over a dark purple dress was littered with dirt from the moldy lumber.

Her cheeks were round, but gray. Above them, her brow was furrowed with lines of pain, and a large bruise was already darkening near her left temple. The length of wood beside her must have struck her, knocking her senseless.

He knelt to examine the boards that had tumbled onto her. He guessed she'd managed to jump away because only a few lay on top of her. Through God's grace, she hadn't been pierced by any of the rusty nails protruding from the wood. Some were grazing her, so he must be careful when he lifted them away in a bizarre and dangerous game of pick-up sticks. Worse, he had to make sure none of the other teetering boards cascaded on them.

"Daisy?" The woman's voice was a whisper.

"She's outside. She's fine," he said to reassure her. "Don't move."

"Don't…?" Her eyes, which could define the color blue, popped open, and she started to raise her left hand to shield them from the light pouring through a broken skylight. She halted with a moan.

"What hurts?"

"My shoulder." With quivering fingers, she tried to reach her left shoulder, but boards blocked her way. "What happened?"

"It looks as if a stack of wood fell on you. Let me get them off."

"I can—"

"You need to be as still as you can while I move the boards."

He half expected her to protest further, but she was more patient than he guessed he could have been if their circumstances had been reversed. He checked each board before he shifted it. Praying he wouldn't make a mistake and cause her more harm, he kept working.

Breathing another prayer, this one of gratitude, as he

tossed aside the last board, he helped her sit. She hung her head and sighed with obvious pain. He guessed she'd have a lot more bruises in addition to the one on her head.

"Daisy?" she murmured. "Are you all right?"

"She's fine. She's waiting outside."

"I should—" Another moan slipped past her pursed lips as she continued to stare at the floor. "My shoulder. It hurts. Really bad."

"You need to see a *doktor*. Is there one nearby?"

She started to shrug, then groaned. "I don't know. I moved here two days ago." She opened her eyes, and he wondered if they were able to focus because she swayed. "Don't you know where there's one?"

"No."

"Daisy has our cell phone." She closed her eyes and cupped her left elbow with her right hand. Gritting her teeth, she said, "For emergencies."

"I'll get it."

"Danki..."

"Benjamin," he supplied as he got to his feet. Before he could add more, he heard rubber tires on the concrete floor. "Don't come over here," he said at the same time Mattie did.

His and Mattie's eyes met for the first time, and a zing of recognition cut like a bolt of lightning through him. A woman named Mattie with a sister who had Down syndrome. Sharrell Albrecht, the woman who'd led him on and broken his naive heart had a younger sister named Mattie and another sister with Down syndrome. Had her name been Daisy? He'd been so caught in his fantasy of having found his perfect woman that he hadn't paid much attention to Sharrell's siblings. But he remembered Mattie, who'd made sure he had an extra piece of pie or the last cookie. She'd had blond hair.

Like this woman.

She'd had apple-round cheeks.

Like this woman.

She'd had bright blue eyes.

Like this woman.

Bile filled his throat as he asked, "Mattie? Is your name Mattie Albrecht?"

He prayed she'd say no. He'd spent the last five years pushing aside his vexation with his brother's dictates and living under Menno's thumb so he could try to bury his horrible, humiliating memories about how Sharrell and her family had duped him.

Had that hiding from his own shame for failing to see what had been right in front of him been for nothing?

Trying to focus on shallow breaths, so the pain in her left shoulder didn't sear across her collarbone, Mattie Albrecht struggled to keep the darkness nibbling at the edge of her vision from sucking her into it. How could she have gotten injured *now*? She, her sister and their three cousins had come to Prince Edward Island to make a fresh start in the new plain settlement. Mark Yutzy was their unspoken leader, though he was a year younger than Mattie. Lucas and Juan Kuepfer had joined them, pooling what funds they had to buy three farms. With what had been left, they'd purchased the ruined building and two rusting greenhouses. Before she'd left Ontario, they'd assured her that she could easily get all three buildings repaired, then she'd seen the reality this morning.

A shudder raced through her, and she couldn't hold

back the moan as her shoulder resonated in agony. How could her cousins expect her and Daisy to get the shop open by the end of April, just over seven weeks away? After running a farm stand which sold vegetables, baked goods and a few craft items at her family's farm in Ontario, she'd been the obvious choice to handle the shop. She had a lot to learn, but knew getting items ordered and displayed would require weeks, even if the shop had been in pristine condition. As it was...

She groaned again, but not because of the pain. How was she going to do the impossible? If she failed to turn a profit quickly, there wouldn't be enough money left for payments on the farm mortgages. She'd be letting her cousins down as well as her own family.

"Are you?" asked the man who'd pulled the lumber off her. His deep voice pounded against her skull and her damaged shoulder.

"Am I what?" she whispered, wishing he'd speak more quietly.

"Are you Mattie Albrecht?"

Wondering why her name was important to him, she said, "*Ja.*"

He muttered something under his breath, but turned to her sister who peeked around the stacked boxes. "I need your phone."

"Mattie says it's for emergencies," Daisy said.

"Your sister is hurt. Isn't that an emergency?"

"If Mattie says so. If she says it's an emergency, I can use the phone."

"Daisy, let him use the phone," Mattie urged.

Her sister didn't take offense at the sharp edge on her voice. Daisy seldom did, though she'd faced many challenges in the fourteen years since she'd been born with

Down syndrome and then lost her ability to walk after jumping from the hayloft when she was ten years old. Her round face was usually lit with a smile. It glittered in her blue eyes. Her hair, several shades lighter than Mattie's, was as soft as milkweed and refused to stay beneath her *kapp*. Its wisps framed her pudgy cheeks and wove along her *kapp*'s strings.

Pain swelled over Mattie again, and she almost sank into the darkness. From beyond it, she heard the rumble of Benjamin's voice and Daisy's lighter one. She wasn't sure when she curled up again on the cold concrete floor, but her head had become too heavy for her left shoulder. With her hand under her right cheek, she closed her eyes as hot contorting lines of pain ricocheted down her left arm.

Seconds, minutes, hours... Mattie had no idea how much later she heard new voices. They were cautioning each other to be careful around the debris.

Someone patted her cheek and called her name. Grateful the person hadn't touched her shoulder, she looked at a woman who was wearing a uniform.

"Can you sit, Mattie?" the woman asked.

"I think so."

"Let me help you."

She was about to say she was fine, but she wasn't. Even with the woman's help, she collapsed as she moved her left shoulder. If she couldn't sit on her own, how was she going to get the shop open in a little more than seven weeks? Tears sprang into her eyes as she imagined her cousins losing their farms because she'd been as clumsy as usual.

Telling the woman what had happened and where

she hurt, she looked around for her sister. As if she'd spoken aloud, the woman reassured her Daisy was fine.

"Your name?" asked a man.

Mattie was about to reply when she realized the man who held a small computer was speaking to Benjamin. The man and the woman must be paramedics.

"Benjamin Kuhns." Benjamin answered.

No!

She started to jerk her head, but froze when agony raced along every nerve again. Shifting her eyes, she peered through her eyelashes at the man beside Daisy's wheelchair.

Pain must have blinded her. Otherwise, she would have recognized the man who'd filled too many of her dreams during the past five years. He'd walked out with Sharrell, paying no attention to Mattie. She hadn't been surprised that he never noticed her. Men noticed Sharrell who knew the right thing to say and moved with a birdlike grace.

Mattie, on the other hand, had never stood out among her eight siblings. She fumbled with words when she was nervous. She wasn't graceful. Everyone joked it was easy to figure out where to sweep the floor because Mattie could trip over the smallest crumb.

Benjamin's dark brown eyes focused on the male paramedic. She couldn't let him guess how she'd wished he'd look at her the way he had Sharrell. That had been before her sister had married another man while *Mamm* had been planning, after more than sixty years of the plain life, to jump the fence and abandon her husband and family.

"Can you move your arm without pain?" asked the female paramedic.

Mattie focused her eyes on the woman's name tag. Erin. She kept her gaze on it as she tried to obey the paramedic's request. Any motion brought torment.

"I think you're going to need to have that shoulder x-rayed because it might be dislocated," Erin said. "Let me help you get up."

As she did, Mattie asked, "If my shoulder's dislocated, how long will it take to heal?"

"It's hard to say before a doctor can see what's happened in there. If muscles or tendons were damaged, it can be a month or two before you can have full use of the arm again."

"A month or two?" The words came out in a frightened squeak. "I don't have a month or two. I've got to get the Celtic Knoll Farm Shop open again."

From where he stood beside her sister, Benjamin gasped. "*This* is the farm shop?"

She grimaced as Erin guided her toward the door. Her foot caught on the edge of a board and her heel dropped to the concrete floor, jarring every bone. Swallowing her pain, she said in a strangled voice, "It will be once we get it cleaned."

"Honey," Erin said, steering her around another pile of wood that glittered with pieces of broken glass, "you aren't going to be doing any cleaning anytime soon. You need to give that shoulder time to heal."

"But I have to get the shop open by the end of April."

If she failed…

No, she couldn't.

As she emerged into the sunshine to see an ambulance parked in front of the shop, she heard Benjamin say, "I'll help." Her dismay at the idea of him hanging around must have been visible on her face because he added, "That's why I came over today. Your cousin Mark asked for extra hands to help."

The paramedics exchanged a look that was easy to read. They thought it would be impossible to make the Quonset hut into anything other than the garbage dump it was.

"That's good news," Erin said in a chirpy tone as she motioned toward the lowered stretcher beside the door. "Let's get you to the hospital and get you x-rayed, and maybe you'll get more good news."

As soon as Mattie sat and swung her feet onto the sheet, the paramedics raised the gurney and began pushing it toward the ambulance.

"Wait a minute!" she cried. "I can't leave Daisy."

"I'll watch her," Benjamin said, walking over to the vehicle. "And I'll bring her over to your house. I'm sure she'll want to be there when you come home."

"Don't leave her alone."

"I won't."

Mattie's uncertainty must have been on her face, because Erin asked, "Is that okay with you if your sister goes with him?"

"She knows me, ain't so?" He scowled at Mattie as if daring her to deny the truth. "Like I said, I'm helping get this place into shape. Isn't that right, Mattie?"

She wanted to say she didn't need his help, but that would have been a lie. Before the stack of boards had fallen, she'd been praying God would send her help. He had, and she couldn't let her pride get in the way of making sure the plans she and her cousins had made succeeded. Benjamin would be there only a short time.

She could live with the open wound from her past until the shop opened.

Couldn't she?

Chapter Two

Mattie had barely noticed anything about the bustling hospital when brought in by the paramedics. The slight bounce as the gurney had gone over the threshold at the entrance to the emergency room had slammed more pain across her left shoulder. She'd thought she heard a soft "Sorry," but hadn't been sure as she fought to hold on to consciousness as darkness licked at the edges of her vision.

After she'd been wheeled into a space filled with equipment she didn't recognize, she'd rested her head against the pillow and stared at the ceiling light. The paramedics had moved her to another table, and she almost fainted at the agony. She'd started to nod when they said the *doktor* would be in soon, but the motion was too much.

She managed to breathe her thanks before they'd left. She'd struggled to sit, but the pain had been too much and she'd collapsed against the pillow. Breathing shallowly had seemed to help, so she did, taking care not to move.

Two hours later, she sat in a wheelchair in the waiting

room. Her left arm was in a sling, and her head wobbled as she fought to focus her eyes. She hadn't wanted to take pain medication, but the no-nonsense nurse had insisted before taking Mattie to have her shoulder x-rayed.

Mattie had to admit the nurse had been right. Having her dislocated shoulder shifted into place by the *doktor* who apologized for hurting her would have been excruciating without medicine to soften the serrated edges of pain.

The whole procedure had felt like a bad dream. She'd heard questions, but it had seemed to take hours before her brain could send an answer to her lips. Her voice had sounded odd and her words garbled. The *doktor* must have gotten the answers he needed because he arranged for her discharge.

Now she waited near the emergency room door, a stack of papers with prescriptions, instructions and an order for physical therapy balanced on her lap beneath her right hand. She didn't dare to let the pages slip, because she doubted she could pick them up without falling onto her face.

"They're not here yet?" asked a gray-haired lady in a bright pink lab coat.

"Not yet," Mattie replied in a strained whisper.

"Didn't you call someone?"

"I did." She didn't add she'd left a message on the answering machine in the barn at her cousin Mark's farm. She knew he'd check it, but wasn't sure when. He might not return to the barn until it was time to start milking. It would be at least an hour traveling by buggy to get to the hospital in Montague which was twenty kilometers from the shop.

"Are they on their way?" the gray-haired lady persisted.

"I'm sure they are," she replied, though she wasn't. Had Benjamin alerted her cousins when he dropped Daisy off at home? That would have been far quicker than waiting for one of her cousins to check the answering machine. Why hadn't she thought to suggest that to him?

She shivered as the door opened, letting cold air sweep in. The motion sent renewed agony through her left shoulder, and she groaned in spite of her determination to hide her pain.

"You poor dear." She didn't ask Mattie's permission before she grasped the wheelchair and drew her around a corner where a half-closed door blocked the breeze. "Do you want me to check with the nurse about more meds for you?"

"No. Most of the time, my shoulder doesn't hurt too bad." Not wanting to be caught in a lie, she hurried to add, "It's bearable."

"You don't want to let the pain get ahead of you because it can become overwhelming. Let me know if you want me to alert a nurse or put in another call to your family. All right?"

"*Danki*," she replied, appreciating the woman's kindness, but wanting to put an end to the conversation so she could sink into her cocoon of not thinking about anything. Not even the ache in her left shoulder.

The lady walked away, but Mattie's thoughts pingponged through her mind, exacerbating her headache. How was she going to get the shop open on time when she couldn't use her left arm for…? She glanced at the top page on her lap, but her eyes refused to let her read how long she was supposed to rest her shoulder. Leaning her head against the wheelchair, she stared at the ceiling and tried not to let weak tears dribble down her cheeks.

She should have been more careful. She might have doomed not only her dreams but Daisy's and her cousins' because she'd been caught up in imagining how the shop could look and hadn't paid attention to the stacks of wood.

"There she is!"

Her sister's voice startled Mattie awake. She hadn't realized she'd drifted off. She looked around for Daisy. The motion made her head spin, but she didn't care when she saw Daisy pushing her own wheelchair toward her at top speed.

"Are you ready to leave?" Daisy asked. "Are you okay? We've been so worried."

"I'm ready to go home, and I'll be okay soon." She looked past her sister, expecting to see one of her cousins.

Her eyes widened when Benjamin Kuhns strode toward her. He looked taller from where she sat. He was built like a mountain, and his muscles moved smoothly beneath his pale green shirt. Yet, she couldn't mistake the genuine concern imprinted on his face.

"What are you doing here?" Mattie blurted before *gut* sense could halt her.

"Daisy refused to go and wait at your house. She insisted we come to pick you up, so I took her to my friend James's house and got his buggy." He gave her a lopsided grin. "I learned a long time ago that trying to tell an Albrecht woman no is a waste of time."

His words were a reminder of how he'd courted and

then left her sister Sharrell. Another spear of pain cut into her left shoulder, and she wished she could keep from reacting to everything he said. She needed to be more like Sharrell who had put him out of her mind and moved on with her life after Benjamin had gone home. If Sharrell could forgive and forget him breaking her heart, Mattie needed to, as well.

But how? Maybe if she'd been honest about her yearning for him five years ago, she could have worked out her grief and put it behind her as Sharrell had. She hadn't, and she had no idea how to deal with its resurgence.

Mattie was saved from having to dredge up something to say when her three cousins shouldered their way past the half-closed door. None of them had ever been able to stand being the last one coming into a room, so they jostled one another as they had since they'd been five years old.

The threesome were handsome and turned heads wherever they went. Mark Yutzy's hair was pale against his well-tanned skin, but he had eyes the brilliant blue of sunlight on the sea. Lucas and Juan Kuepfer were brothers, but most people wouldn't have guessed that. Lucas, the older by two years, resembled his black-haired, brown-eyed *grossmammi*, whom his *grossdawdi* had married when the Kuepfer family had lived in Mexico in the early twentieth century. The family had returned twenty years ago to Aylmer, Ontario, and Juan had inherited his looks from his Amish *mamm*'s family. His medium brown hair fell over eyes the same bright blue as his cousin's.

What people often neglected to notice because of her cousins' *gut* looks were their calloused hands and wind-roughened faces that spoke of long hours of hard work. The few who failed to realize how smart her cousins were soon discovered their mistake.

"What happened?" asked Mark, taking the lead as he often did.

Again Mattie was too slow to answer. Daisy gave a quick overview of how the stack of wood had fallen. Her sister colored the simple facts with her own reactions, and Mattie realized how terrified Daisy had been when she couldn't wake Mattie and had gone to look for help.

When Daisy mentioned Benjamin had appeared to help her and Mattie, Juan, the youngest cousin, interrupted to say, "And you're Benjamin?"

Benjamin nodded. "Benjamin Kuhns. I'm visiting a friend."

"Nice to meet you. I…" Mark's voice faded off, and he exchanged a look with his cousins.

"Kuhns?" asked Lucas. "Are you the Benjamin Kuhns who lives in Goshen, Indiana?"

"That's where I used to live. My brother, sister and I moved to Harmony Creek in northern New York State a couple of years ago."

"But you're the Benjamin Kuhns who came to Aylmer about five or six years ago, ain't so?"

"I am."

Turning to his brother and cousin, Lucas asked, "Don't you know who he is? He's the one who walked out with Mattie's sister Sharrell."

Juan whooped a laugh. "Wow, you are one brave man, Benjamin. Sharrell is a bulldozer, cutting a swath through life. No wonder you hightailed it back to the States."

Several hospital employees glanced at them with reproving gazes, and Juan apologized for being loud. It was something, Mattie knew, he'd been doing all his life. His exuberance was as much a part of him as his blue eyes.

Her cousins introduced themselves to Benjamin, acting as if they didn't see his discomfort. Like Daisy, her cousins were candid and curious.

"Mattie left a message in the dairy barn," Mark was saying when she forced herself to focus on the conversation again.

"So you're planning to have dairy farms here?" Benjamin asked.

"I am," Lucas replied. "Juan and Mark are going to grow seed potatoes and soybeans. Once we get our first crops harvested, we'll have cash to invest in a herd." He gave Mattie the smile one of her childhood friends had described as *dangerous as a heart attack*. "We're grateful Mattie agreed to open the shop to keep us afloat."

"You're helping Mattie, Benjamin," Daisy said as she rolled forward.

"I am." Benjamin smiled at her sister as he took the handles on Mattie's chair and started pushing it toward the emergency room doors.

Mattie was surprised when a pulse of envy rushed through her. How she wished she could be as at ease with people, whether they were friends or strangers, as her sister was. Daisy was interested in everyone she met, and she assumed they were as interested in her. So many people looked at her sister with pity because of her Down syndrome, but Mattie knew God had given Daisy special gifts to go along with her challenges.

"You're helping Lucas and Juan and Mark, too," continued Daisy.

"I am." Benjamin slowed the wheelchair as they approached the automatic doors.

As the doors moved and cold air rushed in, Daisy asked, "How 'bout helping me and Boppi Lynn, too?"

"Who?" he asked.

"Boppi Lynn. You met her at the shop." Daisy lifted the doll she always carried on her lap. Unlike most Amish dolls, it had eyes, a nose and a mouth. Any color on its face had been worn away by the kisses Daisy had given her beloved doll. "She needs a family. A whole family. Everybody should have a *daed* and a *mamm* to love them. I'm not old enough to get married." She hooked a thumb toward Mattie. "But she can." Her eyes filled with abrupt tears. "Will you help me find someone to ask my sister to be his wife?"

Benjamin was wide-eyed with shock, and Mattie was sure she heard her cousins trying to stifle their chuckles.

But Mattie didn't feel like laughing. Pain exploded inside her. Not from her shoulder, but from hearing the grief in her sister's voice. *Mamm* had tossed them aside to find the life she believed she'd been denied. Daisy was desperate for a family again.

But why had Daisy asked *Benjamin* that question?

A coat settled on her shoulders, and she looked in surprise at him. She quickly shifted her eyes away, not wanting him to guess her thoughts. Nor did she want him to think she'd had anything to do with Daisy's outrageous question.

His hand lingered on her right shoulder. "Daisy, I don't think your sister will have any trouble finding a man when she's ready to marry."

"*Mamm* says it's too late for her," argued Daisy, then paused. "But *Mamm* doesn't know everything, ain't so?

She couldn't have known it was wrong to leave all of us, or she wouldn't have. Ain't so?"

"Daisy," Mattie said, "let's talk about this later. I want to get home. Okay?"

"Home with *Daed*?" Hope burst into her sister's voice.

"Home here."

"Oh." A soft sound too much like a sob came from Daisy.

Mattie closed her eyes and prayed she hadn't made a mistake bringing her youngest sibling to the Island with her.

Benjamin must have heard it, too, because he said, "Daisy, lead the way. You remember where we parked, don't you?"

"I do." Pride swept away the pain in her sister's voice. "Follow me."

"*Danki*," Mattie said as her sister spun the wheels of her chair along the asphalt.

"She was frantic about you." He halted Daisy's chair as a car pulled out of the lot. "As you are about her. Relax."

"I know." She tried to do as he suggested, but too many thoughts tumbled through her head, most gone before they registered. She wondered how long it would take for the pain medication to wear off. "*Danki* for bringing her."

He chuckled. "Like I said, she insisted she wasn't going to stay behind. Trying to figure out how to get her wheelchair in my friend's buggy delayed us getting here."

"My buggy has been refitted to hold it."

"So Daisy told me *after* I spent an hour trying to

figure out how to get it in James's buggy. I asked her why she hadn't mentioned that earlier, and she told me that you said everyone has to try before letting someone else help."

"I did tell her that because her physical therapist was insistent she learn to do things on her own. I'm sorry that—" Her words became a groan as the wheelchair bounced.

"Sorry," he hurried to say. "I didn't see that hole in the asphalt."

"You don't need to apologize. I guess it's my turn for PT. I know it's going to be a lot of hard work."

"Just like clearing out the shop."

"*Ja.* I know that's going to be hard work, too, and I also know the best things can't be done the easy way."

He didn't say anything as he slowed the chair next to her buggy where Daisy waited. There wasn't any reason to reply. The gargantuan task of getting the shop ready on time had been made more complicated by her injury.

After taking Mattie and Daisy to the small house where they lived on Lucas Kuepfer's farm, Benjamin walked east on the road along the shore. The narrow strip of blacktop was edged by no more than a couple of yards of grass before dropping a few steps to the thin strip of beach. He wondered if he'd ever get accustomed to seeing red sand that glistened like a handful of ketchup had been mixed in with the grains.

It was astounding to realize five hours had passed since he'd been sauntering in the other direction, eager to offer a hand to a neighbor in need. His world had been turned on its ear by the day's events.

Mattie Albrecht couldn't really expect to have a shop

in that battered Quonset hut by the end of next month. The determination in her eyes and the stern set of her mouth when she insisted she would get the job done told him she wouldn't be swayed by logic.

You wanted an adventure when you came here, a voice murmured from deep in his mind.

That was true, but he hadn't imagined it would take the form of helping his ex-girlfriend's family get their business started. It wasn't going to be easy to spend time with Mattie and her sister and the memories of their older sister. Sharrell had been out of his life for a long time, but it didn't feel that way now.

He sighed as he turned his back on Shushan Bay and walked toward a squat cottage that needed repainting. Its small windows protected against winter winds, but offered stunning views of the bay. At one end of the Cape-Cod-style house, a former owner had built an addition that looked like a gigantic buoy. The roof of the round ground floor contracted into an upper octagonal room that was no more than six feet in diameter. James had cared less about the house and its condition than the open-front barn behind it which offered space for his forge and tools.

When James had announced he was returning to Canada, Benjamin had been shocked. He'd been sure James would never go back to Ontario where his older brothers insisted he do as they demanded. Sometimes Benjamin wondered if he and James would have become *gut* friends so quickly if they didn't both have overbearing older brothers.

But James hadn't been heading home to Milverton. He'd planned to come to Prince Edward Island and asked Benjamin to join him for a few weeks. The invitation offered a chance to get away from Menno and think about what he wanted to do. Most men Benjamin's age had families. He'd never met anyone who was *gut* enough in Menno's opinion. Benjamin couldn't let more time drift by because he didn't want to rock the boat. Seeing Mattie Albrecht on his first day on the Island had reminded him how much time he'd wasted.

Benjamin went to the side door. He could hear the clank of metal tools from the barn where James was setting up his smithy.

"I'll get supper started," Benjamin shouted before opening the kitchen door.

Boxes were stacked everywhere. There was a sink and a narrow stove with four burners closely set together. The floor rippled where the linoleum had bubbled and cracked. There were only two cabinets. The one below the sink was draped by cotton that looked as if it'd been nibbled by mice. The other cupboard ran from floor to ceiling and had a bifold louvered door that wouldn't stay closed.

He went to the tall one and pulled out a loaf of bread. From the refrigerator that sounded like a jet taking off each time its motor ran, he gathered sliced meat and mustard and mayonnaise. He set them on the kitchen table, hoping its flimsy legs wouldn't collapse. The table and its mismatched pair of chairs had been left behind along with a few other pieces of furniture in the house. James had been thrilled to buy a furnished house, but Benjamin's opinion was the furniture was only *gut* for kindling.

When James came into the kitchen, he grinned though fatigue had drawn lines into his cheeks. He needed a haircut, because he kept sweeping his blond hair away from his green eyes. He was taller than Benjamin, but as thin as one of the nails he made.

"How did it go?" James asked as he went to the sink to wash his hands.

"Not like I expected." The words slipped out before he could halt himself.

James turned. "What do you mean?"

"You didn't tell me the person needing help was Mattie Albrecht."

"I'm sure I did." After rinsing soap off his hands, he reached for the towel hanging by the sink. "Sorry if I didn't, but why's that a problem?"

Benjamin motioned toward the table. "Let's eat. I'll tell you about my day, and you can tell me how things are going with you."

James looked confused, but, after grabbing two plates, he pulled out a chair and sat.

Benjamin found a couple of knives and filled two glasses with water before sitting on the other chair. He followed James's lead when his friend bent his head to thank God for the food on their table. But finding the right prayer wasn't easy. His thoughts were too scattered. For weeks, he'd been seeking God's guidance to know if he should come to Prince Edward Island. He was here, and one of the first people he'd encountered reminded him of the past he wanted to forget.

Guilt assailed him. His prayers should have focused on gratitude that Mattie hadn't been injured worse and her recovery would be swift. Was he as selfish as Menno had claimed he was when Benjamin announced he was visiting James? If his brother had been right about that, was Menno correct that Benjamin's life should be focused on running the sawmill, too?

He murmured a quick *danki* when James raised his head and reached for the half loaf of bread. James cut four thick slices while he talked about his work.

As he handed two pieces of bread to Benjamin, he asked, "So what happened at the shop?"

Benjamin gave him an abbreviated account of the day's events. When his friend paused with two slices of bologna halfway between the package and his plate, Benjamin realized his story sounded like a tall tale.

James was silent after Benjamin finished. As he slathered mustard on his meat and bread, he kept his eyes on his task. Benjamin knew his friend well enough, however, to know that James's thoughts weren't on his sandwich.

That was confirmed when James said, "It sounds as if they're going to need you even more now."

"Ja."

"You don't need to sound as if you're being sent to be hanged. I thought you were looking for something different to do while you're here. Cleaning that building isn't like working in the sawmill."

"It's more alike it than I'd guessed. There's a bunch of wood to be moved."

"You've got experience with that, so it's *gut* God brought you here when He did." James slapped his sandwich together before adding, "So how is it over there?"

"I'm sure it'll be great if it opens."

"If?"

"The place is a disaster."

"Hey, weren't you the one who wanted an adventure when you left Harmony Creek Hollow? You've got one. Making the impossible possible."

Benjamin reached for the mustard. "You're closer to the truth than you think."

"The mess—"

"It's more than the mess." He spread a thin layer of mustard on his sandwich.

"It's working with Mattie and her family, ain't so? What's the problem?"

He didn't bother to ask how his friend had guessed the root of his concerns. James was insightful. "You don't know these Albrecht women. They smile prettily, but they've got their own agendas."

"And her agenda is to open a store so people along the bay don't have to drive into Shushan or Montague." He shook his head. "Accusing her of something nefarious doesn't make sense."

It didn't.

He started to say so, but James wasn't finished. "You said Mattie Albrecht is pretty?"

"I guess so."

"You guess so?" James snorted. "Are you trying to get me to believe you didn't get a *gut* look at her while you waited for the ambulance and while you took her and her sister home?"

"Okay, you're right. I had plenty of time to look at her. She's easy on the eyes when she's not scowling at me."

"Which it sounds like you gave her plenty of excuses to do. You seem to know how to push her buttons."

Benjamin tried again. "When Sharrell—"

"We're talking about Mattie Albrecht, not her sister. They're different people, ain't so?"

Usually Benjamin appreciated his friend's rationality, but it irritated him. Not because James was pointing out what he knew. It bothered him James had highlighted what Benjamin didn't know. He didn't know much about Mattie because, before today, she hadn't said more than two words in a row to him.

"I guess I'm going to find out."

"So you're still planning to help get the store open?"

"I said I would, and I won't go back on my word."

"You'll be glad you didn't."

He wished he could be as certain as James sounded.

Chapter Three

Mattie walked into the Quonset hut after carrying out two disintegrating cardboard boxes. Water flowed into the rear of the store from melting snow. Mark had promised to dig a trench to divert it, but he hadn't yet. She hoped he would before he began milking tonight.

Putting a hand onto the doorjamb, she waited for her eyes to focus. They threatened to betray her every time she moved. If she let Daisy see, her sister would alert their cousins, and they would insist she stop working.

She must not. The time was short enough already to get the job done. She'd promised herself that she would take frequent breaks, but it wasn't easy when each time she stopped to regain her equilibrium she noticed something more that she could do.

Benjamin had frowned when he came in this morning, but hadn't said anything but "*gute mariye*" before starting work. She was grateful he hadn't demanded that she go home and rest, but at the same time, she was bothered by what seemed to be indifference. After how anxious he'd appeared at the hospital, she'd been shocked by his cool greeting.

She sighed as she looked around. Only a tiny area had been cleared. The rear of the store was piled to the ceiling with debris, though she and Daisy had started to clear paths before she was hurt. She wanted to check if anything could be salvaged. She'd found a few unbroken shelves, but she doubted they'd hold more than the dust caked on them.

Paper and cardboard were tossed on top of bulging food cans and empty soda and beer cans. Furniture had been left in corners, and she guessed at least one of the reeking sofas with torn upholstery was the home of critters she didn't want to come face-to-face with.

Mattie had to wonder how long people had been using the building as a dump. Before she'd come to the Island, Mark and the Kuepfers had told her that she'd be in charge of the budget for the shop. She hadn't seen yet what Lucas had put together. When she'd asked him about it, he'd told her he'd given the paperwork to Mark to double-check his numbers. She'd been too caught in the whirl of getting started at the shop and then hurting her shoulder to pursue the issue further.

Had her cousins considered budgeting to have this trash removed by truck? She needed to ask Lucas tonight and see if they could arrange to have a large dumpster delivered. That would make their job easier because the wood and garbage and broken furniture could be tossed right into it.

Hearing Daisy's voice at the back, Mattie didn't head in that direction. She guessed by the rise and fall of her sister's words that she was teasing Benjamin.

Mattie stumbled when her toe caught on a discarded can. She bit back her moan as a hot spear of pain cut through her left shoulder.

"Watch where you're going," she murmured to herself. She knew time would never turn her into the elegant swan Sharrell was. Tripping over something she'd walked past a half-dozen times already today was proof of that.

"Are you okay?" asked Benjamin.

The heat in her shoulder exploded up her face, and she prayed she wasn't blushing. She should have guessed he'd seen her clumsiness…again.

"I'm fine."

When his brows shot up, she realized her answer had been too curt. His own voice was emotionless. "I hope you're not risking your shoulder."

"I'm doing my best." She managed a half smile. It was all she could do.

It must have been enough because the tension fell away from his face. "I don't want to hover over you, but you need to know I can toss out this junk without you supervising me. Daisy is already doing a *gut* job of telling me what I should do."

"I can talk to her about being bossy. She—"

He grinned. "It's okay, Mattie. She's keeping me on my toes with her questions."

As he turned to head back to work, she said, "Benjamin."

"Ja?" He looked over his shoulder.

"What Daisy asked you at the hospital…" She faltered, not wanting to repeat her sister's request that Benjamin help find Mattie a husband.

He faced her. "Don't let that bother you, Mattie. I'm sure she was joking."

"She wasn't, and she'll expect you to keep your word."

"I didn't realize that." He rubbed his freshly shaven chin. "Tell you what. I'll find a way to do as I promised without any matchmaking."

"She's not stupid. She'll see right through half-hearted attempts."

"What if I'm the most incompetent matchmaker she's ever met? Do you think that will work?"

"It might." She prayed the ruse would satisfy her sister.

"*Gut.* Give me a call if you need help. Take it easy and sit if you need to. Daisy and I are removing that stack of two-by-twelve boards near the side door."

She took a step toward him and lowered her voice. "Don't let her overdo it either. She doesn't always know when she should stop."

"Sounds like her big sister."

She started to frown at the reference to Sharrell, then realized by his widening grin he was referring to her. She needed to remind herself that though she hadn't escaped the sorrow left by his departure five years ago, he'd moved on. He asked about her family, but when she'd changed the subject, he hadn't persisted.

"*Ja,* we're two of a kind." She tried to inject humor into her words.

He laughed for a moment, then asked in not much more than a whisper, "Does she have heart issues? I know lots of folks with Down syndrome do."

"She did when she was born, but her heart was repaired when she was a tiny *boppli.* You don't have to worry about that."

"*Gut* to know. I'll make sure she takes breaks. Like now. I sent her off to get water for us."

"*Danki.*"

"I'm glad to have her help."

Mattie surprised herself by putting her hand on his arm. "That's not what I meant. I'm grateful you're treating her like a regular kid. Not everyone does."

"Plain folks believe—"

"That these kids are a special gift from God." She half turned to look in the direction where Daisy was talking to her doll. She didn't want her sister to overhear what she was about to say. "But Daisy doesn't want to be special in any way. What she wants is to be like you and me."

He looked at where her fingers had lingered on his sleeve. "What she wants is for you to be happy, Mattie."

"She wants everyone to be happy." She stepped away, clasping her hands in front of her.

"True, but most of all, she wants *you* to be happy. She thinks her big sister is the one who's pretty special." He gave her a playful wink. "And I think she's right."

Mattie clamped her lips closed before she could stutter over an answer to his unexpected compliment. She was relieved when he strode to where he'd been working. She wasn't sure if he was teasing her as he did Daisy or if his words had been sincere.

He whistled a cheerful tune as he returned to his work.

Knowing she needed to do the same, Mattie tried to put Benjamin out of her mind. It wasn't possible when the lilting melody he whistled bounced off the curved ceiling. She decided to focus on picking up the can that had tripped her as well as the others scattered across the floor.

But how? She couldn't hold a garbage bag and reach for cans at the same time. Glancing around, she smiled when she saw a rusty metal bucket. It would sit on the floor while she tossed cans in.

She twice filled the pail and emptied it into the metal barrel Juan had left by the side door. Then she picked up a can and choked back a shocked cry when liquid ran down her apron and dress.

Her nose wrinkled at the odor of sour beer. She frowned as more golden liquid splattered her black sneakers. She grabbed the can and threw it into the bucket. It rattled against other cans, and beer spilled out.

She sighed when she saw puddles on the floor. Whoever had brought the beer in hadn't finished it. Or, more likely, the cans had been left behind by underage kids who'd run away before they were caught.

The call of a starling, its cry sharp and shrill, caught her ear, and she glanced out through the filthy windows at the front of the hut. The sunshine iced the waters in the bay, sparkling on the tip of every wave in the narrow open channel. The dancing light urged her to rush out the door and pretend she'd never set eyes on the disaster inside the Quonset hut. She could walk along the narrow beach while she savored the sunshine and the sea. She could imagine the reddish sand warm and soft between her bare toes, though she'd have to wait a few months to experience that.

She could imagine *someone else* doing that. Not Mattie Albrecht. Work first, then, if there was any time left, she could have fun.

Another shiver ached across her shoulders when her memory spewed out Karl Redden's voice saying, while they were walking out together, she wasn't any fun, that she'd rather do chores than walk out with him. That it had been true was something she hadn't wanted to admit. She'd spent time with him because her *mamm* had insisted she should be grateful someone was willing to consider a woman in her late twenties as a wife. That had been three years before, and at thirty-one, she was unwed. She was happier single than she would have been as Karl's wife. After all, she couldn't love him when her heart belonged to someone else.

That ache tightened along her right shoulder to match the pain in her left, but she halted more memories from bursting forward. She was here to help her family build new lives, and she shouldn't be thinking of the past. Only the future, and she couldn't get there if she went for walks along the water. At least here she could have taken that walk without worrying about running into someone she knew. In Ontario, everyone she met wore a face she knew well, but she wasn't in Aylmer any longer.

She was grateful for that. Nobody here looked at her with pity because her *mamm* had shocked everyone, including her own *kinder*, by jumping the fence after sixty years of a plain life. Here, no one asked why Emmaline Albrecht had left. Nor did Mattie have to face others who were curious why Mattie hadn't gone with her *mamm* as five of her siblings had. A few people had been bold enough to say they were glad she and two of her brothers and Daisy had remained with *Daed*. She wondered what those people had thought when she and Daisy left the farm a week ago. She was certain plenty of tongues had wagged, but not as hard as they had when *Mamm* walked out of her house and marriage.

Mattie wished she could stop thinking about how her *mamm* had splintered their family when she'd abandoned her husband and her *kinder* and *kins-kinder*. As the exact middle *kind*, Mattie had been torn apart by wanting her parents to reunite. And still was.

If there was something she could do to make things better...

She stood straighter. She could get the shop open while *Daed* and her brothers sold the farm in Ontario and arranged to move to the Island.

"What did you do?" Daisy grimaced. "You stink!"

"I spilled beer on myself." She forced herself to laugh and then realized it felt *gut*. How long had it been since the last time she'd allowed herself a chuckle? "I should have guessed not *all* the cans would be empty."

"Someone had quite the party here," Benjamin said, joining them. He tossed long pieces of lumber out the door, then wiped his hands on his dusty trousers.

"A lot of parties to judge by the number of cans." Mattie hefted the pail. "This fills up fast."

His brow threaded, and his voice deepened. "You aren't overdoing it, are you?"

"No." She regretted her terse answer, but couldn't think of anything else to add. Maybe it'd been better when he hadn't said more than a greeting. Everything else he'd said that morning had reminded her of what a decent man he was, even if he'd dumped her sister and trod on Mattie's own heart.

"I'm keeping an eye on her," Daisy piped up. "Don't worry, Benjamin. She'll listen to me."

"And not to me, ain't so?" His jesting words were for her sister, but his gaze was aimed at Mattie.

She didn't want to know what he was thinking. Or maybe she did... No, she didn't want to! His concern pierced the coolness she tried to project around him. If she allowed herself to appreciate his kindnesses, she was afraid her heart would be laid bare another time. She must not open herself to that kind of pain again.

Benjamin leaned one hand against the curved wall and stared across the water at the clouds building on the horizon past the bay's far side. He missed the views of Green Mountains that rose to the north and east of Harmony Creek Hollow. He hadn't known how much he'd come to appreciate their vibrant summer greens and myriad autumn colors. Prince Edward Island, or at least the small part he'd seen so far, had rolling hills, but nothing taller.

But the vistas of the sea in constant motion more than made up for the lack of mountains. He could have stood there and watched its restless movement for hours. He understood the need to be going somewhere, doing something, exploring new places. Wasn't that why he'd come to the Island in the first place?

A shiver ran along his spine, and he almost laughed. He should have waited another few months before visiting James, who'd assured him more than once that July would be glorious on the Island with a pale carpet of lupines woven among the grass along the roads.

It wasn't more than a few degrees above freezing outside; yet his shirt beneath his black coat was stuck to him. He hadn't bothered to count the number of times he'd gone back and forth with armfuls of trash and broken lumber. While the piles outside seemed to be growing into the Island's first mountain range, the amount of debris inside didn't appear to be any less.

"When was the last time someone used this place as a business?" he asked as Mattie came toward him with a bottle of water. He took it and downed a big swig before thanking her.

"I'm not sure. Mark could tell you." She gave him one of her rare smiles. "Mark learned everything he could about these properties before he arranged for us to invest here." Walking away, she bent to get her bucket that was filled to the brim with empty cans.

"Let me help you with that."

"Danki." She stepped aside. "Be careful. We don't need you smelling like a brewery, too."

"It might be an improvement after all the boards covered with mold and mildew." He chuckled. "And more than a few mushrooms. We could have made several superlarge pizzas from all the fungi I've found."

"Edible ones?"

"I didn't recognize them. That's why I tossed them out the door." After lifting the pail, he emptied it into the large bin by the door. "Have you given any thought to tearing down this place and starting from scratch?"

"Every minute of the day."

Laughing as he handed her the empty pail, he said, "I'm not surprised. The thought has crossed my mind more than once."

"If we start from scratch, we won't be open by the end of next month."

"Even if…" He cleared his throat, wishing he'd thought before he spoke.

Her face fell, and he knew she was as dubious as he was that the shop would be ready in time. As he started to apologize, she waved his words away.

"You don't have to choose your words carefully around me, Benjamin. I can see what a disaster this is and how small our chances are of having it ready on time."

"Yet you keep working."

She nodded, careful not to jostle her shoulder. *"Ja."*

"Because you don't have any choice?"

"Because I do."

His brows lowered toward each other. "You've lost me."

"I've got the choice of doing what I said I'd do or not doing it. God gives us choices. It's up to us to discover which one will lead us on the journey He has set for us."

"Could you walk away and leave your cousins in the lurch?"

"No."

"You didn't hesitate."

"There's no reason to hesitate when I know what I'm going to do." She ran her hand along the side of the Quonset hut, then grimaced at her fingers that were covered with a thick layer of dirt. "I told my cousins I'd help, and that's what I intend to do. I may not have said it before, but I'm glad you're here to help. There's no way we could have moved those big pieces of wood."

"I'm glad to help."

"But why are you spending your holiday time here instead of exploring the Island?"

"We plain folk help others."

"I know that, but why are *you* here when you're not part of our community?"

He considered giving her another glib answer. That was his usual way of responding to questions. His brother didn't want to hear about anyone else's hopes and dreams. Sarah, his sister, had listened to him, but she was living her own dream after marrying and having a *kind*. And Sharrell? She'd been more like his brother, focused solely on what she wanted.

As he opened his lips to give Mattie a teasing retort, the words dried in his mouth. He barely knew her, but was certain she'd be more likely to listen than his brother had. Should he tell her about his yearning to use the woodworking skills he'd learned through hard labor? People paid *gut* money for well-made items they could display in their homes. Friends had asked for him to build items, most often clocks, and he'd spent many happy hours in his shop. Yet, did he want to share his dreams without knowing whether she'd ridicule them?

As he was debating with himself, Benjamin said, "I thought if I helped you with the cleanup, you could teach me about running a retail shop."

"Don't you have a Christmas tree farm in New York? What you did to sell Christmas trees wouldn't be much different from what I'm going to do selling vegetables and groceries."

"And crafts," Daisy added with a grin as she rolled over to them. "Don't forget those, Mattie."

"Never." Her smile for her sister was genuine and warm. Would she react the same way if he told her how he wanted to make clocks and sell them? "And I won't forget who's going to be in charge of that."

"Me!" She giggled as she pushed her chair toward the entrance again.

He watched her go, amazed how the girl found joy in mundane things.

"I envy her view of the world," Mattie said as if he'd spoken his thoughts aloud. "She sees the best in everything and in everyone."

"Even me?"

Her smile vanished. "I didn't say that."

"I know you didn't. I was teasing."

"Were you?" She waved aside her words before wincing when the motion pulled her shoulder. "I'm sorry. I shouldn't be so sharp."

"No need to apologize. I shouldn't be teasing you when you're feeling lousy." He hefted a nearby board onto his shoulder. "Where do you want these to go?"

"If any are beyond being used, put them out by the greenhouses. Juan plans to chip the ruined boards into mulch."

"That's a *gut* idea. You've given this a lot of thought. The rest of us could learn from that." He grinned. "And I hope to. So will you help me learn to run a shop?"

She continued to regard him with a somber expression. That told him how reluctant she was to agree, so he was surprised when she said *ja*.

She walked away, leaving him to wonder if he should have kept his mouth shut.

Chapter Four

Mattie rolled her sister's wheelchair out of the back of their market buggy the next afternoon. It hadn't been easy using one hand to drive the buggy, but she'd managed it after Lucas had hitched up the horse. The slower-than-usual drive into the small town of Shushan had taken about a half hour, but she'd finally parked the buggy beside the hardware store.

Pushing the chair to the buggy's passenger side, she held it while Daisy swung herself into it. She swallowed a moan when the movement shifted the wheelchair and resonated through her shoulder. But Mattie made sure she had a smile in place when Daisy looked at her. She couldn't let her sister discover something she'd done had hurt Mattie. That would break Daisy's heart.

A fresh breeze brought the strident sound of bagpipes toward them. One of her cousins—she couldn't remember which one—had warned she'd better learn to appreciate Scottish Highlands music if she intended to settle the Island. The instrument, which some folks loved and others despised with a passion, was the centerpiece of many community activities on the Island.

"What's that?" Daisy asked. When Mattie hurried to explain, her sister's mouth twisted. "Sounds like someone strangling a cat."

"Don't say that to anyone around here." Mattie chuckled.

"All right, but that doesn't change how awful it sounds." Daisy gasped. "You like it?"

"I think it's interesting. It combines a goose's honk and a robin's trill. Can't you hear that?"

"You need to make sure your ears are working."

Mattie hoped Daisy, for once, would be circumspect. People in Shushan were going to have to get used to Daisy, as Daisy must learn to hold her tongue around them. Her sister spoke her mind to plain folks and to *Englischers*. Most people realized Daisy never spoke with malice, just honesty.

The trip into the village at the head of Shushan Bay would take most of the afternoon. Her cousins had given her a long list. She'd start at the hardware store and end at the grocery store. In between, she'd find a craft store so she could refill Daisy's art box.

It was a simple file storage box where her sister kept paper and markers and stamps and ink. Daisy and two other teens with Down syndrome shared a circle letter. They had begun it with the help of their occupational therapist two years before, and it was a high point of Daisy's day when she got an envelope filled with letters and artwork from Adan and Zoe. Adan was plain, but Zoe was *Englisch*. It didn't matter. They worked hard to write about what was going on in their lives and to decorate their letters. It wasn't a competition. They'd needed to learn fine motor skills, and using pens and rubber stamps and stickers had provided *gut* practice.

As Mattie helped her sister push her chair toward the hardware store, Daisy seemed to be trying to take in everything at once. It was her sister's first trip into the small village and Mattie's second. Bright buildings edged Main Street which was divided by a bridge over the bay. Most of the businesses on the western side were aimed at tourists while the ones to the east catered to locals. A pair of streets ran along either shore and were filled with homes. A marina holding pleasure-and commercial-fishing boats was downstream from the bridge. Half the moorings were filled, and Mattie could see fishermen working so they'd be ready at first light tomorrow to go out.

Though Mattie needed to visit shops on both sides of the bridge, she'd leave the buggy and Pebbles, their gray horse, in front of the hardware store because it was the only place in town with a hitching rail. One was being built in front of a consignment shop at the far end of town, but it hadn't been completed.

"Let's get going! Boppi Lynn wants to see the store!" Daisy squealed with excitement.

"All right." Mattie guided the wheelchair toward the hardware store. Daisy needed help on the uneven pavement, and Mattie wanted to make sure her sister in her eagerness to see everything didn't roll her chair out in front of oncoming traffic.

As they entered the large building, Mattie let go of the wheelchair and got a cart. She smiled when Daisy rolled along beside her, helping her turn the shopping cart around corners so Mattie didn't have to risk her shoulder. They went through the store that was packed from floor to ceiling with a varied collection of products.

Mattie tried not to pay any attention to the curious

glances aimed in their direction. She smiled at each person they passed while Daisy called out greetings in a voice so filled with enthusiasm that it was contagious. All but a couple of people replied to Daisy and grinned.

It didn't take long to fill the cart with paint for Mark's barn along with new paintbrushes and rollers. Lucas wanted two boxes of drywall screws, and Juan had asked her to buy a five-gallon pail. She wasn't sure what he intended to use it for, but she found a stack. With help from Daisy and a customer who'd been walking past them, she separated one from the others and put it in her basket.

"Do you need a cover, too?" asked the man, stretching to take one from a shelf she couldn't have reached on her own.

"*Ja. Danki*... Thanks." She didn't know if Juan wanted a top for the bucket, but the man was being so kind she didn't want to ask him to put it back.

"Let me know if you need anything else." He gave her a lazy smile before continuing his own shopping.

Daisy leaned toward her and whispered, "He likes you!"

"Oh, don't be silly. He was being nice."

"Because he likes you." Satisfied she'd had the final word on the subject, she motioned for Mattie to lead the way toward the registers. As the family's youngest, Daisy had figured out a way to boss everyone around without being imperious.

Mattie's smile wavered as she wondered if their family would be together again. *Mamm*'s leaving had created a schism Mattie feared would never be repaired.

A few minutes later, Mattie had her emotions under control as they checked out.

The lady at the counter, who wore a bright green name tag with Roxie printed on it, scanned their items while Mattie kept an eye on her sister who'd moved her wheelchair closer to the door to admire the collection of keys on a rack. Many of them had cartoon characters, flowers or maps of the Island embossed on them. Daisy knew she shouldn't leave the store, but Mattie didn't want something to distract her enough to forget common sense.

"Can I take the cart into the parking lot?" Mattie asked.

"Of course." The checkout clerk smiled. "Do you need help getting your purchases in your buggy? I can call one of the stockers to help you."

"We should be fine, but I appreciate the offer."

Roxie leaned forward, her silver braid flopping over her shoulder. "Do you have locks on your buggies?"

"No."

"Are you heading straight home?"

"No. I've got a few more stops to make. Is it a problem to leave my buggy here?"

"Of course it isn't." She lowered her voice as she added, "I'll have the guys keep an eye on your buggy while you finish shopping. There have been car break-ins recently. Everyone's being extra careful until the thieves are caught."

"You're kind," Mattie said.

The woman blushed and waved her hand. "We try to be good neighbors along Shushan Bay."

Thanking Roxie again, Mattie collected her sister and went to the buggy. The crisp wind whipping off the water was a reminder winter wasn't ready to leave. While Mattie unpacked the cart, putting what they'd bought in the back, Daisy kept her arms around Boppi Lynn so there wasn't any chance the doll would be swept away.

Mattie took the cart back inside the store, waved to Roxie and then walked beside her sister's chair which Daisy rolled along the sidewalk with ease. They went toward the bridge and the stores on its far side. She stopped in the middle so Daisy could peer through the railing at the boats below. As the icy wind blew odors of sand and salt toward them, they laughed about the names they could read on the sterns of the boats. Who would have guessed a prosaic fisherman would name his boat *Tiptoe on the Waves*? Or that a fancy yacht all in white and gold would have had the words *Always an Extra Potato* painted on its stern?

Mattie tried not to stare as they passed a man dressed in a kilt and playing the bagpipes on the sidewalk on the other side of the bridge. Then she wondered why she was worried. He turned to let his gaze follow her and Daisy as they crossed the span. She chuckled to herself. It was stranger for the local folks to see a plain person than one decked out in plaid and squeezing a set of pipes.

"What's funny?" Daisy asked.

"I'm just happy on this pretty day."

Her sister gave her a look that suggested Mattie had lost her mind, but Mattie didn't slow as they went along the sidewalk.

Her shoulder was aching worse than she'd expected by the time they reached a stationery shop. It was a few doors past the bridge, but every step seemed to resonate from the soles of her feet to her shoulder. While

Daisy oohed and aahed over the fanciful stickers, Mattie found a package of writing paper that had wide lines on it. The pictures of puppies and kittens delighted Daisy, and she put a package of each along with a box of pens with purple ink into the plastic basket on her lap. Boppi Lynn was propped inside it, standing with her little arms over the edge so she could "see." Daisy had selected several packets of stickers and a box of stamps. Mattie added crayons to the basket. Daisy had left her coloring books in Aylmer, and her sister missed them.

"Ice cream now?" asked Daisy after they'd paid and emerged from the store.

"You want ice cream when it's this cold?" Mattie retorted, though she knew the answer. Her sister enjoyed ice cream whether it was midsummer or midwinter.

"It won't melt fast today."

Mattie started to answer, but halted when she saw Benjamin Kuhns stepping out of an office across the street. Her eyes widened. Why had Benjamin gone into a real estate office? He'd said, hadn't he, that he'd come to the Island to visit his friend. People who didn't plan to stay somewhere wouldn't be paying a visit to a real estate agent.

Or would they? She didn't know.

Don't look for trouble where there isn't any, she warned herself. His friend might have sent Benjamin to handle something for him.

"Mattie! It's Benjamin!" Daisy waved and called, "Benjamin! *Komm* and see what fun Boppi Lynn is having."

He appeared as startled as Mattie felt, but crossed the street after waiting for a line of cars to pass. The wind flipped the corners of his dark coat to reveal his light blue shirt, and he held one hand on top of his hat to keep it from blowing away. When he stopped beside them, he greeted Daisy first and listened when she told him about what Boppi Lynn had liked in the shops.

Mattie was treated to a clear view of his strong profile. He had a stubborn jaw and a straight nose above his mouth that tilted with his smile. She didn't remember him smiling much in Aylmer. Mostly he'd focused on Sharrell, and his expressions had been in reaction to her older sister's changing moods. Now he was laughing along with Daisy as if he didn't have a care in the world.

But she realized that was an act when his dark eyes cut toward her. An explosion of emotions glistened in them, and not a single one appeared to be amusement. Something had him on edge. Something that had happened at the real estate office?

"Mattie, how's the arm doing?" Benjamin asked.

"It hurts when I do something foolish."

"And you're not a foolish person, ain't so?"

She couldn't tell if he was teasing or not. "I try not to be."

"I didn't expect to see you two in town, but I'm glad you felt well enough to drive here." His mouth wavered, then his smile settled into place. "What's that old line? Imagine seeing you in a place like this."

"We had errands to run. Just like you." She thought about saying more but halted herself because he wore the look of a *kind* caught sneaking a candy bar out of a store. Asking why he was visiting a real estate agent would suggest she cared.

She didn't.

At least that's what she told herself. After all, she didn't want to be like the nosy people in Aylmer who'd been hungry for every sordid detail about why her *mamm* had left.

Daisy filled the silence. "Roxie told Mattie about bad guys who are breaking cars and maybe our buggy."

His eyes shifted to Mattie. "Breaking your buggy? Roxie?"

Mattie explained who Roxie was and what she'd said. "They're keeping an eye on the buggy at the hardware store while we finish our shopping." Lowering her voice as Daisy began to point out items in a window to her doll, she added, "I didn't realize Daisy overheard that conversation. I don't want her to get upset over something she doesn't understand."

"Seems like she understood."

"True, but when she's frightened, she has night terrors. She may appear all right during the day, but then she wakes up screaming."

"I had no idea. I—"

"Less said the better."

He nodded, and she was grateful he didn't ask any of the other questions she could see in his gaze. Others hadn't been as circumspect around her sister, acting as if they could ask anything without Daisy comprehending what they were saying.

As Daisy wheeled over to look in the window of a nearby store which sold beach toys, Mattie started to follow.

He halted her by asking, "How's your family in Ontario? I should have asked before."

What did he know? Which rumors had reached him? She silenced the questions she didn't want to ask so as not to let the past invade the future she longed to build for what was left of her family. But how was she going to stop it?

Benjamin was surprised when Mattie seemed to close up like a bank vault. He'd thought talking about her family would be a *gut* way to divert the conversation away from her catching him coming out of the Buy the Bay real estate office after talking to the owner, Ray Bassett, about the property James had insisted Benjamin consider buying.

James had been right. It would be an amazing opportunity for Benjamin to build his own business, though his friend couldn't have guessed how enticing it would be that the property was situated on a well-traveled road between Shushan and Charlottetown, a route used by locals and tourists. It would be the perfect place for him to open a shop to display and sell the clocks he made.

He'd set aside the dream of creating clocks when Menno asked him to move to New York and help with the sawmill, but with each passing day, the yearning to use the skills he'd worked to master ached inside him. With the trees on the property, he'd have materials to carve the clock cases. Ideas for designs filled his mind.

Yet the question remained: Was he willing to give up on adventure before it'd begun? He'd done the right thing, the wise thing, the careful thing all his life. He wanted to discover if there was more out there for him. Still, he hesitated. God had a plan for him, and he doubted it was to waste the talent He'd given Benjamin.

"My family is fine," Mattie said, jerking him from his thoughts. "Or they were when I last saw them. I don't know how they are at this exact moment. If I did,

I'd tell you. That is—" She clamped her lips closed, then said, "I'm sorry. I don't usually babble."

"I know you don't. Is something wrong?"

"I've got a ton of things to do. My brain is skittering here and there."

He had no doubt that was true, but he sensed she wasn't being honest. What else could he expect when he was being as cautious about what he said?

Daisy came to where they were standing. "Ice cream now?"

He thought Mattie would say no, but she nodded. "*Ja.* We've got time enough for a bowl, but then it's back to work."

Daisy smiled at Benjamin. "Do you like ice cream?"

"Doesn't everyone?"

"*Ja.*" She giggled. "Let's get ice cream. *Komm* too, Benjamin?"

Again he glanced at Mattie. Did she always give in to Daisy? As he had before, he reminded himself how little he knew the younger Albrecht sisters.

"If it's okay with Mattie…" he began.

"You're welcome to join us." There wasn't a hint of sarcasm or vexation in her voice.

"*Danki.* I think I will. I didn't know there was an ice-cream shop in Shushan."

"It's a diner," Mattie replied as she grasped one handle on her sister's chair and headed toward the bridge with Daisy pushing the wheels. "They serve delicious ice cream."

He gestured for her to step aside, and he took both handles on the chair and started along the street. He couldn't keep from glancing at the simple navy blue sling that supported Mattie's left arm. It was a constant reminder of why he needed to be at the shop helping her instead of going off to look at a piece of property.

Daisy grinned. "Almost as *gut* as Cows."

"Cows?" he asked.

"It's a chain of ice-cream shops, and we stopped at one in Charlottetown on our way here." Mattie chuckled. "Daisy said it was the best ice cream ever."

"*Ja, wunderbaar* ice cream." She bounced the doll on her lap as they walked toward the bridge. "Love ice cream. Love, love, love it!"

"Does Boppi Lynn like ice cream?"

She gave him a sad smile as if he didn't have an ounce of sense in his head. "She's too little to eat ice cream." She rolled away, then looked over her shoulder. "*Komm mol!* We don't want to get there and have it be all gone."

With a laugh that freed him from his anxiety over the decision he'd need to make soon, Benjamin walked alongside Mattie as they followed her sister. He wasn't surprised when she called to Daisy to slow so she didn't plow over a pedestrian.

Before they reached the bridge, Daisy turned the wheelchair to the right and into a parking lot in front of a small light brown building that looked as if it might have been a fishing hut. A large window commanded the front, and the menu selections were painted in bright colors on boards nailed overhead as well as special flavors listed on sheets set in frames along the counter. However, Mattie pushed the wheelchair past it and two people waiting for their orders.

Benjamin was amazed to see a larger building behind the small one. What he'd assumed was a neighboring business was an old-fashioned diner connected to the hut. Its windows offered a view of the bay, the moored boats and the bridge.

Stepping forward to take the handles of the chair and push Daisy up the ramp, he nodded his thanks when Mattie held the door open. Inside, booths lined the walls. Between them and a U-shaped counter, tables claimed the center. A jukebox that must have been older than he was held court between two windows to the right. Lights moved along its sides in a hypnotic pattern. Pulling his eyes away, he steered Daisy toward a nearby table.

A smiling waitress rushed forward to remove one of the metal chairs so Daisy could edge her wheelchair close to the table. As she set the chair aside, the red-haired girl asked, "Food or just ice cream?"

"Ice cream," Daisy said before either he or Mattie could answer. "And there's no *just* about ice cream."

The waitress laughed. "I like how you think!" Dropping three laminated sheets on the table, she added, "Here's our list of flavors and all the different ways we serve it. I'll be right back with water."

A few minutes later, Benjamin took a sip, then a deeper drink. Setting his half-emptied glass on the table, he said, "Guess I didn't realize how thirsty I was."

"That's the salt in the air." Mattie again wore her pretty smile, and he found it tough to look anywhere else. The expression lit her whole face, wiping away the fatigue he'd seen at the shop and her harried frown on the sidewalk. "You'll find you're thirstier and hungrier. I'm told we'll get used to it once we've been here a while."

"I don't know how long I'm going to be here."

"But you were at the real estate office..." An enticing pink rose in her cheeks. "I'm sorry. I shouldn't be nosy."

"There's no reason not to ask. James goaded me into talking to an agent about a piece of property he thought I might be interested in. It's intriguing, but like I said, I don't know how long I'm going to be here. I—" He halted himself as the waitress returned, ready to take their orders.

"Go ahead," Mattie said, bending to confer with her sister.

"A scoop of maple walnut for me," he said.

As the waitress wrote on her pad, Mattie said, "I've never had maple walnut ice cream before. What's it taste like?"

Daisy rolled her eyes. "What do you think, Mattie? It tastes like maple and walnuts and ice cream."

This time when Mattie smiled, he enjoyed the way her eyes crinkled. She had a face that was meant for joy, but she smiled so seldom. It was as if a black blanket hung over her, smothering her natural tendency for humor. He couldn't help wondering why.

Listening to Daisy talk to the waitress about her doll, Benjamin kept thinking how Ray, the real estate agent, had been enthusiastic about him looking at the property. He'd urged Benjamin several times during their conversation to make an appointment to see it. Benjamin had put him off, saying he needed time to go over the information Ray had shared with him.

He was relieved when, after the waitress left to get their ice cream, Mattie didn't return to the subject of his visit to Buy the Bay. Instead she asked questions about James and when the forge would be open for business. He understood her concerns because his friend had told him the next nearest blacksmith was a two hour drive away, and buggy horses needed their shoes changed and their hooves trimmed every four to six weeks.

"He plans to have it open in a day or two," he said. "It's less complicated than getting your shop cleared out and stocked."

"Don't remind me." She sighed, and he wished he hadn't. He wanted her to smile again.

She did when their ice cream arrived. It was, as Daisy kept reminding him, delicious, and he enjoyed every bite. He was sorry when his bowl was empty. Mattie insisted on paying for hers and Daisy's bowl, and he didn't argue, though he suspected the cousins were stretched thin after investing in the shop and their farms.

Once they were outside, the cold wind whipping around them, he wasn't surprised when Mattie bid him a quick farewell. The weather wasn't conducive for a chat.

"I'll see you later," he said. "I've got a couple of things to get for James, and then I'll come over to help you."

Emotion sped across her face like a ship before a high wind, before being hidden behind a polite mask. "You don't have to feel obligated to come every day. You're on vacation, ain't so? You should take time to enjoy yourself."

"I said I'd help, and I don't plan to go back on my word." His voice was harsher than he'd intended, but he couldn't help being annoyed that she was eager to offer him an excuse not to work with her and her sister.

"All right. *Danki*. We'll see you then." She spun to grasp her sister's wheelchair, then groaned as she held her hand under the sling to support her left shoulder.

Daisy twisted in her chair to look at him. "Why did you upset Mattie?"

Color flashed up Mattie's face again. "Daisy, remember how we talked about not asking other people about how they feel. We should wait for them to tell us."

"I'm not asking how he's feeling. I'm asking why he upset you so you hurt your shoulder."

"It's a *gut* question," he said. "What did I do, Mattie, to upset you enough for you to hurt yourself?"

He'd pushed her too far. He knew that when her lips tightened into two taut parallel lines.

When she began to walk away, with Daisy struggling to keep up, he didn't follow. What could he say? That he was sorry. How could he say that when he didn't know what he'd done?

Or why it was so important to him to find out.

Chapter Five

Over the next week, Benjamin's days fell into a regular pattern. Every morning at five, he rose to make breakfast for James and himself. His friend rarely had much to say during the morning meal, because he was half-asleep. Once, James had almost fallen asleep in his scrambled eggs, saved because Benjamin grabbed him before he planted his face on his plate. His friend was working as hard as Mattie and Daisy.

By seven, Benjamin had done his share of the household chores. James hated doing laundry, so Benjamin had coaxed the ancient washer to work. It wouldn't do more than a few items at time, so most days when he headed to work at what would become the farm shop, he left laundry on the line. By the time he'd gone the short distance to the Quonset hut, the two Albrecht women were there working.

Seeing them and hearing their voices lilt through the clogged building brightened his morning and made his steps lighter as he hurried to where they were working. Every morning he cautioned them to let him lift the heaviest boards and to make a wide berth around the unsteady stacks. Did either of them guess he used that stern warning as a way to hide how much he looked forward to another day with them? He couldn't wait for a chance to hear Daisy tell him more about Boppi Lynn's latest "adventure." He savored every chance he had to spend time with Mattie.

It amazed him that five years ago he hadn't said more than a handful of words to Mattie. He'd been immersed in giving Sharrell the attention she craved and hadn't had time for anyone else. Too late, he'd discovered the real Sharrell behind her apparently sweet smile. Mattie wasted no smiles on him, and he couldn't keep from wondering what she hid behind her pretty face.

A face he thought about far too often when he was walking to and from the shop. A face he yearned to see when he should have been concentrating on work. He didn't have to ask her all the questions he did, but he was drawn to her.

"Like a moth to a flame," he muttered to himself each time he gave in to his craving to talk with her. Everyone knew what happened to the foolish moth that got too close to the fire. Hadn't that happened to him already with her older sister? He should have learned his lesson. He needed to be extra cautious about being lured into the orbit of another Albrecht woman.

He knew he should have been relieved, but he wasn't when Mattie went home for forty-five minutes of physiotherapy every day with the woman who drove out from Shushan. He'd met her physiotherapist, Patty Turner, who was a middle-aged woman with a big laugh and a gentle but assertive manner. Mattie had told him Patty was patient as long as Mattie made her best efforts.

Mattie returned to the shop with lunch for him and

Daisy. She'd found a covered casserole dish in one of the boxes she'd shipped from Ontario. Before she began her session with Patty each day, she put the casserole she'd made the night before into the oven. It remained warm by the time she served their midday meal. In the past week, they'd enjoyed a quick lunch of noodles and beef or chicken pot pie or four-layer pizza bake.

In the middle of the afternoon, Mattie paused to do her exercises which Patty insisted must be done twice more each day. Benjamin wondered if she'd have been so willing to do them if her exercises hadn't offered Daisy an excuse to take a quick nap.

No, Mattie didn't need any excuses to do what was right. While Sharrell could be as distracted as a magpie, Mattie had the unwavering persistence of a snowplow cutting through drifts. Sharrell liked to be the center of attention while Mattie was happy to work in the background. Mattie didn't ask for help, unlike her sister who was glad to let others see her as a delicate flower.

That was why Benjamin hesitated when he came around a stack of broken boards to discover Mattie sitting on an inverted bucket. She was trying to slide her sling off her shoulder, but it had caught on the edge of her apron and dress, twisting them.

Benjamin knew how frustrated Mattie was that she couldn't do what she normally did. Would she want his assistance? He couldn't watch her struggle when she might do further damage to her shoulder, so he asked, "Do you need help?"

"Ja, danki."

He hid his shock at her soft answer. She must be hurting more than she'd let anyone know if she was willing to accept help.

He took a steadying breath as he reached toward the sling. Was she trembling, or was he? Maybe they both were. A tendril of her hair that had escaped her bun slid over his fingers as he drew the sling across her slender shoulder. Its silken caress sent a ripple of unexpected sensation up his arm. Every breath he took was filled with the scent of whatever she used to wash her hair. He couldn't identify the sweet aroma.

"*Danki*," she whispered, her voice as unsteady as he felt.

Had all the air in the building vanished? His heart was hammering against his chest, and he wasn't sure if he remembered how to draw in a deep breath as he thought of the soft skin of her neck.

"You're welcome." The words sounded strangled.

What was he thinking? She had to be around ten years younger than he was, ain't so? Sharrell was close to his age, and there were several *kinder* between Sharrell and Mattie. She should be courted by a young man, not one who was nearing forty.

He watched as she sat on the bucket again. Putting her right hand under her left elbow, she rocked her arms back and forth. Then she did a similar motion, but away from her body and then toward it.

"How's it going?" he asked, though if he had a hint of sense, he'd go to work and end the uneasy conversation.

"Better than yesterday."

"That's *gut*, ain't so?"

"*Ja.*" She faltered and winced.

"Are you okay?"

She didn't answer as Daisy wheeled toward them. She wagged a finger at her sister, then picked up her doll so to make Boppi Lynn do the same.

"Remember?" Daisy asked. "The fiscal therapist said don't do it if it hurts."

He fought not to smile at what she continued to call Patty. Once Daisy got something in her mind, even if it wasn't accurate, she didn't let it go. Was that a trait of the Albrecht family?

"I remember." Mattie smiled at her sister as she kept rocking her arms, but didn't swing them so far.

"You need to listen to Patty," Daisy said.

"I know."

"Gut." Daisy motioned to him. "Let's get to work, Benjamin. Time's a-wastin'."

This time he couldn't hide his grin. "Where did you hear a phrase like *time's a-wastin'*, Daisy?"

"Mattie. Who else?"

Mattie gave him a weak smile when he glanced in her direction. He looked back as he walked away with Daisy. Mattie was focused on her exercises, but he noticed her color was high. She had been as affected by their closeness as he had been.

He wasn't sure if that was *gut* or not.

Benjamin wasn't given a chance to ponder that. Daisy waited until they were out of earshot from Mattie, then crooked a finger at him. When he paused by her chair, she motioned for him to bend so their heads were close.

"Find anyone yet?" she asked. His face must have shown his bafflement because she asked, "Did you find someone to marry Mattie so Boppi Lynn can have a *daed*?"

"Not yet." He went over to the pile of boards that would take him the rest of the afternoon to carry outside.

"Why not? How long should it take for you to find a husband for Mattie?"

He lifted the topmost board and froze as the others rubbed against each other, a sign they weren't as steady as they appeared. "Matters of the heart need to be handled carefully, Daisy. Being careful takes time."

Without a hint of guile, she said, "It didn't take long for Sharrell to get married after you left."

"No, no, it didn't." It wasn't easy to keep his voice even. Though he'd known courting Daisy's older sister any longer would have been foolish, he'd been shocked when he heard how soon Sharrell had married.

"So why is it taking you so long to find a husband for Mattie? Mattie's nicer and prettier than Sharrell, ain't so?"

"Ja." He chuckled. "But don't tell her I said so."

"Why not?"

"Because she might get pickier about potential husbands."

Daisy wore a pensive expression as she thought about his words while he walked toward the rear door to toss the board atop the others that would be chipped later.

He hoped she'd forgotten about finding Mattie a husband. She was too young to understand what he knew to the depths of his bones. If Mattie made the slightest sign she was interested, potential suitors would line up to win her heart.

If he had any idea of what he wanted to do with his life—seek the adventures that were out there waiting for him or settle as his brother expected him to do—he might have been the first in line.

But he'd seen the cost that must be paid when one person in a relationship had a definite future in mind and the other didn't. He'd made that mistake with her sister. He wouldn't let the past repeat itself. He didn't want that heartache again, and he didn't want to inflict it on Mattie.

Listening to Daisy talk while they unpacked boxes in Daisy's room on the first floor in their small house later that afternoon, Mattie smiled. They'd stopped work at the shop early because dark clouds had heralded a snowstorm. Without enough light in the building, one of them could have gotten hurt while trying to navigate the hoarder's paradise.

Mattie hoped Benjamin had reached his friend's house before the nor'easter clamped its wild grip on the Island. If she'd looked out the window, she'd see a curtain of white as the snow blew sideways. The house shuddered when a strong gust struck it as if the wind were trying to push them into the bay.

Daisy was pulling the wrapped items out of the boxes as if nothing was happening beyond the walls. She put them on the bed beside her so Mattie could unwrap them. Keeping up a steady patter as she lifted out each item, the teenager had an opinion on every subject and wasn't afraid to share them. Not because Daisy wanted to dominate the conversation or compel someone to see her side. She was interested in learning what other people had to say, so she assumed everyone else was eager to hear her thoughts.

Mattie sat on the edge of the bed. The springs squeaked as they rubbed against the iron footboard, but she'd grown accustomed to the sound. It was beginning to feel like home. As much as it could when *Daed* and two of her brothers remained in Ontario and the rest of the family was scattered who knew where.

"You're wearing your unhappy thoughts face," Daisy said, bringing Mattie back to the small room. "I don't like when you wear your unhappy thoughts face."

"Me neither." She screwed up her features before asking, "Better?"

"Ja." Daisy remained serious. "Anything's better than your unhappy thoughts face. I wish you wouldn't wear it."

Mattie clasped her sister's hand between hers. "I do, too, but sometimes we're happy and sometimes we're not."

"I want you to be happy all the time, Mattie."

"That's a lovely thought." She squeezed Daisy's hand. "But if I wasn't sad once in a while, how would I know how blessed I am when I'm happy?"

"It says in Ecclesiastes 2:26. 'For *God* giveth to a man that *is* good in his sight wisdom, and knowledge, and joy.'" She giggled. "And He gives that to women, too. *Daed* says so."

"Who am I to argue with you and *Daed*?" She stood and went to another box. She was amazed how Daisy, who found it difficult to read the Bible, could keep so many verses in her head. No, not in her head, but in her heart.

"And God!"

"I'm not going to argue with Him either, because He knows everything, and I don't."

Daisy steered her chair around another stack of boxes. "You know a lot, Mattie. You were smart enough to bring us here."

"That was Mark and Lucas and Juan's doing."

"Okay, but you're smart enough to get Benjamin to help us at the shop."

Mattie smiled. "That was Mark, too."

Frowning, she said, "You're smart enough to make my favorite pie for dessert."

"*That* I was smart enough to do."

"See?" A triumphant smile returned to her sister's face. "I told you you're smart." She put her finger to her lips. "Quiet. Boppi Lynn is taking a nap."

"She's a wise little girl. It's a *gut* time for a nap."

"I think so, too." Daisy yawned. "A very *gut* time."

"Have pretty dreams." Mattie rose, bent to kiss her sister's cheek and gathered a stack of clothing. She closed the door behind herself as she went into the living room and took a deep breath of the *wunderbaar*, pungent aroma of the chili cooking in the kitchen before she climbed the stairs to her own room under the low eaves.

She paused as, when she stepped into her room, another gust shook the house. She went to the gable window that should have offered a view of the Kuepfers' house. The Kuepfer brothers, Juan and Lucas, were living together in the house while they fixed the house on Lucas's farm. They were patching walls and floors, using reclaimed wood from the shop, and taking out the electric wiring as they did. Once they knew someone walking across the floors wouldn't fall through, Lucas would move into his own house on his own farm and keep rebuilding the house after working in the fields each day. Juan would then finish the work on his house next door.

Life was an endless carousel of chores in Prince Edward Island, but Mattie wouldn't have traded it for any place else. Soon, she hoped, *Daed* and her two brothers who hadn't jumped the fence would arrive. Then they'd be a family again. A smaller family which had been torn asunder, but a family nonetheless. *Daed* and Ohmer and Dennis would stay busy with their farm on the Island while Mattie spent time at the shop with Daisy.

You spend too much time with your sister.

She cringed as she heard the echo of Karl's voice in her head. Why was he plaguing her now? She'd told him she didn't want to walk out with him more than a year ago. *Mamm* had insisted he was her perfect match, so Mattie had agreed to let him take her home from a few youth events where they'd been chaperoning the younger ones.

How could Karl have been envious of the time Mattie spent with her sister? His demand that she choose him over her family had made telling him she didn't want to see him again easy…and had allowed her to avoid admitting the truth. Her heart longed to belong to Benjamin Kuhns, though he hadn't known she'd fallen in love with him while he was falling in love with Sharrell.

Her hands dropped, idle, to her lap as she sat on her bed. With each passing day, it was more and more difficult to recall the woman she'd been last year. She could no longer imagine walking out with a man because someone told her she should.

She looked at the sampler she'd hung on the light blue wall so it was the first thing she'd see each morning when she opened her eyes. The verse from the Book of Mark was one she'd learned from her *daed*'s *mamm*. She'd chosen to use it when *Grossmammi* Alma offered to teach her to cross-stitch.

"'And when ye stand praying,'" she whispered, "'forgive, if ye have ought against any: that your Father also which is in heaven may forgive you your trespasses.'"

She sighed. It was easy to say she wanted to forgive *Mamm* for running away from their family—from her—but if Mattie wanted to forgive, why hadn't she? The thought of *Mamm* sent heated anger rising through her like lava in a volcano.

Unable to sit, she opened another box. It was filled with the special quilt *Grossmammi* Alma had made for her. Her *grossmammi* had sewn one for each of her *kinskinder* after they were born. The quilts were meant to be used throughout their lives, but *Mamm* had insisted they be stored away until their wedding days.

"I'm not waiting any longer," she said as if *Mamm* could hear the words from where she was halfway across Canada. "When you left, you said only fools follow rules. Well, I'm not a fool. Or I'm not as much of a fool as I used to be."

Balancing the quilt against her sling so no weight strained her shoulder, she placed it on top of her bed. It wasn't easy spreading it across the mattress with a single hand, but she managed. The pattern, Diamond in the Square, had large swaths of dark blue fabric along the four sides. In the center, set in a field of dark green edged by lines and squares of blue and red, was the diamond. It was a patchwork square with triangles on all four sides. The colors were vibrant and brought her simple bedroom to life.

She was where she was supposed to be.

Something banged against the roof, and she flinched. She cupped her elbow. The slight support eased the pain searing her shoulder after she'd reacted to the unexpected noise.

Should she check the attic? She found a flashlight in the bedside table and rushed to the low door that opened into the attic space. A quick sweep of its light on the underside of the roof didn't show any damage.

Grateful, Mattie walked back to her room. Boppi Lynn and Daisy might have had the best idea. Rest during the fury of the storm and wait for the sunshine to return.

But her thoughts were as turbulent as the winds. They centered on Benjamin and how she'd seen him at the real estate office. Was he thinking about staying here? Why else would he have been visiting the office? She wished she'd asked him while they were having ice cream. She didn't need more puzzles in her life when she was confounded about why *Mamm* had deserted them with no other explanation than she wasn't happy any longer.

Fifteen minutes later, Mattie was tenser than she'd been when she'd decided to rest. She came downstairs to hear someone hammering on the door.

Her heart leaped as she rushed to it. Could it be Benjamin? In this storm? She threw the door open.

The wind almost knocked her off her feet, and a hand settled on her right arm. Nothing zinged across her skin as it had when Benjamin helped her with her sling earlier at the shop.

She was eased aside so her three cousins could enter the small living room. Cold radiated off them, and she stepped away, not wanting to chance a shiver igniting another flame across her shoulder.

"What are you doing out in a blizzard?" she asked, trying to ignore how disappointed she was Benjamin hadn't come to the house. "Have you lost your minds?"

She must have lost hers if she expected Benjamin to come in the middle of a powerful storm. If he had, she would have chided him for being stupid, too. The one thing she hadn't expected when he reappeared in her life was her variety of reactions to him. Some logical, and others, like this evening, utterly illogical.

Mark unwound his scarf and revealed how his face above it had been chafed by the wind. "How are you doing?"

"So far so *gut*." She smiled. "You didn't need to check on us."

"Mattie and me and Boppi Lynn are keeping busy," announced Daisy when she came into the room.

Mattie settled her sister's *kapp* in its proper place. "We've been unpacking since we got home before the storm hit."

"You should have asked one of us to help." Lucas shrugged off his coat and tossed it on the well-worn sofa next to a table holding a Bible and a few other books.

"We're managing fine," Mattie said. "It's not as if you don't have a lot to do, too. But what about something to eat?"

"Is that chili I smell?" asked Juan.

"*Ja*. The family recipe."

That was all her cousins needed to hear. They divested themselves of their outerwear and stampeded into the kitchen which was the largest room in the house. Even so, it only had room for a long table, a few cabinets and basic appliances.

As the wind and snow blew around the house, Mattie worked with her family to get supper ready. It reminded her of how it'd been at home before *Mamm* left, though her brothers seldom came into the kitchen other than to eat. Her cousins pitched in, talking nonstop. She had to wonder if anyone was listening to the others, but she soaked up the contentment of being with her family.

Her cousins along with Daisy insisted she sit and let them put the meal on the table.

"Tell us what to do," Lucas said.

"*Ja*. Pretend you're Mark." Juan laughed as his cousin made a face at him while everyone else chuckled.

Mattie didn't have to do more than explain where plates and silverware were. In quick order, Mark carried the chili pot from the stove and placed it on a trivet Daisy had set on the table. Lucas put the rolls next to it while his brother got butter and chowchow from the refrigerator. Daisy poured water into glasses around the table, then pulled her chair in next to Mattie's.

"You're going to spoil me," Mattie said as her cousins took their seats.

"Not likely." Juan didn't give her a chance to reply before he prompted, "Mark?"

The oldest of the male cousins bowed his head, and the rest of them did the same. Mattie took the time for silent grace to thank the Lord for her cousins who hadn't complained once about how her injury might destroy their dreams of having farms of their own. Might destroy those dreams before they began.

When Mark cleared his throat, the sign grace was finished, Mattie raised her head. Juan with a flourish held out his hand for her bowl. He ladled chili into it and set it in front of her, leaving a few drips across the table. She told him not to be bothered, though she doubted he was.

She smiled as she took a roll from the plate Daisy offered her, then managed to pass it to Lucas who sat on her other side. He winked, and she guessed her delight with being able to do something so simple must have been visible on her face.

"Is it okay to ask how it's going at the shop?" Lucas queried, as always, concerned more about others' feelings than his own.

"Of course, you can ask." Mattie held out the chowchow to his brother. "We're working as fast as we can, but I'm not sure we can be done on time."

It was the first time she'd said those words out loud, and she saw her cousins exchanging worried glances.

"Don't look like that!" Daisy slapped her hand on the table, making water splash out of two glasses. When Mattie jumped to her feet to get a towel before it dripped on someone's lap, Daisy hurried to add, "You saw the mess when you bought the place. We're working as hard and as fast as we can."

"It's all right, Daisy," Mark said in a soothing tone.

She scowled at him. "I'm not a *kind*, Mark! You shouldn't talk to me as if I'm one."

"No," he said, "you're not a *kind*. Not any longer. But an adult doesn't pound the table to make a point."

"I needed your attention." Daisy wasn't about to back down, even when Mattie put a hand on her arm. "You need to come to the shop and see how much we've done. Mattie didn't take a single day off after hurting her shoulder, though her *doktor* told her to."

"He told me," Mattie said, glancing around the table, "not to strain my shoulder, and I've done my best not to."

Daisy wasn't going to be mollified. "And you've done your best to get the place cleaned out. Nobody's going to say otherwise."

"We're sorry, Daisy," Lucas said. "We're distressed because we didn't realize how much work it'd take."

"We wouldn't be as far along as we are if we didn't have Benjamin's help." Mattie looked at Mark. "I don't know if I ever told you *danki* for letting James know we needed help. His asking Benjamin has enabled us to make as much progress as we have."

"I never expected him to put in more than a day or two."

"He said he'd come every day if I'd teach him how to run a store."

"What?" asked all three of her cousins at the same time.

Daisy giggled. "You sound like a bunch of geese."

Laughter rushed around the table, easing the tension that had clamped around them. Again bowls and platters were passed, and Mattie rose, despite protests, to bring the pot of *kaffi* to the table.

As she began to fill the cups, Mark asked, "Did Benjamin explain why he wants to learn to run a store?"

"Not much." She hadn't asked because knowing more about Benjamin threatened to open her heart to him again.

"Is he going to open a place here?"

"Maybe." Seeing the glances her cousins exchanged before she carried the pot to the stove, she added, "I didn't ask." She didn't add that she'd seen Benjamin at the real estate office. Unless she knew for sure he'd gone there for his own purposes and not James's, she couldn't share what she'd seen. "I thought we needed his help enough that agreeing to show him what I learned from running our farm stand in Ontario seemed a small price to pay." As she sat at the table and reached for the sugar, she said, "If you're curious about Benjamin's plans, you could ask him or James."

"I have asked James." Mark rubbed his chin between his thumb and forefinger as he did whenever he was trying to solve a puzzle. "But he says he's got no idea if Benjamin intends to stay or not."

"So why is he asking Mattie to teach him to run a store?" Lucas asked, leaning his elbows on the table.

Everyone looked at her, and all she could say was the truth, "I don't know."

Chapter Six

Benjamin picked his way past another pile of debris, chasing the sound of wood shifting. He hoped Mattie wasn't taking any chances with the stacks. For someone with a lot of common sense, she'd made what he thought were rash decisions too often in her determination to get the shop open. He would have thought, during the past ten days while they'd been working together, that she'd realized her limitations with her dislocated shoulder. She hadn't. She plowed ahead, not willing to let anything slow her.

Not that he could fault her for the accident. He'd nearly been hit by boards several times. Each time, he'd managed to jump aside. Daisy had called warnings when she saw a pile move. Having the girl keep an eye out had been a *gut* idea. Not only was he able to make sure she and her doll were far enough away so they couldn't be struck, but she knew what she was doing was important.

It was impossible to keep as close an eye on Mattie. She worked in a different section of the hut, gathering smaller items because she couldn't use both hands. An efficient working situation, but he could spend the day not saying much more than a morning greeting and an evening farewell to her because they spent the day separated by the debris.

His mouth tightened as he edged around another stack of rotting boards. The problem was she shouldn't be there at all. She should have stayed at home and rested her shoulder. However, each time he'd suggested she finish so she could go home and put heat on her shoulder, she assured him she wasn't overdoing it.

"Stubborn woman," he muttered under his breath.

He had to admire how she did as she'd promised her cousins. She wasn't like his brother with his imperious orders. She thanked him each day for coming. Her gratitude was sincere, but he couldn't miss how she kept him at an arms' length. While Daisy chatted about everything and everyone in her life, Mattie's words were focused on their job.

The unmistakable creak of wood slithering off a pile yanked him out of his thoughts. He rounded the next heap, as Mattie jumped away from a tumbling pile of wood. She hit him hard enough to knock his breath from him, but she'd pushed him aside so he wasn't hit either.

"Be careful," she said.

"I was about to say that to you."

"I am being careful. This time the boards missed me."

As she stepped away from him, it was as if a dark chasm had opened, sucking in his *gut* feelings and leaving him empty. Puzzled, he tried not to think why a simple motion, taking her a single pace away, felt so devastating. He could smell her lavender shampoo and meet her uncompromising eyes in her pretty face. Her cheeks were pale, a sure sign her shoulder was aching.

Her shoulder...

He stared as he exclaimed, "You're not wearing your sling! Is that okay?"

"Ja." A flash of amusement sped through her eyes. "Patty told me to try not wearing it a few hours each day. If the pain doesn't get worse, I should keep it off longer and longer every day."

"That's great. I—"

The sound of wood scratching against wood interrupted him. He wrapped an arm around her waist and lifted her off her feet, carrying her with him as he back-pedaled. She shrieked out a cry of surprise before he set her on her feet, more than a meter from where they'd been standing. A moment later, the wood that had been mounded against the wall tumbled, pieces shattering on the concrete floor. Dust and splinters erupted into the air.

He turned her face against his chest while he hid his own against her head. The sharp sounds of lumber clattering to the floor vanished as he breathed in the scent of the starch in her *kapp*. The whole world disappeared as he savored how she fit into his arms perfectly. Her breath sifted through his shirt to warm a spot right over his heart. Nothing had ever felt so *wunderbaar*.

Then he sneezed.

Hard.

And sneezed again and again.

She stepped back. "Are you okay?"

"Just the dust," he said, waving his arms as if he could knock it out of the air. "Tickled my nose."

She opened her mouth, then sneezed. She winced, and he guessed the simple motion had hurt her shoulder. Her voice was unsteady as she said, "Me, too."

"What happened? That stack was pretty secure against the wall. I checked it yesterday before we left for the night." He hoped she didn't guess how much easier it was to talk about the mundane issue of the falling wood than the special moment—a moment far too fleeting—when he'd held her.

Had she been as astonished as he was by the connection he'd sensed between them? If so, he saw no sign of it on her face and heard nothing in her words. She edged away and cradled her left elbow.

"I don't know what happened. I was walking past, and I heard the wood start to shift."

He frowned as he bent to examine what remained of the pile. "I checked this last night before we left, and the bottom pieces weren't so far from the wall. It looks like they've been moved."

"Of course they have. I told you that I heard the wood moving."

"But why would they move?"

"I don't know."

"It's not as if they can move on their own."

"None of us touched them." She glanced around. He did, too, but saw nothing amiss, so he wasn't surprised when she sighed before saying, "The wood is so rotten, it must be caving in under its own weight. We'll have to be extra cautious until we unstack the rest of it."

"Until *I* do."

"Benjamin, we've talked about this before. I can do—"

"I know you can do anything you put your mind to, but it'll be easier if one of us stands off to the side and keeps an eye on the pile while the other removes the boards. That way, if they start to fall, you can alert me and I can get out of the way. Doesn't that make sense?"

"*Ja.*"

"*Gut.* That's how Daisy and I have been working things."

"Why didn't you say that in the first place?"

He grinned at the vexation in her voice. Did she have any idea how delightful it was to see her eyes snapping like fireflies on a moonless night?

"I thought you knew," he replied. "You've peeked around the corner at us enough times."

When she rolled her eyes, looking as much of a teenager as her sister, he resisted chuckling.

He looked past her. "Where's Daisy today?"

"Boppi Lynn has the sniffles." She scooped a crushed can off the floor and tossed it into the bucket a few feet away.

Had he heard her wrong? Daisy's doll was sick?

She smiled as she straightened. "Our cousin, Mark, brought Daisy three new books from Charlottetown yesterday. She stayed up all night reading. When she's tired, she announces Boppi Lynn has the sniffles and needs to stay in bed."

"And being the *gut mamm* she is, she has to stay in bed, too."

"*Ja.* If you want the truth, I doubt you'll see much of Daisy until she finishes the first three books in the Anne of Green Gables series. They're set right on the Island, so Daisy was fascinated with the stories before she opened the cover of the first one." She motioned toward the rear of the hut. "In the meantime, I'll be glad to be your spotter."

"*Gut.*" As she turned to pick up the bucket, he asked, "Do you think you can take a couple of hours away this afternoon?"

She faced him again. "I shouldn't. I'm not spending enough time here as it is with PT."

He knew that, but he also wanted her opinion on what he'd discussed yesterday evening with James. His friend had been growing impatient with Benjamin's vacillation about whether he intended to stay or return to Harmony Creek Hollow.

"You've got to make up your mind," James had said as they were finishing a supper of leftover beef stew, "if you are going to do what you want to do or what Menno insists you do."

"He wants me back right away. Says the busy season is coming."

"Menno is always seeing a busy season right around the corner." James had taken a reflective sip of his *kaffi*. "I figured Menno was pressuring you when I saw you got a letter from him, and you were glum the rest of the evening."

"He makes sense, James."

His friend had put down his cup and looked at Benjamin. "I'm sure you think he does. He's been telling you what to do for so long you're accustomed to bowing to his edicts without a thought of your own."

"It's not that. He makes sense about the future of the sawmill and how when we bought it, we did so thinking both of us would work there."

"If Menno needs another hand to help, let him hire someone. God has a plan for you, Benjamin. You need to listen to Him, not to Menno."

Benjamin hadn't said anything last night, but he agreed with James. One thing stood in the way of walking away from the sawmill. When he'd promised Menno he'd help his brother build and run the business, Benjamin had been at a low point in his life, not caring what he did. He hadn't considered the long-term consequences.

His word meant so much to him. He was edging close to *hochmut* in being proud that he'd never reneged on a promise. His only promise should be to hold on to his faith in God and live the life Jesus taught.

"I know you shouldn't take time off," Benjamin said, realizing Mattie was waiting for him to say something. "But will you?"

"Benjamin, I hadn't thought it would take so long to clean up this place. We've got to paint and put shelves up and stock those shelves and—"

"I get it! But what if I come in an hour earlier for the next week? I don't mind getting up earlier in the morning."

Again he thought she might disagree, but she said, "All right. I'll come with you. You don't have to come in earlier. You can't work with no light."

"I'll borrow a hanging flashlight from James, and I'll be able to work."

When she looked around the remaining debris, she sighed. "I know I should insist you don't need to do that, but we're all going to have to come in earlier if there's going to be any chance of being finished on time. Let's get what we can done, and then we'll go...where?"

"There's a piece of property I want to look at, and I'd like someone else's thoughts on it."

Mattie's eyes grew wide. "Why mine? If you're looking at property, you should ask Mark or Lucas or Juan or your friend James. They know a lot more about property here than I do."

"I'd like your opinion."

"Why?"

He shoved his hands into his pockets. "You've been curious about why I've been asking you to teach me more about running a shop, ain't so?"

"*Ja.*"

"Well, you'll get your answer if you come out to the property."

"I don't understand."

Resting his elbow on the narrow windowsill, he hoped he looked more casual than he felt. "I want to open a shop on that property. I could use your insight on its location. What do you say?"

He held his breath, waiting for her response. Could she hear how his heart beat hard against his breastbone as she took a moment to think over his request? He didn't want anyone to know how important this decision was to him or how difficult it was proving to be. He hoped he wasn't being foolish to check it out.

Would Mattie be surprised if he said he envied how certain she was that she was where God meant her to be, doing what God wanted her to do? Once he'd thought that way, too, but then his life had turned inside out after his brief courtship with her sister, and he'd begun to question so many aspects of his life. Not his faith, but his lack of comprehension about how God expected him to live his life and where. After working with Menno for the past couple of years at the sawmill in Harmony Creek Hollow, he'd been confident that life wasn't the right one.

But then he received letters from his brother and his sister. Menno's had been the usual litany of complaints. Sarah's had mentioned Menno was having a tougher time than any of them had imagined running the sawmill on his own. She was ready to help him hire an assistant, but should she be looking for a temporary hire or a permanent one? He had to answer her, but he didn't have a response yet. Looking at the property might help him decide.

"All right," Mattie said at last, pulling him out of his quandary. "I'm not sure how valuable my input will be, but I'll be glad to offer it."

As they got to work, he realized she hadn't asked what sort of shop he planned to open, and he was grateful. He wouldn't have lied, but he wasn't ready yet to share his dream of selling his handmade clocks.

He didn't want her to laugh. He didn't want Mattie belittling his dreams as Menno had when Benjamin had been silly enough to reveal them. He couldn't endure another person whose opinion he respected telling him that he'd be wasting his time and money.

Keeping her right hand under her left elbow so she didn't jar her shoulder as she stepped out of the buggy by the side of a busy road, Mattie heard frozen grass crunch beneath her boots. She was amazed how different the weather could be a few miles away from Shushan Bay. Every inch of the Island was affected by the temperature of the water surrounding it and the wind blowing across it. Her sheltered bay was already showing signs of winter departing, despite the recent snowstorm, but here on the road to Charlottetown, the frigid grip hadn't loosened.

She looked around. Snow clung to the shadowed places beneath the trees as if the icy bits were hiding from the sunshine so they weren't melted into oblivion. Two buildings faced each other from opposite sides of the road, one a barn and the other a dilapidated house. Not a speck of paint could be seen on either. Trees were clumped behind the buildings, and the tangled wiry arms of briars and weeds surrounded the house. The area around the barn had been cleared, the ground frozen in contortions left from a vehicle with tracks instead of wheels.

"Which side of the road are you looking at?" she asked as Benjamin came around the buggy.

"The property is on both sides." He rubbed his gloved hands together. "There's not anything to see inside the house. It looks like your shop, only worse because the walls and the ceilings have fallen in. Tearing it down might be the best idea."

"And the barn?"

"It's in a bit better condition, and you don't need a machete to get to the door. Do you want to see inside it?"

"That's what we came here to do, ain't so?"

"*Ja* and no. I'm not as interested in the buildings as I am in the land itself."

Though she wanted to ask him to explain that last statement, he was walking toward the barn before she had a chance. She followed and was amazed to discover the entry was wide open. One door lay on the frozen grass to the right of the doorway. The other wasn't in sight.

The barn's interior was as battered as the outside. Grooves in the wooden floors showed where loaded wagons had come in and been stored for decades. Each step she took sent dust and bits of hay rising to swirl like miniature whirlwinds in the beam of sunlight cas-

cading from the window in the gable. Scents of feed
and animals were like long-ago memories.

She walked to a stable box. The door hung by one
hinge. Had a horse sheltered in the box where hay was
decomposing on the concrete floor? Or had it been a
pony used by the *kinder* to pull a cart around the farm?

Farther along, she saw the stanchions which went
around a cow's neck while being milked. The water
bowls were empty. She looked up a ladder to the loft
and wondered if cats still hid their litters there.

But she noticed how the boards along the walls were
warped, some so badly they seemed about ready to escape from the nails holding them in place. Wind blew
through, rattling the joists and tugging at the walls. The
wood was so dry, even with the snow and ice around
the barn, that a single spark would set the whole building alight in minutes.

"Are you thinking of this building for your shop?"
she asked.

"For the shop and everything else." He pointed at the
loft. "There's a lot of hay up there, so the floor must
be able to hold weight. I can live there and work here."

Her gloved fingers lingered against the hand-hewn
supports, and she looked at the beams overhead. From
where she stood she could see the marks left when the
wood had been shaped into rafters. The bones of the
building were *wunderbaar*, and as Benjamin outlined
how he'd use the space, she could imagine it. So much
work would be required, but every ounce of sweat eq-
uity could be worth it. The soaring lines of the roof and
the structure inside could be left open. Large windows
replacing the missing doors in the entry would send
sunshine through the whole building.

"It'll be beautiful," she said.

"That's what I thought." Benjamin grinned. "That's the main road going between Charlottetown and Shushan, so it'll get a lot of traffic in the summer when tourists are circling the Island. A sign outside might convince them to stop."

"Do you plan to cater primarily to tourists?"

"*Ja.*"

"What are you going to sell?"

"Clocks."

"Clocks?" She stared in amazement. She'd been certain he intended to open a farm stand of his own or something similar. Her cousins had believed that and had been puzzled that Benjamin was helping them when his business could become their competition.

"*Ja*, clocks." He stared at the joists supporting the hayloft. "Making clocks is something I've been interested in for a long time, but Menno has needed my assistance with the sawmill and the tree farm."

"But why here?"

"Why not?"

"Answering a question with a question doesn't get either of us any closer to the truth."

"You sound like Daisy when you say things like that." He shook his head when she opened her mouth to retort. "Don't shoot daggers with your eyes. I meant that as a compliment. Your sister speaks her mind without beating around the bush. I admire that about her."

Knowing she couldn't look for hidden negativity in everything he said, she nodded. "I do as well, but too much honesty can be a bad thing."

He opened his mouth to reply, then halted as the sound of boots came from the entry. A man walked toward them. He had a thick gray mustache and a long beard that reached the second button on his overcoat. Everything about him was long and thin, and when he moved, all she could think of was a scarecrow that had come off its pole to wander through the countryside.

"Can I help you?" he called.

"We're looking around," Benjamin said, crossing the barn to meet the man. "I'm considering purchasing this property."

"I'm Henry LaPierre. I own the farm next door." He stepped forward, and the sunshine glistened off his bald pate. Her eyes were caught by his gigantic mustache. It grew over his lower lip and halfway to his chin. She wondered how he managed to eat with it in the way. "You can see my place past the trees this time of year." He pointed toward a white house with a wide wrap-around porch that would be the perfect place to sit in a rocker at day's end.

"I'm Benjamin Kuhns." He gestured toward her. "And this is Mattie Albrecht."

"I shouldn't stick my nose in where it doesn't belong," Mr. LaPierre said, "but I'm sure you've noticed the land wouldn't be much *gut* for growing potatoes."

"I'm not a farmer."

"No?" Mr. LaPierre eyed him up and down again. "If you don't want to farm the land, what do you want it for?"

"The wood lot and the barn."

"Ah." He nodded as if the few words had explained everything. Clearly wanting to ask more questions, he halted when a woman came out on the porch of the farmhouse and called his name. "Time to go. I made one rule when I got married: Never be late for any meal my wife has prepared." He wagged a finger at Benjamin, then winked at Mattie as he said, "Wisdom I'm glad to pass on to you two."

Mattie felt heat on her cheeks. Had Mr. LaPierre somehow sensed her thoughts about the barn's renovations? How she'd imagined herself standing in the vast space, watching the sunlight dance through the uneven glass in the windows while Benjamin built his clocks?

She backed into a shadowed area, pretending to be intrigued by a water trough that had fallen into pieces. She knew with every sense when Benjamin came to stand behind her. He didn't touch her, but her skin was as aware of him as if he'd run his hands along her arms.

"*Danki* for coming today," he said, his words ruffling the small hairs beneath the bottom of her bonnet.

She didn't look at him. "It's been fun to see more of the Island."

"So what do you think of my idea of opening a shop?"

Though she didn't want to turn when he stood so close, she did. Her breath threatened to explode out of her, but she forced herself to sound calm. "As long as you've thought through all the work ahead of you—"

"I've thought of little else for the last year. I've been praying for guidance, and He's led me here. I've got to admit I hadn't considered having a shop in Prince Edward Island, but the opportunity is in front of me. I've heard that God opens doors in unexpected places."

"In a place without a door?"

He grinned. "Are you always so literal?"

"Daisy is, and I thought you were missing her input."

His grin became a laugh. "I should know better than to try to trade words with an Albrecht woman. You keep a guy on his toes."

She shifted her eyes away from his gaze as she had each time he referred, even obliquely, to Sharrell. If he saw a hint of her dismay on her face, he was sure to ask what he'd said to upset her. How could she admit that, after five long years, she regretted how stupid she'd been to pine for a man who hadn't noticed her?

Benjamin walked out of the barn, and Mattie bent her head as she followed. The wind was beginning to stiffen again, so she should have been glad to get in the warm buggy. It seemed too intimate with them sitting side by side. He didn't touch her, but again she was conscious of each motion he made as if she was a puppet connected to him by invisible strings.

Her disquiet must have been obvious because, as he took the reins, Benjamin said, "This is the first time we've done something without Daisy joining us."

"No, it's not. It's—" She halted herself when she realized he was right. Every other time they'd been together, Daisy had been with them. Even the times when Daisy had taken a nap in the back room. "Well, there was the time I went off to the hospital on my own."

"Don't remind me of that. I see you lying under that wood when I close my eyes. I thought you were dead."

"I'm sorry."

"For what?"

"For you having to come to my rescue."

"Don't spout nonsense. You would have done the same for me, though I hope you never have to." He steered the buggy along the road, drawing it to the right along the uneven dirt shoulder whenever a car came behind them. "It seems strange not to have Daisy with us. You two are a matched set."

Was he going to chide her as Karl had about making

Daisy a priority in her life? If so, she was going to tell him that if he didn't like how she and Daisy were close, then he didn't need to bother coming to the shop again.

Her whole body seemed to spasm at her own thought. They needed Benjamin if there was any hope of them meeting the deadline Mark had set. That was the cause of her reaction, she told herself. It didn't have anything to do with how much she looked forward to seeing him each day.

He chuckled, startling her. "I miss her teasing me."

"You miss her?" she choked out.

"Sure. In a lot of ways, she reminds me of my younger sister. Never having much respect for her older brother."

She was amazed. She'd been so sure he was going to complain like Karl, that her mind was having trouble grasping his words. He appreciated having Daisy around?

"Daisy likes you, too," she said.

"And you? How do you feel about me hanging around and getting in your way?"

Any hesitation in answering would suggest she had to give the questions a lot of thought. Because she wasn't prepared to answer them or because she was too uncertain about her feelings for him? She *was* uncertain, but she didn't want to reveal that.

"First of all," she replied in a tone that suggested he was silly to ask, "you don't hang around. You've been working hard. And if you hadn't 'gotten in my way,' as you put it, who knows how long I would have lain under those boards with a damaged shoulder?"

"That's in the past. I'm talking about now."

"You don't hang around." She looked across the

buggy to find his gaze focused on her. Caught by its intensity, she doubted she could have looked away.

Not that she wanted to. It was easy to accept the invitation in his deep brown eyes and let her own gaze linger while she discovered more about the man who'd reappeared in her life at the very moment she needed him. How ironic, when she'd prided herself as a woman who wouldn't ever need to be rescued!

"And you don't mind me being underfoot?" he asked in little more than a whisper.

Words of how his presence in her life again was an unexpected gift begged to escape her lips. She halted them. Though he'd brought her out to look at the property along the Charlottetown road, he hadn't hidden how he wasn't sure whether he would stay or go home. He had hurried home after he and Sharrell broke up, instead of staying to mend whatever had broken between them. Would he take off again, as *Mamm* had, if things didn't go his way on the Island?

She couldn't risk her heart on a man who had already left her behind once.

Chapter Seven

Wiggling her fingers, Mattie relished how pain didn't rush to her shoulder any longer whenever she moved her left arm or hand. It was a *wunderbaar* change after almost four weeks. She'd been glad to leave March and its pain behind, but turning the calendar's page had been a reminder that the shop must be open by month's end.

She walked around the large, cleared space inside the front half of the Quonset hut. No, she wasn't going to think of it as a hut anymore. She needed to call it the Celtic Knoll Farm Shop when talking with prospective customers. At least a score of people had stopped in as the weather had warmed to above freezing. They wanted to see the progress. Each one had expressed excitement about having a shop closer than Shushan. Several were grateful the cousins had purchased the landmark building and were rehabbing it.

One young man and his wife had asked about buying pieces of the old lumber. Mattie urged them to take as much as they wanted. They'd been delighted when she told them they didn't need to worry about paying.

"You're saving us from being charged to take it

away," she'd told them. "We've got all we need, so help yourself to whatever's out front."

They'd thanked her, telling her they were looking for old cedar boards to turn into shakes for the cottage they were building at the mouth of the bay.

But ridding the building of so much of the debris had led to other problems. Mattie hadn't guessed there would be a massive hole, deep enough to hold one of the stacks, near the back door. The concrete floor must be repaired before they went much further. She didn't want to chance her sister's chair rolling into it or her klutzy self tripping into it.

"You klutzy?" asked Benjamin as he used a broom to sweep trash into piles he could scoop into the bag Daisy held. "What gave you that idea?"

Mattie pointed to her left shoulder. "This for a starter."

"You were in the wrong place at the wrong time. That's all."

Waving aside his words, she said, "Be careful until we can get the cement company here tomorrow."

Once the big hole was filled, she'd arranged for the large truck to deliver more cement for a sidewalk to the front door from the road. Next week, the trucks were scheduled to lay a concrete driveway that would allow supply trucks to reach the storage rooms at the rear.

"So what do you want us to do today while we wait?" he asked.

Before she could answer, Daisy said, "I know what we should do."

"What's that?" Mattie asked.

"Have a picnic."

"A what?"

Benjamin laughed. "If you don't know what a picnic is, Mattie, you've been working too hard for too long."

"I know what a picnic is." She looked out the door. "There's snow on the ground. Picnics are meant for warm, sunny days."

"It's sunny." Daisy bounced her doll on her knees. "Boppi Lynn wants to go across the road and have a picnic by the water."

"Boppi Lynn will freeze her little toes right off."

Pulling out a small cloth bag from between her hip and the side of her chair, Daisy opened it. She lifted out tiny crocheted socks and slipped them on her doll's feet. "Nice and warm. So can we go?"

Benjamin said, "Mattie's right. It's too cold for a picnic, but what if we take a look at the bay?"

"Can we?"

"As long as it's okay with Mattie."

"Mattie?" Her upturned face glowed with anticipation.

Smiling, Mattie replied, "That sounds like fun, but not for long. I don't want to freeze my nose off."

Daisy laughed. "You'd look so different without a nose."

"*Ja*," Benjamin interjected. "How would we know if we said or did something you thought was silly if we can't see your nose wrinkle?"

"I don't—"

"All the time," crowed Daisy as she and Benjamin laughed.

"Okay, let's go," Mattie said, eager to switch the conversation away from herself.

"I'm getting our coats!" Daisy rushed away toward the storage room where they left their outerwear and lunch boxes. Her song floated to them. "Toes and noses. Noses and toes. Don't freeze them. Might need them. Toes and noses. Noses and toes."

"That's a big grin." Benjamin chuckled.

"She's thrilled, ain't so?" Mattie replied.

"I'm not talking about Daisy. I'm talking about your grin. I can't believe it's because you're letting her talk you into going outside and sitting in the cold."

"No, it's not. I'm happy how easily Daisy drew the socks onto Boppi Lynn's feet. You may think it's a simple thing, but it hasn't always been easy for her to do. She began working with an occupational therapist as a toddler, and one of her first tasks was learning how to put on socks. Not just hers. She practiced on everyone until our older siblings made sure they had their shoes on before they came downstairs."

"Because they didn't want to wait for her to get their socks on?"

"A couple have ticklish feet." Her smile faded. "*Daed* is ticklish, too, but he never begrudged Daisy a chance to practice, even when it took her more than an hour to get his socks on. He always has had time for each of his *kinder*, though there were nine of us and he had the farm. I can't say the same for *Mamm*."

"She left, ain't so?"

"*Ja.*" She should have guessed he would have heard about the Albrecht family's shame. Thinking the tale wouldn't follow her and Daisy had been naive. Would the truth cast a pall over the shop and keep customers from coming? She closed her eyes before tears could spill over. Had all their hard work been worthless before they'd begun? If nobody came…

As if she'd spoken her thoughts aloud, Benjamin

said, "It was her choice to go, not anyone else's. Nobody should judge any other member of your family by her actions."

"Plenty have."

"People who know you and your family well?"

"No," she admitted. "Most people who know us have made efforts to treat us the same as before she left."

"It'll be like that here."

"But people don't know us yet."

"They'll get to know you here in the shop and through community events. You've already met your neighbors at church, ain't so?"

He was making sense, and she was letting her fears control her when she should be depending on her faith in God's plans for her and her family.

"*Danki*, Benjamin, for saying what I needed to hear." She put her fingers to the middle of the dusty bib on her apron. "I know that in my heart, but sometimes it's easier to worry than to heed the truth."

"Glad to help." He chuckled, lightening the moment. "Do the same for me if I open my shop and wonder whether anyone will come."

She nodded, but went to meet Daisy who was bringing their coats. *If I open my shop.* When was Benjamin going to decide whether to stay or to go? If he stayed, she must be careful. He'd left her sister. Knowing she was making too much of her attraction to him— again!—she reminded herself she and Benjamin were only working together. He wasn't walking out with her as he had with Sharrell.

Daisy's chatter and Benjamin's answers buoyed Mattie out of her low spirits while they left the shop. The wind had dropped to a gentle breeze, but it didn't offer much hint of impending spring warmth. She dipped her face into her scarf, then raised it when the air sifting through the thick knit was stale.

They waited for two cars to pass, then crossed the road toward the bay. Benjamin grabbed the handles on Daisy's wheelchair. With care, he helped her navigate through the thick grass that had become matted beneath the snow during the winter.

"I hear the waves!" Daisy looked at her doll. "Do you hear them, Boppi Lynn?" She grinned. "Boppi Lynn likes the sound of the waves. It's like they're whispering."

"I like them, too." Mattie watched her own steps as they edged down the gently sloping bank.

"Oops!" Benjamin chuckled and added, "It's more slippery than I'd guessed. Ice isn't just on the water, ain't so?"

"It's all around the Island," Daisy said before pointing out a gull to her doll.

"Most of the way," Mattie said with a smile.

"Maybe next winter, it'll be all the way around." Daisy chuckled. "If it gets thick enough, Juan said he'll put skis on my wheels so I can go ice skating with him."

"That sounds like fun." Benjamin winked at her. "Warn me when you're coming because I know how you like to go fast."

Mattie glanced at him as her sister began to tell Boppi Lynn how much the doll would love skating. Unlike others, Benjamin treated Daisy as if she was a regular kid and listened as if it was ordinary to talk about a doll in ice skates. She wondered if her sister realized what a precious gift it was.

Maybe so. Maybe not.

But Mattie did, and knowing endangered her heart more.

* * *

Benjamin threw a stone into the water beyond the red sand beach. He'd aimed at the ice, but missed. The waves swallowed its ripples. He listened as Mattie and Daisy spoke about the ruddy sand and the blue water skimmed with thinning ice.

Mattie was at ease as she seldom was. He'd begun to relax, too, when he reminded himself she wouldn't be so calm if she'd overheard his conversation with Daisy while he'd been sweeping.

Daisy was growing anxious he didn't have suitors for Mattie. Would the girl become so frustrated that she'd inadvertently say something to embarrass her sister?

To avoid that, he'd decided to offer names Daisy would reject out of hand. Men far too old or too young or with no hint of a sense of humor or someone who'd offended Daisy by treating her as if she was a *boppli*.

Each time, Daisy had shaken her head. "Remember, Benjamin. She's got to fall in love with him. Can't you find someone better for her?"

"I'll try," he'd replied and reassured her that his next suggestion would be the perfect match for Mattie.

The problem was, of the single men he'd met in the new settlement, not one of them seemed like the right potential husband for her. Most, like Mattie and her cousins, were too busy trying to establish new lives and livelihoods on the Island.

Benjamin watched as Daisy tried to copy his motions and throw stones at the ice. He'd collected a handful of pebbles and given them to her. She was "teaching" Boppi Lynn how to toss them.

"She's so patient with her little one," he said to Mattie

who stood beside him. He didn't want to use either Daisy's name or her doll's and draw attention to his words.

"She is. She's compassionate when others have trouble learning something."

"Something few people learn when they're as young as she is." He faced Mattie who had one foot on a tree trunk that must have fallen years ago because it was bleached white. "But something you learned young, too."

"I'm not so young. I turned thirty-one in December."

He stared at her in shock. "You're thirty-one?" He'd almost added that he'd been certain she was much younger than that, but he wasn't sure if she'd be complimented or insulted if he said that.

"How old did you think I am?"

He held up his hands in a pose of surrender. "No way am I going to answer that question. A man should never discuss a woman's age."

"*You* aren't discussing it. I am." She chuckled, surprising him. He heard her laugh so seldom, though Daisy spoke often about Mattie giggling as if the two were the same age. "I'm thirty-one, and Daisy mentioned that you're a few years older than that."

"Thirty-seven."

"So at that ripe, old age, you've amassed a lot of wisdom, ain't so?"

He couldn't hold in his roar of laughter that was swept out over the water by the breeze. "You couldn't be more mistaken, Mattie."

"So you haven't amassed wisdom?"

"Not much."

"What have you learned?"

"One thing, and it was from my *grossdawdi* when I

was young. He said that nothing lasts forever, not even our troubles."

"I like that saying, though I used to believe that things like love and faith lasted forever."

"They can, and for a lot of people they do."

She gave a terse laugh as she sat on the log. "Not for my *mamm*. She tossed aside everything she had."

"For what?"

"I'm not sure." She pulled her knees close to her and wrapped her arms around them. She drew back her left arm, and he realized she'd strained her shoulder. How badly? He couldn't tell because her voice had already been filled with pain as she spoke of her *mamm*. "She left a rambling letter behind, but I only got a quick look at it. *Daed* put it somewhere, and I never saw it again."

"Are you sure he still has it?"

She drew in a deep breath and released it in a long, slow sigh. "I don't know, Benjamin. I do know I hope it gets lost somewhere between Ontario and here. Thinking about it makes me sad."

"I'm sorry. I shouldn't be asking questions about something so raw."

"No, I'm glad you're asking. It's easier to answer questions than to have people tiptoe around me as if they're afraid the wrong word will cause me to shatter like glass."

Sitting beside her, he selected another stone and tossed it into the water. "I can't imagine you shattering, Mattie. You're strong."

"Too strong according to *Mamm*. She worried I would become an *alt maedel* because I could do everything myself. Worried too much about it." Her nose wrinkled.

Benjamin missed her next few words as he enjoyed the view of her cute expression. Cute. That was the perfect word to describe Mattie Albrecht. She wasn't as classically beautiful as her older sisters. But he didn't like to hear her disparage herself.

"Well, that makes us two of a kind," he said. "You're an *alt maedel*, and I'm whatever the male version would be."

Again her nose crinkled. "A confirmed bachelor, ain't so?"

"Confirmed how?"

"You tell me."

"I don't have the slightest idea." He stood and wiped off his trousers. "Maybe there was paperwork I was supposed to fill out."

Again she laughed. "You're being ridiculous."

"You sound surprised."

"I am," she answered. "It's because, other than when you and Daisy are teasing each other, you're serious about everything you do."

"In that way I'm like my brother. Menno doesn't smile much, and he worries too much."

"What has he said about your idea of staying here?"

"Nothing." He held out his hand to her. "Because I haven't told him. There's no reason to get him upset until I know, for sure, what I plan to do."

"Oh."

He waited for her to add more, but she didn't. The easy camaraderie between them had vanished. Because she didn't want him to go? Or because she was disappointed in how he was sneaking around behind his brother's back to get information on the property?

No, those were the reasons bothering him. He had no idea what disturbed her about his simple explanation.

When he helped her to her feet, she released his hand as she thanked him. He had to wonder. Had she over-heard his conversation with Daisy? No, she wouldn't have been able to hide her reaction. As she motioned for Daisy and him to come to the shop, he went to help Daisy get her chair up the knoll.

As soon as he reached her, Daisy said, "I've got a *gut* idea."

"What is it? Would your sister approve?"

"I hope so." She pushed the rest of the pebbles and dust off her lap and onto the shoulder of the road. "What about your friend James? He seems nice."

"You've met him?"

"I saw him at the last church Sunday services, but I didn't talk to him."

"You could talk to him at the services this weekend."

"Why do I need to? What you say about him sounds nice."

"You're right. James is a nice man."

"So why haven't you suggested him as a match for my sister?"

Why hadn't he? Because James was focused on get-ting his business going and was too busy to walk out with a woman? In Harmony Creek Hollow, Benjamin had seen his friend talking with the new schoolteacher quite a few times, but that had ended in the fall before James decided to move to Prince Edward Island.

Amazed, he wondered if James had been running away from a broken heart. His friend hadn't spoken of it. Had James been as humbled as Benjamin had been when his relationship with Sharrell Albrecht fell apart?

It was too late to ask. To probe six months later could have been like picking at a healed scab, bringing back a sharp pain that had been forgotten.

"You need to find Mattie a husband," Daisy said, bringing his attention back to her. "Boppi Lynn is growing sadder every day because she doesn't have a real family."

"You should remind Boppi Lynn that she has you. Both of you have Mattie and your cousins. They love you."

"But she needs a *daed*! Not a cousin. Every *kind* should have a *mamm* and a *daed*. That's right, ain't so?"

He wasn't sure how to answer. If he reminded Daisy that many *kinder*, plain and *Englisch*, didn't have both parents living, she might keep arguing with him.

As she grasped the wheels and pushed herself across the road, he remained on the shoulder. Daisy might be patient with her doll, but she wasn't going to wait much longer for him to do as she'd asked. She was so determined to have a family that she might take matters into her own hands. That could lead to humiliating Mattie before her new neighbors.

He must do what he could to avoid that, even if it meant finding possible suitors to discuss with Daisy.

Chapter Eight

The idea started simply enough when Mattie greeted her Kuepfer cousins as they came to the shop later that afternoon. She hadn't expected to see them during the middle of the day.

Lucas smiled as they stacked a pile of garbage bags by the front door. "We thought it was long past time for us to stop in and see how things are going."

"And see if there was any more of that pie I made for supper last night."

He gave her what he considered his most charming grin. She wanted to tell him not to bother to waste his winsome smile on her. She'd grown immune to it years ago.

His smile faded as he looked around. "You've done so much, but there's no way you can get this done in the next two weeks."

"Two and a half weeks," Daisy said.

"Even if you had a month," Juan argued, "you couldn't get this ready. Why didn't you let us know?"

"I've been giving you updates," Mattie said as she

wiped her dirty hands on her apron. "It's much better than it was. We're doing our best."

"I know you are," Lucas said, "but we shouldn't have left it all to you. It's too much." Turning to Benjamin, he added, "And we're grateful you're helping us."

"A job divided into many hands is a job done," Benjamin replied. "My *daed* used to say that."

"My *daed* liked saying that nobody can do everything."

"We'll get it done," Mattie said to draw them back to the problem at hand. She picked up a garbage bag, not straining her left shoulder. She tossed it on top of other bags waiting to be picked up.

Coming inside, she was almost run down by Daisy's chair. Daisy was crying.

"What's wrong?" Mattie asked.

"They—they th-th-think we're useless," her sister whimpered.

"They don't mean that."

"They—they s-s-said they shouldn't have given us the job." Tears ran down her full cheeks. "We've worked so hard. You got hurt, and you didn't stop working. How could they be ungrateful?"

She knelt so she could look into her sister's eyes. "Daisy, you know they're grateful. They're worried the shop won't open on time."

"It will. I know it will."

"It will if that's God's will."

Daisy frowned. "God wants us to succeed. Remember what was preached at the last service? 'I can do all things through Christ which strengtheneth me.' Philippians 4:13."

"I remember." It was one of Daisy's favorite verses

among the many she'd memorized. Trust her sister to know the exact one for any occasion.

Benjamin came to stand behind the wheelchair. "I remember, too. The sermon was about working together by God's grace. There was much to take away from that lesson."

"*Ja.* I..." Mattie's voice trailed off as she looked from her sister to Benjamin. Coming to her feet, she said, "That's it."

"That's what?" asked Benjamin as Daisy stared at her, puzzled.

"The answer to the problem." Calling her cousins inside to join them, she said, "I've got the solution." She smiled at Benjamin and her sister. "*We*'ve got the solution."

"We do?" asked Benjamin. "What is it?"

"A work frolic."

All three men turned and looked at her in shock. Lucas spoke first. "What did you say?"

"You heard her," Daisy said, coming to her defense as if they'd denounced her words. "She said we should have a work frolic at the shop. That would be a lot of fun, ain't so?"

Again her cousins exchanged a glance she couldn't read, but Benjamin interjected, "That's an amazing idea, Mattie. There are what? Ten families in the community along the bay?"

"An even dozen, I think," Mattie said.

"No, more than that." Daisy started counting them off on her fingers. "There are the Zooks and the Gerbers and the Petersheims and us, of course, and James and two Oatney families and the bishop's family and the minister's family. And three Miller families."

120   *Building Her Amish Dream*

"If half of them could spare a few hours, we could get the shop fixtures done in no time." Juan warmed to the idea. "We've got a couple of weeks before we're scheduled to open." He grinned at Daisy. "We've got *two and a half* weeks. If we can finish clearing this space, get shelves up and run the propane lines during the frolic, will you have time to paint the shelves, Benjamin?"

"Plenty, but there are also the windows to be replaced, too."

Lucas groaned. "All of them have broken panes."

"There are only a dozen of those," Mattie said. "The frames are fine. We need to cut glass to size and glaze them into place. I can do that except for the top panes."

"We've got a plan then." Lucas bent his head and said, "We should thank God for inspiring Mattie and easing our way to getting the store open."

"Amen," she whispered as she took the first easy breath she had since she'd seen the disaster inside their future shop. It might be possible to open on time.

I can do all things through Christ which strengtheneth me. The verse resonated through her mind as she thanked God for her family.

And for Benjamin, who'd inspired her when she'd least expected it.

Everything came together for the work frolic at the Celtic Knoll Farm Shop quickly. Word spread through the community. The frolic was scheduled for Saturday, the day before their next church service.

Mattie was astonished when, on Saturday, a line of buggies arrived. Families from their local settlement, as well as families from two other communities closer to Montague, more than an hour away by buggy.

She welcomed each participant and found everybody jobs that fit their skills before joining other women washing the metal walls while the men started rebuilding the interior. The plans she'd devised for setting up the shop had been copied and shared. When her cousins let Benjamin oversee the project, it was an acknowledgment of all his work.

Daisy gathered the *kinder* in one corner. She led them in games and singing. Making sure they had cookies and *millich* when the adults took a break in the middle of the morning, she kept the youngsters happy and out from underfoot.

After enjoying a few of the cookies herself, Mattie returned to work. Beside her was a dark-haired woman who looked to be in her midtwenties.

After Mattie had introduced herself, the woman said with a shy smile, "I'm Kirsten Petersheim. I'm here with my *aenti* and my cousins."

"Those guys over there are my cousins." Mattie motioned toward where Mark, Juan and Lucas were trying to lift a heavy cabinet into place. Benjamin jumped to join them. "We're going to be running the store together. *Danki* for coming to help today."

"*Aenti* Helga never misses a work frolic, and I didn't want her to drive out here from Shushan on her own."

Knowing Kirsten was downplaying her own participation as most plain folks would, Mattie asked, "You live near Shushan? I thought the plain community was out here along the bay."

"We live about a half mile from here, but we work at one of the resorts at the edge of town. We do housekeeping there."

"It must be interesting meeting tourists."

Kirsten didn't quite smile. "We don't often encounter the guests, but we've had strange interactions on those few occasions."

"I'd love to hear about them, and I'll tell you about the doozies at the farm stand we had in Ontario."

"You're from Ontario?"

"*Ja.* You?"

She answered with downcast eyes. *"Ja."*

"Have you been here long?"

"Almost a year." Each word seemed more reluctant.

Mattie couldn't figure out why. They weren't talking about anything different from several other conversations she'd already had that day. It was the Amish way, upon meeting someone new, to establish where they were from and if they were related to anyone in common.

"My sister Daisy and I would love to have all of you stop by sometime soon. There's so much we don't know about living here, and—"

"I— Let me talk to my *aenti*. She— That is, our work schedule—I'll have to let you know."

"Of course," Mattie began, then realized she was talking to Kirsten's back in the seconds before the woman disappeared into the crowd.

"Who was that?" asked Mark.

She hadn't noticed him coming to stand beside her. His gaze was focused in the direction the young woman had gone.

"Her name's Kirsten Petersheim," Mattie answered. "She's here with her *aenti*."

"I should thank them for—"

She grabbed his sleeve without thinking, then winced when the motion jarred her shoulder. Reassuring her cousin that she was all right, she said, "If you do thank her, do it by yourself."

"Are you playing matchmaker, Mattie? That's not like you."

She didn't return his grin. "I'm not joking, Mark. She seems as timid as a fawn. When I suggested she and her *aenti* might want to stop by the house to have a chat so we could get to know each other, she couldn't flee fast enough."

"Timid, huh?" He didn't say anything else, but he turned on his heel and walked in the opposite direction.

She wondered what had triggered his reaction. She didn't ask because several volunteers had questions about what she wanted them to do next. By the time she finished finding jobs for each of them, her cousin's odd reaction had vanished from her mind.

Benjamin was exhausted at day's end. The *gut* kind of exhausted that was the result of a hard day's work with excellent results. Shelving units had been raised along the length of the building.

Windmilling his arms, he heard a soft pop in his right shoulder as the muscles stretched. He'd been holding shelf units against the wall while others secured them. It had been a puzzle to figure out how to arrange them best. The curved walls of the Quonset hut meant the taller sections couldn't be used anywhere but in the center of the building. It became obvious they had too many tall shelving units and not enough the necessary size to run along the walls.

His friend James and Hosea Thacker, an elderly man who was an experienced carpenter, had devised a simple way to cut the shelves to fit. The parts that weren't used along the wall were joined together to offer a variety of heights. Paint would disguise that the shelves had been jury-rigged.

In a day's time, the building began to look like a shop, albeit an empty one without a morsel of food in sight. The generous spread Mattie and the other women had provided was long gone, consumed as if by a swarm of locusts.

The shop was emptying as the folks who'd come for the frolic were leaving for their own homes and chores. In the past ten hours, more work had been done than he, Mattie and Daisy could have finished in two weeks.

"*Danki*, Father," he breathed as he bent his head.

He didn't add more to his prayer because his sleeve was grabbed and tugged.

"I found him!" Daisy cried.

"Him who?" He looked around, but nobody else seemed to be listening. Despite that, he motioned for Daisy to lower her voice.

She did. "The man for Mattie to marry. He'd make a great *daed* for Boppi Lynn."

"Who?" He couldn't help wondering what old man or young boy Daisy had chosen this time.

"Quinton Hass!"

His stomach tightened so hard, he gasped. He'd met the farmer on several occasions and had worked with him early in the day. Quinton's *gut* looks caught women's eyes, whether they were *maedels* or married. More than six feet tall, muscular and with black hair that had a tendency to curl at the exact spot to emphasize his sharp cheekbones and the cleft in his chin, he looked like the hero on the cover of a book.

The idea of Benjamin finding Mattie a husband

wasn't funny, but he didn't want to explain to Daisy—
or to himself—why.

It should be simple. Daisy had picked a man whose
temperament seemed to match her sister's. Both were
hardworking and uncomplaining. Both possessed a
strong faith, if he was to judge by how many people
whispered Quinton's name was sure to be in the lot
when an additional minister was chosen later in the
spring. Quinton's farm wasn't far from the shop, so it
would be convenient for Mattie to work there as long
as her cousins needed her.

Most important of all, Daisy approved of him. Her
sister's happiness meant the world to Mattie, and she
would give Quinton Hass a more serious look because
Daisy seemed to think he'd be a *gut* match.

That should be the best reason for him to approach
the man. He couldn't. He didn't want Mattie to marry
because her sister approved of the man. Mattie deserved
a man who loved her. A man who knew what she needed
before she did.

She wasn't like him. While he craved the chance for
a few adventures before he was too old, she was seeking contentment and family and the self-assurance she
was surrounded by those who loved her and whom she
loved.

"Shh!" warned Daisy, though he hadn't said anything.

Benjamin understood when he saw Mattie walking
toward him. Fatigue slowed her steps, but a happy smile
warmed her face. He wished he could capture that sight
and keep it forever.

"*Danki* to you two, too," Mattie said, bending to give
her sister a quick hug. As she straightened, he made sure

he wasn't looking at her. She mustn't see how much he wished she'd embrace him, as well.

"It was a *gut* work frolic," Daisy said. "We got a lot done, ain't so?"

"A lot." Mattie wiped a few strands of hair from her face. "I don't know why I didn't think of a work frolic before."

Benjamin shook his head. "Can you imagine all those people in here with the rickety piles of wood? We would have been jumping out of the way more than we would have been working. It was a *gut* idea and at the right time." He went to the table where the last of the drinks remained. He got three bottles of water. Handing one to Daisy, he undid the top on a second one before he gave it to Mattie.

"*Danki* again," she said, taking a deep swig.

"How's your shoulder doing?" he asked.

"Tired…like the rest of me." She smiled at her sister. "Daisy, do you think you and Boppi Lynn can get our coats?"

Daisy pushed away, but Benjamin noticed that the chair was moving far more slowly than usual. They all were tuckered out by the long day's work.

"If you want to check the doors, Benjamin," Mattie continued, "I'd appreciate it. Now that there's something of value in here, we should make sure they're locked."

"All right."

"*Gut*, and I'll—"

They moved at the same time and collided. Water spilled out of her bottle as it fell from her hand. Most of it struck him in the chest, but he paid it no mind. Instead he reached out, then cupped her elbows to keep her from tumbling backward and injuring her shoulder more.

She gave a soft cry and used the hem of her apron to pat his shirt. He put his hands over hers to halt her before her innocent touch persuaded him to pull her to him and sample her lips that looked so sweet.

"It's fine, Mattie," he said. "It's just water."

"I'm so sorry. I'm so clumsy." She drew her hands back before touching her left shoulder and grimacing.

"You've seen me trip over my own feet a few times," he said, "while I'm toting out the lumber. We all do that sometimes."

"I do it more than sometimes. My older sisters are graceful, and I'm a clod-footed dolt."

Searching through his memories, he tried to picture Mattie as she'd been five years ago. He realized he couldn't recall much about her. Had he been so besotted with Sharrell that he hadn't noticed anything or anyone else? It seemed impossible that he hadn't noticed Mattie more. She was so vital, so caring, so…alive, grasping on to every minute of every day and treasuring it as a gift from God.

"You're more than a clod-footed dolt." He wasn't surprised when her eyes cut to him when he didn't deny her assertion. Holding her gaze, he hoped she would hear—really hear—his next words and heed them. "Look what you made happen today."

"With a lot of help."

"*Ja*, but whose idea was it to ask for help?"

"Yours."

"Mine?" He shook his head. "No, you were the one who suggested a work frolic."

"I suggested it because you talked about many hands getting a job done."

"I'm glad I could inspire you. You've certainly inspired me."

"To do what?"

"To open my own shop."

Her bright blue eyes grew round. "Are you going to do that?"

"Maybe."

"I thought you liked the land with the wood lot."

"I do like it, but there are a lot of things to consider before I make my decision. I'm sure you and your cousins thought long and hard while you made your plans to come to the Island."

"Some days I wonder if we should have thought longer and harder."

"About opening a shop?"

"About everything." She didn't add more as she walked to where Daisy was rolling toward them.

What had he said wrong? He replayed the conversation in his mind, but everything he'd said had been the truth. He'd berated himself before for not being honest with her about opening a shop to sell his clocks. Now that he had been, he'd expected to feel better.

He didn't.

In fact, he felt worse, and he couldn't figure out why.

Chapter Nine

Two days later, Benjamin was no closer to finding an answer to the problem puzzling him than he'd been yesterday evening when he'd felt guilty for avoiding Quinton Hass at the Sunday service. He was worn out today, not having been able to sleep as he tossed and turned from one side to the other in a futile attempt to find a comfortable place in his pillow.

He couldn't blame his pillow. His own thoughts had kept him awake. Should he have talked to Quinton Hass after church about paying a call at the Albrechts' house to get to know Mattie? He'd mentioned the man's name to James over breakfast this morning, and his friend had had only *gut* things to say about the farmer.

Benjamin wished he was doing something more physical than painting shelves. With unfocused energy spiraling through him, he would have been better suited to clearing stacks of wood. He struggled to hold his brush steady so he didn't leave more paint on the walls and floor than the shelves. More than fifty feet of shelving awaited his paintbrush. Painting it wouldn't help him unwind the taut coil deep in his gut, but Mattie was depending on him to finish the job.

He stifled a yawn as he bent to open a new paint container. He'd calculated that at least six more gallons of paint would be required for the shelving as well as the moldings around the doors and the windows.

"Did you talk to him?" asked Daisy as she stopped beside him. "Is he interested in marrying my sister?"

"*Gute mariye* to you," he said, trying not to yawn again.

"*Ja, ja, gute mariye.*" Impatience rang through her voice. "Did you talk to him?"

Benjamin appraised the shelves he'd put into place along the center of the building. They were low enough so Mattie could reach the uppermost shelf to restock the groceries she intended to put there.

"Who was I supposed to talk to?" he asked, though he knew what she was going to answer. He hoped the few seconds of delay would give him a chance to compose his thoughts that were mired in exhaustion.

"You know who."

"I do?"

"*Ja.* Quinton Hass." She leaned forward in her chair and locked her fingers together on her knee. The motion made her arms an effective dam so her doll couldn't slide off her lap. "You did speak to him, ain't so?"

"Not yet."

She frowned. "He was at church services yesterday, and you were, too. Why didn't you speak with him?"

"The time and the place have to be right. When others were around, I couldn't ask him if he was interested in Mattie." His stomach tightened as he spoke what should have been commonplace words. Because he was telling a half-truth? He could have asked Quinton to speak privately. "These matters are delicate."

"I know." She sank into her chair and held Boppi Lynn to her heart. "Don't wait forever, Benjamin. Mattie isn't getting any younger, and Boppi Lynn cried herself to sleep last night because she doesn't have a real family anymore."

Benjamin wasn't sure which remark to respond to first, so he nodded. He hated the thought of Daisy being so upset about the disintegration of her family that she'd wept into her pillow. Had that really happened? Sometimes when Daisy spoke about Boppi Lynn and her "feelings," she was talking about herself. Other times, she was imagining how her doll might have reacted. It was impossible for him to tell which she meant.

Just as it was impossible for him to explain to the girl why he was hesitant about approaching Quinton Hass about walking out with Mattie. Maybe if he could explain it to himself, it might be simpler.

You don't want to explain it to yourself, chided the small voice of his conscience. *And you know why.*

That was true. He did know why. He enjoyed spending time with Mattie. The afternoon they'd gone to check on the property on the Charlottetown road had been the most fun he'd had in longer than he could remember. Seeing her joy during the work frolic had made him smile more than he had in years. She was a delight for the eyes, and she kept him on his toes with her insightful questions and the humor she allowed to show so seldom.

More than once, when he'd woken from a dream of her pretty smile, he'd asked himself if he should pursue more than friendship with Mattie. Two things held him back. One was that he wasn't sure how she'd react if he expressed his interest in her after he'd walked out with her older sister. Though she seldom spoke of that time, he'd heard enough to know she was bothered by what had happened then. He couldn't help thinking of Daisy and how protective the sisters were of each other. Did Mattie feel the same way about Sharrell? He knew how important family was to Mattie, but it had been ripped apart by her *mamm* leaving. Her cousins had hinted there was a lot they could tell him, but he'd resisted. He wanted to hear the truth from Mattie, not her cousins.

Looking at Daisy, who was waiting for him to answer, he said, "Boppi Lynn will have a family because she has you."

"But she wants more. A *daed* as well as a *mamm*, who'll never leave her." Her voice broke on the last words.

When he bent toward her, she threw her arms around his waist and held on as if she feared she'd be washed out to sea with the next wave lapping the shore. He held her without speaking. He wasn't sure what he could say to ease her grief that Mattie must share, though he seldom saw any hint of her feelings toward her *mamm*'s leaving.

When Daisy was more composed, he began to tease her. It took longer than he'd hoped for her smile to return, but she began picking on him, as well. The brief storm was past, but he knew it wasn't gone.

He prayed for the words to ease Daisy's broken heart, but none came to him. Were there any, or must she find a way to heal her heart on her own? That seemed cruel for the girl who'd suffered so much, but God had His reasons for everything that happened.

Benjamin wished he knew God's reasons for bringing him to the Maritimes. He hadn't come here to settle down. If he was going to cause a possible rift between him and Menno, he didn't want it to be because he'd abandoned his dream of finding the adventure he hadn't sought as a teenager.

His vacillating had kept him from buying the property along the Charlottetown road. He'd gone to look at it after church on Sunday, hoping a second visit would help him decide. It should have been perfect, but he couldn't commit to making an offer.

Hearing Mattie's voice calling them to lunch, Benjamin was shocked how quickly the morning had gone. He washed his hands, but couldn't scrub off all the spots of paint. Joining the two women, he sat on one of the empty folding chairs someone had left after the work frolic. He smiled when Mattie handed him a roast beef sandwich.

"It smells *wunderbaar*," he said.

"Everything Mattie cooks is delicious." Daisy took a big bite, then said around her mouthful, "You should mention that."

"Mention it?" Mattie's brows lowered. "To whom? Daisy, you're not matchmaking again, are you?"

"Me? No." She didn't look in Benjamin's direction. "This is really *gut*, Mattie."

Mattie's frown didn't lessen, so Benjamin asked as soon as they'd finished their lunch, "How was the physio session today?"

"I can explain in one word. Ouch." She touched her shoulder.

"Ouch worse or ouch better?"

She smiled wanly. "I think *ouch* should explain it pretty much. But I can do more today than I could a couple of days ago. Patty wants me to push to where it begins to hurt, no further."

"But you push into the pain." He put the containers that had held the sandwiches into her red plastic tote.

"It's not easy to know the exact spot to stop until it starts to hurt."

"How much longer will you be working with Patty?"

"We should be finishing around the time when the shop opens." She scanned the space. "Wow! You've been busy."

"All the shelves on the right side have one coat on them." He put the tote by the door. "Let's take a walk along the bay."

"I've got to—"

"You've got to let this paint finish drying before you can do anything in the shop. Wouldn't you rather enjoy the views along the bay than stand here and watch paint dry?"

"I've got to admit I've never stood and watched paint dry."

He smiled, glad to hear the lightness return to her voice. He understood her desperate need to do as she'd promised her cousins, but she would be useless to them if she continued to work herself so hard. Once the shop opened, she would have to spend long hours serving customers.

And he… Where would he be after the Celtic Knoll Farm Shop was in business? He wasn't leaving before the grand opening, but what about afterward?

Benjamin didn't try to answer that question as Mattie called to her sister. Daisy was excited to go along. When he told her he'd found a path a short distance along the road that would allow her to get close to the water, she sped out the door. Mattie went to get her sister's coat and her own and followed.

He pulled on his jacket and scanned the interior that reeked of fresh paint. They'd achieved so much. The holes in the concrete floors had been filled, and the windows were intact. Shelving had been set in place and the front counter built. A lot of work remained, but he began to believe they'd finish it by Mattie's deadline.

And then what?

Benjamin walked away from the shop and his own question. The sun was shining, the air was a bit warmer and he didn't want to think about anything but this moment when he walked between Mattie and Daisy along the deserted road.

He savored Daisy's delight when he showed her the dirt path to the sand. Though she needed his and Mattie's help to push her chair out to the water, she giggled and pointed out everything with a *kind*'s wonder. He lifted a piece of driftwood about the length of his forearm from the red sand and offered it to her.

"Look over there!" Daisy jabbed a finger toward where the beach curved. "That's more wood, ain't so?"

"I think you're right." He loped along the sand and bent to pick up a long length of bleached wood. It forked in two different directions. Carrying it to where Daisy and Mattie were examining the first piece, he said, "This is a *gut* one. See how many colors are in the wood?"

"It's gray." Mattie laughed.

Enjoying the sound of her laughter, he leaned the end of the large piece of driftwood on the sand, holding it tight so he didn't reach out and hug Mattie as he had Daisy earlier. No, it wouldn't have been at all like hugging Daisy. Daisy was a kid. Mattie was a lovely, enticing woman, and he would have been a fool to think he could hold her the same way.

"True," he said as he ran a finger along the smoothed wood, "but see the different shades of gray?"

Daisy grew serious. "Shades of gray? *Gut* thing *Mamm* isn't here. Mattie says she can't see any shades of gray. Mattie says if she could have, she wouldn't have left us all." She flung the piece as far as she could. "I hate gray!"

He heard a muffled gasp and discovered Mattie's face had become the color of the wood he held. If he hadn't guessed before, her expression showed that, though she hid it well, she was as brokenhearted about her *mamm*'s leaving as Daisy was.

And he had no idea how to help either of them.

Mattie didn't follow when Daisy asked Benjamin to wheel her to a large rock at the edge of the water. When she heard his footfalls crunching on the dirt and sand, she looked over her shoulder, amazed he'd left Daisy sitting by the boulder.

"The paint needs another fifteen minutes or so before I can put on the second coat," he said as he came to stand beside where she'd been staring out at the thin ice clinging to the far side of the bay.

"All right." What else could she say?

"Daisy asked me to tell you that she's worried Boppi Lynn will get too cold if she stays out much longer."

"I should—"

"Leave her be for a few minutes. She wants to be alone."

"As *Mamm* must have. I didn't know she was so unhappy." She wrapped her arms around herself as a cold blast struck them. "I should have paid more attention. I shouldn't have let other things distract me."

She saw curiosity in his eyes, but he didn't ask what other things she'd had on her mind. Did he suspect the "things" had been him?

"Maybe," he said, "there wasn't anything for you to pay attention to."

"What do you mean?" She faced him, hopeful that he'd give her a way to forgive herself for not easing the pain that had driven Emmaline Albrecht away from her family.

"I mean some people don't share their feelings when they're about to make a huge decision." He shuffled his feet in the sand. "Sometimes, they need to mull them over and consider all the ramifications. Other times, they're afraid they'll look foolish if they speak about what's on their minds. But often people want to keep that decision to themselves because they don't want to take the chance of someone talking them out of it."

"You've met *Mamm*, Benjamin. Do you think anyone could have talked her out of doing what she wanted to do?"

He gave her a wry smile. "She's a force of nature. A lot like you."

"Me?" She stared at him in shock. "I don't feel like listening to your teasing." She walked away, but heard Benjamin following her along the shore.

He used the driftwood as if it was a walking stick. As soon as he'd caught up with her, he said, "You are a force of nature yourself. A benign one, it's true, but once you set your mind on a course of action, I pity whoever attempts to stand in your way."

"I've got to be single-minded. Everyone and everything depends on me getting the shop open."

"It will open."

"On time."

"On time." He chuckled, though she wondered what he found amusing about her greatest fear. "It won't take long to get the rest of the painting done. All that remains after that is arranging the stock, right?"

They continued walking as she listed the tasks waiting to be done, including having the vegetable scales certified as accurate and having several different inspections completed.

"I had no idea all of that had to be done," he said. "I wonder if I should give up on opening my own shop."

"You won't have to do all that, because you won't be selling food. You'll need to get approvals to open a business in the barn."

"And to sell Christmas trees?"

She stopped and faced him, making sure she was away from the waves that were encroaching farther onto the shore as the tide came in. "You're going to sell those, too?"

"I enjoy working outside as well as in the wood shop. It's a treat to see the happy faces of the *kinder* as they pick out their favorite tree to decorate for Christmas. You can see what an important tradition it is for *Englischers*." His expression grew distant as if he was looking at the tree farm he'd overseen in Harmony Creek Hollow. "I'd miss the rush of tree seekers in December."

"Does that mean you're staying on the Island?" Her voice might have been calm, but her insides were doing leaps in every direction.

"It means I'm thinking about it."

When he didn't meet her eyes, she knew it would be foolish to press him. He wasn't trying to give her the runaround. He didn't know, and it wasn't easy for her to understand why it was hard for him to make up his mind. When she had to make a decision, she made it.

She sighed and looked at the sky where low, dark clouds were gathering. A lone seabird was calling out. She didn't see it, but could hear its distant cries. "I should get Daisy before that storm gets here."

"*Ja.* I can start on the next coat of paint."

Mattie nodded and matched his steps as they walked toward where they'd left Daisy. The cries from the bird got louder.

No! Not cries from a bird.

Daisy!

Mattie ran to her sister. What was wrong?

Benjamin must have realized there was a problem at the same time she did. He tossed the driftwood into the brown grass and raced after her. Seeing Daisy's chair surrounded by salt water, Mattie splashed through it to her sister.

Daisy clutched her in fright. "Where did you go? You left me here, and my chair is stuck in the wet sand. I could have been stranded here."

"You wouldn't have," Benjamin said.

Mattie released the breath she'd been holding. His answer had eased the fear on her sister's face.

Keeping her own voice light, she said, "That's right, Daisy. We wouldn't have left you here on your own."

"That's not what I meant." He grasped her chair and tugged it out of the sand so hard he almost rocked off his feet. "You wouldn't have sat here, Daisy Albrecht, until you floated away. You would have climbed out and onto the grass. Or knowing you, you would have found a way to climb a cliff."

"I don't know how." Her voice remained filled with fear.

He leaned one hand on her chair. "I could teach you."

"Really?" Daisy's fright had disappeared as if it'd never existed. "Say *ja*, Mattie. Let Benjamin teach me to climb a cliff."

Was Benjamin out of his mind? He wanted to take Daisy climbing the cliffs?

Mattie looked from one eager face to the other. Daisy couldn't use her legs to help her balance as she pulled herself up the sheer face of a red cliff.

Grasping her sister's chair, she wrestled it to the dirt road, then pushed it toward the shop. She tried not to listen to Daisy's pleas to learn to scale a cliff.

"No!" Mattie said. "I'm responsible for you, and I won't agree to such nonsense." The chair bounced into a pothole, and Mattie groaned when her shoulder was jostled.

Benjamin's broad hands reached past hers and drew the chair out of the hole. "Daisy should be able to handle it from here. Daisy, your sister and I need to talk."

Daisy took off as if she'd hooked rockets to her chair.

Mattie faced him as she supported her left elbow to ease the strain on her shoulder. "Don't waste your breath, Benjamin. There's nothing you could say to make me change my mind."

"I know you don't like to change it."

"At least, I make up my mind." She wished she could pull back the words when his mouth tightened into a straight line.

But instead of firing heated words, he said, "I'm not

talking about an actual cliff. Have you heard of climbing walls?"

"*Ja*," she admitted. Two of her brothers had gone to one several times with *Englisch* friends. They'd spoken of how tough it was to climb all the way to the top. In fact, one of them had come home with a sprained ankle which he struggled to hide from their parents who wouldn't have been pleased to discover what he'd been doing. "I want her to do everything she can, but I don't want to risk her getting hurt again."

"Because you believe her accident was your fault?"

Every instinct ordered her to leave. If he could see that truth she'd buried in her heart, what else could he discern about her?

She didn't move, discovering how much she ached to talk about her guilt. "*Ja.* I should have kept a closer eye on her."

"If Daisy was the same then as she is now, she wouldn't have been talked out of jumping from the loft."

"I'm the big sister."

He put his hands toward her shoulders, then drew them back. She wasn't sure if it was because he was anxious not to hurt her injured shoulder, or if he'd realized touching her like that might lead to a situation they should avoid.

"Didn't you say she was with one of your brothers?" he asked, shoving his hands into his pockets.

"Two of them." She sighed. "But Ohmer and Jerry aren't much older than she is. None of them should have been in the hayloft unsupervised either."

"You said they were jumping out into the hay piled beneath the loft. It sounds as if they'd done it before."

"We all did. It was a rite of passage to be brave

enough to jump." Raising her gaze to meet his, she curled her fingers into her palms so she didn't reach out to draw his arms around her. "But *Mamm* told me to watch over the younger ones. It was my job, and I failed."

"Because you were busy, too?"

Mattie thought of that day. "It was a hot day in mid-August, and I was in the kitchen, canning beans. The steam left me wrung out every day that week. *Mamm* was at her sewing machine. She was always really busy in the weeks before another school year."

"So both of you were there, and both of you were busy."

"*Ja.*"

"Then why was it your fault only?"

"Because I could have protected her. She's my youngest sister, and she already had enough challenges."

He said with a gentle smile, "I don't think Daisy would agree. She's eager to do the same things everyone else does. You can't be overprotective, Mattie, to make up for your belief—your mistaken belief—that you didn't protect her enough. Let me take her wall-climbing. She's worked hard at the shop. She's a *kind*, so she should be having fun, too."

"I know." She dared to put her fingers on his sleeve. "*Danki* for caring so much about Daisy."

"It isn't hard to, as it isn't hard to care about you, Mattie. You care so much about others you make it easy. I..." He slanted toward her, his face lowering.

She held her breath, wondering, hoping, praying he was going to kiss her. She tilted her own face toward his and closed her eyes as her senses focused on him.

That was why she jumped when she heard Juan call

her name. Her head almost hit Benjamin's nose, but he moved away, as her cousin came toward them.

Juan grabbed her arm without slowing and began asking questions about what craft vendors she'd found for the shop.

"None yet," she replied, wanting to check if Benjamin had followed.

"*Gut,*" her cousin said. "I've heard of an artisans' co-op in Shushan that's looking for a place to display their work. I thought we could meet with their representatives to see if we should invite them to use our shop. What do you think?"

I think I wish you'd come by five minutes later. I think I wish Benjamin had kissed me.

She didn't say that, as she agreed to a meeting the following morning with the co-op's representatives. She faltered when Benjamin walked past them. Her gaze was caught by his for a second, but it was long enough for her to discover he was as disappointed with the timing of Juan's visit as she was.

And that made her happier than she'd been in a long time, even as she reminded herself about the possible heartbreak ahead. For the first time, that risk didn't seem like too high a price in exchange for his kiss.

Chapter Ten

"You're sure you know how to do this?" Mattie stood in the center of a high-ceiling room at a resort hotel south of Shushan. The sprawling complex had what they called an "adventure dome" that was filled with swimming pools and carnival rides. A fake mountain that didn't match the Island's flat landscape had water slides on one side. The other was a climbing wall.

Benjamin straightened from helping Daisy hook her plastic helmet under her chin. As the girl rolled her chair over to speak to one of the people assisting at the climbing wall, he said, "*Ja.* I learned how to do this as part of my volunteer firefighter training. Where I live in New York is between the foothills of the Adirondacks and the Green Mountains. We've got plenty of cliffs there. While I wasn't expected to do the actual climbing myself in an emergency, I had to assist others. Our fire chief used rock climbing walls like these to give us the training we needed."

"I had no idea. Did you enjoy it?" She was stalling to give herself time to devise an excuse why Daisy shouldn't attempt the wall. She didn't want to say her sister couldn't do it because she was in a wheelchair, not after all the times when Mattie had insisted Daisy could do whatever she put her mind to.

When the concrete floors at the shop had been finished with an epoxy coating yesterday, she hadn't guessed that any work there would have to wait twenty-four hours. The floors wouldn't be cured for a week, but after a day, they could go inside and finish the painting. The day away from the shop had given Daisy the excuse she needed to ask Benjamin to take her wall-climbing.

So here they were, and Mattie had to clench her hands so she didn't grab her sister's chair and run out of the building.

"It's fun, and it's safe." Benjamin motioned toward the people holding ropes while others clambered up the wall.

Mattie looked around again. She saw glances in their direction. They were the only plain people near the climbing wall, and *Englischers* weren't accustomed to seeing them.

One young woman came over to Daisy. "Are you ready?" she asked.

"*Ja!*" Daisy answered so enthusiastically that everyone grinned.

The woman, who wore khaki pants and a white polo shirt with a name tag that said Sage, looked at Mattie, her gaze dropping to her skirt. "Are all three of you climbing?"

"Just those two." Mattie tried to smile and failed. "But if Daisy can't climb in a dress—"

"Daisy will be using a platform she can sit on, so she doesn't have to worry about her modesty." Sage motioned for Daisy and Benjamin to follow her. "Let's get you ready for your climb."

While Benjamin and Daisy were fitted with safety harnesses, Mattie was given a sheaf of papers to read and sign. She almost reneged on her agreement when she saw most of the information would hold the resort harmless if her sister was injured. She didn't because she saw how eager Daisy was to try something new. She signed them and gave them to an employee before going to where her sister waited to move from her chair to the platform.

Mattie gave Daisy a hug. "Listen to what they tell you, and do what they say."

"I'm going to listen to what Benjamin tells me." She cradled her doll as if it was a newborn and handed her to Mattie. "Don't let Boppi Lynn watch. She gets scared."

"That's because she's a *boppli*. They grow up fast, and then they want to try new things."

"Don't let her watch."

"I won't." Mattie didn't add that she would have preferred not to watch either.

But her eyes were glued to her sister as Daisy was helped onto the platform that was balanced by a man holding ropes and standing off to the side. Moved closer to the wall, Daisy grinned as she gripped two brightly colored projections in front of her.

Benjamin quietly instructed her. He wore a plastic helmet, too, and was belted to a rope offset by another man who was talking to the man with Daisy's rope.

Mattie wanted to shout to the men to pay more attention, but her mouth dropped open as Daisy reached for two different projections. She pulled herself and the platform up. Her smile was so wide it seemed impossible for her face to contain it.

"There you go," Benjamin said. "One hand at a time." He gripped his ropes with one hand and reached out to steady Daisy with his other.

"Don't let me fall," she said, and Mattie's heart jumped into her throat.

Benjamin remained calm as he climbed beside her. "I won't. Go ahead and find another handhold."

Daisy stared at him for a long moment, then reached to grasp the next protrusion on the wall. She shot a grin at Mattie before continuing.

Far faster than Mattie had imagined her sister could scale the wall, Daisy reached the top and then came down to her chair. While Mattie handed Boppi Lynn to Daisy, Benjamin handed their equipment to a staff member who took it with a flirtatious smile. He thanked her as if he hadn't noticed her reaction. The woman shrugged and turned to store the equipment as he walked to where Mattie stood.

"*Danki*," Mattie said as she watched her sister jabber with excitement to the staff at the same time. "This is something she'll never forget."

"Me neither." He shook his head. "That girl doesn't have an ounce of fear in her. Nothing scares her."

"That's not true," she retorted more heatedly than she intended.

She couldn't help the sharp edge to her voice. Benjamin had hit a sensitive nerve. She and Daisy kept up an unrelenting facade that they were fine with the mess their lives had become.

"I'm sorry," she went on when he didn't answer. "I

appreciate what you've done for Daisy. My reaction wasn't about you."

"I know." He gave her a sympathetic smile as Daisy wheeled over to them, and Mattie recalled how he had family issues, too. Not the same as hers, but as tough to deal with.

Linking arms with her sister and with him, Mattie said, "I heard someone mention there's a place selling ice cream around the corner. What do you say we check it out? My treat."

"How can we resist such an offer?" asked Daisy. "Right, Benjamin?"

"Right. It's impossible to resist." The warmth in his eyes flared, and Mattie wondered if he still was talking about having ice cream.

She hoped not.

Benjamin heard raised voices from outside the shop the next day. Putting aside the push broom he'd been using to clean the floors one more time after cutting a few more shelves to put into an alcove by the side storage room door, he walked to the front. In astonishment, he realized Mattie and Daisy were arguing.

Daisy shook her finger at Mattie before bursting into tears. For once, Mattie didn't give her a hug to console her. Mattie, instead, crossed her arms.

"You've got to be reasonable, Daisy," she said in a tone Benjamin had never heard her use with her sister. It was filled more with frustration than anger.

"No, I don't!" Daisy retorted. "Why should I be reasonable when nobody else is? I'm tired of you trying to protect me from the truth, Mattie. I can see it. Why can't you?"

She didn't wait for an answer, but spun her chair's wheels to send her toward the road. Benjamin expected to hear a squeal of rubber as the chair took a sharp turn toward the Albrechts' house.

Throwing her hands in the air, Mattie stormed in the opposite direction.

"Wait, Mattie," he called.

He wasn't sure if she would turn around or keep on walking. When she turned toward him, her eyes were luminous with unshed tears. He could respect the amount of willpower it was taking to keep those tears from falling down her face. She was one of the strongest people he'd ever met, but he didn't say that. Any compliment made her close up further.

"Is there anything I can do to help?" he asked, hoping it was the right question.

She shook her head and looked past him in the direction Daisy had gone. "Unless you can reach into Daisy's brain and pull out the ridiculous assumptions she's made, there isn't anything any of us can do."

"What assumptions?"

"She won't stop believing that *Mamm* left because of something she did."

Benjamin scowled, though his expression wasn't for Mattie or her sister. If he ever had the chance to tell Emmaline Albrecht what the terrible cost of her selfish decision had become for her family, he doubted he'd be able to stop himself.

"That's nonsense," he said.

"I know that, and so do you." Her shoulders eased from their taut stance, and a riffle of discomfort crossed her wan face. Her left shoulder must still be tender. "Though Daisy assures me she believes it's nonsense, too, she clings to the idea that if she hadn't been injured, *Mamm* would have stayed."

"But she was hurt years ago, ain't so?"

"More than four years ago. *Mamm* left last year. But logic doesn't have anything to do with how Daisy feels."

"That's too much of a burden for a young girl."

"If you've got any ideas on how to ease it, I'd love to hear them."

He closed his eyes and sent a quick prayer to God. He needed the right words to help Mattie and Daisy. Mattie hadn't spoken of her feelings. She seldom did, but he'd guessed she was torn up inside about her sister taking the blame for their *mamm*'s decisions.

Because Mattie thinks she *is the cause of her* mamm *leaving.* He corrected himself. Mattie didn't think she was the cause, but she believed she should have been able to find a way to keep Emmaline from jumping the fence. He couldn't guess why, and he halted himself from asking. She was already upset. He must not add to her pain.

"Have you had Daisy talk to a minister?" he asked, realizing he didn't have any easy answers.

"Ministers, deacon, bishop." Mattie sighed. "They all came to speak with what remained of our family." Her voice hardened. "One of them, the first time they came, seemed more interested in placing blame than helping, but the others must have told him that blame wasn't what we needed then. After that, they all did their best to help." She raised her tear-glistening eyes to him. "And they did, but nobody could fill the void after *Mamm* and the others left. Not in our house and not in our hearts. I don't want Daisy to be hurt again."

"You can't decide that. Only God knows what lies ahead for us."

"But He expects us to take responsibility for ourselves and to help others." Her mouth tightened.

"He does, but He also knows our limitations. After all, He made us in His image. He didn't make us His equals."

"I know that, Benjamin."

He sighed as she had. "I know you know that, but I'm finding it tough to find words to help."

"As I'm having a tough time with finding the words to help Daisy." She wrapped her arms around herself. "Letting pain control us day after day and month after month leaves us hollow inside. I learned that the hard way after you left five years ago."

"I hurt you?" He stared at her, wanting to believe that he'd misheard her.

"I don't expect you to remember." She moved toward the shop. "I should get back to work."

He blocked her way. "You can't make a statement like I hurt you and then walk away without explaining."

"What's to explain?" She didn't meet his eyes. "I had a crush on you."

"You did?" Shock pierced him, and he almost blurted out a question to ask if she still had feelings for him.

"*Ja*, but you were too obsessed with Sharrell to notice me."

"I noticed you." His retort was automatic, but as he said the words, he wondered if she was right. More than once since he'd seen her again, he'd recalled how little he knew about her.

But then he'd known too little about her sister, as well. He'd been blinded by Sharrell's enticing smile and his own hopes for a future with her. A future, he'd learned, that was nothing like she'd planned for herself.

"You barely noticed me," Mattie said, but there wasn't any accusation in her words. She was speaking what she believed were indisputable facts.

"Nobody could be oblivious to you, Mattie Albrecht."

She grimaced as if he'd insulted her. "It doesn't matter, Benjamin. The past is the past."

"The past is what makes us what we are today." He took her arm and drew her toward the shop, surprising her. "I brought something over today to show you, and now is as *gut* a time as any."

When she didn't ask what he'd brought, more regret swept through him. Her memories stood between them. He'd been foolish to try to deny the truth. He couldn't change their past, and he couldn't tell her how he envied her knowledge of what she wanted to do with her life.

The floors beneath their feet shone with the epoxy that would reflect the propane lights that had been installed over the aisles and by each door so no place in the shop would be lost to shadows. Her cousins had brought four simple tables they'd constructed to showcase the handicrafts and art that would be available for sale along with groceries and fresh produce.

Benjamin stopped by one of the tables and bent over to collect a cardboard box he'd put there this morning. He'd assumed Mattie and Daisy would be curious about what was inside it, but they'd been too busy.

"Here's what I wanted to show you." He prayed his voice wasn't trembling like his hands were as he drew a maple mantel clock out and set it in the center of the table.

He stepped back before he could snatch the clock

away and hide it in the box he'd carried it in to the Island. His sister had admired his work, but Menno had dismissed it as a frivolous hobby that kept Benjamin from spending time in the sawmill.

Mattie reached out to touch the carving of a bird along the side of the plain dial. Her finger traced the vine curving toward the splayed base. He moved out of the way as she walked around the table so she could see the other side of the clock. Without speaking, she unlatched the back and opened the door to reveal the coils and spring that brought the clock to life.

He pulled out a key, inserted it in the front under the dial and gave it a couple of turns. The soft tick-tick-tick of the mechanism filled the shop as she leaned closer to look at the workings.

How he wanted to ask what she thought of the clock! He knit his fingers together while he waited for her to say something.

When she straightened, the tension had fled from her face. Instead her eyes glowed as if twin stars peeked out of them.

"It's beautiful," Mattie said. "Is this one of yours?"

"Ja." Her reaction sent pleasure flooding through him, buoying his hopes that he wasn't wrong to spend his time building clocks.

"How long did it take you to make this?"

"About four months. I can make simpler clocks in a few days, but this one I took longer with so I could do the more intricate carving."

Again she touched the bird on the front. "It looks like cuckoo clocks I've seen."

"I learned woodworking from an elderly man named Joas. When he began teaching me to carve wood and design clocks, he told me how he learned from his *gross-dawdi* who'd learned from his *grossdawdi* who learned from…" He chuckled. "You get the idea. Anyhow, one of his ancestors had been apprenticed to a clockmaker in the Black Forest who worked on the earliest cuckoo clocks in the seventeenth century. Those techniques were passed through the family and on to me. I like working with walnut or linden as the first clockmakers did, but it's not easy to find. So I use maple or pine."

"The property on the Charlottetown road has a wood lot."

"*Ja*. Not only are there trees I could use, but there's plenty of room to plant black walnut trees. It'll take about thirty years for the black walnuts to mature, but in the meantime, I can also plant faster growing trees like pine."

She looked from the clock to him. "So why haven't you put an offer on the property?"

He started to tell her how often Menno had decried his dreams as silly and selfish. Instead he gave her a trite answer of not being certain if he should leave his brother to run the sawmill in Harmony Creek Hollow alone.

She nodded, thanked him for showing her the clock and then went to the front of the shop to check the list of suppliers from whom she might purchase groceries and other goods. He watched her walk away, her smile fading, and he berated himself.

Mattie was an astute woman, and she must have sensed how he'd skated around her question. Not lying, but also not telling her the whole truth.

Why didn't you?

He had no answer, even for himself. He'd been set

to be honest with her, telling her how he was trying to decide if he'd come to regret settling down in Prince Edward Island when he hoped there were adventures waiting for him.

What if you told her the truth?

Another question he didn't want to answer. He knew why. If he told her the truth, she might rebuke him as a fool. That could confirm his fears that her sister and his brother were right. He'd been devastated when Sharrell denounced his plans as ludicrous.

And how much worse would it hurt if Mattie said the same?

Chapter Eleven

Mattie wiggled her fingers and grinned. After having them feel numb for so long, it was a blessing to be able to feel each motion. She tapped each finger against her thumb. Her smile widened. She could feel each one, and the motion didn't hurt as much as it had.

That was on top of the *gut* news that *Daed* had sold the farm and would be coming to the Island soon. She guessed the first thing they'd want to do was find a nearby farm to buy because they'd be as eager as her cousins to get their crops planted.

She couldn't wait to see them. Since she'd come to the Island, she'd tried to push them out of her mind and focus on the shop so she didn't miss them so much. Now she could think of little else.

"But you need to!" Mattie told herself as she glanced at the stack of boxes waiting to be unpacked and the contents put on the shelves. Her primary distributor had arrived with twenty cases of various types of canned and bulk food. The driver had left them stacked by the rear door. She should unpack them before the rest of the order arrived tomorrow morning, but straining her shoulder would be stupid. However, she could do an inventory to find out what had been delivered and what hadn't.

Pulling off a pen she'd hooked onto the bib of her apron, she flipped a page on the shipping manifest and looked at the first box. She could hold the paperwork in her left hand without any pain. Every morning and before bed each night, she did her exercises to keep the damaged muscles loose. She must be extra cautious. She'd inventory the boxes, then open a single one and unpack what was inside. After giving her shoulder a rest, she'd do the next one.

Mattie glanced at the clock near the front door before beginning her inventory. It was three. Benjamin and Daisy should be back soon. They'd gone into Shushan to get another box of nails to finish the ramp they were building by the side door. It would make it easier for someone with mobility challenges to reach the fresh produce.

Did Benjamin realize how important he'd become in Daisy's life? By letting Daisy join him on errands, he'd become a substitute for their brothers who were dispersed throughout eastern Canada. She flinched as she realized she wasn't sure where any of them were. Tonight, she'd write a short note to each at the most recent address she had. She didn't want to lose track of them.

Cold air swirled through the shop, and Mattie saw three people at the front of the store.

"We're not open yet," she called, not looking up from her list.

She didn't get an answer.

Her eyes widened as three *Englisch* boys walked toward her. They were in their late teens, probably a year or two older than Daisy. They swaggered, but couldn't hide their surprise as they looked around. Did that mean they'd been inside the building before? When she'd first come to the Quonset hut, the debris of leaves and twigs scattered near each entrance had been proof that the doors had often been left open.

Dressed in identical outfits of blue jeans and puffy black winter coats, none of them wore hats and they had their hands stuffed in their pockets so she guessed they hadn't put on gloves either despite the blustery day. The heels of their boots grew louder with every step on the concrete floor.

Curiosity battled with uneasiness inside her, but she said again, "I'm sorry. We aren't open yet."

"We didn't come here to buy anything." The one in the middle spoke, and his lip curled. "You don't have anything in this junky place we want."

"Other than the building," said the teen to his left. He rapped his knuckles against the building's metal shell.

"What?" She stared at them. Were they out of their minds?

"You heard us, lady."

"I heard you, but I don't understand what you're getting at." She focused her eyes on them. That steady stare had worked with her brothers when they were teens, and she prayed it would be as effective with these *Englisch* boys.

It wasn't.

The teen in the middle took a step toward her. "Don't play dumb with us. Get out of here, lady!"

"I'm not leaving, but if you don't, I'm going to call the police." She hoped they didn't know much about the Amish and wouldn't guess she didn't carry a cell phone like the ones she could see sticking out of their jeans' pockets.

He ignored her threat as he moved another step closer. "This is our place. It's been our place for years. You're the trespasser."

She raised her chin as she began, "We don't want trouble."

"Then leave."

"We don't want trouble," she tried again, but again he cut her off.

"Don't you understand English?" He stuck his face close to hers, and she could smell the strong scent of whatever sandwich meat he'd had for lunch. "How about French? *Sors d'ici.*"

"I don't speak French."

The shortest teen tugged on the most aggressive boy's arm. "Don't you know? They speak German, Owen."

"Don't use my name!" the other boy snarled.

"Why don't you want him to use your name?" asked Mattie, hoping the small schism between them would be her chance to convince them to leave. "Owen is a *gut* name."

"*Gut?*" mocked the rudest teen. "Told you they speak German."

"This is Prince Edward Island, lady," said the shortest boy. "Here we speak English or French. None of that German stuff."

"I'm not speaking German, though it might sound that way to you," she said in what she hoped sounded like a conversational tone. The longer she could stall the teens from doing what they'd come in planning to do, the better the chance was that someone else might come along. She hoped it wouldn't be Benjamin and Daisy. That could escalate the situation.

"Look, lady," Owen said, flicking a finger at her *kapp*. "We've asked you nicely to leave. Don't make us ask you not so nicely."

She scanned their faces. The shortest boy glanced with unease at the other two boys. Was he as eager as she was to put a peaceful end to the confrontation? How could she convince him to take his friends and go?

The tallest teen, the one who hadn't spoken, darted forward and shoved a box off one pile. As it crashed to the floor, he poked a finger in her direction. "You're next, lady."

She closed her eyes and murmured a quick prayer when she heard raindrops hitting the skylights. Hoping she wasn't being a fool for not running away as fast as she could, she said, "Please leave. We're not open yet."

Owen clenched his hand into a fist, but he didn't raise it as the door opened.

"Are you three looking for something other than trouble?" came Benjamin's voice from the front of the store.

As he walked toward them, the boys froze, shooting fearful glances at one another. Benjamin didn't say another word. He acted as if he didn't notice the rain dripping off the brim of his hat and his hair.

All three boys' eyes grew so round she could see white around the irises. With his broad shoulders and work-hardened hands, Benjamin would seem like a walking monolith to the teens. He strode past them without speaking. Only when he stood beside her, facing them, did he say, "I asked you a question. Are you three looking for something other than trouble?"

The shortest boy turned on his heels and ran out of the shop followed by Owen. The third, the one who'd knocked over the box, opened his mouth but closed it so hard his teeth clicked. Moving back one step, then another, he whirled and followed his buddies through the open door and into the storm.

Mattie gave chase.

Benjamin shouted, "Where are you going?"

"Daisy's out there in your buggy, ain't so? If they see her…" She didn't have to finish because he rushed past her.

Moments later, she heard her sister's laugh along with Benjamin's as they came in the side door. The tension along Mattie's shoulders eased, and a sharp pain coursed down her left arm. She ignored it as she ran to her sister and hugged her.

"Daisy, you're all right!"

"What's going on, Mattie?" her sister asked as she tried to wiggle free. "First, I see three *Englischers* running out of the store like they were being chased by a bear. You're acting weird."

Mattie glanced at Benjamin who gave her a terse nod. Daisy hadn't guessed the teens had tried to cause trouble in the shop, and Mattie wouldn't tell her.

"Sorry," Mattie said. "I was thinking you two got lost."

"The storm slowed us," Daisy said. "That rain is mixed with ice, and Benjamin didn't want us sliding." Without a pause, she looked at him. "Speaking of sliding, I couldn't get any traction on our new ramp. My wheels spun and spun."

"Tomorrow," he said, "I'll put down rough material to give your wheels a better grip when it's wet."

Mattie went to where a roll of paper towels stood on the front counter. Peeling off several, she gave half to her sister and the other half to Benjamin. "You're dripping." She got more towels and handed them to Daisy so she could wipe off her doll.

"That rain felt like ice cubes down my back." Daisy wrapped her doll in the paper towels. "Poor Boppi Lynn was shivering, and she was scared she'd be stuck in the storm." Raising her eyes, she said, "*Danki*, Benjamin, for rescuing us."

"Rescuing everyone," Mattie added.

Benjamin motioned with his head toward the front of the shop, and she nodded. After urging her sister to toss the soaked towels in the storage room bin, Mattie crossed the shop to where Benjamin waited for her by the counter.

"Are you all right?" he asked. "Are you *really* all right?"

"*Ja.*" She unrolled more towels and handed them to him so he could wipe more rain off his face. "You sent them on their way before they could find the courage to do more than push over a box."

He scowled as he dried his face. She watched the motions, wishing her fingers were tracing those firm planes instead of a paper towel.

His sharp retort shattered that fun fantasy. "They were brave enough to try to intimidate a woman, but not face a man."

"I wasn't intimidated!"

"I said they *tried*." He frowned. "Don't bite off my head."

"I'm sorry to be sharp. I guess I was a little intimidated."

He chuckled as he tossed the used towels on the

counter. "You'd have to be a fool not to be wary of three teenagers with mischief on their minds, and I know you're not a fool, Mattie."

"Not today, at least." She reached out and put her fingertips on his chest. His heart hammered as hard as hers had when she faced the teens. It jumped to a faster beat as she said, "*Danki*, Benjamin."

"I didn't do anything but give them a chance to remember their manners."

"I'm glad you were here."

"I am, too." His fingers rose toward her face, but he jerked them back as he said in an uneven voice, "Those boxes won't unpack themselves."

He walked away before she had a chance to reply. She guessed it was for the best, because she didn't have any idea what she might have said. She'd dared to believe his swift heartbeat was because she'd touched him. She must have been wrong.

Fool!

Stupid fool!

Stupid, witless fool!

Benjamin continued to berate himself as he opened another box. This one contained jars of spaghetti sauce. It took all his self-control not to slam them on the shelf. How could he have been so brainless when Mattie thanked him half an hour ago for coming to her rescue? She'd been standing right in front of him, and he wouldn't have had to stretch out his arm to bring her against him. She would have offered him the chance he'd dreamed of to explore her lips.

And he'd walked away.

Fool!

Stupid fool!

Stupid, witless fool!

Instead of accepting her unspoken offer, he'd scurried away like those teens had when he'd challenged them. It'd been a reflex, one that he hadn't realized he'd developed until now…after he'd messed up. He'd tried not to look in Mattie's direction while she finished her inventory of the boxes. He hadn't needed to. He was as aware of her hurt as if she wore a sign around her neck.

How he wished he could explain to her! Even if he could find the words, whatever he said was sure to make her feel worse.

Then Mattie had gone to do another task, leaving him alone with the boxes. His opportunity to apologize had vanished. He'd been as cowardly as those kids.

"Have you found anyone?"

Daisy's voice shook him out of his self-incriminations. She hadn't seen the teens who'd threatened her sister. So if she wasn't talking about them, then who?

"Found anyone…?" he asked.

"For a husband for Mattie. What did you think I was talking about?"

He struggled to keep his expression serene. "You know I've been busy, Daisy."

"Not too busy to fulfill a promise, ain't so?"

With a sigh, he wondered how he'd ever let himself be roped into a bizarre situation. He'd been lost in thoughts of kissing Mattie seconds ago. Daisy wanted him to help her find another man to marry her sister. It was time to put an end to this absurdity.

"Daisy, I don't think there's anything else I can do."

She gripped the arms of her chair. Her eyes snapped. "That's not true. There are two guys I want you to talk to this week at church. They're nice guys. That's what Lucas and Juan said."

"You're asking your cousins to play matchmaker, too?"

She rolled her eyes. "No. I asked *you* to help me find her a husband, so Boppi Lynn can have a *daed*. Why would I ask them?"

"I don't know." That was the truth, but he didn't add he had no idea why she'd tapped him to be her assistant in her quest. After all, he knew fewer people on the Island than she did.

"Talk to them after church, Benjamin."

It broke his heart, but he shook his head. "No, I don't think that's a *gut* idea."

"But you said you'd help."

"I have helped. As much as I can, but I've failed."

She stared at him for a long moment, then whispered, "But you said you'd help."

"I'm sorry, Daisy. If there was something else I could do, I would."

"But you said you'd help." Her voice broke, and tears rushed down her face. She whirled her chair around and rolled away before he could respond.

He watched her disappear into the storage room at the back, far from him and far from her sister. How many others had made promises to Daisy and then hadn't kept them?

At least one other. Her *mamm*.

He wished there was way to convince her that he'd tried.

But you haven't. The small voice of his conscience chided him. *You never tried because you didn't want to see another man woo a woman who's touched your heart.*

He stared at the closed storage room door, then put down the jar of sauce he held. He walked out, half hoping that Mattie would call after him to discover what was wrong.

She didn't, and he had to wonder if she'd be glad at this point if he kept walking straight back to Harmony Creek Hollow.

Chapter Twelve

James gave the metal hook one final clanging hit on his anvil before he took the strip of iron and put it into the charcoal on his forge. He stirred the fire, making sure the iron heated again. Once it reached the proper temperature, James would take it out and twist a pattern in it.

Benjamin put the other hooks that James had made that afternoon into a small box. The bishop had ordered the hooks for his wife to use in her kitchen. The one James was making would be the final one in the set of four.

"*Danki* for your help today," James said as he hung a hammer he'd been using on the wall where he kept his tools. "I didn't expect it. I figured you'd be helping at Celtic Knoll Farm Shop again today. They open soon, ain't so?"

"*Ja.* On Friday." He kept his head down so he didn't have to meet his friend's eyes. "But I figured I should spend at least one day helping you as I told you I would." *I didn't want to break another promise.*

His hands tightened on the iron hooks so hard he

hoped he wouldn't bend them. He knew that was impossible, but the unhappiness in him was so powerful it seemed as if it could crush everything like it was pulverizing him. How could he have hurt Mattie and Daisy in the same hour?

"I appreciate it, Benjamin." His friend pulled the iron hook out of the fire and placed it on his anvil. As he shaped it with taps and sharp turns, he added, "Don't take this the wrong way, but I think the shop could use you more than I do. Blacksmithing is pretty much a one-person job."

"So I've just been in the way today?"

James grinned. "No, you've been great to have around to talk to. It can get lonely out here with only a horse to talk to, and most horses aren't inclined to chat when I'm changing their shoes."

Benjamin laughed because that was what his friend expected. "I guess if they started talking to you, then you'd really have something to worry about."

"Well, one thing I don't have to worry about is supper tonight." He held up the hook, examined it and then stuck it into the water basin beside his anvil. Steam sizzled. "We've been invited to our neighbors' for supper."

"Which neighbors?"

"The Kuepfer brothers." James's lips tipped in a grin. "And their cousins. I hear Mattie is a *gut* cook." He tapped his chin. "Who told me that? *Ach, ja,* I remember. It was you. You know, I'm still waiting for those leftovers you promised you'd share with me."

"As soon as there is any food left over, I'll share it." He kept his tone light, though his stomach was vibrating like a fiddle string beneath a bow.

Spending the evening with Mattie and her sister?

How could he eat a single bite while he looked at their faces. Daisy's would be bright with disappointment while Mattie's would be blank. Not that he needed to see her expression to know how she must be feeling.

He'd hurt her five years ago without realizing it, but he'd inflicted pain on her yesterday aware of what he was doing. She could have yelled at him, telling him her heart deserved better. She hadn't. She'd crawled more deeply within herself, shutting out the rest of the world.

"Mattie must be a *gut* cook," James said as he inspected the hook again.

"*Ja.*"

"I guess I'll find out myself soon enough." He stoked the fire in his forge, then gestured toward the door. "This is done, so grab your coat and hat, and let's go treat my taste buds."

"I probably—"

James stopped in midstep. "Don't tell me you're trying to think of an excuse not to go. Mark said they're going to be celebrating the progress on the shop. You can't miss the celebration that's partly in your honor."

"No, I guess I can't." But how he wanted to!

Pulling on his coat, Benjamin walked with his friend along the shore road. The air was fresh and tasting of salt. The last of the day's light flitted on the water like hundreds of dragonflies. A hint of warmth was in the breeze, a herald of the coming spring. It would be a lovely evening, but he couldn't enjoy it.

What was he going to say to Mattie when he walked into her cousins' house? To Daisy? Apologizing hadn't worked with Daisy, and he couldn't tell Mattie how much he regretted not kissing her. Not when her sister and her cousins would overhear.

Two hours later, Benjamin realized he shouldn't have worried—at least not about when he arrived—because neither Mattie nor Daisy was in sight when he and James came into the long narrow entrance hall that split the Kuepfers' large farmhouse in half. Stairs rose from the rear, giving him a view of the reverse side of the risers. A coatrack waited under the stairs along with a dower chest. The colors painted on the chest's front panel had cracked and faded long before he was born.

Mattie's three cousins came to welcome James and him. They were ushered into a sparsely furnished living room big enough to hold church for two districts. Benjamin took a glass of cider and tipped it back. Its chill flowed down his throat, but he could hardly taste its sweetness.

When Daisy rolled into the room to let them know supper was on the table, she had a genuine smile for James, but it grew brittle when she glanced at Benjamin. He rose along with the others to follow her wheelchair into the dining room, feeling as much dread as a man on his way to his execution.

Lord, show me the way to mend the damage I've done.

He repeated that prayer over and over while he sat in the chair pointed out to him at the long oak table in the white dining room. It echoed in his head while Mattie brought a platter with two roasted chickens waiting to be carved and set them among the bowls of vegetables and potatoes and gravy. It ran through his head the whole time they shared a silent prayer before they ate. He should have been thanking God for the bounty Mattie and her sister had put on the table, but he thought of bridging the chasm his actions—his inaction—had opened between him and Mattie.

Grateful he wasn't sitting across from either Mattie or her sister, Benjamin moved his food around on his plate with a piece of bread so it would look as if he'd eaten what he'd been served. Her cousins and James dug in with gusto while they talked with equal enthusiasm about their hopes for the new settlement. At the end of the table Mattie and Daisy were quiet, though he heard Daisy speak to her doll a couple of times. He was stuck in the middle, neither part of the conversation among the men nor invited to join the women in their silence.

"You've been a godsend to us, Benjamin," Mark said, pulling him into the discussion he hadn't been following.

"I'm glad I could help." He glanced around the table, but halted when his gaze reached Mattie. He willed her to look at him, but she kept her attention on her plate. "Each of you would have done the same for me. You know that we're blessed by being a blessing for others."

At his words, Mattie's head jerked up. He caught her eyes before she could look away again. Was there a way he could ask her forgiveness without words? If so, he had no idea how. He wanted them to be focused only on each other, letting the rest of the world melt away.

The moment passed when Daisy said something. He thought it was happenstance but wasn't sure when Daisy shot a glare in his direction. The sisters were protective of each other. He'd never imagined they'd be shielding each other from him.

His heart sank into his empty stomach. Was there any way to return to that sweet cocoon with Mattie? If he got her talking to him… Yet, if he forced a conversation, somebody might get the wrong idea.

Or the right one, corrected his conscience.

Telling himself not to get mired in an argument with

himself, he pushed aside his plate as Lucas announced Mattie had made them something special for dessert.

"What is it?" James asked.

"You'll see soon enough." Lucas chuckled.

James patted his stomach. "Not soon enough for me."

When Mattie rose and collected their plates, she urged each person to hold on to his or her fork. Benjamin might have said something to try to make her smile, but he remained silent. Her smiles were saved for her family tonight.

"Any hints, Daisy?" Benjamin asked when Mattie went through the swinging door and into the light green kitchen.

"You'll have to wait and see." Her voice could have chilled James's forge, and her cousins stared, their questions unspoken.

Mattie came from the kitchen with a chocolate cake topped by pecan-coconut frosting. As she leaned between Mark and Lucas to put it on the table, the front door opened without a knock. He saw confused looks exchanged among the cousins. They weren't expecting anyone, and their neighbors would have come to the kitchen door, not the front one.

Chairs clattered against the floor as all three of Mattie's cousins pushed back from the table. They started to rise, but froze halfway between sitting and standing as a gray-haired *Englisch* woman walked into the dining room. She wore a sweatshirt with a University of Winnipeg logo beneath a bright blue vest jacket. Her jeans had stylish holes in the knees above her high black suede boots. Her cropped hair was tinted with blue to match the frames on her glasses.

Daisy drew in a shuddering breath, and Mattie's face turned a sickish color. No one spoke. No one moved.

Benjamin reached around Lucas to draw Mattie toward him, wanting to ask why everyone was reacting so strangely to their caller. She didn't resist, and her gaze remained centered on the *Englischer*. Standing, he bent closer to her, trying to ignore the enthralling scent of her skin.

Everyone began to speak at once.

"What's wrong?" Benjamin whispered near Mattie's ear. "Who is that?"

She broke her mesmerism with the gray-haired woman. When she turned her eyes toward him, he saw disbelief and hope in them. "Don't you recognize her?"

He shook his head. He couldn't recall meeting the *Englisch* woman. "Do you?"

"Of course. It's *Mamm*."

Mamm? That *Englischer* was Emmaline Albrecht?

Beside him, Mattie was wringing her hands so hard she was going to make them raw. He reached out and put his fingers on top of hers. She froze, except for her eyes that looked at him in surprise. He had to wonder if she'd forgotten he was there. With her life flipped upside down and inside out, he shouldn't be surprised. As shocked as he was at the sight of her *mamm*, she must have been knocked even more off-kilter.

But he knew she was thinking the same thing he was: what was Emmaline doing here?

"*Mamm!*" cried Daisy. She almost ran over Mattie's feet as she spun her chair away from the table and sped toward the woman. "You've come back!"

Mattie held her breath as she waited for *Mamm* to

answer. So many questions demanded to be asked. Why had *Mamm* left Ontario last year? Why was she here? Was she returning to a plain life so their family could be complete once more? Was the rest of the family…?

Looking past *Mamm*, Mattie saw no one else. Were her sisters and brothers who'd left with *Mamm* waiting on the porch? She glanced out the window. A small red pickup was parked in the yard, but nobody stood near it.

Mamm was driving a truck?

"*Aenti* Emmaline," asked Juan, his voice choked with shock, "is that you?"

With a feigned laugh, *Mamm* said, "It's me. Your *aenti*." She turned to Daisy. "And your *mamm*." She looked past Daisy at Mattie.

Mattie didn't move or speak. She couldn't. Every inch of her was numb. Just as it had been when her *grossmammi* died. Just as it had been when she'd discovered *Mamm* wasn't returning. And exactly as it had been after Benjamin left before she got the nerve to tell him how she felt.

Her eyes cut to where he stood beside her. Was she making the same error again? So determined to protect her heart that she wasn't prepared to take the slightest risk with it?

No, she couldn't think about that. Not when *Mamm* was standing in the dining room doorway, her smile and assumption of welcome unchanged.

Mattie forced her attention to her *mamm*. Daisy had flung her arms around her and was talking so fast Mattie doubted *Mamm* could understand a single word.

Just as Mattie couldn't understand what was going on.

Emmaline Albrecht had changed. She'd lost weight,

no longer the roly-poly *mamm* and *grossmammi* who'd had a lap meant for cuddling *kinder*. Her gray bun was gone along with the long tresses that Mattie had loved to touch when she'd been young. Wisps curled around her ears. There was no hint that once she'd worn a *kapp* along with a simple cape dress and apron. The purse hanging from her shoulder was decorated with a bright print of a variety of animals, all with rhinestones for their eyes. Matching glitter decorated *Mamm*'s eyelids. Mattie had never imagined her *mamm* wearing any sort of makeup.

Everything about her shouted that she had put her plain life behind her, and she wasn't looking back. Yet, if that was so, why had *Mamm* come to the Island?

A gentle hand cupped her elbow, and Mattie tore her eyes away from *Mamm* and Daisy to look at the broad fingers steadying her. Her gaze rose along Benjamin's arm to his face. A mixture of emotions blazed there. Was he feeling as discombobulated as she was?

"Aren't you going to offer me a piece of that delicious-looking cake?" asked *Mamm*, smiling as if no time had passed since the last time she'd spoken to Mattie. As if she hadn't stepped out the door and never come back.

"*Komm* in, *Aenti* Emmaline," Juan said with a strained smile. "Would you like *kaffi*, too?"

"A cup would be nice. It's cold out there." *Mamm* gave an emoted shiver. "Are you sure you want to live so close to the ocean? It'll take forever before spring gets here."

"I'll get the *kaffi*," Mattie said and rushed from the room before anyone could halt her.

In the kitchen, she leaned her hands on the patched

orange countertop and closed her eyes. *Let this be a nightmare, God, and let me wake up.* She knew it was a futile prayer. Her *mamm* was in the dining room, acting like nothing out of the ordinary had occurred last year.

Benjamin walked in. "Are you okay?"

Her heart quivered at his voice. She hoped he couldn't guess how she was wishing *Mamm*'s arrival was just a bad dream.

"No. I—" She clamped her lips closed when the door opened again.

Daisy came in, grinning. She went to Benjamin and said, "It's all right, Benjamin. I forgive you for not finding a husband for Mattie. It doesn't matter any longer. Boppi Lynn doesn't need to find a family. She's got one." She rushed out, her chair aimed at the end of the table where *Mamm* was sitting and monopolizing the conversation.

"She's so happy," Benjamin murmured.

"What happens when *Mamm* disappears again?"

He stepped aside as she began to look for cups to serve the *kaffi*. "She's seeing what she wants to see, Mattie," he said. "She's a *kind* in so many ways, and she's overlooking your *mamm*'s appearance and how she's acting."

"I don't want her hurt again." Where were the cups? Her cousins should have put them next to the dinner plates and bowls, but they weren't there. How about by the glasses? She reached for the next door.

"I know."

"Daisy was devastated when *Mamm* left. If it happens again and—" Her voice hardened as she opened another door and saw no sign of cups. "—*when Mamm* leaves us again, Daisy is going to feel even worse. It took me months to convince her that nothing she'd said or done had caused *Mamm* to desert us."

"I'm sorry, Mattie."

Where were the cups? She'd opened all the top cabinets. Bending, she grabbed the knob of a bottom cabinet. "Why is she here? Do you think she's heard *Daed* has sold the farm in Ontario?"

"I didn't realize that. You must be thrilled."

She waved away his words. She wasn't thrilled *Daed* would be here soon. She wasn't angry that *Mamm* was here now. She was numb. If she could find the stupid *kaffi* cups...

"Does *Mamm* know *Daed* is coming to invest in our projects here?" She grabbed a knob. "Or does she hope she can get money from him?"

"She may have rights to the money Wendell made from selling the farm, even if she's filed for a divorce or separation." He sighed. "That's the law."

"How do you know that much about divorce?" She tugged on the door, but it refused to open.

"You'd be surprised what you hear while folks are shopping for Christmas trees." His smile vanished when she scowled at him. "I'm sorry, Mattie. I know this has got to be tough for you."

She tried pulling on the door again. Harder. It didn't budge. "I don't know why I'm worrying about this," she said through gritted teeth. "If we don't get customers at the shop, it may take every penny *Daed* has to keep our farms from going into foreclosure."

"It's not the money that's bothering you, ain't so?"

It's this cupboard and my cousins and their inability to put cups in the proper place. She didn't say any of that. Instead she tugged on the cupboard so hard that the knob popped out of the door, sending a crack down the wood. She stared at her hand where blood was oozing from two of her fingers. She didn't feel any pain. Just disbelief.

Benjamin snatched a rag from a pile under the sink. She continued to stare at her bloodied hand until he grabbed her other hand and pulled her to the sink. Holding her injured hand under the water, he murmured an apology if he was hurting her. He wasn't. The pain of slicing two fingers couldn't pierce the hard wall she'd built around her grief. He tore the rag in half and wrapped a piece around each finger.

"I'll pour the *kaffi*," Benjamin said. "You go in the other room and sit."

"You need cups. I don't know where they are."

"Right there." He pointed to a small cupboard on the far side of the stove.

Emotion exploded through her, refusing to remain pent up any longer. She flung the knob across the kitchen. It hit a plastic bucket and bounced away, then rolled against the door.

"Mattie..."

She ignored Benjamin's consoling, reasonable tone. She didn't want to be consoled. She didn't want to be reasonable. She wanted to rip the powerful frustration and rage out of her and throw it away as she had the knob.

"You don't understand!" she exclaimed. "I don't either. I don't understand why *Mamm* is here, and I don't understand how she could have abandoned us in the first place without telling us she was going. Oh, she told most of my siblings and convinced them to go with her. I've found that out in the past year."

"But she didn't ask you?"

"No. Why," she asked, her voice cracking, "did *Mamm* leave without asking me and Daisy if we wanted to go, too?"

She pressed her face against his chest as sobs erupted out of her. Her weeping threatened to buckle her knees as powerful emotions she couldn't control flooded her. Gripping the front of his shirt, she tried to anchor herself so she wasn't washed away by the tempest within her.

His arms enveloped her as he whispered her name over and over against her hair. She prayed he'd never let her go. Once she was out of his arms, she must face the reality waiting in the dining room.

When his finger traced her jaw to her chin, she tilted her face to answer his silent invitation. His lips brushed hers with a gentleness that eased her splintered heart. He lifted his mouth away after the briefest touch, and she steered it back to hers, wanting more.

He wrapped her in his arms, and she leaned into him and their kiss. As his lips etched sparks across her cheeks, she knew this was what she wanted, the promise of a lifetime together with...

Mattie jerked herself away, horrified that she'd let her emotions betray her into throwing herself at him. Dashing the tears away from her eyes, she picked up the *kaffi* pot.

"Mattie, I shouldn't—"

"I've got to serve the *kaffi* before the cake is gone," she said. She'd had to interrupt Benjamin before he could say their kisses had been a mistake. They might have been, but she needed to hold on to the illusion he hadn't kissed her because he felt sorry for her. After five years of pining for him, she yearned to believe he'd wanted the kiss as much as she had.

As she hurried through the swinging door to return to the dining room, she caught his determined expression from the corner of her eye. He didn't intend to leave what he had to say unspoken, so she'd have to make an extra effort not to give him a chance.

Chapter Thirteen

Nothing went as it should the next morning.

Though Mattie had risen before the sun to make breakfast, nobody had come to the table. She wondered how anyone could sleep when the wind howled around the chimney and rattled the windows and doors. It would be a cold walk to the shop because the wind blew from the north.

While eating her own breakfast, she kept the pancakes warm in the oven until they were as dried out and hard as the plate they were stacked on. Throwing them into the bucket to slop Lucas's new pig, she tossed the desiccated scrambled eggs on top of them.

Daisy came down an hour late with dark circles under her eyes. She grumbled about being too excited most of the night to sleep. Mattie served her freshly made pancakes and eggs and a few slices of bacon along with a large cup of *kaffi*. Daisy must have been tired because she skipped her regular half-and-half mixture of *kaffi* and *millich*. Instead, she'd tossed a teaspoon of sugar into the cup and gulped it black.

Mamm didn't appear until it was time for Mattie to

leave to open the store. The older woman was dressed in blue jeans and a sweatshirt that was emblazoned with the words Manitoba Moose. A logo with a belligerent looking moose glared at everyone. She waved aside the offer of food, but filled the biggest cup she could find with *kaffi*.

Mattie wondered if *Mamm* had any plain clothes in the big suitcase Lucas had put in the spare room. Mark and Juan had delivered a bed frame and a mattress for *Mamm* to use. After finding extra sheets, Mattie had made the bed, taking the quilt her *grossmammi* had made off her own bed to put it on *Mamm*'s. If *Mamm* recognized it, she hadn't said.

Mattie was grateful everyone thought her out-of-character silence was shock from *Mamm*'s arrival. She didn't want to talk about when Benjamin had kissed her.

Or why.

Her fingers trembled as she put the batter and the eggs and bacon into the refrigerator. Taking her coat and bonnet from the pegs by the rear door, she said, "I'll see you later. Make yourself at home, *Mamm*."

"Where are you going?" Her *mamm* peered at her with narrowed eyes over the top of her *kaffi* cup.

"Daisy and I are heading over to the shop." She forced herself not to look at Daisy because she knew her sister must have been wearing a similar expression of disbelief that *Mamm* didn't seem to remember what they'd been working on. Daisy had talked about it a lot last night. "We need to get a bunch of things done so the shop can open the day after tomorrow."

Happiness created excitement that flared for a moment against the darkness wrapped around her heart. After weeks of work, they were going to throw open the doors and welcome customers. It seemed impossible that it was finally happening, but it was.

Because Benjamin helped you. Why are you okay with him helping at the shop, but not with him helping you last night by holding you while you cried?

Mattie jammed her arms into her coat, annoyed with her own thoughts. She had to find a way to silence them so she could finish the work waiting for her at the shop. "See you later, *Mamm*."

"Aren't you going to invite me to see what you've been working on?" demanded her *mamm*.

Though she wanted to retort that the shop wasn't a school project and she wasn't a scholar getting ready to recite on the last day of school before the summer break, Mattie knew saying that would be petty. Her vexation with *Mamm* was deepening so fast she wasn't sure how long she could control her hurt and angry words.

"Of course," Mattie said. Getting upset wouldn't solve anything.

Once Daisy had finished her breakfast and was ready, she and *Mamm* pulled on their coats. Mattie saw something flash through *Mamm*'s eyes when Daisy took the time to wrap Boppi Lynn as if swaddling a living *boppli*. How many times had Mattie defended Daisy's doll when *Mamm* complained about it? Too many to count, and Mattie was amazed she'd forgotten about that.

Nobody spoke on the walk to the shop. The wind whistled around Mattie's bonnet and tried to tug it off her head. She kept one hand on it and the other on Daisy's chair to help her roll into the powerful gusts. *Mamm* strolled along beside them, taking in the sights and acting as if she was alone.

Mattie was tempted to ask *Mamm* why she'd come to the Island—or with them to the shop—but curbed her tongue. The tension grew tauter when they reached the shop and *Mamm* insisted Mattie give her a tour. With every step, her *mamm* asked why Mattie had chosen to do things as she had, and had Mattie considered doing things differently? Doing them exactly as *Mamm* would have.

Giving noncommital answers, Mattie sought any way to change the subject. The one time she managed to and began talking about how many gallons of paint they'd used on the building and the shelves, *Mamm* continued to find fault with the colors she'd chosen and how she'd set up the store and every other detail.

A sigh of relief slipped past Mattie's tight lips when *Mamm* left after an hour of dogging Mattie's steps. It'd been impossible to get anything done when *Mamm* criticized everything. Saying she was bored and wanted to sightsee, *Mamm* returned to the house to get her truck.

The last of their order was delivered in midmorning, and Benjamin was kept busy helping Daisy with inventory and shelving what had arrived. That gave Mattie the excuse to learn how to use the cash register by the front door. Electricity ran it as well as the coolers and freezer. Lighting and heat in the building came from the propane tank out back near the ruined greenhouses. Once the weather turned warm, the doors would be opened to let the breezes off the water cool the shop.

Something tickled Mattie's nose. She sniffed, trying to avoid a sneeze, but the sensation continued. Looking up from the manual she'd been reading to learn about the cash register, she gasped as she realized what was teasing her nose.

"Smoke!" she cried.

"Fire!" Benjamin's shout rang through the building. He seized Daisy's wheelchair. "*Komm mol!* We've got to get out of here."

Mattie froze. The fire was in her shop? All their work? All their dreams? Had they been for nothing?

As if she'd asked that out loud, Benjamin yelled, "We've to stop the fire before it reaches the shop."

His words broke her free. She ran after them, pausing to grab a case of bottled water. It might not be enough to put out the fire, but wetting the metal building might halt the flames from destroying it and everything inside.

Sirens shrieked in the distance as Mattie burst from the shop. She saw a red line of fire in the grassy field beyond the building. It was fifty yards away, but in the high wind, embers were swirling toward them.

She set the case of water on Daisy's knees, making sure her sister could balance it as Mattie and Benjamin yanked bottles out and opened them. They flung the water over the side of the Quonset hut, aiming at embers that had fallen on the metal.

Two fire trucks and a tank truck roared to a stop close to the blaze. Firefighters jumped out. Some began to hook a hose to the tank truck while the rest pulled out shovels and other equipment. Before Mattie could catch her breath, water was shooting out of the hose, creating thick clouds of smoke as it hit the flames.

"Get out of the way," bellowed a firefighter as a trio aimed another section of hose at the shop.

Mattie rolled her sister away from the building. The last of the water bottles crashed off her lap. Daisy reached out to grab one.

"Don't worry about them!" Mattie said as the wheel-chair careened down the knoll.

Seconds later, Mattie was on the other side of the road, watching the firefighters put out the blaze. The huge fountains of water coming out of the two hoses astonished her.

Benjamin moved next to her. "Are you okay?"

"I will be if they get the fire out." Thick smoke billowed toward them, and she turned away, putting her hands over her face. Others in the growing crowd of curious onlookers did the same. "I hope the water lasts long enough."

"They know what they're doing. They've got about ten minutes of water between the three vehicles. It shouldn't take any longer to knock the fire down."

"If they run out, there's the bay."

He shook his head. "They won't want to use seawater if they can avoid it. Salt messes up pumps." He gestured toward the flames. "Look! They're getting ahead of it already."

"You want to work with them, ain't so?" Mattie was surprised how easy it was to ask the question when she'd intended to avoid any conversations with him until she'd come to terms with what happened in her cousins' kitchen.

"*Ja*, I miss being a volunteer firefighter." He craned his neck to see past two tall men who'd shifted in front of them, stepping aside to let Daisy get a better vantage point. "But they're a well-practiced team, and the last thing they need is me getting in the way."

Faster than Mattie would have thought possible, the firefighters had put out the blaze. Smoke lingered, and she saw several people with shovels turning over dirt on hot spots.

A police officer wearing a light blue shirt and a dark vest with the word Police in white across his chest walked toward them. His hat and his trousers were decorated with the gold braid of the Royal Canadian Mounted Police.

"Are you the owners of this building?" he asked.

"I own it with my sister and cousins," Mattie answered. "I'm Mattie Albrecht."

"Constable Boulanger," the police officer replied after Benjamin introduced himself. "I'll be handling the preliminary investigation."

"Investigation of what?" she asked.

"Arson."

She gasped, "You think the fire was set?"

"Yes. Fires don't start in the middle of fields all on their own." He flipped open a notebook. "Have you seen anyone hanging around?"

"No," Mattie said at the same time Benjamin said, "*Ja.*"

"Which one is it?" the constable asked.

When Benjamin explained about the three teenagers who'd come into the shop to threaten her, Constable Boulanger nodded and scribbled notes before asking, "Owen, you say?"

"*Ja.*" Benjamin added, "We didn't hear any other names, and Owen was annoyed his name was used."

After asking them to describe the boys, the officer told them he might return with further questions. "You said three of you were there when the boys came? Who's the other person?"

"My younger sister." Mattie raised her voice when

she realized Daisy wasn't with them. "Daisy, where are you?" She stepped out on the road so she had a clear view in both directions. "Daisy!"

Heads turned, but her sister didn't appear. As Mattie began to hurry in one direction along the road, she heard Benjamin describing Daisy to Constable Boulanger. They rushed in the opposite direction.

Had Daisy gone home to talk with *Mamm*? It wasn't like her to miss out on a second of excitement. Where was she?

Mattie ran toward home, praying nothing had happened to her sister.

Benjamin didn't need to search far. He knew one place where Daisy might be. Sure enough, he found her sitting on the path to the shore where the water lapped its soft song. When he called to her, she didn't answer. She didn't acknowledge him when he slid to a stop by her chair.

"Daisy, Mattie is worried about you." He shivered as the icy wind swirled around them.

She didn't answer him as she hunched into her chair. "Daisy?"

No answer other than heartrending sobs.

The trails of tears along her face brought forth the image of Mattie weeping last night. Was Daisy upset because of her *mamm*, too?

When she didn't reply to his question, he sighed. He couldn't remain here when Mattie was frantic with fear for her sister. Leaving Daisy by the beach could lead to her getting stranded in the rising tide. It was cold, and she was bent double with her arms wrapped around her.

He gripped the handles on Daisy's chair and pushed

her along the access path. He'd expected her to tell him to stop, but she said nothing. While he took her to the shop, he tried again and again to get her to talk.

Nothing but soft sobs.

As Benjamin steered Daisy into the shop, Mattie cried out in joy, "You found her!"

He stepped out of the way as Mattie flung her arms around her sister, embracing her and trying to comfort her. Daisy didn't move, sitting hunched in her chair as she sobbed.

"You're safe. Thank God, you're safe." Mattie smoothed strands of her sister's hair from her wet cheeks. "We're all together again."

"Not...not...not all," Daisy moaned as she straightened, letting her arms fall by her sides.

Benjamin gasped. Daisy's lap was empty.

"Where's Boppi Lynn?" he asked.

"Gone."

"Where?"

"I don't know." She raised tear-filled eyes toward him. "I thought she might go to the beach. Boppi Lynn likes the beach." Her voice hardened. "But she wasn't at the beach. She's run away. Like *Mamm*. Boppi Lynn ran away without me." She hid her face in her hands and wept.

Mattie recoiled as if she'd run full tilt into a stone wall. Benjamin put out a hand, unsure if she would tumble off her feet. She seized his hand, holding it so tightly her fingernails cut into his palm.

He ignored the discomfort as he looked from one sister to the other. He'd never realized how much alike Mattie and her sister were. He'd been focused on how different Mattie was from Sharrell and had overlooked how she and Daisy both hid their wounds behind smiles intended to make others feel better.

He squatted beside the wheelchair. The renewed sound of Daisy's sobs hammered him.

"Daisy, Boppi Lynn didn't run away," Benjamin said.

"How do you know?" She glanced sideways at him, then at her hands on her empty lap.

"She's a *boppli*. She can't run." He tipped her chin up. "She can't crawl yet. She's a *boppli*."

Her eyes widened, and her sobs grew softer. "She's a *boppli*, ain't so? She's got to learn to crawl first, ain't so?"

"*Ja*, you're right. I'm going to go and look for Boppi Lynn. Someone will be taking *gut* care of her, I know. Everybody loves little ones." He stood, his gaze colliding with Mattie's. How much more pain could she endure? He longed to put his arm around her shoulders, being careful not to touch her tender left one. Then he wondered if there wasn't a single part of her that wasn't tender, most especially her heart.

Words failed him as he recalled how he'd done damage to her heart without realizing it. Last night, he'd surrendered to his dream of kissing her, and he'd hurt her again. He wasn't sure exactly how because she'd been wondrous in his arms, but he couldn't forget how she'd preferred to face the *mamm* who'd abandoned her to the man who was falling in love with her.

"I'll get others to help search," he said.

"*Danki*." She turned to her sister.

He trotted out of the shop. Finding the cousins, he explained what had happened and asked them to search and to get others to do the same. He had to retrace the way Daisy had gone. He discovered the water bottles that had fallen off Daisy's lap and followed them like a trail of breadcrumbs until he reached where the wheelchair's tracks had been obliterated beneath the thicker wheels of the firefighting equipment. If one of the trucks had run over the doll… No, he wasn't going to let negative thoughts into his head. He'd told Daisy he'd find her beloved doll, and he was going to do it.

No matter how long it took.

Chapter Fourteen

"Has Benjamin gotten here yet?" Daisy strained to look around the vegetable bins and out the shop's front door the following morning.

All the doors were open because deliveries were arriving every few minutes. In less than twenty-four hours, the Celtic Knoll Farm Shop would open. Everything inside must be ready before then.

Mattie pulled her coat around her, because the wind off the bay was cold. She paged through the signs she'd made showing the prices for the vegetables they'd be selling on opening day. So much needed to be done.

"I haven't seen him yet," Mattie replied.

"He's bringing Boppi Lynn to me. He said he would."

"I know." She wished she could say something more to console her sister, but she wouldn't lie to her.

Daisy left to go check with *Mamm* who'd insisted on coming to the shop again, though she'd spent most of her time talking to the vendors who were bringing the fresh fruit and vegetables. *Mamm* had become someone Mattie didn't recognize.

Mattie was grateful to the vendors who took time

to chat with *Mamm*. While they kept *Mamm* diverted, Mattie could do her work without constant critique.

She was finishing checking the signs when Daisy returned and asked, "Is Benjamin here yet?"

"I haven't seen him," replied Mattie as she had before.

"Do you think he's found Boppi Lynn?"

"I wish I could say *ja*, but I don't know."

The conversation played over and over in various forms through the morning. Each time, Mattie prayed she'd soon be able to answer her sister's anxious questions. It wasn't easy when her mind was reeling with so many conflicting emotions. She shouldn't be thinking about how sweetly Benjamin had kissed her. Instead she must focus on taping the signs listing the cost of each vegetable onto the bins. She couldn't, and she'd put the price of onions on the bin holding green beans.

Right after midday, Benjamin arrived. His hair was windblown, and she wondered if he'd run along the shore road because he sounded breathless. "I'm sorry I'm late. James had work he needed my help with." He looked around. "Where's Daisy? Has Boppi Lynn been found?"

"She's outside with *Mamm*. Nobody's found Boppi Lynn." She held the signs close to her, hoping they concealed her yearning to have him hold her and keep her sorrow at bay.

"I've looked over every inch of the road between here and your house. I went to the beach twice more. I've crisscrossed the field and spoken to anyone I've met. One of your neighbors thought he'd found Boppi Lynn. The doll was smaller, and it had dark hair. I'll keep looking." He ran his fingers through his hair.

Her own yearned to copy his motion. Locking her hands around the signs, she refused to give in to her own longings. They'd betrayed her with him too often in the past. She couldn't keep making the same mistake.

"*Danki*, Benjamin," she said before moving around the bins to post the signs on the other side.

"That's it?"

She frowned. "What do you mean?"

"I mean I didn't expect you to treat me like a leper because we kissed."

Mattie cut her eyes toward the side door where *Mamm* was in conversation with a man Mattie didn't know. Daisy was intently listening to them, so they might not have heard Benjamin.

"I don't want to talk about this now or here," Mattie said.

"But I do."

"I don't have time today, Benjamin."

He edged in front of her, blocking her from hanging up the next sign. "I know you've got a ton of things to do, but the first one should be saving our friendship."

"Friendship?" She choked on the word. "Do you think I go around kissing my *friends*?"

"I said friendship because the way you've been acting I figured any chance for more than that is gone."

Pain rushed through her, stronger and more devastating than any she suffered from her shoulder. "Is this how you dumped my sister?"

"You think I dumped Sharrell?" His eyes grew wide with what looked like genuine astonishment.

"*Ja.*"

"Why would you think that?"

Mattie didn't want to say how she couldn't imagine

anyone in their right mind ending a relationship with a man like Benjamin Kuhns, but she swallowed those words. Instead she whispered, "She said her heart was broken."

"If so, it wasn't my doing. Her heart didn't belong to me. It never did. That was the reason I left. She wanted to pit me against the man she loved in the hopes that we'd battle for her affections."

"That's preposterous."

"I agree, and that's why I went home. I didn't want to be part of any game where I knew I was going to come out the loser. All of her efforts were aimed at getting Barry Duerksen jealous enough to propose." A lopsided grin eased his tense face. "She might still be waiting if I hadn't spoken to him and warned him that he could lose her to someone else."

She stared at him, amazed. "I never heard about that."

"None of us was eager to broadcast the convoluted craziness we'd gotten caught up in, thanks to Sharrell."

She comprehended what he wasn't saying. Sharrell had been scolded by *Daed* often for her *hochmut* of believing she deserved to be the center of attention. Pride could betray a plain woman, but her sister was no longer living a plain life. Mattie wondered if Sharrell now displayed her pride for the whole world to see.

"I owe you an apology," Mattie said.

He shook his head. "You don't have to apologize when you trusted your sister to tell you the truth. I'm sure she did…from her point of view."

The tight straps that had been wrapped around her heart loosened. He was not only willing to forgive Sharrell, but forgive her, too, for believing the worst about him.

Mattie heard a hubbub outside the shop. Turning, she gasped. A crowd had gathered between the shop and the neighboring field where scorched black ground marked the boundaries of the grass fire. In the center of the crowd was *Mamm*, talking a blue streak. She looked as if she was having the best time ever, though each time she paused to take a breath, questions were fired at her from someone in the circle around her.

What was going on?

Where was Daisy?

Mattie relaxed when she saw her sister pushing her chair up the ramp and into the store. Running to Daisy, Mattie asked, "What's going on?"

"They don't want to help find Boppi Lynn." Two thick tears ran down Daisy's cheek. "All they want to do is talk about the fire."

"What about the fire?" Benjamin asked from behind Mattie.

Daisy shrugged. "I don't know and I don't care."

Mattie groaned when she looked past the gathered people to see three vans with logos painted on their sides. Each one had letters and numbers along with the word News. Looking at the crowd, she saw several of the people facing her *mamm* were holding out microphones. Someone shifted, and she saw a trio of other people with cameras on their shoulders.

Television cameras!

Mamm was talking to television reporters and letting them film her instead of concealing her face as plain people did when confronted by cameras. In Mattie's head, she heard her *mamm* telling her to make sure she always turned her face away if someone aimed a camera at her.

"Where's my Boppi Lynn, Benjamin?" Daisy asked.

"I don't know." When Daisy let out a wail, he hurried to say, "But I'm trying to find out."

"Now would be a *gut* time," Mattie said, catching Benjamin's eyes and trying to convey how important it was to get Daisy away from the prying eyes of the media.

He nodded and convinced Daisy to come with him to search on the far side of the building where they wouldn't be seen. As he walked away with her sister, he gave Mattie a rigid smile.

Grateful he'd understood her unspoken request, Mattie faced the crowd outside the shop. She paused to grab her bonnet and tied it in place. It would shadow her face, helping to conceal it from the cameras. She strode out of the shop and to where her *mamm* was smiling at an *Englisch* man who held a microphone out to her.

Mattie spoke to nobody as she hooked her arm through *Mamm*'s and turned her toward the shop.

Mamm planted her feet, refusing to move until she waved to the cameras and called, "That's all for now!"

Trying not to gnash her teeth to nubs, Mattie steered her *mamm* into the shop. She closed and locked the door behind them, before doing the same with the others. Before Mattie could reach the front door, a woman with a camera in tow opened it. Mattie shooed her and another woman out by saying the shop wasn't open to the public until the next day.

"Well done!" crowed *Mamm* as Mattie locked the doors.

"What do you mean?" Peering out the windows, Mattie saw the crowd dispersing and the news vehicles pulling away.

"You got them to tape your announcement of the shop opening tomorrow. Think of the free publicity you're going to get."

Mattie heard a knock on the side door and realized she'd locked Benjamin and Daisy out. Or was it someone else trying to gain access to the shop? She looked out and was glad to see Benjamin and Daisy. Mattie threw open the door to let them in, then secured it again.

Marching to her *mamm*, Mattie said, "You shouldn't be talking to those newspaper people."

"Not just newspaper. Television." She grinned as if she was younger than Daisy. "Imagine that! Emmaline Albrecht being interviewed on TV."

"*Mamm*, what's wrong with you?" The words were out of Mattie's mouth before she could halt them.

"Nothing is wrong with me. I'm happy."

"How can you be happy when you've given up the life you and *Daed* have had for all these years?" Mattie looked past the older woman to see Benjamin going with Daisy into the storage room. How could she have thought poorly of him when he was protecting her sister? Daisy didn't need to hear what Mattie must say to their *mamm*.

"You don't understand, Mattie." *Mamm* shrugged off her coat and tossed it on top of a bin.

Mattie lifted it off before the winter coat's weight damaged the tomatoes. Folding it over her arm, she faced her *mamm*. "You're right. I don't understand how you could have thrown aside everything that you spent years building. And for what? Why did you leave?"

"Because I couldn't stay any longer."

Mattie frowned and tightened her hold on the coat. "You would never have accepted an excuse like that from me. Why would you expect me to be satisfied with such an explanation from you?"

"Whether you're satisfied or not, Mattie, the truth is I wasn't happy. My parents insisted on me getting married to a man they chose."

"As you tried to do with me when you told me I had to walk out with Karl."

She laughed, shocking Mattie. "I never was a *gut* matchmaker for my daughters. I did much better with my sons."

"You tried to make matches for Sharrell and Beth? I didn't know that."

"Of course you did. I tried to match Beth with one of the boys next door. That didn't work when she decided she needed to marry the youngest Stoll son. I failed worse with Sharrell."

"Sharrell didn't need help finding a husband."

"I wanted her to have a *gut* husband, not the slug she married."

"Mamm!"

"Well, Barry was no catch. Not like Benjamin. I knew he was the perfect match for Sharrell the first time I met him." Her mouth hardened. "You're like Wendell. He never could understand me. He was happy to live out every single one of his days on a farm, never looking beyond its borders. I didn't want to waste my life that way."

"Waste? Are you saying we're all a waste of your life?"

"That's not what I'm saying. Don't put words into my mouth as your *daed* does." She grabbed her coat from Mattie who released it when she heard threads snap.

"Then tell me why you left, *Mamm*. Tell me why you abandoned us."

"I told you. Wendell never understood me. He thought

I should be content to live with every day like the one before it. That's not how I want to live. God has given us an infinite number of choices. There are so many different types of people, and so many different types of places. I want to see as many of them as possible, not be stuck on a farm. I want adventure, Mattie."

Hearing Benjamin make a muffled sound, Mattie glanced over her shoulder. She hadn't realized he was listening. Daisy? Her sister must still be in the storage room.

Benjamin avoided her gaze, but she couldn't mistake the disappointment on his face. She remembered how he'd told her that his primary emotion when Sharrell ended their relationship was disappointment that she'd used him to win her now husband's heart.

Was the memory of that moment why he wouldn't meet her eyes? Did he think that all the Albrecht family were as indifferent to others' feelings as her sister... and her *mamm*?

The disloyalty of that thought struck her like a blow. She shouldn't be finding fault with *Mamm*. How long had *Mamm* been unhappy being a housewife and overseeing her family? Lost in her own grief when Benjamin left without ever knowing how he'd touched her heart, Mattie had failed to notice. That didn't excuse what *Mamm* had done, but Mattie wished *Mamm* had spoken with her before running away.

Mattie opened her mouth to calm her *mamm*, but it was too late. *Mamm* was storming toward the front door. She tugged on the knob. When it didn't open, she spoke words that Mattie hadn't realized her *mamm* knew before she unlocked the door and left, slamming it in her wake.

Before Mattie could chase after her, she heard Daisy cry, "Our family is all gone."

Mamm would have to wait.

"That's not true, Daisy." Mattie knelt by her sister's wheelchair and folded her hands over Daisy's on the arm. "We've got a family right here. You and me and Mark and Lucas and Juan are a family. We've worked together to open the store, because that's what families do."

"But Boppi Lynn is gone."

"Keep praying. We can't guess what God has in store for us."

Daisy gave her a watery smile. "Maybe He knows a family who needs Boppi Lynn more than we do. Maybe He's going to give her to that family."

Mattie faltered. What could she say to reassure her sister and yet not be false with her? Benjamin! He'd found the right things to say to Daisy before. Could he again?

She looked over her shoulder. Where was he? She heard a door click closed at the rear of the shop.

"Why did Benjamin leave?" Daisy asked.

Coming to her feet, Mattie stared past the areas Benjamin had worked so hard to clear, past the shelves he'd built and hung during the work frolic, past the floors he'd coated to protect them from further damage. Everywhere she looked, she saw Benjamin's fingerprints.

But he was gone.

Horror gripped serrated fingers around her throat, making it impossible to breathe. Had hearing about the disaster her family had become been the final straw for him? He'd put up with so much from her sister, her *mamm*…from Mattie herself. Had he decided he didn't want to be part of the drama anymore?

When Daisy's hand slipped into hers, Mattie looked at her sister and whispered, "I don't know why he left."

"He's coming back, ain't so?"

"I don't know." And her poorly patched heart splintered into countless pieces all over again.

Benjamin closed his fingers into a fist on the wall of his bedroom before leaning his head next to it. Anger and frustration made it tough to breathe. He'd gone to his room so he didn't have to explain to James why he was home from the shop so early instead of staying to finish last-minute details before tomorrow's opening.

What could he say to James? That he wished he'd never come to the Island? That staying under his brother's thumb was better than escaping and drowning in regret and longing? That he'd complained for years about not being able to follow his dream, but didn't have the guts to grab it when it was right in front of him?

When *she* was right in front of him.

His regret and longing had nothing to do with opening his own shop where he sold his clocks. It was about Mattie Albrecht.

"Are you in there?" asked James after knocking on his door.

"Ja." He didn't move.

"There's a message for you on the phone in the smithy."

Though he didn't want to, Benjamin opened the door. His friend stared at him with sympathy, a sure sign that his thoughts were emblazoned on his face.

"What's the message?" Benjamin asked.

"It may not be important any longer." James looked past him. "Have you already started packing?"

"No."

"So you aren't leaving?"

"I haven't decided."

"The message is from the real estate agent you talked to in Shushan. An offer may be coming in on the property you're interested in. The call was a heads-up if you wanted to put in an offer for it yourself. Here's the office's number." His friend handed him a slip of paper with smoke smudges on it. "But if you're leaving, it doesn't matter, ain't so?"

Benjamin didn't answer as he took the slip of paper. He didn't look at it as James walked down the stairs.

What a fool he'd been! Thinking he knew what he should do with his life instead of heeding God's will for him. But he had no idea what God wanted him to do. Benjamin couldn't follow his brother's orders any longer. Not after defying him by coming to the Island. He'd discovered Mattie here and lost his heart.

Yet Emmaline had held up a mirror to him, and he didn't like what he'd seen. She'd spoken of having adventures, something she was so desperate to grab that she'd thrown away everything important in her life.

He wasn't any different, was he? He'd come here on a whim. Instead of confronting his brother, he'd run away.

Just as Emmaline had.

He hadn't given a single thought to what he'd lose.

Just as Emmaline had.

He'd selfishly thought of what he didn't have rather than what he did.

Just as Emmaline had.

And now he'd hurt Mattie far worse than her *mamm* ever could have.

* * *

Adjusting a loaf of bread here and an apple there, Mattie walked along the long aisle at the center of the store the next morning. The Celtic Knoll Farm Shop's doors would be thrown open in five minutes, and she wanted everything to be perfect. Her suppliers had done a great job of making sure she had enough produce and canned goods to make the shelves look enticing. Their products filled the bulk area in the rear where everything from flour and sugar to beans and rice awaited frugal shoppers.

She glanced at the clock over the front door and gasped. There weren't five minutes before the store's grand opening.

There was just one!

Calling to Daisy to join her at the front of the store, she wished she could find a smile for her sister. In the past forty-eight hours, ever since Boppi Lynn had been lost, Daisy hadn't smiled once. She'd stopped teasing everyone. She'd barely spoken. She'd become a Daisy statue with no life inside her. It'd been worse after Benjamin left yesterday, and *Mamm* had disappeared again.

According to their cousins, *Mamm* was staying at a nearby motel. Mattie had to wonder where *Mamm* had found the money to pay for it, but she pushed the thought away. For now, she had to get the doors open.

Tears burned in Mattie's eyes as she walked to unlock the front door, but she blinked them back. If she cried, she'd upset Daisy more. They'd worked so hard for this day, and it wasn't anything like Mattie had hoped.

"*Wilkomm*," she called as she opened the door. Her eyes widened when a parade of shoppers came through it…and kept coming and kept coming.

Within minutes, she found herself at the cash register as she checked out her first customers. She didn't have to refer to the register's manual once while she greeted more customers and bagged groceries. The shoppers were a *gut* mix of plain and *Englisch*. She knew many were curious to see the inside of the Quonset hut, but few left without purchasing something. She hoped most would return.

Mattie stepped away from the register an hour later to answer a question and point to where the baked goods were displayed. The shop was full beyond her expectations. Sending a prayer to thank God for making it possible for them to get the store open on time, she added a quick *danki* for all the people who'd come.

But Benjamin wasn't there that morning. He should have been part of Celtic Knoll Farm Shop's grand opening. He'd worked as hard as anyone else to ensure its success. Not having him in the shop on this all-important day left a void so deep she wasn't sure she could keep from falling in.

Daisy was doing her best to help customers. She'd promised not to ask each person who came in if they'd seen Boppi Lynn, but only because Mattie had agreed to put flyers about the missing doll by the register.

The shop was doing great, so Mattie tried to concentrate on that and assisting shoppers. She knew not to assume that every day would be as busy as this one, but she couldn't appear glum and chase potential customers away.

"Daed!"

Mattie whirled at Daisy's joyous cry. She pressed her fingers over her mouth so she didn't shout herself when she saw *Daed* standing in the side doorway at the top of the ramp. Her eyes widened when she noticed that he held a cane. When had he started using one?

People got out of the way as Daisy rolled toward *Daed*. Those she passed began to grin as they realized what was happening. Other customers peered around the end of the aisles, not wanting to miss the reunion.

Reunion...

Mattie couldn't move from behind the register. What would her parents do if they ran into each other in the shop? *Mamm* knew *Daed* would be coming to the Island, because the cousins had mentioned it while devouring the chocolate cake the night of *Mamm*'s arrival.

However, *Daed* might have no idea his wife was on the island. What would he do or say when he discovered that fact?

Daed hugged Daisy, then looked around. When he saw Mattie standing by the counter, he asked, "Don't you want to greet your old *daed*?"

She rushed to him. Hugging him, she wished he wasn't so thin. "How was your trip?"

"Long and, by God's *gut* grace, over."

Daisy asked, "Where are Ohmer and Dennis?"

"Your brothers went straight to the house." He touched Daisy's hair with love. "They couldn't wait to talk to your cousins about possible properties we can buy." He appraised the shop. "You've done a *wunderbaar* job, Mattie."

"*Danki*." She had to get back to the till, but she bent toward him to whisper, "*Daed*, *Mamm* is here."

"I suspected that might be so." He sighed. "It's no secret the farm has been sold. Your *mamm* isn't a stupid woman."

She just does stupid things. Mattie didn't say that aloud. It would hurt *Daed* more.

Leaving him to talk with Daisy who was grinning for the first time in two days, Mattie returned to work. The morning sped past, and right before lunch, the crowd began to thin. Mattie took the time to refill the shelves between customers at the register. She began with the jams, which had been popular. She made a mental note of which ones had sold best. She'd add extras of those to her next order.

She smiled when her cousins burst past the back door. They'd assured her they would be stopping by for lunch and an update on how the opening was going. She was pleased to see they'd cleaned the mud off their boots after a morning in the fields.

"*Onkel* Wendell!" Lucas pumped *Daed*'s hand. "Why didn't you let us know you were coming today?"

"I sent a letter, but it looks as if I got here before it did." *Daed* smiled at the shoppers in the store. "This is amazing."

"You can thank your daughters and Benjamin. They pulled it off."

"Benjamin?" *Daed*'s brow threaded. "Who's Benjamin?"

"Benjamin Kuhns. He's here on the Island visiting a friend and pitched in to help us." Mattie glanced at Lucas and realized she wasn't the only one holding her breath, waiting for *Daed*'s reaction.

"The same Benjamin who walked out with your sister?" Not giving them a chance to answer, *Daed* answered his own question, "I've always thought he was a *gut* man. Hardworking and with a generous heart. I never understood why your sister tossed him aside for the guy she married."

"She loves Barry," Mattie said.

"Sometimes love isn't enough." *Daed* sighed, and she guessed he was thinking of how *Mamm* had walked away after so many years of what everyone—including *Daed*—had believed was a happy marriage.

She wanted to sigh, too. It hurt her to see *Daed* so beaten down by the direction his life had taken. She prayed now that he was there, he'd rebuild his life with the family he had remaining.

And she could, too.

Chapter Fifteen

Benjamin paused as the big silvery Quonset hut came into sight. He saw a long line of cars parked along the road. Interspersed with them were buggies that hadn't fit at the hitching rail between the building and the delivery road that curved behind it. People were gathered outside, talking and enjoying the day that was going to be much warmer than the past few. Every person, he noted, was carrying a bag with the words Celtic Knoll Farm Shop imprinted in dark blue letters.

The shop was a success. Mattie had worked through pain and overcome every trial she'd faced. She'd watched over her sister and helped her cousins.

And she'd stolen his heart. No, she hadn't stolen it. He wanted to give it to her, but it might be too late. His indecision could have cost him what he wanted most. He hoped talking to her and getting her advice would guide him to the right choice. After long hours on his knees last night, beseeching God to help him, he'd been pushed toward her. It was a direction he wanted to go, though he didn't know if she'd be as pleased to see him after he left her to handle the mess with her *mamm* and finish the final details for the opening.

As he reached the path to the shop, a police vehicle pulled into the driveway. Every conversation stopped, but resumed when Constable Boulanger stepped out, holding a small tote. Was the constable coming to shop, too? He nodded to the people gathered outside as he settled his hat on his head.

Benjamin greeted the constable at the door. "Any news on the fire?"

"Not that I can share, but things are moving forward with the investigation." He went inside.

Again silence dropped on the shop as if Constable Boulanger was carrying a gun in his hand instead of a grocery bag. Acting as if he hadn't noticed, he smiled at Mattie who stood behind the counter.

"Is Daisy here?" the police officer asked.

"Ja." Mattie glanced at Benjamin before she stepped around the counter, but he couldn't read her blank expression. Was she hiding her reaction at seeing Constable Boulanger or him? "Let me find her."

Moments later, Mattie returned with Daisy who said, "Hi, Constable. Did you come to see our new store?"

"It looks great," the constable replied. "But it's not the reason I'm here. This is." He smiled as he opened the tote bag and lifted out a bedraggled Boppi Lynn. Someone—Benjamin guessed it'd been the constable himself—had made an attempt to clean the doll, but her clothes had dark stains.

"Boppi Lynn!" Daisy swept the doll into her arms and hugged her close. *"Danki, danki, danki* for bringing her home, Constable. Don't ever go away again, my sweet Boppi Lynn!"

Benjamin stepped back as Mattie embraced her sister. Neither spoke a word, but the connection between the two of them was so palpable that it was as if a warm wave had swept through the store.

The constable said, "I found the doll about a mile from here. It looks as if she was picked up by someone and then tossed away. Too bad we didn't find her first."

Mattie came to thank the constable. He started to congratulate her on the shop's success, but his radio crackled with words Benjamin couldn't catch. Sirens split the air. A police car skidded to a stop in front of the store. Another officer ran to Constable Boulanger and spoke in a tense whisper.

"You ask outside," the constable said. "I'll check in here."

The other officer ran outside, calling for attention.

At the same time, Constable Boulanger asked, "Does anyone here have climbing experience?"

"I do!" Daisy raised her hand, keeping her other arm around Boppi Lynn. "I climbed the wall. Benjamin helped me."

The constable turned to Benjamin. "Wall-climbing? Like at the resort?"

"I've climbed there, but I've also had training with the fire department in Salem, New York." He listed the skills he'd practiced over and over with the other volunteers, then asked, "What's going on, Constable?"

"We've got someone stuck in a soybean silo."

Gasps of dismay came from every direction.

"It's a woman," Constable Boulanger went on. "Says her name is Emma. I'm not sure about her last name. Lime or something like that."

Mattie gave a soft cry. "Do you mean Emmaline?"

"It could be. Sounds are strange when they echo up the silo."

"*Mamm* is in a silo?" cried Daisy.

The constable flinched. "You know this woman?"

Mattie answered, her voice trembling. "My *mamm*'s name is Emmaline Albrecht, but it can't be her."

"The report is that the woman has short gray hair and is in her sixties. Wearing a sweatshirt with what looks like a moose on it. Does that sound familiar?"

Instead of answering the constable, Mattie whirled to face Benjamin. "You've got to save my *mamm*."

"It can't be her!" Benjamin argued. "Why would she be in someone's silo? That doesn't make sense."

"Nothing about her makes sense." Mattie seized his hand and clasped it between hers. "I know God brought you here at this exact moment because *Mamm* needs your help. Help her please."

He nodded, though he longed to draw her closer and sample her soft lips again. Wishing he could be as certain of God's will as she was, he released her fingers as he nodded to Constable Boulanger.

Everything went into fast-forward as the constable hurried him toward his patrol car. They careened along the road, the sirens blaring and the lights flashing and the trees beside the tarmac a blur. More information crackled through the car's radio, but the strange code words used by the police force made no sense to Benjamin.

Neither did the idea that Emmaline was stuck in a silo. The reports had to be wrong, but if he could help whoever it was, he would.

Benjamin was slammed against the door as the constable made a sharp turn onto a farm lane. He jumped out before the car came to a full stop. Its forward motion propelled him toward the barn and storage silo so fast he almost tumbled onto his face. He got his feet under him and ran toward where a crowd was already gathering.

"Whose farm is this?" he called.

A tall thin man, his face as weathered as the boards on his barn, raised his arm. "Mine!"

"Is there an auger in the silo?" He didn't know much about soybean storage, but he did know about storing silage and corn. In both cases, the silo could have an auger that would disgorge the silo's contents into a concrete pit where it could be shoveled out for use.

"Yes," the *Englisch* farmer said, his face blanching. "And it's on."

His stomach clenched. "Turn it off. Now! If she falls into it, it'll rip her to shreds."

"It's far below where she should be."

"If she's getting sucked into the beans, she could reach it faster than we might guess."

The man nodded and rushed away, shouting to the others gathered around the silo.

Benjamin looked around to see who was in charge of the firefighters who had come to help with the rescue, but couldn't tell as the milling crowd grew bigger by the second.

"Are you Benjamin Kuhns?" asked someone from behind him.

He saw a woman wearing a fire chief's regalia. *"Ja."*

"I'm Kelsey Davenport. This way." The fire chief waved her arms, and a path opened among the firefighters and the growing crowd. When one person didn't step aside, he was yanked back before the chief reached him. Without breaking her stride, the dark-haired chief said, "I've been told you've got vertical rescue training."

"*Ja*, but I've never been on an actual rescue. Just training."

"That's more than the rest of us have." She gave him a quick smile. "I've scheduled our training for next month. Won't do us much good today, though."

"Who's your best climber?"

Looking to her right, she put two fingers into her mouth and whistled. A man who didn't look like he was much more than a teen loped to her side. Benjamin was glad to see the firefighter was trim and muscular. Both would be an asset while they rescued Mattie's *mamm*… or whoever was in the silo.

"Benjamin, this is Logan Bancroft," she said. "He's been clambering over the shore cliffs his whole life."

"*Gut.*" He looked at the younger man. "I'll need your help with ropes for climbing into the silo."

"You're climbing inside it?" asked the chief. "Won't that be too dangerous with the beans slipping all over the place?"

"I won't be going all the way down. I'll—"

"Do what you need to! We don't have time for you to explain."

Benjamin seized a length of rope before he ran toward the silo to climb the ladder. Logan carried another section of rope over his shoulder as he tailed Benjamin up the ladder.

Wishing he could scamper like a squirrel, Benjamin saw two men shoveling soybeans from an opening at the base. They were working hard, but he guessed they wouldn't be able to remove enough in time.

The silo stopped reverberating against him, and he

shot up a quick prayer of thanks that the auger had been turned off. That was one threat they wouldn't have to worry about. He had no idea what impact turning it off would have on the beans, but he wasn't going to look for more trouble.

Shrieks burst from inside the silo as he continued up the ladder. The sound was harsh, but female. Could it really be Emmaline in there? If so, her throat was raw from crying out for help.

Reaching the top, he grabbed the edge, being cautious not to cut his hands on the rough perimeter. He peered in and groaned. Mattie's *mamm* was in the silo. Had she lost her mind? He started to call out to her, then caught his hat before it fell. Spinning it away like a *kind*'s toy, he watched it sail onto Daisy's lap as she and Mattie and the rest of their family emerged from other emergency vehicles. Daisy held two thumbs up to him, grinning.

Beside her, Mattie stood with her hand on Daisy's chair. Her expression was grim, but when her sister turned to say something to her, she smiled. He knew she didn't want to distress Daisy further. Again, he was struck by how different she was from her *mamm* and Sharrell. Those women thought only of themselves. If he'd continued to let his impressions of the family be colored by Emmaline and her oldest daughter, he…

No, he couldn't let his thoughts linger on the past. He needed to think about saving Emmaline's life.

He bent over the top.

"Can you see her?" Logan asked from behind him.

Turning to the man who'd paused a few rungs lower on the ladder, he said, "Yes. She's stuck more than halfway down."

Benjamin gauged the scene below him. The soybeans were in constant motion, though she wasn't fighting to escape them. Dust rose to tickle his nose. He didn't dare to sneeze, fearful the slightest sound would send the soybeans into a green avalanche.

At last, she looked up. "The beans are sliding from under my feet." She moaned in fear. "They're like quicksand."

He risked answering her. "Stand as still as you can, Emmaline! Hold on!"

"To what?"

He turned away before she could see his involuntary grin when she sounded like the literal Daisy. Handing one end of the rope he carried to Logan, he ordered the firefighter to secure it on the ladder. At the same time he began lowering the other end toward Emmaline.

"I'm dropping a rope," Benjamin called. "Tie it under your arms." He continued lowering it. "No! Don't reach for it. Any motion you make could dislodge the soybeans farther. Wait for the rope to come to you. There you go."

He instructed her how to secure the rope under her arms. When he assured her that tightening it around her would mean she couldn't fall any deeper into beans, she hurried to follow his instructions.

"Can you move your legs?" he called.

"No." She winced. "And the beans are getting tighter and tighter around them."

"We can take care of that. Just give us a few minutes."

"I don't know if—"

"Stay calm, Emmaline!"

Hoping she'd heed him and not thrash around, he

took the plastic panel Logan passed to him. Several more were on their way up the silo as the firefighters made a human chain. He balanced the panel on the top as he straddled the side. Seeing interior rungs a few feet to his right, he inched in that direction. He took a deep breath before he put his foot on the uppermost one. Before he shifted onto the ladder inside the silo, he scanned the ground below.

Even if she hadn't been standing beside her sister's wheelchair, he could have picked out Mattie. It was as if he was seeing with his heart rather than his eyes.

The distance didn't seem to matter as she gazed at him. He could sense her worry and her prayers flying past him to God, and her belief that He'd brought Benjamin to this place and time to save her *mamm*.

Lord, don't let me disappoint her. Not again.

The process was simple because he'd practiced it in New York. He pressed the panel into the soybeans behind Emmaline, warning her several times not to touch it. He kept up a steady monologue about what he was doing, how he was building a temporary silo within the real one so they could keep the rest of the soybeans away from her during the rescue.

He climbed up and took the next plastic panel. Slowly, each motion calculated to keep the soybeans from shifting, he hooked the panel to the previous one. The final two panels snapped together to form a box without a top or bottom.

"I'm going to push this down around you," he said.

Emmaline's head lolled to the side, and he wondered if she'd lost consciousness.

Then she whispered, "All right."

Benjamin held his breath as he got the plastic box in

place, then signaled to Logan at the top. Slowly the rope wrapped around Emmaline became taut. She kicked her feet as if swimming upward, but the soybeans clung to her. The men shouted to pull harder.

At last, she was freed. Benjamin climbed beside her as he had Daisy. He steadied the rope so it wouldn't spin, bashing Emmaline against the walls of the silo.

Cheers burst out from the ground as Emmaline's head became visible over the top of the silo. With the help of Logan and the other firefighters, she was transferred to the ladder truck where another firefighter helped guide her toward the ground. Logan scampered down the ladder on the silo.

Benjamin grasped the top of the plastic box. The beans didn't release it. He almost fell off the ladder, but caught himself before he'd have to be rescued, too. When he reached the top, he handed the panels to a firefighter who'd taken Logan's place.

As he climbed out, more cheers met his appearance, but he heard one voice over the others because it resonated in his heart.

Mattie.

Benjamin rushed down the ladder, thanking the firefighters and accepting their congratulations. He cut through the crowd to find Mattie.

She put her fingers on his arm and gazed at him. She didn't speak, but she didn't need to. Unlike ever before, she wasn't trying to hide her emotions from the world.

He understood, for the first time, how she'd submerged her true feelings so she could be strong for what remained of her family. While her *daed* and siblings had fallen apart, grieving for what had been lost and might never be part of their lives again, she'd gone on. She'd tended to everyday matters and eased their sorrow while stanching her own pain until the day arrived when she could let it go.

Because she hadn't shown her anguish didn't mean she hadn't felt it. Knowing her as he hadn't before, he realized how she'd suffered in silence. How lonely it must have been for her to shoulder that burden alone and never once complain.

"*Danki*," she whispered.

"I'm glad I could help."

Mattie's name was called by someone close to the ambulance where her *mamm* sat in the back. She squeezed his arm. "Don't go."

She didn't add anything else before she rushed away to tend to Emmaline, but those two words had been enough so he finally knew what he should do.

Mattie brought another bottle of water for *Mamm* who was frowning at the fire chief and several police officers. They were asking questions, and it was obvious *Mamm* didn't want to answer them. Mattie guessed it was because answers would show everyone how careless *Mamm* had been.

"I never suspected there would be a problem," *Mamm* asserted. "He said he's done it a dozen times, and he's never had any problem."

"He who?" asked Constable Boulanger.

She shrugged, then winced. "A guy I met at your store yesterday, Mattie. He was telling me about great extreme adventure things he's done. He said he'd come with me."

"Where is he?" Mattie asked.

"I don't know."

"He's not in the silo, is he?" The constable frowned.

"No. He never showed up, so I went on my own."

Mattie wanted to roll her eyes at her *mamm*'s foolishness, but she didn't. There wasn't anything funny about what had happened.

"That was stupid, *Mamm*," Daisy said in a voice that carried over the crowd that seemed eager to see every last bit of the drama. "You told us to think twice before doing something that could be dangerous, and then you went and did this. You needed to think twice." She snorted as *Mamm* had done so often when she was disappointed in them. "You needed to think *once*!"

Mamm puffed in indignation. "I don't need a lecture from my own *kind*."

"*Ja*, you do."

Mattie saw Benjamin's lips twitching, and she had to fight to keep her own still as Daisy scolded *Mamm* as if she had no more sense than Boppi Lynn. A guffaw came from the crowd when Daisy reminded *Mamm* how many times she'd told her *kinder* to look before they leaped.

"If you'd done that, *Mamm*, Benjamin wouldn't have had to risk his life to save you." Daisy frowned. "He's a *gut* guy. I thought I needed him to help me and Boppi Lynn find her a *daed*, but *Daed* is back."

"Wendell is here?" *Mamm*'s head swiveled to let her look in every direction.

Mattie couldn't guess if *Mamm* hoped to see *Daed* or to avoid him.

"I'm back, too," *Mamm* added. "Your doll can have a *mamm*."

"She doesn't need you to be her *mamm*." Daisy shook her head as she said with quiet dignity, "She's got me!

And I think about her before I think about myself. I won't ever leave her without a second thought."

Standing, *Mamm* then strode away without another word. The constable followed, and Mattie knew there would be consequences for what *Mamm* had done, though she had no idea what.

Mattie started to follow, too, then halted. Nothing she said would make a difference to *Mamm* who couldn't see the grief and pain she'd left in her wake.

Instead, she hugged Daisy. "Do you know what?"

"What?" asked her sister.

"You say the smartest things."

"Me?" She looked astonished.

Mattie smiled. "*Ja.* You told *Mamm* what she had to hear. No wonder Boppi Lynn loves having you for her *mamm* so much."

Daisy's grin widened, crinkling her eyes. "And I love being her *mamm.*"

Behind Mattie, Benjamin cleared his throat. "Is this a private conversation about the ones you love, or can anyone join in?"

"Join in!" Daisy stretched out her hand, and he took it. With another face-lighting grin, she grabbed Mattie's hand and shifted it into Benjamin's. "What are you waiting for?"

He didn't release Mattie's hand. "For you to give us a minute of privacy."

"One minute," Daisy agreed. "That should be all you need, Benjamin." Giggling, she rolled to where she could listen while *Mamm* talked to the constable.

When Benjamin took her other hand, he turned Mattie to face him. "One minute? I don't think that will be enough."

She put her finger to his lips. "Let me say this." When he nodded, she lowered her finger. "I'm grateful to God for Him having you here to save her, Benjamin. And I know He would want me to forgive *Mamm*, because in spite of everything she's done and said, she's my *mamm* and I love her."

"Can you truly forgive her for everything she's put you through?"

"I'm going to try. It won't be easy, but I know the best things can't be done the easy way." She raised her gaze to meet his eyes that glowed with strong emotions. "And I want you to know that I've forgiven myself for believing the worst of you for the past five years."

"You know I never intended to break your heart."

"I know that *now*, but then all I could do was hate myself for being foolish enough to fall in love with a man who didn't notice me."

"I noticed, Mattie." He released her hand and let his fingers uncurl along her cheek. "Trust me, I noticed. Maybe not enough then, but definitely now. You've never been as invisible as you seem to think you are. In fact, if you ask me, you've always been pretty special, loved by those who love you."

She put her hand over his, pressing it to her face. "I'm learning I can't be someone else's special person unless I come to realize that I'm special, too, in God's eyes."

"And in mine." He bent so his forehead was against hers. "I'm sorry I walked away yesterday and left you with all the last-minute details at the shop. When Emmaline talked about adventures and how she craved them, I was amazed how absurd she sounded. And then I realized how stupid my yearning for adventure was when I could have all the adventure I wanted if I stayed here, bought that property, opened my shop and married the woman I've loved longer than I've known." He moved so their gazes could meet and meld them together. "*Ich liebe dich.* Will you marry me, Mattie?"

Her heart danced with joy as he said he loved her. She'd tell him the same...soon. But for now all she could say was, "*Ja.*"

With ease, his mouth found hers. His kiss was as gentle as a spring breeze, but deepened as her arms rose to curve along his back. At her touch, his lips entreated hers to soften beneath them. When he drew away, his palm grazed her face. A shiver of delight danced through her as his lips brushed her other cheek.

A giggle broke them apart. Mattie turned to see Daisy bending over her doll. "See?" Daisy asked. "What did I tell you? I didn't need anyone's help, Boppi Lynn. We found a match for Mattie on our own."

Laughing, Mattie hugged her sister, then watched Benjamin do the same.

"I thought," Mattie said, "I'd lost my family before I came here." She smiled at the man she loved with all her heart and her sweet sister. "But I've found a more precious one with you, Benjamin, and with you, Daisy."

"Don't forget Boppi Lynn!" Daisy held up the battered doll.

"Never!" Benjamin enveloped them in a hug that sealed their promise of love.

Epilogue

"Mattie?"

Turning from where she was taking an apple pie out of the oven in the kitchen that would be hers only a short time longer, Mattie saw Daisy rolling toward her in her wheelchair. Benjamin stood behind her sister, grinning.

Smiling was easy now. In fact, it was much harder *not* to smile since she and Benjamin had spoken their vows in front of all the families in their burgeoning community four months ago. Since then, the two of them—along with Daisy—had been immersed in getting their businesses off the ground. The Celtic Knoll Farm Shop was open six days a week and had become a favorite shopping place for plain folks and *Englisch*. Tourists, exploring every corner of the Island, had stopped in. There hadn't been any trouble from the three teenagers. She suspected Constable Boulanger had given them a stern warning to behave. No one had admitted to picking up Boppi Lynn, and Mattie knew it didn't matter because the doll had been returned to Daisy who doted on her as she always had.

Benjamin's clock shop in the barn on the Charlottetown road was due to open in another couple of months. In the meantime, he divided his time between building his beautiful clocks and fixing the tumbledown house across the road. Mattie couldn't wait until the day they moved out of the house behind her cousins' and into their own home. She intended to continue to work at the shop until there was enough money to hire a full-time manager. After that, she'd work side by side with her husband in his shop.

Husband. The word delighted her. She'd come to believe *Mamm* was right, and she'd remain an *alt maedel*. Now she was Benjamin's beloved wife, and Emmaline had hurried back to Manitoba after paying a small fine for trespassing.

Their wedding had been *wunderbaar* because she was marrying the man of her dreams. Not her childish dreams of a fairy-tale ending from five years ago, but a real love that wasn't one-sided. Now they shared a love created by two hearts.

Every member of her family and their spouses had attended the wedding, except for *Mamm* who had decided to cut herself off from her husband and *kinder* at least for now. She'd left Prince Edward Island after paying her fine of nearly five hundred dollars for trespassing with money she borrowed from *Daed*.

The wedding ceremony had been, Mattie hoped, the beginning of a reconciliation for her family. Sharrell had come with her husband, Barry, and their three *kinder*. Mattie had been pleased how happy her oldest sister was for her and Benjamin.

"I'm glad Benjamin's found the happiness he deserves," Sharrell had said before the ceremony began. "A happiness I never could have given him when I fell in love with Barry after I began walking out with Benjamin."

"You've never done anything the easy way," Mattie had replied, and they'd laughed, the differences between them healed and forgiven.

The only disappointment that day had been the absence of Benjamin's family. His sister had been too pregnant with her second *kind* to travel from northern New York, and his brother had replied to their invitation with a terse "I can't come. Benjamin understands why."

But Benjamin hadn't. So many times, when someone mentioned the wedding, Mattie had seen the sorrow in his eyes that his brother had chosen not to attend.

"Is it true?" Daisy asked, bringing Mattie into the present. "Benjamin says I'm going to be an Island *aenti*."

"An Island *aenti*?" Mattie put the dish towel she'd used to protect her hands from the hot pan onto the counter. "How is that different from being an *aenti* in Ontario?"

Daisy threw her arms around Mattie's waist. "Because we live on the Island, silly."

"*Ach*, I am silly. As silly as a goose."

"You're not a goose," the always literal teenager said. "You're a *mamm*." Her face crumpled. "You won't go away, will you, Mattie, now that you're a *mamm*?"

Mattie cupped Daisy's chin. "Never. I'll never leave you. I'm going to be stuck to you like a burr in a dog's tail. Our *boppli* is going to adore you, as I do."

"Have you picked a name?"

"How about, if it's a boy, we call him Benjamin, Junior?" teased Benjamin.

"Benjamin's a long name for a little *kind* to spell."

Daisy was as serious as a judge, then she brightened. "What if it's a girl?"

"I thought about Boppi Lynn," Mattie said, trying not to grin.

"My *boppli*'s name is Boppi Lynn. You need to have another name for your *boppli*."

"That's true. We could call her something like Shelley Lynn. What do you think?"

"Two Lynns?" Daisy considered it for a moment, then grinned. "That'll be *gut*. We can take care of our Lynns together."

"That's what I thought, and they'll become *gut* friends."

"Like you and me, Mattie. Friends and sisters."

Benjamin crossed the kitchen to put his arms around Mattie as Daisy rolled into the living room, chattering to her doll about how Boppi Lynn could help with the *boppli*.

"She's as excited," he murmured against Mattie's *kapp*, "as you and I are."

"I'm glad." She clasped her hands behind his nape and gazed into his loving eyes. "A new husband and a new *boppli*."

"And soon a new, well newly renovated, home of our own."

She leaned her head on his chest, savoring the sound of his heartbeat that bounced when her cheek rested against his shirt. She was about to suggest he should kiss her when the door opened, and a stranger walked in.

The man was shorter than Benjamin, and strands of gray had faded the color of his hair at his temples. His gold-rimmed glasses had thick lenses, but they couldn't lessen his intense gaze.

As she was about to ask his name, Benjamin exclaimed, "Menno! Why didn't you tell us that you were coming?"

She looked from one man to the other, biting her lower lip to keep the questions bubbling in her mind from popping out. The first one was why Menno had come now when he hadn't attended his brother's wedding.

"I wrote to you." Menno's gravelly voice sounded as if he hadn't spoken in months. She wondered if the rasp was caused by sawdust. "I told you I couldn't get away when you were married. I assumed you'd realize that I would come as soon as I could."

"No," Benjamin said. "I didn't assume that."

"You should have. You're my brother, and I want to make sure you're doing well." He looked past Benjamin and appraised Mattie. "I would say you are if you're his wife."

She didn't have a chance to answer before Daisy pushed into the kitchen. "And I'm his sister-in-law. Did you hear the *gut* news? I'm going to be an Island *aenti*."

Menno's brows rose toward his receding hairline. "Is this true? You're going to have a *boppli*?"

"It's supposed to be a secret," Mattie said. "Remember, Daisy?"

"But we don't keep secrets from family, ain't so?" Daisy steered her chair closer to Menno. "And you're family. My one-and-only brother-in-law named Menno."

Mattie saw her shock on Benjamin's face when his brother grinned. "And you're my one-and-only sister-in-law named Daisy."

As her sister and Benjamin's brother laughed together, Mattie gestured toward the dining room table. "Will you join us? We're going to have pie and *kaffi*?"

"Got any ice cream?" Menno asked.

Mattie startled everyone, including herself, when she hugged him. "If I wasn't sure before, I'd know now that you two are brothers. Both of you love ice cream. Go on in and sit and rest from your trip. I'll bring you pie and ice cream."

Menno went into other room with Daisy following him, asking question after question which he was answering with a patience that Mattie could see shocked Benjamin.

"People change," Mattie murmured as she took out plates for them. "Even your brother."

"So it would seem." Benjamin put his arms around her still slender waist and leaned his chin on her head. "You're right about that, but not about something else."

"What's that?" she asked, enjoying his teasing tone.

"I might like ice cream, but you, Mattie, are what I love." He brought her to face him and silenced her retort with a kiss.

She decided she couldn't have found a better way to answer. Not then or not during all the years to come.

* * * * *

THE AMISH ANIMAL DOCTOR

Patrice Lewis

To my husband and daughters, my greatest earthly joy.
To Jesus, for His redeeming grace.
To God, who has blessed me
more than I could possibly deserve.

For as we have many members in one body, and all members have not the same office: So we, being many, are one body in Christ, and every one members one of another. Having then gifts differing according to the grace that is given to us.

—*Romans* 12:4–6

Chapter One

Dimly, through the fog of sleep, Abigail Mast heard a pounding at the front door.

She opened her eyes into the dark room and smelled the cool summer night through her open screened window. A glimmer of pale light had barely seeped over the eastern horizon. It was dawn, but the nighttime frogs and crickets still chirped. She heard the deep hoot of great horned owls from the nearby forest that surrounded her mother's rental cottage, a few miles outside the tiny town of Pierce, Montana.

The pounding on the door came again. From the other bedroom, Abigail heard her mother's weakened call. "Abigail? *Liebling*, someone is at the door."

"*Ja, Mamm*. I'll see who it is." Abigail pushed back the blanket, swung her feet to the floor and snatched a bathrobe to cover her nightgown. She slid her feet into slippers and hurried into the dark living room, yawning. She'd finished nearly a week of hard driving, coming all the way from Indiana, and had only made it in around midnight. Now, this...

On the porch, barely visible in the fading night, appeared the figure of a disheveled man. He wore no hat, his shirt was untucked and his features were too shadowed to see. He breathed hard, as if he'd been running… or carrying a heavy load. "Are you Esther Mast's daughter Abigail?" he asked, panting.

"Ja," she replied.

"I understand you're a veterinarian—is that true?"

"Ja, but—"

"I have a dog with a broken leg." He gestured toward the yard. "Can you help her?"

Abigail peered through the gray dawn light and saw a huge bundle of white fur lying on the grass. But rather than approaching the animal, she drew her robe tighter around her, as if to shield herself from the man's plea. "There is a vet clinic in town."

"It's too far away and it would hurt the dog to transport her there by buggy. Besides…" A note of bitterness crept into his voice. "They're *Englisch*."

Well, of course they are, she thought, but didn't say it out loud. Instead she fought the waves of sickening insecurity that had plagued her professional judgment since she had nearly lost a prized dog because of her ineptness last month.

"Bitte?" the man asked again. "Please?"

From the yard, Abigail heard the dog whimper in pain, and in that moment she knew she had no choice. *Gott* had given her the gift of healing animals. She could not deny a creature in pain.

"I have very few vet supplies with me," she explained. "But I'll do what I can. Bring her onto the porch and let me get what I have."

He nodded and turned. Abigail retreated into the

house and dragged out her truck of veterinarian supplies, which she'd had the forethought to bring with her.

"Who is it?" called her mother.

"I don't know, but he has a dog with a broken leg," she called back. "Stay there, *Mamm*, I'll just be on the front porch."

"*Ja, gut.*"

The man had carried the dog to the porch and now squatted down, smoothing the animal's fur.

Abigail tried to forget she was attired in nightclothes. She was conscious that her hair was not properly tucked up under a *kapp*, but hung in a long loose braid to her waist. Instead, she focused with laser intensity, as she always did, to help an animal in need. She kneeled down and touched the injured foreleg. "How did she break it?"

"I don't know. I heard her cry from the field, where she guards my cows. I don't think she tussled with a coyote or a wolf—she'd have bite marks if she did."

"Is she a Great Pyrenees?"

"*Ja.* A livestock guardian."

Abigail noticed something, and ran a hand over the dog's belly. "And she's pregnant."

"*Ja.* The puppies are due in a month."

She bit her lip. "I don't have an X-ray machine," she warned him. "I'm just running on instinct. Will you trust me?"

"Of course. Do what you can."

Knowing the animal might bite her from sheer pain, Abigail rummaged among her supplies and drew out a muzzle, which she expertly wrapped around the dog's snout before the animal could object. But in the dim light, the dog's deep brown eyes—though tinged with pain—only looked at her with calmness.

"Ach," breathed the man. "You've a good touch with animals. I see she trusts you already."

"My gift from *Gott*," Abigail muttered. Without picking up the limb, she gently probed the animal's foreleg. "Ulna isn't broken, but the radius is snapped. Clean break. No skin penetration. Perhaps a cow stepped on her leg, or kicked her. Can't tell if there are bone fragments, but—" She pressed gently and the dog whimpered.

The man continued to bury his hands in the dog's thick white neck fur, soothing and restraining at the same time.

Abigail looked up at him. "I'm going to take a chance and cast her leg, but I strongly recommend you bring her to the vet clinic in town for X-rays to confirm there are no bone fragments. I can't tell for certain, but the break feels very clean. If I had all the tools at my disposal, I'd give her an external fixator for the fracture, where I put pins through the skin and into the bone. That would allow the fracture to heal while letting her use her leg in a normal way. But about all I can do right now, with what supplies I have here, is to cast the leg, then fit her with a cone around her neck so she can't chew at the cast."

"Ja, please. Anything."

Abigail nodded, wondering why he wouldn't simply take the animal to town, where the vets could provide the best of care. Besides, a shock big enough to fracture a leg bone might have caused damage to other organs as well…and this dog was pregnant.

She sighed. "All right, I'll do my best."

For the next half hour, as the sky lightened and dawn broke, Abigail treated the dog's leg. In the end, the cast was in place—it was damp but firm—and she was able to find a plastic cone to fit around the dog's neck.

She also took the opportunity to examine the man unobtrusively. His dark hair was curly and his beardless chin had a bit of stubble on it, probably from his all-night vigil. But the laugh lines at the corners of his dark blue eyes—shadowed from lack of sleep—showed he had good humor, and his gentle touch with his dog indicated a caring disposition. He also looked familiar somehow.

"There. That's the best I can do," she said at last. "Let's get her up." She stood up, stretching her cramped limbs.

The man also stood, grunting a bit as he unfolded himself from his position restraining the dog on the porch. The enormous Pyrenees rolled onto her belly and tried to sniff at the cast, but the plastic cone prevented her. She wagged her tail when Abigail bent to pet her. "What a beauty," she crooned.

"Her name is Lydia. She's my favorite dog. *Ach*, there's a *gut* girl…" he added, as the dog gingerly got to her feet. She balanced herself on three legs and lightly touched the paw of the injured leg onto the ground as if testing it.

Abigail stroked the animal's long fur. "I'll give you some pain pills for her. I haven't spent much time around Pyrenees. There aren't so many predators in Indiana, where I worked, so most farmers didn't have guardians for their herds. She's gorgeous."

"We have a lot of predators out here—cougars and coyotes and bears and wolves. I lost a calf my first year here, but since getting Pyrenees, my cows have been safe. Now everyone else in church wants some, too, for their herds." He held out his hand. "I'm Benjamin

Troyer, by the way. I remember you from when we both lived in Grand Creek."

Abigail shook his hand, peering at him more closely. "Benjamin! Of course. I remember you now. Goodness, it's been a long time. Last I heard you were…" She trailed off and had to restrain herself from smacking her forehead.

Last she heard, he'd been courting a pretty young woman named Barbara, but his beardless face stopped her from saying anything. If he'd married the woman, he would have grown a beard. She felt herself blush at nearly bringing up what could be an embarrassing topic.

"Wh-what brings you to Montana?" she stuttered instead, hoping he hadn't noticed her blunder.

"Land prices, what else?" he replied. "Farmland in Indiana was getting scarce and expensive, as you well know. That's why so many church members decided to up and move here to Pierce, to start a new church and some new farms."

"*Ja.* My mother, she wanted a bit of an adventure after *Daed* passed away five years ago."

"I think that was the motivation for quite a number of people. Your *mamm*, she rents this house from me."

"Oh! So you own all this?" She gestured across the porch, toward the fields and forests around them.

"*Ja.* I have sixty acres, and it came with a number of outbuildings, as you can see. This one was outfitted as a guest house, and Esther said it's all she needed."

"*Mamm* didn't expect her hip to give out as quickly as it did." Abigail stroked the dog's flank. "I'm just glad I had a chance to come out here and help her recuperate after her surgery."

"She's been talking of little else than your visit. The whole church knows you're here to take care of her."

Abigail wasn't sure she liked being the subject of church gossip, but she supposed it was natural. She was an oddity. Most Amish women didn't disappear from the community for ten years to obtain a veterinarian degree.

Whether she would remain in the community was still a question she couldn't answer. Her excuse to travel to Montana was to help her mother recover from surgery. But her unspoken reason was to make an extraordinarily difficult decision—whether to return to her childhood faith, or remain forever in the *Englisch* world.

"Well…" She retied her bathrobe more firmly around her middle. "I hope you don't expect me to act like a veterinarian while I'm here. I—I don't think I'm that skilled. That's another reason you should bring this dog to someone more competent than I am." A note of bitterness crept into her voice. "After all, that's why I'm back here taking care of my mother. I couldn't hack it in the *Englisch* world."

Benjamin was startled by the tone of self-recrimination in Abigail's voice. He'd just watched her set Lydia's leg with gentleness and precision, yet she thought she was inept? There was a story there. He wondered why he cared.

He remembered her as a child back in Indiana. Consumed as he was by the woman he was courting, he recalled Abigail as an idealistic kid, obsessed with animals and determined to help them no matter what. He hardly noticed when she'd left to go to college, because he was too busy courting Barbara. And then… Barbara was gone, sucked into the *Englisch* world, lured by its brightness and glitter.

And then his beloved older sister had also left the Amish to become a nurse. Benjamin had a big reason to distrust the *Englisch* world and all its temptations, especially with the women he loved.

Now here was that formerly gawky kid he remembered, all grown up. Abigail's thick honey-colored braid hung to her waist. She had large chocolate-brown eyes, which were unusual among the Amish, and they gave her face a graceful beauty. She was a small woman, only a couple inches over five feet, but her size didn't hamper her skill.

But he was done with women who were in any way connected to the outside. While grateful for Abigail's competence with his dog, her very presence reminded him of the losses in his life, both with Barbara and with his sister.

"—these dogs?" she asked.

Benjamin blinked himself back to the present. "I'm sorry, what did you say?"

"I said, so you're breeding these dogs?"

"*Ja.* There's a huge demand right now, especially since I'm not the only one who has lost an animal to predators." He buried his hand in his dog's magnificent mane. "Lydia here, she and her mate guard my cows. This is her second litter, and every last puppy is already spoken for, however many she has. I'm thinking on getting a second female, more as a household pet, but which I can also breed. There are many farmers in our church whose livestock need protection."

He heard a voice from inside. Abigail cocked her head. "Excuse me, *Mamm* is calling."

"*Ja*, see how she's doing. I'm sorry to take so much of your time."

Abigail nodded and ducked inside. He was just starting to help Lydia down the porch steps when she reappeared. "*Mamm* asked me if you wanted coffee."

"Oh." He drew himself up. "*Ja*, sure."

"*Mamm* also said the dog is welcome inside. There's a comfortable mat she can rest on."

"*Danke.*"

He followed Abigail indoors and saw Esther, dressed in a bathrobe, seated at the table in the cheerful cream-and-sage kitchen. "*Guder mariye*, Esther. How are you feeling today?"

"I've felt better. Mighty glad Abigail is here to help me. I'm just sorry I can't cook for you."

He saw Abigail's eyebrows raise in surprise. "You've been cooking for him, *Mamm*?"

"*Ja*. It's part of my rent."

"I'm not much of a cook," Benjamin explained.

"*Ach*, I didn't know that. I'd be happy to help in that department. Um, excuse me." She glanced down at her bathrobe. "I should get dressed." She turned and disappeared.

"You look *gut* for being a week out of the hospital." Benjamin sat down opposite Esther and patted her hand.

"*Danke*. Things hurt right now, but I know I'll get better. Especially since my *boppli* is home." Esther's eyes took on a misty look of maternal love.

Benjamin chuckled. "You missed her that much?"

"*Ja*, of course. I've seen her very little since she left, and not at all since I moved here to Montana."

"How long will she stay?"

"I don't know." Esther's faraway look vanished and

a troubled expression took its place. "She told me she could stay about two months. I'm hoping she'll stay longer."

Benjamin was sorry he'd brought up the subject. Evidently there was a complication about Abigail's visit he knew nothing about. He rose and moved toward the wood cookstove. "I can at least manage coffee. Have you had any yet?"

"Nein." The older woman managed a rusty chuckle. "It was all I could do to hobble from my bed to this chair. I'm still learning to use the walker." She gestured toward the wheeled implement.

Benjamin added a stick of wood to the stove and put the coffee percolator on the burner. He paused, not sure where the coffee cups were. Then the bedroom door whisked open and Abigail emerged, properly dressed in a dark green dress with a black apron, and was pinning her *kapp* over her tucked-up hair. In his eyes, there was no prettier clothing for a woman. Or maybe it was the woman wearing them.

"Where do you keep the coffee cups?" he asked.

"I've no idea. I didn't get in until late last night." Abigail looked at her mother. *"Mamm?* Where will I find things?"

"Cups are in that cupboard over there." Esther pointed. "And I keep coffee in that can on the counter."

Benjamin returned to the kitchen table as Abigail bustled around, pulling together the beverage. Within a few minutes the percolator was boiling, and she poured out cups, placing them on the table with a jar of fresh milk and a bowl of sugar.

"Ah, *danke*." Benjamin took a sip. "It's been a long night."

"*Ja*, for all of us." He watched as she took a reverent sip of the beverage. "I woke *Mamm* up when I got in around…what, *Mamm*, midnight or so?"

"Something like that." Esther's eyes crinkled. "I know I was sound asleep."

"How did you get here?" Benjamin asked. "The nearest airport is in Missoula."

"I drove." She gestured behind the house. "My pickup truck is parked out back."

His eyes widened. "You can drive?"

"*Ja*. I've lived in the *Englisch* world long enough. I had no choice."

To Benjamin, it was another indicator that Abigail was not Amish, no matter how much she looked the part. She might have grown up into a beautiful woman, but he wasn't about to become interested in someone with both feet planted firmly elsewhere. To cover his dismay at that realization, he added, "It must have been a long drive from Indiana."

"It was. It took me five long days. But I had a large trunk of vet supplies I wanted to bring, as well as a fair amount of my household luggage, so it was more efficient than anything else. By the way, I owe you an apology. If I'd been thinking straight earlier, I would have offered to drive you and the dog into town to see the vet."

"I think you did a fine job." He looked over at Lydia, asleep on the mat, her cone flattened on the floor under her neck. "I think she's exhausted from the pain and stress, but you did a fine job with her."

"Oh, I almost forgot. Let me get you some pain medication for her." She stood up and went to the open trunk, which he could see held a variety of veterinary items.

She rummaged around until she found a large bottle, which she brought back to the table. "I think two pills a day for a week should be enough." She poured some pills out on the table and counted them out. "*Mamm*, do you have something I can put these in?"

"I have some jars in the cupboard over there."

She fetched a small jar with a lid and transferred the pills to it, then pushed the jar toward him. "There you go."

"*Danke.*" He picked up the jars and looked at the small pink pills. "That's quite a collection of supplies you have. Do you plan to open a clinic or something while you're here?"

He saw her face shutter. "No. I'm just here to help *Mamm* recuperate from surgery."

He didn't ask why she thought it was necessary to schlep a huge trunk of veterinarian supplies across the country if she was only here to help her mother for a couple of months. There were some undercurrents here he didn't understand, and frankly didn't want to.

"Well." He stood up. "In that case, I'd best get home. I have cows to milk and chickens to feed."

"Abigail can bring you some lunch later on," offered Esther.

He saw Abigail glance at him. "*Ja*, sure. I'll bring you some lunch, if that's the agreement between you and *Mamm*."

"*Danke.* And I can't tell you how grateful I am for setting Lydia's leg. Can she walk home, do you suppose, or shall I carry her?"

"How far away is your house?" Abigail asked.

"Just about a hundred yards, that way." He pointed.

"Do you want me to drive you back with the dog?"

That was the last thing he wanted. "No, I'll manage. If she can't walk, I'll carry her."

"She's a big dog to be carried!"

"I carried her here."

"Well, see if she can walk. Go slowly. If not, then try carrying her."

Benjamin coaxed his dog out of her sleep. The animal took a few shaky steps, but gained confidence as she moved across the room.

"I'll go slowly," he told Abigail. "*Vielen Dank* for everything."

He matched his pace with the hobbling dog, making sure not to go faster than she could manage. He found he was anxious to get out of the house, away from Abigail. She was entirely too attractive, and he had no intention of cultivating a personal interest in her.

After Barbara had left him high and dry and disappeared into the *Englisch* world, and after his sister had done the same thing, he had schooled himself to be alone. He had never courted another woman. He liked his solitude. He liked breeding his dogs. He liked his profession as a furniture craftsman. He liked his new home here in Montana. In short, he had built himself a solid, respectable life…alone. He had his faith and his church community, and that was enough.

He didn't want to contemplate the alternative—what it might be like to *not* live alone.

Chapter Two

After Benjamin left, Esther said, "It's such a beautiful morning, let's go sit on the porch. We have a lot of catching up to do."

Abigail didn't have to be urged. She had arrived after dark and barely had a chance to glimpse anything of the stunning scenery around them. So she settled her mother as comfortably as possible into a rocking chair on the porch, then stood and looked out at the view.

Tall muscular mountains, capped with snow, rose above a rim of conifers to the west. Green meadows punctuated by groves of pine and fir trees surrounded them, spangled with flowers. A flock of garish black-and-white magpies, their exaggerated tails trailing behind, passed nearby. Scattered Jersey cows grazed in the pasture. She saw a huge white dog, doubtless Lydia's mate, lying near a fence among the cows. The air was fresh and sweet.

Benjamin's house was, as he'd said, not more than a hundred yards away. It was a picturesque one-story log cabin with a broad front porch and smaller back porch.

"I wondered why you wanted to come to Montana,"

she ventured, "but I think I understand now. It's beautiful."

"*Ja*, I haven't had any regrets. It's wilder than Indiana, and somehow—lurking around corners—there's a tiny element of danger. Not from people, but from animals." Esther set her rocking chair in motion. "I like it here. I've seen moose and elk and bears and coyotes. Eva Hostetler—do you remember her? She was Eva Miller. She lives down the road now. She's sure she saw a couple of wolves last fall. I never thought I'd become an animal watcher like you, but it seems I have." Esther chuckled.

"I remember Eva. She's only two years older than me. I liked her." Abigail pulled another rocker over next to her mother and sat down with a sigh. "*Ach*, what a busy morning."

"And not much sleep for you last night—getting in around midnight and then being woken before dawn to fix the dog's leg."

"I'm just glad it was a clean break and an easy fix, though I wonder why Benjamin refused to go to the clinic in town."

"He can be an odd duck, Benjamin."

"In what way?"

"He just seems to be a loner. Doesn't get out much, though I know he sells some dairy items to the Yoders' store in town. Otherwise he stays close to home."

"Is he baptized?"

"*Ja*, sure. He's been baptized for years."

"Why isn't he married?"

"I don't know. I gather something happened in his past, but he's never told me what it might be. He can be moody sometimes. I don't ask why, since it's none of my business. He's an easy man to cook for and he hardly charges me anything for rent, so it's a situation that's worked out well for us. I'm grateful to him."

"How did you come to rent this little house to begin with? It's cute." Abigail gestured upward, taking in the clapboard construction and modest porch, all painted a soft pale yellow.

"I was rooming with the bishop and his wife," explained Esther, "but when you're older like me, you need your own kitchen. Plus I had already made arrangements to make baked goods for the Yoders' store, and for that I needed room to work. Benjamin offered me this cottage and I accepted."

"It was the bishop's wife who took care of you just after you got out of the hospital, *ja*?"

"*Ja*. Lois, she's a *gut* woman. I was in sorry shape the first day or two, and she stayed with me day and night until yesterday, when she knew you were arriving."

"I'll have to do something to thank her." Abigail patted her mother's hand. "To be honest, I'm surprised you're up and about as much as you are. I thought a hip replacement would take longer to recover from."

"Actually, except for the pain of the surgery itself, I can already tell I'll be better soon. Stronger. The surgery was a *gut* thing." Esther paused. "As for this morning, you did a fine job with Benjamin's dog, *liebling*."

"She's a beautiful animal. If I had plans to stick around, I might be interested in having one of those puppies for myself. If any were available, that is."

"So you *don't* have plans to stick around?" inquired Esther.

Abigail winced. "I don't know yet, *Mamm*. I'm happy to be here for a couple months, but after that..."

"You have time to think about it. This little cottage is plenty big enough for us both for the time being. And the kitchen is big enough so once I'm back on my feet, I can continue baking for the Yoders."

"That's Abe and Mabel Yoder, *ja*? I remember they ran a little store in Indiana."

"*Ja*, the same couple. Two of their daughters came out here with them when the church moved, and they help run the store. Quite a number of us in the church contribute things to sell. The store is doing very well."

"Do you like making baked goods for the store?"

"It was a little hard being on my feet all day," Esther admitted. "But it gives me a nice bit of income and makes me feel useful. I can make things at home and bring them to the bakery. It's a nice chance to meet some of the *Englischer* in town, too. As a new church, we need to make sure we contribute to the community and are helpful."

"Are you going to make things for the bakery again?"

"*Ja*, as soon as I can." Esther waved a hand. "But that's in the future. You're here now. Tell me what happened, *liebling.* Why did you leave your job?"

Abigail knew this conversation was unavoidable. She shrugged with a nonchalance she did not feel. "You know pretty much all of it. I nearly lost a valuable dog because of my incompetence. Robert—the senior vet in the clinic where I worked—was able to save him, and then he chewed me out royally for messing up." What she didn't admit to her mother was how much she'd fancied herself in love with Robert. That little fantasy had come crashing down in a hurry. Instead, she added, "I was glad to take a leave of absence with the excuse of taking care of you."

"And that one experience with the dog was enough to make you doubt your gift? You've always had a way with animals, *lieb*. What is one mistake after years of success?"

Abigail didn't want to confess how much her love-lorn thoughts for Robert were entwined with her professional humiliation, so she just said, "I guess coming from my boss made it all the worse."

"Well, whatever the issue, I'm glad you're home for a bit. It's nice to have my *boppli* back."

Abigail smiled at the mother she'd missed so much. "It's nice to be back with you, *Mamm*. There hasn't been anyone to fuss over me since I left home ten years ago."

Esther chuckled. "But you're the one taking care of me, not the other way around."

"Just long enough for you to get better. I know you, *Mamm*. Tell me the truth—you're just chafing to run a marathon, *ja*?"

Her *mamm* blushed slightly. "Maybe not a marathon, but I like cooking and baking. Are you up for doing that for both Benjamin and myself while you're here?"

"*Ja*, sure. That's what I'm here for, to make myself useful." She felt momentarily uneasy, like the feeling of inadequacy that had overcome her when Robert had yelled at her after her failure with the dog. "Should I have made him breakfast?"

Esther waved a hand. "You just set his dog's broken leg. I think that was enough. But normally what I do is bring lunch to his house. Sometimes he comes here for dinner, but not always. As I said, he often seems to prefer being alone."

"I don't have your skills in the kitchen, *Mamm*, especially since I've spent ten years not practicing enough. You'll have to guide me."

"That's fine. You've spent ten years acquiring different skills. Do you feel like you've developed your gift from *Gott*?"

Abigail silently blessed her mother. Esther was one of the few people who truly understood why she'd left the Amish, left the security of the church community. Abigail's love for animals wasn't just a girlish whimsy; it was her gift from *Gott* that she sought to develop by training as a veterinarian.

So she answered the question with the seriousness it deserved. "*Ja*. A part of me knows you're right, *Mamm*. That mistake with the dog was just one mistake, and thanks to Robert's skill, the animal fully recovered. I don't know why that one issue made me lack confidence in my own abilities, though."

"Well, now that you're here, perhaps you should look for a *hutband*."

Abigail felt herself blush. After her debacle with Robert, a husband was the last thing on her mind. She'd always known the senior veterinarian had a volatile temper, but he'd never directed it at her before. It was far more devastating than she was willing to admit, and it made her realize she wouldn't want a husband like that.

"I don't know, *Mamm*…"

"Do you want a *hutband* at all?" persisted Esther.

Abigail smiled at her mother's transparent interest in matchmaking. "I spent so many years wrapped up in animal medicine that I've hardly had a chance to think about it."

"Well, you're here now, *liebling*. Maybe you'll have time to put your mind to it."

"Maybe. But remember, *Mamm*, I'm not baptized. No Amish man will consider me seriously for that reason." She sighed. "It's like I'm straddling two worlds. It feels *gut* to dress this way again—" she smoothed her apron "—but it makes me feel like a fraud."

"*Gott* will direct your way," her mother said with a smile. "He's had His hand on you all these years you were in the *Englisch* world becoming a vet. Why would He abandon you now?"

"*Ja*, you're right. That's another thing I'm looking forward to while here—attending Sabbath services and being back among people of faith."

"Was it truly so bad, being away from the church?"

"*Nein*, not bad. Just…different. I got used to it because I had to, but it took a lot of adjustment…"

Esther tried to reposition herself in the porch chair, and Abigail saw her mother wince in pain. Instantly her own troubles were forgotten. "*Mamm*, I'm sorry. I'm so busy yammering about my own issues. Have you taken your pain medication this morning? Can I help you back into bed?"

Her mother's smile was a bit strained. "*Nein*, I haven't taken my pain pills yet. They're on the kitchen counter. As for going back to bed, I've spent enough time in there already. Instead help me back into the house and I'll guide you on making lunch. I have an idea of what Benjamin likes now."

Abigail helped her mother rise carefully, and she let the older woman lean on her heavily while she shuffled into the house. Remembering how active and vigorous her mother used to be made Abigail swallow hard. She supposed it was natural to dread the thought of parents getting older, but having lost her father already, she didn't want to think about losing her mother, too.

It made her wonder if returning to the *Englisch* world was worth the separation from her only remaining parent. Her father had passed away while she was gone. Her brothers and sisters were all married and living back in Indiana. She didn't want to think about not being here for her mother.

But once Esther had swallowed the pain medication and settled into a kitchen chair, she seemed to improve. "Are you used to cooking in a microwave now?" she teased.

Abigail chuckled. "I confess I never got used to that," she replied. "And it's nice to see a proper cookstove again. Okay, tell me what Benjamin likes to eat for lunch."

Benjamin ran a planer over a piece of oak. He squinted down the length of the wood and straightened up, satisfied.

Next to him on the shop floor, Lydia rested on a blanket. The dog was lying with her head down, the plastic cone flattened around her, with her leg cast a bit awkwardly to the side. But her eyes were alert, and that awful strain of pain was gone.

The dog suddenly jerked up her head and whined. Her tail swished and she tried to rise to her feet. Alarmed that she might hurt herself, Benjamin dropped his tools and started for the dog until he saw what had gotten the animal's attention. Abigail walked into the shop building, a covered basket in her hands.

His heart thumped unreasonably. "Oh, hello! I wasn't expecting you."

"I'm bringing you lunch in *Mamm*'s place." She placed the basket on a workbench, then kneeled down next to Lydia and stroked the dog. She chuckled. "I don't think I've ever seen such a beautiful dog."

Benjamin looked down at the woman crouching next to his pet. Her white *kapp* was tidy on her hair, and her black apron and green dress puddled around her knees as she fussed over the animal. "She certainly seems to like you. It's as if she understood you're the one who helped her."

"How has she been behaving? Any whimpering or acting agitated?" Gently, she probed the dog's injured leg around the cast.

"*Nein*. On the contrary, she's been calm and alert."

"I think it's safe to say she has no bone chips, then. A good, clean break." She ran her hand over the dog's belly, carefully feeling. "But you'll need to watch her when her due date gets near. I'd hate for her to have any complications when she whelps." She rose to her feet. "For the time being, I don't think it will be necessary for me to drive her to the vet clinic in town."

Mention of her vehicle was like a splash of cold water over Benjamin's face. It was a blatant reminder of the gulf between them—that Abigail was not Amish, despite her appearance. A little bit of his heart shriveled up inside him.

He strove to keep his voice level and dispassionate. "Have you considered opening a veterinary clinic for church members?"

Abigail looked startled. "*Nein*, of course not! What gave you that idea?"

He shrugged. "You might find a fair number of people might prefer to bring their animals to you than to the *Englisch* clinic in town."

"Why? What's wrong with the clinic in town?"

"N-nothing. It's just that…" He trailed off.

He saw Abigail's lips tighten. "It's because they're *Englisch*, is that it?"

"Maybe."

"Benjamin, this branch of our church is new in the area. We are the ambassadors of our faith. Yet you make it sound as if we plan to shun the local businesses, the very people who welcomed us to the area."

"*Ja*, I know." He turned away and fiddled with the planer. Not for anything would he admit his reasons for not wanting to associate with the local townspeople. Yet he was also aware of his hypocrisy, since a portion of his business was dependent on them.

He sighed. "You're right. I'm feeling unaccountably hostile toward the townspeople, for no *gut* reason. Everyone I've met so far has been kind and welcoming. Since I provide products to the Yoders' store, I can hardly complain. And the bishop is working to make sure I conquer any hostility I may have."

He saw her startle. "The bishop? What can he do to make you less hostile toward the *Englisch*?"

"He assigned me a task." He fingered a rough piece of wood on the worktable. "The town of Pierce has a yearly festival they call Mountain Days. It's a fairly big deal and attracts people from all over the region. This year the organizers came to the bishop and asked if we could put together a demonstration area featuring Amish skills and crafts. The bishop is anxious to make sure we establish the church community on *gut* terms with the town, so he agreed." He tightened his lips. "And guess who he put in charge of organizing it?"

"You?"

"*Ja*, me. He said it was because I don't have a wife and *kinner*, so I have fewer commitments than a family man might. But I agreed because I thought it might help my furniture-making business. I have some orders from church members, but not enough to keep me solvent. So I guess you could say I have an ulterior motive in taking on the task." He hoped that didn't sound too mercenary. In fact, he was barely making ends meet, and perhaps was pinning too much hope on the demo. "I plan to have a booth where I demonstrate how to construct a rocking chair. It's straightforward and I'm sure people will be interested, hopefully enough to order some furniture."

"I'm sure they will. The *Englisch* can be very generous, and they like handmade things. Your business should flourish."

Benjamin didn't like how allied she seemed to be with the outside world. "Do you say that because you feel you're one of them? One of the *Englisch*?"

"Sometimes." She looked defensive. "I can hardly help it. I spent my adult years among them. How else did you expect me to feel?" She plucked at her dress. "Outside appearances and inside feelings are two different things."

For a brief moment, he felt sorry for her. She was obviously not comfortable in her own skin. "You're torn," he murmured.

"Of course I'm torn. You would be, too, in my position."

"*Ja*, maybe, except I wouldn't have *put* myself in your

position in the first place." The moment the words were out of his mouth, he felt ashamed. He slapped a hand to his forehead. "*Ach*, that was rude. I'm sorry."

His apology seemed to deflate her defensiveness. Her smile was tinged with sadness. "Let's just say I'm taking this opportunity to help *Mamm* after her surgery to do a lot of thinking. I'm looking forward to attending Sabbath services. It wasn't always easy to attend church when I was in school or working."

"That's a start," he commented.

"A start?" she responded. "Of what?"

"The start of transforming you back into an Amish woman."

She shrank back a bit. "I *am* an Amish woman. No, I *was* an Amish woman…" She trailed off, then asked in a small voice, "Do I act *Englisch*? Am I so very different than I was?"

"I can't really say," he replied. "I hardly remembered you when we were *youngies*. I was too involved with—" He stopped. With great difficulty, he prevented himself from swiping a hand over his eyes. Of all people, why did he have to bring up Barbara? "Never mind," he muttered.

She didn't push or probe. Instead, she merely said, "Sounds like we both have regrets about our past."

"*Ja*, who doesn't?" To cover his blunder, he continued, "That's another question, I suppose. Which do you prefer, the *Englisch* or the Amish world?"

If he expected more defensiveness, he didn't get it. Instead she stared through the open workshop doors across the pasture, where cows were grazing. A large bird silently flew overhead. She tracked its trajectory with her eyes.

"Bald eagle." She pointed, then sighed. "I don't know which I prefer yet. I spent eight years training to be a vet. I spent two years working in a clinic. I'm just home for a little while to help *Mamm*. I didn't realize…"

"Realize what?" he prompted, when she remained silent.

"Realize how much I missed my people." She glanced at him, then focused back on the pasture. "There's a lot to be said for the *Englisch* world. There are many things to do, many opportunities for everyone. But here, there's peace. There's faith. There's purpose. There's…well, there's *Gott*."

He was startled. "*Gott* is everywhere."

"*Ja*, of course. But it's not always easy to seek Him out. It's too easy to get distracted with other things… which is precisely why, of course, we Amish discourage higher education. And that, in a nutshell, is what I'm facing—the tug between my calling and my faith."

Calling. That's what she termed her veterinary training. He wanted to ask just what she meant by that, but it seemed too personal a subject.

Besides, for him there *was* no conflict. Faith always came first, job second. How could it be otherwise for her?

"I must get back to keep an eye on *Mamm*." She turned to go, then spoke over her shoulder. "Are you coming for dinner? *Mamm* says you do, sometimes."

"If it's convenient, *ja*, I'd like to. What time?"

"How about sixish?"

"Sixish, then."

Without another word, she walked out the barn door.

He watched her slender figure as she headed back toward her mother's cottage. He could see her observing everything as she went—birds overhead, the cows in the field, his other dog, who was guarding the cows in his mate's absence. Animals always seemed to dominate her thoughts. He'd never met anyone with such an affinity for nonhuman creatures.

Abigail was dangerous. She was smart, compassionate, skilled…and pretty. She also had one foot firmly in the *Englisch* world. That alone was reason enough to leave her alone.

He'd lost two loved ones to the *Englisch* world. He stayed in fond touch with his sister Miriam—she was now a nurse—but Barbara was irrevocably lost to him. She had long ago married some *Englischer* and, as far as he knew, never regretted her decision to leave the church. How could he have been so blind as a younger man to fall for a woman intent on leaving?

And now here was Abigail, a woman he'd known since childhood but had never paid much attention to.

He drew his lips tight. Ten years since Barbara left— that's how long he'd been alone. Ten years of wondering if it was something he'd said or done to make her think the *Englisch* world was more attractive than the Amish community. Ten years of watching his cohorts pair off and marry and have children.

It was no accident that he'd volunteered to move with the church to Montana. Anything to leave behind his sour memories, and perhaps meet a woman who wouldn't mind a man still unmarried at age thirty.

But he'd met no such woman. Until now.

Chapter Three

Abigail took a bubbling dish of macaroni and cheese from the oven. As she placed it on a hot pad in the center of the table, she heard a knock at the door.

"That will be Benjamin." Esther tried to hoist herself out of a kitchen chair, but sank back down with a grunt of pain.

"Stay there, *Mamm*," ordered Abigail. "I'll let him in."

She padded in bare feet toward the front door of the cottage and whisked it open. He had a dusting of sawdust on his shirt. "*Gut'n owed*, Benjamin."

"*Gut'n owed.*" He removed his straw hat and sniffed the air. "Whatever's cooking smells *gut*."

"Macaroni and cheese. *Komm—Mamm* is in the kitchen." She turned and led the way through the house.

Benjamin entered the kitchen and hooked his hat over a chair back. "*Gut'n owed*, Esther. Any improvement today?"

"*Ja*, as long as I don't try to get up to let you in." The older woman smiled.

Abigail detected the faintest flirtatious note in her mother's voice, and it made her smile. Losing her husband had been hard on her mother, she knew. Whatever her reasons for moving to Montana, proximity to Benjamin seemed to have had a beneficial influence on the older woman.

"I brought your mail." Benjamin proffered several envelopes and a newspaper.

"Ach, danke." Esther took the envelopes and scanned them. "Ah, how nice. A letter from my sister in Indiana. I'll read it after dinner."

"There's no mail service here?" inquired Abigail.

"Nein, not to this cabin. It all comes to my house," explained Benjamin. "Your *mamm*'s cabin is on my property, that's why."

After the silent blessing, Abigail dished out the food. Trying to make polite conversation, she asked Benjamin, "The furniture you make—do you sell it at the Yoders' store in town?"

"Nein." He paused to chew and swallow a bite. "Most of the furniture I make is for church members. I've been too busy with that to expand elsewhere. What I sell at the Yoders' is dairy products—cheese, yogurt, butter. You might say dairy products are my evening job. I'll be delivering some tomorrow, in fact."

"You mean you make furniture *and* dairy products *and* breed Great Pyrenees?" She stared. "You're a busy man, Benjamin."

He shrugged. "Right now my furniture business is slow, so dairy products fill my time since—since I have no family."

She felt a shaft of curiosity about why he was still unmarried, but it wasn't her place to ask.

Before the pause could get awkward, Esther piped up. "How is the planning going for the Mountain Days event?"

"Slowly." Benjamin poked at his plate with, Abigail thought, a trace of defensiveness. "I sometimes wonder if I'm the right man for the job."

"Maybe you should recruit my *boppli* here to help you." Esther jerked her head toward Abigail.

"Mamm," warned Abigail. "I'm here to help *you*, remember?"

"Well, I don't need you to dance attendance on me every hour of the day," Esther replied with some asperity. "Helping with the Mountain Days event might be *gut* for you, *liebling*."

Abigail was loath to commit herself. Instead, she changed the subject. "You said you were getting low on coffee, *Mamm*. I can go into town tomorrow and get some, if you like."

"Ja, danke. And I wouldn't mind some lemons, too, if they have some. Lemonade is a perfect summer drink."

"Since I'm bringing some things to the Yoders' store tomorrow, I can give you a lift," said Benjamin.

Abigail knew she couldn't suggest the use of her pickup instead of Benjamin's buggy. Driving a motorized vehicle would widen the chasm between herself and her church community. She needed to blend in as much as possible.

"Danke, that would be nice," she said instead. "What time?"

"Morning, probably. The Yoders' store opens at eight a.m., so if you want to come by around that time, we can drive in."

"Ja, gut."

The next morning dawned fresh and clear. Abigail finished her short shopping list, gathered some money and kissed Esther on the cheek. "I doubt I'll be long," she said. "Don't run a marathon, *ja*?"

Her mother smiled at what was becoming a standing joke. "I promise."

Abigail made sure her *kapp* was firmly pinned in place, then set off on the short walk toward Benjamin's. A cheerful chorus of birdsong filled the cool air. She watched as a pair of evening grosbeaks swooped across her path before landing on a nearby conifer. The huge male Great Pyrenees guarding the cattle loped along the inside of the fence as she walked near.

"You're a beauty, do you know that?" she crooned as she reached through the fence wire and scratched the massive animal under the chin. "Your mate will be ready to join you again in a few weeks."

The dog pressed his ruff to the fence as she buried her hands in his coat. What an absolutely beautiful breed of dog, she thought. After a minute or two of bonding, she gave him a final pat and made her way toward Benjamin's cabin.

To her surprise, he was waiting for her on the front porch. "Elijah seems to like you," he observed.

Abigail blushed a bit at the thought of her quiet moment with the majestic dog being observed. "Is that the dog's name, Elijah? He's gorgeous. I don't know why this breed was never on my radar, but I really like them. How's Lydia?"

"Big and ungainly from carrying the puppies, but she's walking better. She hates that cone around her neck, though."

"I know, but we can't risk her gnawing off her cast before the bone is properly set. I'll remove the cone when she's whelping her puppies. Looks like you're ready to go," she added, glimpsing his horse already hitched to the buggy.

"*Ja*, I was just loading some items. Here, would you like to carry this basket of cheeses? I've got some jars of milk in the cooler."

Abigail helped him load the rest of his dairy products into the wagon, then climbed aboard the seat as he unhitched the horse. With a small jolt, he guided the animal onto the road.

"How far away is the town?" she asked.

"About three miles. Don't you remember? You drove through it a couple nights ago when you arrived."

"It was close to midnight and I was exhausted. It was just a dim blur to me."

"It won't take long to get there." He was silent a moment, then added, "I hope Esther didn't put you on the spot when she recommended you help with the Mountain Days event."

Abigail shrugged. "She did, a little. I think that's just the nature of mothers, ain't so? But if you need help, I suppose I can do something."

"I don't quite know what you could do."

She grew curious. "What exactly does your project entail? I mean, how are you going about convincing church members to make an appearance at this festival?"

"It's not quite as hard as you think," he replied. "First of all, the bishop is encouraging everyone to participate so we're viewed as cooperative members of the town. It's not like I'm getting a hostile reaction from any of the church members…"

"But you just don't want to do this, is that it?"

"It's outside my comfort zone." His expression suggested the admission was difficult. "But since I'm hoping it will give a boost to my business, I guess I don't mind."

"Well, I'm happy to help however I can, but since I've never done anything like this before, I don't know what to suggest."

"And it's not like you really know anyone anymore."

"*Ja*, there's that." She stared at the surrounding scenery. Benjamin's obvious observation depressed her for some reason. He was right. She hardly knew anyone anymore. "I've been away so long," she murmured.

"Does it bother you to be back?"

"*Nein*, it doesn't bother me. It's just…different. Being back in an Amish community is a big contrast. Everyone is more relaxed, less stressed here. I just have to get used to it."

"Since most of the people who moved here are ones you knew growing up, it won't take you long to slip back into the community."

"If I'm here long enough."

She saw him stiffen. "*Ja*, if you're here long enough. Look, there's the edge of town."

Abigail saw a simple grid of buildings. The road transitioned to pavement instead of gravel, and the horse's hooves clip-clopped on the asphalt with a bright sound. They came in from a side street through a series of quiet suburban homes. As they approached Main Street, she saw that it was lined with sturdy-looking older buildings—storefronts and offices—with more homes spreading out from the core. The town had a comfortable, settled air about it.

"How many people are in Pierce?" she asked.

"About twenty-five hundred." Benjamin waved at

another buggy going the other direction. "Because the town is so isolated, it has a lot of the amenities people need—hardware store, grocery, a small hospital, things like that. There are now two buildings in town owned by church members. The Yoders opened their mercantile in a vacant storefront on Main Street and the city council was very glad to have them there. Apparently it's been vacant for quite some time." He pointed. "See? They even installed hitches for buggies."

Abigail saw a wide storefront with Yoder's Mercantile pained in a large sign across the awning. A Western-style rail had been installed for hitching horses. "What's the other building?"

"Eli and Anna Miller bought an old run-down building. I think it used to be a tiny hotel or something." He pointed. "They've spent the last year renovating it into a combination bed-and-breakfast, boardinghouse and meeting area. They're still working on it, but they've taken in a few early guests. They've also hosted two weddings for church members so far, since no one has a home big enough to handle it. That's another difference between settling here in Montana and our old place in Indiana—we have to adapt."

Abigail gazed at the Western-themed two-story building with a sign proclaiming Miller's Lodging.

"It looks *gut*. Do they live there?"

"No, because Eli won't give up his cows and they don't allow cows within city limits. So one of their sons lives there—do you remember Matthew Miller? He's doing the day-to-day work and getting used to the hospitality industry."

"It seems like the *Englisch* are very glad the church moved here," she observed.

"*Ja*, it seems that way. I gather the town was slowly dying, with many young people moving away to look for work. Having extra people means more revenue for the town."

"What's the main source of income for the area? It seems too forested for farming."

"Logging. That's the main source of revenue. That and cattle ranching, I believe."

He guided the horse toward the hitch in front of Yoder's Mercantile. Abigail climbed down from the buggy and reached in back for the basket of cheese while Benjamin hoisted the cooler filled with clanking jars of milk.

The storefront had a wide, covered wooden porch with stairs on one side and a ramp on the other. Outdoor buckets held colorful displays of cut flowers for sale. The windows were filled with attractive displays of merchandise—crafts, fabrics, antiques, quilts. "Looks like they sell a little of everything," she observed, glancing over the display. "Just like in Indiana."

"*Ja*. The *Englisch* love it." He turned and pushed the door open with his back, then held it while she slipped through.

In a moment she saw the store was arranged similarly to the Yoders' old store in Indiana, with a general mix of dry goods with a few select groceries, local produce and a dairy case. There was one new addition—a coffee area. Several older *Englisch* men in overalls and ball caps were sitting there with mugs and muffins, laughing and talking. A younger man sat before a laptop computer, earnestly typing, a mug of tea at his elbow. The smells of fresh bread and coffee filled the air.

"Nice," she observed, taking in the wooden flooring and gleaming glass display cases in a glance.

"*Ja*, the Yoders have always had a touch for retail. This place has become the logical spot to sell all the local Amish-made goods, but the Yoders also reached out to *Englisch* crafters and townspeople. The flowers out front, for example—they're grown by an *Englisch* family that lives outside of town. The store has to have electricity, of course, to legally sell dairy products and such. *Guder mariye*, Mabel," he added, lowering his ice chest to the floor.

Abigail turned and saw an older woman, plump and cheerful, in a black apron and pink dress.

"*Guder mariye*, Benjamin. And… Abigail? Abigail Mast? I heard you were visiting! *Welkom!*" Her face creased into a huge smile.

Abigail put her basket on the floor and embraced the woman. "*Danke!* It's *gut* to see you again!"

Mabel's warm greeting echoed through the store, and within moments several other Amish people crowded over to greet her. Abigail felt a warm flush at their enthusiasm as she renewed the acquaintances of several people from her youth. When the interest finally died down, she noticed a woman a few years older than her lingering in the background. Abigail did a double take. "Eva? Eva Miller?"

"*Ja!*" The woman catapulted forward and gave Abigail a hug. "But it's Eva Hostetler now. *Ach*, it's so good to see you!"

Benjamin lingered near Mabel, whose husband, Abe, bustled over to unload the jars of fresh milk. But as he helped unpack the cheese and butter, he watched as Abigail chattered with her long-lost friend. Eva Hostetler, he remembered, had grown up just a short distance away from Abigail when they were children in Indiana.

"It seems like she's fitting back in without a problem," Mabel murmured in his ear.

"*Ja*. But she says she doesn't know if she will stay yet." The words held more pathos than he would have liked.

Mabel gave him a sharp look before bending her head to write some information on her inventory sheet. Benjamin wanted to kick himself. The last thing he needed was some of the older women in the church playing matchmaker, especially with an unavailable woman. He would have to watch himself.

It took fifteen minutes for Mabel and Abe Yoder to log in the dairy products he'd brought, and Abigail spent the whole time talking with Eva Hostetler. He was certain Abigail could use a friend, so it pleased him to see her making a connection.

When his business was finished, he walked up to the two women. "*Guder mariye*, Eva. Abigail, I'm finished. Are you ready to go?"

"Oh, I forgot about my shopping. *Mamm* needs a few items. Eva, let's get together later on, *ja*?"

"*Ja, gut*. I'd like that." With a warm smile, the other woman walked away.

"I won't be long," Abigail told him. She pulled a small piece of paper from her pocket. "Coffee, lemons, ginger and salt. That's all I need." She snatched a plastic basket from a stand and moved around the store, selecting her groceries.

Benjamin went outside to load the empty cooler and baskets into the buggy. By the time he was finished,

Abigail came out carrying a paper bag. She climbed into the buggy as he unhitched the horse.

Her gaze tracked down the street and suddenly she went very still. "Look." She pointed.

Benjamin looked. The town's veterinary clinic was half a block from the Millers' bed-and-breakfast building. "What about it?"

"Nothing." She sat silent as he climbed into the seat and clucked to the horse. After a moment she added, "Except I wonder if I shouldn't go in and introduce myself."

He frowned. It was a reminder of the tug she felt toward the *Englisch* world. But he just said, "Are you hoping they'll hire you?"

"Nein!" She fell silent again as he directed his horse to mesh with moving traffic. *"Nein,"* she repeated more quietly. "I'm not licensed in Montana. They couldn't hire me."

"Do you want to get licensed?"

"I don't know. I don't think so. Oh, I don't know!" The last words came out on a note of despair.

He glanced at her and saw a bleak expression on her face. "Abigail, are you going to be okay here in Montana? It seems you're torn up inside."

"I'll be okay." She straightened her shoulders. *"Mamm* needs me. Going into the vet clinic will only make things worse. I won't think about it."

He gave a noncommittal grunt and focused on directing the horse out of town. He sighed in relief when the road turned to gravel. In his mind, the end of pavement meant he was away from the *Englisch* world... including the vet clinic.

"Mamm told me this morning Eva is married," mused

Abigail after a few minutes of comfortable silence. "It's not surprising since she's a bit older than I am. She looks happy. She said she has two children so far, a boy and a girl."

"She's, what, two years older than you?"

"*Ja.* If you remember, she lived only a short distance away from us in Indiana. We were never terribly close because I had friends nearer my own age, but it's awfully nice to reconnect with her. Our lives took such different directions," she added.

"Any regrets about the path you chose?"

"*Nein.* I suppose. I mean, I've given up a lot. Eva never gave up anything."

"But you've gained a lot, too. Eva never took the opportunities you did."

"The opportunity to do what? Leave behind everything that's comfortable and familiar?"

He was surprised at the bitter tone in her voice. "The opportunity to do something you always wanted to do," he reminded her.

"*Ja*, I know you're right." She took a deep breath. "There are just times I forget. It's *gut* to be here, Benjamin. Not just to help *Mamm* when she needs it, but because I needed to get away from my practice. I needed to—to de-stress, as the *Englisch* put it."

Another buggy approached, heading toward town. They both waved at the older man, who waved back. "That was Bishop Beiler," he told her.

"Samuel Beiler?"

"*Ja.*"

"I remember him from when I was a *youngie*. I didn't realize he'd become the bishop."

"He's a *gut* man, fair and understanding. Everyone likes him." Benjamin grinned. "And he loves his cats."

"A man who loves animals can never be that bad." To his relief, she chuckled, seemingly over her earlier dark mood. "Oh! I forgot to tell you. Eva asked about participating in the Mountain Days demo. She said she might be interested in showcasing some baby quilts she makes."

"That's *gut*! She makes beautiful quilts. *Danke*, I've been meaning to ask her if she wanted to contribute."

"So many skills," Abigail murmured. "I have a feeling all the girls I grew up with went on to learn some amazing skills. I'm behind on so many things."

"Except a veterinarian degree," he reminded her.

"*Ja*, but that doesn't count for much when it comes time to cook dinner or sew a quilt. Although I wasn't bad at sewing," she added. "Sometimes I think I suture as well as I do because of my early training in sewing."

"We each have our own gifts."

"*Ja*, we do." Her words sounded a bit strangled.

Benjamin wondered at the reaction to what seemed like an ordinary comment, but he didn't pursue it. Something was bothering her, and it wasn't his business to probe.

Instead he reverted back to his assignment from the bishop. "I have quite a few people lined up so far for the Mountain Days festival." He started ticking off names. "Tom Miller said he can demonstrate horseshoeing. Peter and Michael Stoltzfus will do some plowing—the *Englisch* seem especially interested in plowing with horses. I have people who said they would demonstrate leather-working, making soap and laundry detergent, and now Eva with her quilting." He rubbed his chin.

"I'll admit, I've taken for granted the amazing variety of talent we have in the church. When you grow up with it, it doesn't seem like anything out of the ordinary. But I've been trying to see things in a different way—what unique demonstrations might interest the *Englisch*."

"It sounds like you've at least come to terms with the bishop's request."

"*Ja*, I suppose. I wasn't pleased at first, but I must admit the people organizing the festival have been very appreciative with what I've done so far."

He pulled up to his cabin and climbed down from the buggy. He turned to assist Abigail, but she had already gotten down.

To his surprise, she faced him and said, "Look, if you want me to help recruit some other demos for the Mountain Days festival, let me know. Alternately, since I have so much more experience with the *Englisch*, I might be able to act as a go-between. I can suggest displays that might be of interest, or something like that."

He suppressed the little frisson of pleasure her offer gave him. "*Danke!* I would appreciate that. But at the risk of looking a gift horse in the mouth, why the offer? As you've said before, you came here to help your mother."

She shrugged and looked at the bag of groceries in her hands. "*Mamm* is right. I would probably drive her nuts if I spent twenty-four hours a day with her. I don't mind having an extra project to keep busy."

"Then what I may ask you to do is keep in mind what kinds of demonstrations the women of the church can do, and I'll concentrate on the men. Would that work?"

"*Ja*, that would work. And it would give me an excuse to reacquaint myself with so many people I used to know."

"*Gut. Danke*, Abigail."

He turned to lead the horse to the barn and watched as Abigail headed back to her mother's house.

"It's a start," he murmured. And he wondered if she would ever become fully Amish.

Chapter Four

Abigail finished pinning her *kapp* over her hair and
gave her mother a concerned look. "Are you sure you'll
be all right by yourself?"

Esther flapped a hand. "*Ja*, sure. I don't intend to do
anything except knit while you're gone. Besides, I'm
getting along okay with the walker. It will be *gut* for
you to attend the Sabbath service, *liebling*. So many are
curious to see you again."

That was part of her reluctance to attend a Sabbath
service. It's not that she was dreading it, exactly. But she
knew her arrival in town had caused a buzz of specu-
lation. About two-thirds of this new Montana Amish
church was from her old hometown in Indiana, and the
rest came from various other churches around the country. This meant two thirds of the people attending the
service would remember her as a teenager.

So far no one had condemned her for leaving, but it
certainly set her apart in a way she found uncomfortable. She realized, deep down, that she craved the good
opinion of the church.

And doubtless everyone would want to know if she

intended to remain—it was a question she could not yet answer.

She caught her mother's eye. With uncanny precision, Esther observed, "You're nervous about attending the service, aren't you?"

"Maybe." Abigail dropped down into a chair next to her mother. "It's been so long, *Mamm*. I don't know what everyone thinks of me. I find myself feeling defensive about the choices I've made."

"Don't borrow trouble," Esther advised. "Maybe it's because they know I'm your *mamm*, but I haven't heard anything bad about you—just wild curiosity now that you're back."

Abigail sighed. "You're right. Maybe I've built everything up in my mind to be bigger than it is. It's just that—that I've led such an unconventional life, and part of me expects to be condemned for it."

"You aren't baptized. You broke no vows or oaths," Esther said gently. "You've just been on your own journey, *liebling*. Many of us do the same thing."

"I know." Abigail toyed with the strings of her *kapp*. "And I have to stop assuming the worst. I chose to leave, and now I chose to come back for a bit. That's all."

"Remember that. Now go on, you don't want to be late."

Abigail should have known her mother would impart hardheaded common sense. *Mamm* was right—there was no reason to avoid attending a Sabbath service, which was the heart blood of the Amish community. And truth be told, she needed to be reminded of her spiritual roots that, all too often, got lost in the secular world.

"All right, I'll go," she told Esther. "But don't try anything fancy while I'm gone, *ja*?"

Esther chuckled. Abigail made sure her mother had the things she needed within easy reach. Then, taking hold of a basket of food for the after-service meal, she set out for the home of Amos and June Stoltzfus, who were hosting the week's service. Esther had told her where she would find the house.

The weather was magnificent. Ever attuned to animal life, Abigail noted white-tailed deer, turkeys—some with long-legged chicks in their wake—magpies, robins, pheasant and quail.

This land was wilder than Indiana, but the church members were actively creating farms from the open land all around. She saw herds of dairy and beef cattle, a few places with goats or pigpens, many with hives of bees, and fields of corn and wheat. Every place had young fruit trees and flourishing gardens. Except for the towering mountains to the west, and the forests of conifers that edged them in, it looked like a typical thriving Amish community that might be found anywhere in the Midwest.

She wasn't alone in making her way toward the Stoltzfus farm. She heard the clip-clop of hooves pulling buggies. Ahead and behind her, clusters of people walked, most carrying baskets. But she walked alone… and wondered at the significance of that.

But she wasn't alone for long. As soon as she drew near the Stoltzfus farm, her friend Eva Hostetler—flanked by two young children—beckoned her over. "Abigail! Come sit with me."

"*Danke!* I will." Abigail deposited her basket of food

on one of the tables set up under the shade of several magnificent fir trees. "Are these your children?"

"*Ja*, Jacob and Mildred."

"Oh, what lovely names." The children looked to be about three and five years of age. "Where is your husband? I haven't met him yet."

"He's over there. His name is Daniel."

Daniel was a pleasant-looking man, about the same height as his wife, with cheerful blue eyes over his chestnut beard. He shook her hand. "So nice to meet you. Eva has spoken of little else since bumping into you at the Yoders' store a few days ago."

"I don't remember you from our old church in Indiana," said Abigail.

"That's because I'm from Ohio," he explained. "I came to visit some family in Indiana, and that's how Eva and I met." He swung his son into his arms and planted a noisy kiss on the child's cheek. "*Komm*, I think we're seating ourselves."

Eva took her daughter by the hand and turned toward the farm's large barn, where the Sabbath service was being held. "It's so *gut* to have you back with us, Abigail."

Abigail followed Eva into the shadowy interior and found a place at a bench on the women's side.

The interior of the barn was bright and clean. "Newly built," Eva told her. "We've been having barn raisings a couple times a month since everyone is still getting their farms up and running."

"It's lovely." Abigail glanced over the benches, which were neatly set up. She nodded at Benjamin as he found a place on a bench on the men's side. "It's like our old church in Indiana was transported right here to Montana."

Eva pulled little Mildred onto her lap. "One or two families returned to Indiana because they preferred it there, but most of us like this new place. We're all starting to build up our businesses and farms. And the *Englisch* community has been wonderful."

They had no time for further chatter as Bishop Beiler stood up to announce the first hymn.

As the service progressed, Abigail realized with a sharp pang how much she missed her spiritual roots. The unity within the barn as everyone sang the familiar hymns, and then as the bishop gave his sermon, created a longing within her. She hadn't expected to be impacted so strongly by the combined kilowatts of faith.

Later, at the meal following the service, she sat among a group of women she remembered from her youth. Most of the women her age had young children and attentive husbands. Whom did she have? Nobody.

Out of the corner of her eye, she saw a black Lab belonging to the Stoltzfus children, a cheerful, healthy-looking animal…except something seemed wrong with his feet. She excused herself from the table and approached the dog, who greeted her with the enthusiasm of all Labrador retrievers.

The animal's toenails had overgrown severely, which made him walk gingerly. It was an easy fix and she had nail clippers back at the house.

"You would trim them for me?" said June Stoltzfus, when Abigail thanked her for hosting the Sabbath service and offered to treat the dog.

"*Ja*, sure. If you want to bring the dog to *Mamm*'s house anytime this week, it won't take much time to trim them. Besides, I'm sure *Mamm* would love to see you." She leaned down and tousled the dog's ears. "He seems like such a nice boy."

"Oh, he is. Our kids love him. *Ja*, I'll bring him by. Tomorrow, perhaps?"

"*Ja*, tomorrow will work fine. Afternoon would be best."

"And I'll have a chance to visit with your mother, too. *Danke*, Abigail. It's so nice to have you back."

Abigail gathered up her basket and the empty food containers, then started on the road back home.

"How was your first Sabbath service?" called a voice from behind.

Startled, she turned. Benjamin jogged to catch up with her. She waited until he was next to her before answering. "Fine. It was nice to see everyone again. Everyone wanted to know if I'm staying."

He fell into step beside her, which created a certain intimacy. She was uneasily aware that courting couples often walked home from church together.

"So…have you made up your mind?" he asked. "About whether you're staying?"

"How can I?" She glared at him. "I've only been here a couple weeks. That's not something I can decide in such a short amount of time."

"What's holding you back?"

"A doctorate in veterinary science and two years of active practicing," she snapped.

"Don't take it out on me," he said mildly.

Her pride deflated in a heartbeat. "*Ja*, you're right. I'm sorry, Benjamin. It's a touchy subject for me. I spent years and years in school, and I finally got to achieve my dream of working with animals."

"But at what cost?"

The simple question nearly undid her. The *cost* had been readily apparent at the Sabbath service—a loving husband, a gaggle of children, a solid place within the church community. The cost, in fact, was enormous. Her eyes prickled. "Let's talk about something else."

"*Ja*, sure." Benjamin gestured around them. "Did you notice that most of the farms belonging to church members are clustered in this little valley?"

Distracted, she followed his motion. "*Nein*, not really. Why is that?"

"Because the church bought a huge ranch that was up for sale, and parceled it out to church members. The only downside is not many have homes big enough to host Sabbath services or other events, so poor Amos and June Stoltzfus end up hosting more often than they'd like, since they have a large house and barn."

"You said sometimes people meet at the Millers' building in town?"

"*Ja*, but we prefer to keep Sabbath services closer in. In many ways buying up that big ranch was an ideal arrangement—it keeps us all clustered close together, where we can help each other, and caused no hard feelings among the *Englisch* in town. I may not be fond of the *Englisch*, but I must admit we've had no problems with them."

Abigail drew her eyebrows together. "You've mentioned several times you're not fond of the *Englisch*, yet each time you also admit everyone in town has been open and welcoming. That's quite a contradiction, Benjamin. What have the *Englisch* ever done to you?"

Benjamin was momentarily broadsided by Abigail's blunt question. He didn't feel like getting into his romantic past or the issue with his older sister.

But before he could answer, a buggy came up from behind and slowed beside them. Benjamin saw the earnest face of Eva Hostetler's father, Eli Miller.

Abigail paused. *"Guder nammidaag*, Eli."

"Guder nammidaag. I meant to ask you something at the Sabbath service, but I forgot. I have a cow whose mastitis is worsening. Can you look at her tomorrow?"

"Ja, sure." He saw her frown. "Is it urgent? Should I come today?"

"Nein, tomorrow should be fine."

"Tell me, does she have a calf on her at all?"

"Ja. I only milk her once a day, in the morning. The rest of the time she has a calf on her."

Her expression cleared. *"Gut.* I think I have some cephalosporin in my kit. What time do you want me there?"

"Morning might be best."

"I'll be there."

"Vielen Dank." Eli tipped his hat, turned the buggy and headed in the other direction.

"Mastitis with a calf," she murmured.

"Is that unusual?"

"Ja. Mastitis most often happens when cows don't have calves on them. But the constant nursing of a calf can clear up a mild case of mastitis quickly. I'll have to see the situation when I get there tomorrow." She started walking again.

He kept pace with her. "Here's something to think about. You said you weren't interested in being hired by the local veterinarian clinic. But have you thought about opening up your own clinic just for the church community?"

She arched her eyebrows. "But I told you, I'm not licensed in Montana. That would be against the law."

"Not if you don't charge anything."

"Benjamin, what are you talking about?"

"I mean, people are already asking you for help with their animals. I know I did, when Lydia broke her leg. Opening up a temporary clinic might be a *gut* way to keep your skills fresh while caring for your *mamm*. It would also…well, it might be a shortcut way to gain respect with the church community. A way of proving you did the right thing by becoming a vet, if you will."

She lifted her chin. "I don't think I did the wrong thing by becoming a vet."

He sighed. "I didn't say you did. I'm not here to argue, Abigail. I'm just making a point."

"You're right." She let out a deep breath. "Sorry. I feel like an outsider. It's just a personal issue I have to deal with."

"We're nearly home, so look over there." He pointed. "See that small shed? I'm not using it, but it's in fairly *gut* shape. I could outfit that for you as a sort of ad hoc clinic, if you're interested. We can look at it tomorrow afternoon, if you want."

"I don't know…" she hedged. "There's only so much I can do if I don't have the proper equipment at my disposal. X-ray machine, surgical facilities…"

"Do you always underrate yourself this way?"

She snapped her mouth shut and looked a bit shell-shocked. Then she gave him a rueful smile. "I didn't used to. All right, let's look at it tomorrow."

He accompanied her to the guesthouse and followed her indoors. Esther was sitting by the open window, knitting.

"*Mamm?* How are you feeling?" Abigail placed her basket on the floor, then bent and kissed the older woman's cheek.

"*Gut.* Fairly *gut. Guder nammidaag*, Benjamin. How was the Sabbath service?"

"Excellent. Everyone asked about you." He smiled at her. "And your daughter has an appointment to see Eli Miller's cow tomorrow about a case of mastitis."

"Ain't so?" Esther turned toward Abigail. "So your concerns about people shunning you because you left aren't coming true, then?"

"It appears not." Abigail glanced at him. "Also, June Stoltzfus is coming over tomorrow so I can clip her dog's nails. They're badly overgrown. I told her you'd enjoy visiting with her."

"*Ach, ja.* June is such a nice woman."

Benjamin nodded. "Apparently I'm not the only one who needs her expertise when it comes to injuries," he said. "In fact, tomorrow we're going to look at a small outbuilding I have that might work as an ad hoc vet clinic."

"Vet clinic! But I thought—"

"I know what you thought, *Mamm*, because I thought it, too," Abigail interrupted. "I'm not licensed here, so I can't charge anything. Plus, I'm limited in what I can do because I don't have any equipment. But maybe I'm being pushed in this direction since everyone keeps asking for help with their animals."

"Perhaps *guided* is the better word," Esther said gently. "Don't underestimate your gifts, *liebling.*" She flapped a hand. "I'm fine sitting here, so why don't you go look at the shed right now? I'm curious to hear about it."

Benjamin lifted an eyebrow and glanced at her. "Will that work? We can look at it now."

She shrugged. "Sure."

"We won't be long," he told Esther.

He led the way toward a shed with a low peaked roof about twenty feet square. "There are lots of little outbuildings on this property," he explained as they approached the structure. "I actually have more than I need, so I've never used this one. But it has easy road access for buggies or wagons."

"And it has a little corral in back." Abigail approached the fence of the corral and rested her hands on the top rail. "An injured horse or cow could stay here for treatment."

"*Ja*, and I could build a small shelter right there for protection."

"You would do that?" She angled a glance in his direction.

"Let's call it a gratitude payment for setting Lydia's leg."

She bit her lip, then said, "Let's look inside."

The shed was cool and dark inside, with a wooden floor, bare stud walls and no wallboard. He looked around. "Somebody had plans for this place," he noted. "See? The walls are insulated." He pointed to the pink fiberglass batting covered with clear plastic. "And I don't see any water damage, so it looks like the roof is tight."

Abigail glanced around. "It would need a few windows for light."

"I have some old windows that were left in the barn when I bought this place. They wouldn't be hard to install."

"I can probably scrounge some furniture and tables."

"Or I could make some. I'm a carpenter, remember?"

She looked around, then crossed her arms and hugged herself. "It might work!" Her eyes sparkled in the dimness of the room.

He chuckled. "I don't think I've seen you so happy since you got here." Her whole face was lit up, as if with an inner light. "Have you missed practicing animal medicine that much?"

"It's not so much a matter of *missing* it as being *called* toward it." She scanned the small room. "Thank you, Benjamin. I don't know how much use I'll make of this as a clinic, but it will be nice to have a place set up."

"You might look through my barn at some point, too." He angled his head toward the doorway to a large older wooden barn, weathered and sturdy. "When the church bought this ranch, whoever was living here left behind many useful things I haven't needed so far. The windows, for example. I can install several in here without much problem."

"I don't want to take you away from your own work," said Abigail, frowning. "It sounds like this whole Mountain Days exhibition stuff you're doing takes a lot out of you." She fiddled with the strings of her *kapp*. "But maybe turnabout's fair play. If you help me set this place up as a clinic, I'll do what I can to help you organize the Mountain Days exhibits and demonstrations. I have more experience dealing with the *Englisch*, so it's not such an onerous task for me."

He felt simultaneously relieved and disturbed. Relieved, because it would be nice to share the burden of the project, and disturbed because it was a clear reminder that Abigail wasn't Amish.

"Ja, danke" was all he said. "Maybe you could talk to Eli Miller tomorrow when you look at his cow. He and his oldest son do leatherworking for bridles and harnesses. I've been try to talk them into setting up an exhibit about how they work leather, but they say it's *hochmut*. Proud."

"Ja, sure, I'll see what I can do." Abigail met his eyes in the gloom of the building. "The *Englisch* aren't so bad, Benjamin. Don't make them into a bigger problem than they are. I met many wonderful *Englisch* during my time away, and I've come to appreciate them. Sure, there are a few bad eggs, but aren't there a few of those within our own church, too?"

"I suppose." He looked at his shoes and scuffed some dirt on the floor, then muttered, "I just wish they'd give back what they swallow sometimes."

"I came back, didn't I?"

Startled, he looked up. "But you're not back," he said flatly. "Not really. You're here to help Esther, and when she's well you'll be swallowed up again, too, just like—" He stopped.

Abigail reached out and touched his arm, then dropped her hand. "Tell me about it someday," she said quietly. "For now, I must make sure *Mamm* has everything she needs. *Danke*, Benjamin."

And she was gone. He stared after her slender figure as she picked her way across a rough patch of driveway, ever alert to the sights and sounds of nature around her.

For just a moment, he saw Barbara walking away. Then he blinked away the memory and realized Abigail—at least so far—was still here.

Chapter Five

Abigail rummaged through her trunk of veterinary supplies, pulling out everything related to mastitis in cows and packing it into a basket. "I'm going to have to order more supplies if this keeps up," she remarked to her mother. "This may look like a lot, but overall it's not much more than a first-aid kit. But I find myself looking forward to setting up a free clinic, even if I'm limited in what I can do."

Esther looked up from her seat at the table, where she was making piecrust cookies. "Just as I'm looking forward to June Stoltzfus coming over this afternoon. I know you'll be trimming her dog's nails, but it seems like ages since I had a *gut* chat with someone besides you and Benjamin."

"You're getting more mobile, so having visitors should be fine." Abigail leaned forward and kissed her mother's cheek. "I'll be back before June comes by, so don't worry about making tea. I can do it when I get back."

She picked up the basket of vet supplies and took off for the Miller farm, which Esther had told her was about a mile away. Puffy clouds piled up and it looked likely to rain later in the day, so she was glad to take care of the cow while the weather held.

Eva's parents, Eli and Anna Miller, had a lovely white clapboard house with a barn that looked newly built. Abigail recalled what Eva had said, about barn raisings taking place frequently as the church community built up their farms. She saw a large and tidy garden, a yard bordered by colorful flowers, a coop with chickens and a number of handsome Jersey cows grazing with calves alongside them. The Millers might be new to the area, but they'd gone a long way toward setting up a workable farm.

"*Guder mariye*, Abigail," greeted Anna, who came to the door with a dusting of flour on her apron. "Thank you for coming by. Eli is in the barn. *Komm*, I'll show you where."

Abigail followed Anna's plump figure through the barn door into the shadowy interior. Eli, a pitchfork in hand, was cleaning stalls.

"*Guder mariye.*" He leaned the pitchfork against a wall and brushed off his hands. "Let me show you where the cow is."

"Is she a Jersey?" asked Abigail, picking her way amid a clutter of barnyard tools Eli evidently stored wherever he wished. "I saw other Jerseys in your pasture."

"*Ja.* She's four years old. This is her second calf."

"Did she have mastitis with her first calf?"

"*Ja*, and I treated it with intramammary infusions until it cleared up. But this time it seems more stubborn. Here she is," he added.

Abigail put her basket on the barn floor and leaned

on the gate top. A buff-colored animal, her huge brown eyes gentle and patient, regarded her while chewing her cud. A calf, darker in color, was lying near its mother.

"Her eyes look good," noted Abigail. "A bad infection can often dull their eyes. Is she eating well?"

"*Ja.* I'm keeping her separated from the other cows. I don't want any cross contamination."

Abigail silently blessed the diligent farmer for his caution. She'd met many livestock owners who were not nearly as careful, then blamed the vet when infections spread.

She rummaged in her basket and withdrew a thermometer and a test cup with a snap-down lid, then opened the gate and stepped inside the stall. With a heave, the cow rose to her feet. The calf scampered to a far corner and stood, watching. After petting the large animal, Abigail ran a hand over her lymph nodes. She worked her way over the cow's body until she reached the udder. She probed and squeezed, extracting milk from each quarter into the test cup. Three of the quarters were fine; the fourth quarter had the telltale squiggly indications of mastitis. But the squiggles were white and not brown, and the smell wasn't strong. The animal's temperature was a bit elevated, but not badly so.

"She's in fairly *gut* shape," she told Eli. "The mastitis might be persistent, but it's not a bad infection. She'll need monitoring. Keep the calf with her at all times—don't separate them at night—and let's see how she does. I have some antibiotics, but I'd rather not use them if possible. Better to let nature heal her. But if you notice a change for the worse, let me know immediately and we'll take a more aggressive approach." Abigail scratched the animal on her forehead. "She's a sweet girl. I can see why you're fond of her."

"*Ja*, I am. Up until this point, she's been my best milker, too."

"We'll see if we can return her to that state." Abigail wiped down the thermometer and snapped the lid on the test cup. She didn't want to risk infected milk spilling anywhere. "I understand you own the building in town that takes in lodgers. Do you run it as a motel?"

Eli rubbed his chin. "Not quite. It's become more of a meeting hall and a place for church members to stay when they visit from out of town. But we've taken *Englisch* guests, too. I guess you could say it's more like a bed-and-breakfast. Our middle son, Matthew, is doing the day-to-day operations. He says it keeps him from milking cows, so he's happy." His eyes twinkled.

Abigail chuckled. "But you won't give up your cows?"

"*Nein.* I love them too much." He slapped the bovine affectionately on the flank.

Abigail repacked her vet supplies into the basket. Then, remembering her promise to Benjamin, she said, "And you're a leather worker, *ja*?"

"That's right. My oldest son and I make harnesses and bridles." Eli pointed to the halter on the cow's head. "Halters, too. That's one of the ones we made."

Abigail examined the halter, which was well-made and fit the cow perfectly. "Where do you get your leather?"

"I get donated hides and we work it ourselves."

Surprised, Abigail turned to him. "You work the leather from start to finish? You don't purchase your leather already cured?"

"*Nein*, I like to work it a certain way for harnesses

and reins, and I can't purchase the quality of leather I prefer. Or perhaps I should say, the quality of leather I prefer is too expensive. Better to work it myself." He gave a rueful smile.

"Have you thought about showing your technique at the Mountain Days demonstration?"

Eli frowned. "Benjamin already talked to me about that. I don't think so. That would be *hochmut*. Proud. And the *Englisch* would likely have cameras."

"I wonder," mused Abigail, "if Benjamin could put up a sign for no photography? I think it would be easier for many church members to participate if they knew cameras weren't permitted."

"He could put up a sign, but I don't know if it will do any *gut*," said Eli. "Taking pictures seems to be too popular to stop by putting up a sign."

"Ja." Abigail rubbed her chin and decided on a little honesty. "But, Eli, I think Benjamin is trying his best to do what the bishop asked. He didn't especially want this assignment to work on the Mountain Days demo, but the bishop wanted him to showcase as many skills as possible from the church community. I think he would consider it a personal favor if you were to do some sort of leather demonstration."

Eli looked a bit guilt-stricken. "I didn't think of that. *Ja*, I'd forgotten the bishop asked Benjamin to organize this." He sighed. "I suppose my son and I can pull something together."

Abigail kept her face serious, but inside she was smiling. "I'm certain both Benjamin and Bishop Beiler would be grateful," she told him.

"And Anna, she makes soft candies," Eli volunteered unexpectedly. "I suppose she could put together a demonstration on that. We have a propane burner for heating the sugar."

"*Danke!* I'm sure that would be welcome." Abigail thought it best to beat a hasty retreat before Eli changed his mind. She gave the cow a gentle slap on the back. "Keep me posted about this lady, but something tells me she'll be fine. I'll come back in a week to check her out."

"*Vielen Dank.*" He opened the pen gate for her. "Are you planning on opening up a clinic while you're here?"

"Funny you should ask," she replied. "I can't legally work here in Montana because I'm only licensed in Indiana, but I don't mind doing some unpaid things here and there. I might be setting up a temporary clinic in a small building near *Mamm*'s house. I can't do anything complicated because I don't have much equipment, but I suppose I can do some things. However, I can't be paid."

"Then consider the leather demonstration as payment." Eli smiled.

Abigail grinned. "*Danke!* That's more than enough. Benjamin has been very *gut* to my mother, so I've been helping him out on this project."

She took her basket and walked back down the road, enjoying the scenery, sniffing the fresh mountain air, listening to the birdsong. She liked this little corner of Montana. Above all, it was good to be out of the busy Indianapolis clinic where she'd been practicing and back among farms.

And the church community. A place where she understood the people, and they understood her.

Her mother was improving. Soon Esther wouldn't need any help around the household at all, certainly within the two months Abigail was supposed to stay here. What then? How long could she use her mother's health to avoid thinking about her own future?

She frowned. She hadn't been fired after her tiff with Robert, so in theory she could return to the Indiana clinic and continue doing what she did best: caring for animals. But feminine instinct told her she would never again be comfortable working for him—not just because of his volatile temper, but also because her own emotions had been too tied up with her work situation.

Her mind turned toward the vet clinic in the town of Pierce. She hadn't yet gone in to talk with anyone, but she wondered if they were hiring. Then again, did she want to be so close to the church community but not be a baptized member? She wasn't certain baptism would be permitted for someone in her position—a working professional.

Maybe it was time to talk to the bishop.

"You did what?" Benjamin stared at Abigail as she placed a lunch basket on his workbench and bent down to pet Lydia, whose tail swished in welcome.

She smiled. "I talked Eli and Anna Miller both into participating in the Mountain Days demos. Eli will demonstrate how he works leather, and Anna will be making some soft candies."

He dropped onto a stool and stared at her. "I've been after Eli for a month now, but he's refused to participate. He's been a tough nut to crack. How did you do it?"

"I think part of it was as a sort of payment for looking at his cow this morning. But his biggest concerns were *hochmut* and photography. I reminded him it was the bishop who asked you to arrange these demonstrations, so participating wouldn't be a matter of *hochmut*.

And I suggested you might put up prominent signage—for all the good it may do—asking people to refrain from taking photos."

"*Ja, gut,* I can do that." He looked at her with admiration. She had an impish sparkle in her eyes and he could tell she was pleased by her morning's work. He rubbed his chin. "Since you've gotten here, three new people have agreed to do demonstrations—both the Millers, and Eva Hostetler as well. And all thanks to you."

"Well, it's just one family, when you think about it."

"But still." He smiled. "This project might turn out better than I'd hoped. I'm beginning to sense a bit of enthusiasm from people."

"And from you, too."

"Me?"

"*Ja,* you." Abigail opened the lunch basket and took out some containers, which she set out for him. "Your attitude appears to be changing. When you first mentioned this assignment from the bishop, quite honestly you weren't happy about it. Now you seem different."

"Hmm." It pained him to admit she might be right. "As I said, I'm hoping it will revitalize my business."

"Or maybe it's because you have a penchant for organization," she replied. "You said you thought the bishop chose you to organize these demonstrations because you were unmarried and had more time, but I wonder if he didn't ask you because you have a talent you didn't know you had?" She smiled. "See you at dinner." After placing the basket on the floor, she gave the dog one last pat, then walked out the shop door.

He stared after her. Could she be right? Did he have a penchant for organization? Could he have invented his resentment toward this assignment from the bishop as a means to overcome his aversion to the *Englisch*, when in fact the bishop simply recognized a talent instead? It was something to mull over.

He ate lunch, then set aside the empty containers and resumed his work building kitchen seating for the large Graber family, who had requested a dozen chairs. He methodically slotted the wood and inserted pegs to join the pieces for the chair frames while thinking about the fascinating woman who'd entered his life. If he wasn't careful, he could let Abigail occupy a good portion of his thoughts. If only...

If only Abigail hadn't followed the same path as the woman he'd courted so long ago, lured into the wider world by the glittering possibilities it offered. Glitter. That was the word he used to describe it. The glitter of a career, the glitter of fashion, the glitter of automobiles and cell phones and movies and all the things he shunned. Barbara had succumbed to that glitter, and that's the only reason he could think Abigail had left the church as well—the allure of a career as a veterinarian.

Could he persuade her to stay? Could a quiet life outside of a small town in Montana compete with the glitter of her work in Indiana? Did he dare risk his heart with a woman for whom the glittering *Englisch* world was an attraction?

He stood back and looked at his handiwork. Twelve partially finished chair frames leaned against the wall, pegged with oak and strengthened with wood glue. He couldn't do much more until the glue dried. He looked at the empty food containers Abigail had left for his lunch, and decided to return them. He could talk with her about plans for the ad hoc clinic. Deep down he knew it was just an excuse to see her.

He placed the empty containers in the basket, pocketed a tape measure and small notepad, and started down the path toward Esther's cottage.

From a distance, he saw Abigail sitting on the front porch, her back against a post and one leg dangling off the edge. Something was with her. Curious, he slipped behind a tree and peered around for a closer look.

A handsome black dog, a Labrador, was lying beside her with his head in her lap. She absently stroked the animal's fur while gazing out at the scenery.

For some reason he felt his throat close up. He was spying on her during a private moment, but her pose epitomized so much about this woman. The dog's trusting position, with his head in her lap, demonstrated Abigail's absolute affinity for animals.

She didn't look like the type to be pulled away by the glittering outside world, but what other explanation was there?

He squared his shoulders and continued down the drive, his feet crunching on the gravel. Both Abigail and the dog turned to watch him approach.

"I thought I'd bring the basket back early," he said. "I have some chairs half-finished in the shop and can't do anything more until they're dry."

"I see." The dog dropped his head back in her lap, watching him with alert chocolate-brown eyes.

"Who's this guy?" Benjamin bent down to pet the dog before sitting on the porch as well.

"He belongs to Amos and June Stoltzfus. June brought him over so I could trim his nails, and stayed to visit with *Mamm*."

Through the open window, he could hear the murmur of feminine voices and the clink of tea things. "I'm glad Esther has a visitor. I imagine she was getting a bit lonely."

"I thought so, too." She stroked the dog's fur. "That's why I invited June over. I thought it best to stay out of their way and let them visit."

"Then we have a chance to discuss your clinic." He gestured toward the outbuilding a short distance away. "I brought a tape measure and notepad, so we can talk about specifics."

"*Ja!* I'd like that."

"I can start putting a little time into it each afternoon to retrofit it," he offered. "I'll start with windows, since those will need to be done first. I also have a roll of linoleum that was left in my barn. I can use that for the flooring if you want—it will be waterproof."

"I can't believe you're willing to do all this work for me."

He was silent a moment. "I've got time," he admitted. "My business is slow at the moment. I don't have enough orders to fill my day. Besides, I can't tell you how grateful I am you helped Lydia. She's my favorite dog."

"Glad to help. How long before her puppies are due?"

"A couple weeks."

"Come and get me when she goes into labor. I want to be there just in case."

"So...do you want to walk over and look at the clinic building?"

"Sure." She rose and dusted off the back of her dress, then stepped toward the open window. "*Mamm?* I'm walking over to look at that outbuilding with Benjamin. June, I'll take the dog with me. He'll enjoy the walk."

"*Ja, danke,*" June replied from inside.

"So I wonder," Abigail remarked as they stepped off the porch, followed by the eager dog, "what are June's skills that could be demonstrated?"

"You mean, for the Mountain Days event?"

"*Ja*, what else?"

"Hmm." He stroked his chin. "She makes the best pies in the church. She sells them in the Yoders' store. But it's not like she can put on a pie-making demo."

"Why not? If her pies sell, it's because people may prefer to buy them ready-made than make their own. Maybe she could put up a demo showing why her pies are especially *gut*."

He chuckled, then stopped when he realized she was serious. "Do you think she would agree?"

"All you can do is ask." She smiled.

"Abigail, you're amazing." He grinned back. "At this rate, the whole church community will be participating."

"That's what you want, isn't it? Or at least, what the bishop wants."

"*Ja*." He was silent a moment, envisioning the variety of booths that might be set up in the demonstration area. In his mind's eye, he could see colorful bunting, clear signage and interested visitors. "It will be *gut*," he murmured to himself.

"What, the demo?"

"*Ja*. I'm just envisioning how it would look."

"I'm thinking it will turn out much better than you might think. Come on, Benjamin. Do you really think anyone who agreed to participate will let you down? And once this demo is over, maybe you won't be so hostile to *me*."

He nearly staggered backward. "Hostile toward *you*? Have I shown myself to be hostile toward you?"

She shrugged. "Maybe not me personally, but I'm a lot more *Englisch* than you like, and you don't like the *Englisch*." She glanced at him, then looked at the ground.

"Glitter," he muttered.

"What?"

"Nothing."

She crossed her arms. "Would you care to explain yourself? Because you're being hostile again."

He felt a shaft of anger. "Deal with it."

"Fine." She turned and started to stomp away.

Benjamin's anger turned to shame. "Abigail, wait."

She stopped but kept her rigid back toward him. The silence lengthened. Finally she said, "Well?"

"Look, I'm wary of the *Englisch* world for reasons of my own, There's just too much glitter out there. It pulls people away from the community."

She looked at him. "What do you mean by glitter?"

"Attractions. Excitement. Change. Cars, electronics, movies, fashion, jewelry, shopping. All the things we shun. It entices those who might already have a rebellious streak, those with a determination to see the wider world. I know now we shun those things for *gut* reason. They pull people away. You're no different," he added, then immediately wanted to snatch back the words.

The utter shock on her face made him sorry he'd brought up the whole matter, but now there was no going back.

"Is that what you think?" she finally choked out. "Do you honestly think it was 'glitter' that took me away from my family and my church when I was eighteen?"

"Wasn't it?"

"Nein!" She glared at him. "I've come to admire many things in the *Englisch* world, but leaving the Amish had nothing to do with all that. I left to go to school and become a vet!"

"Hochmut," he muttered.

She poked an index finger against his chest. "Don't accuse me of *hochmut* without evidence, Benjamin."

"But that's part of why you succeeded, isn't it? *Hochmut?*"

"Wrong again." She shook her head and leaned against a fence rail. "You're making a lot of assumptions."

"Then why did you leave? What caused you to want to be a vet if it wasn't *hochmut* or the attractions of the *Englisch* world?"

"It was *Gott.*" She lifted her chin.

He stared. *"Gott* told you to leave our church?"

"In a manner of speaking." She sighed. "Let me explain."

Chapter Six

Abigail dropped down to sit on a long length of log near the fence. The black Lab selected a stick and lay down to gnaw it. "Did *Mamm* ever tell you anything about how much I loved animals as a child?"

Benjamin straddled the log and picked at some bark. "A bit, but everyone knew it. You were always doing something with dogs, or cows, or cats. Didn't you once fix a bird's broken wing?"

"*Ja.* I'm surprised you remember that. But I think it stems from when I was seven or eight years old. One of my favorite cows was sick, and a veterinarian came out to look at her. Next thing I remember, the cow was fine. It was an amazing moment for me, realizing that a person could cure an animal. From that moment on, I knew I wanted to do the same thing. Not because of *hochmut*, but because *Gott* called me to be a vet."

"How can you be so sure it was *Gott*?" He looked skeptical.

"Because I've prayed on it. I spent years praying on it. It wasn't a whimsical decision or a rebellious phase. *Gott* gave me my affinity for animals from when I was a child, and medicine is the best use of that gift. Vet school was tough, but I always felt I had a higher purpose. A calling. A gift."

He shook his head. "I find that hard to believe."

"Have you never had a calling, Benjamin?" She met his eyes. "It's a powerful thing, sometimes a frightening thing. It's a gift, yes—but it can also be a torment. To follow my calling, I had to leave my family and my church. That wasn't easy to do at eighteen. But if I hadn't left, I would have felt I wasn't doing what *Gott* directed me to do."

"Are you glad you left?"

"Ja. Nein." She looked at the ground. "It's complicated. I'm glad to have developed the skills, but I've given up so much…" She trailed off.

"Ja, you're alone," he said bluntly. "You have no *hutband,* no children. For an Amish woman, those are serious sacrifices."

She turned away and focused on the mountains to the west. He was right. She had denied those yearnings for many years, which was easy in the *Englisch* world, with its emphasis on career. But would that denial haunt her as she grew older?

"I had no choice," she said softly. "It's what *Gott* wanted me to do."

"Is that a decision you'll be happy with ten years from now? Twenty years? Thirty years?"

"How could I turn down my gift?" She felt a flare of anger inside her and strove to keep her voice from reflecting it. "It's all over the Scriptures that we have different gifts from *Gott,* and we have to use those gifts to His glory. How can I throw my gift back in His face?"

"So you're staying if you stopped being a veterinarian to raise a family, that would be a decision you'd regret," stated Benjamin.

"Maybe." She noted a bald eagle sitting on a distant tree, and kept her gaze focused on the magnificent bird. "*Ja*, I'm sure of it. In a way, that's why it's such an adjustment to be back in the church community. Here, career is subsumed by faith and cooperation. I've missed that. But am I willing to sacrifice what I've worked ten years to achieve? Being a vet is not just a career, not just a job. It's *Gott*'s gift to me, and I can't push it aside."

"Let me ask you something." Benjamin continued to pick at the bark on the log. "Let's say for the sake of argument you could practice being a vet here, as an Amish woman. Would you want to?"

"*Ja*, sure, of course. But I can't. It's not acceptable. Amish women are encouraged to put family first, and if I was a practicing veterinarian, that wouldn't be possible."

"With *Gott*, all things are possible," he intoned. "But I think you're being a little too rigid. You're making assumptions that may not apply. Maybe you should talk to the bishop to see what your options are."

She felt a gleam of wry humor. "I've avoided the bishop since arriving here in town. I know precisely what he would say, and maybe I just don't want to hear it in person."

"You're going to have to talk to him at some point, anyway," he warned.

"Not if I leave again." She saw his face shutter.

"And is that what you want?"

"Benjamin, you know I'm not here for the long term. I'm just here to heal…" Her voice trailed off. She hadn't meant to say that.

Sure enough, he looked at her sharply. "Heal? Heal what?"

"Nothing."

"Abigail, lying is a sin. You know that." She heard a faint note of teasing in his voice.

She felt pressure build up inside, a need to confess. She sighed and reached down to pet the comforting dog at her feet. "Did *Mamm* tell you why I came home?"

"Your *mamm* doesn't gossip, so all I know is you came home to take care of her after her hip surgery."

"Let's just say the timing was perfect." Her voice cracked. "I messed up, Benjamin. I made a professional mistake in the clinic in which I worked, and a beautiful dog nearly died as a result. My boss—his name is Robert—was able to save him, and he dressed me down for my incompetence. As a result, I got to where I lacked confidence in my own skills. I had to leave for a while. Let's call it a leave of absence." Embarrassed, she felt herself blush. She didn't want Benjamin to know she had fancied herself in love with Robert.

To her annoyance, Benjamin stated the obvious. "You're blushing. Was that *all* that happened?"

She felt her blush deepen. "*Ja*, that's all," she snapped.

"Why do I think you're lying again? Or at least omitting something?"

"It's none of your business, Benjamin."

"As you say." He quirked a smile at her. "Though it occurs to me there might be a man involved."

She glared, then abruptly laughed. "You're incorrigible. Okay, if you want the truth, I fancied myself in love with Robert. I created a whole scenario in my mind of us marrying. It seemed so right—two professionals sharing a mutual love of animal medicine. Then when he yelled at me after nearly losing the dog, my little fantasy went right down the drain. It's like the blinders were stripped off my eyes and I saw him for what he was truly like—a man with a volatile temper who would have made a terrible *hutband*. And don't you *dare* tell *Mamm* I said that," she added fiercely.

"I wouldn't dream of it." His tone was definitely teasing. "Did this Robert ever court you or indicate he was romantically interested in you?"

"*Nein*, not at all. I was painting romantic scenarios about a man who was really, at the heart of it, very professional. There was no harassment or inappropriate behavior at all. He just had a nasty temper, something most of us in the office were willing to put up with because he paid well and we knew he was a brilliant veterinarian."

"But what happens now? Is your job still open?"

"*Ja.* I took a two-month leave of absence to care for *Mamm* just about the time they hired a junior vet fresh out of school. The clinic is growing. But they want someone with more experience and told me my job will be waiting for me when I go back."

"And *are* you going back?"

She sighed, gazing at the mountains. "I don't know. I mean, I *do* know. Yes, I'll be going back...but I'll have mixed feelings about it. Here, it's easy to immerse myself back in the church community, and it's like going from one extreme to another. I turned my back on the church when I left. I didn't leave my faith behind, but I left my culture behind. I had to learn how to live like the *Englisch*, and I came to appreciate all the opportunities I had and the things I saw. It's magnetic, really. But now that I'm back..." She paused.

"Now that you're back...?" he prompted.

"I miss it." She blurted the words. "I've missed the Sabbath services. I've missed *Mamm*. I've missed the camaraderie and sense of community, the cooperation and lack of competitiveness. There's so much I've missed out on."

"Including a *hutband* and children."

"*Ja*. Seeing Eva Hostetler was an eye-opener. She's so happy. Am I happy? I don't know. That's why I'm so confused. The tug of practicing my profession is still strong. But so is the tug of the community." She peeled a piece of bark off the log and chucked it into the grasses in a petulant gesture.

Thoughts of Robert had receded in her mind since returning to the church community and reacquainting herself with some of the people she grew up with. Attending the Sabbath services was a reminder of how much she had sacrificed in her quest to develop her gift.

A thought flickered through her consciousness... Could some of the reason Robert had receded from her mind have to do with the man now sitting opposite her on a log at the edge of a Montana forest?

Benjamin was glad to hear Abigail wasn't stuck on some *Englisch* man. It didn't seem likely any romantic interests might pull her away, even though she still faced professional conflicts. He sat quietly, momentarily lost in thought.

"Now what about you?" she asked. "There's something I want to know."

"*Ja*, sure," he said absently. "What?"

"Why you're so hostile to the *Englisch*."

He snapped out of his reverie. "I'm not—"

"Benjamin, lying is a sin." She smiled as she parroted his words back to him. "You know that. And just because I bared my heart to you doesn't mean you're obligated to return the sentiment." Her words dripped sarcasm.

"Ach." He took her rebuke in the spirit it was intended and gave her a wry smile. "Okay, I'll tell you. Do you remember my sister Miriam?"

"Ja. She's your oldest sister, isn't she?"

"Middle sister. She's two years older than me, and we were always close. She wanted to become a nurse, but to do that she had to leave the church community. My parents weren't happy with her decision, of course, but they understood she had a calling from *Gott*, so they were supportive. I was less understanding. I argued with her. I said she should stay and be baptized. I was probably obnoxious about it in the way teenage boys can be obnoxious. But in the end she left and became a nurse."

"How old were you when she left?"

"Sixteen. I took it pretty hard. For a time, I didn't have anything *gut* to say about the *Englisch*, I can tell you that. It got to the point where our old bishop in Indiana had to call me in to chastise me for my attitude. I stopped badmouthing people after that, but inside, it festered."

"Oh, Benjamin…" She gave him a sympathetic look.

He continued. "I couldn't forgive. I felt hatred for the first time in my life, and it hurt. None of these feelings were directed at my sister—I love her too much for that—but I blamed the *Englisch*, unfairly and unreasonably. I've always wondered if my attitude pushed my sister away, and deep down I blamed myself. Did I not argue enough? Did I argue too much? Was my adolescent snarkiness the final spur behind her decision to leave? And then…" He lifted his gaze toward a distant horizon and bitter memories rose.

The silence lengthened. "And then…?" Abigail prompted.

"It wasn't just my sister," he said, gritting out the words. "Do you remember Barbara Eicher? We were courting about the time you left the church community and went to college."

"*Ja*, I remember her. Nice young woman. I've always wondered why you didn't marry her."

"I wanted to. Dear *Gott*, I wanted to. But she was restless. She wanted to see the *Englisch* world during her *rumspringa*. I didn't want her to go. All I could see was the same thing happening all over again as what happened to my sister—I would lose someone I loved to the *Englisch*. But this time it was the woman I wanted to marry."

"And so she left." It was a statement, not a question.

"*Ja*, she left. She moved to the city, got a job, made friends. She ended up marrying an *Englisch* man. As far as I know she's happy, but I don't stay in touch with her so I don't know for certain." A hard look crept into his eyes. "The bottom line is, I've lost two people I love to the *Englisch* world. So I question my own temperament and my ability to chase people away."

"Is that what you think?" She stared at him. "That you chased away your sister and Barbara?"

"*Ja*. It's what I think. Maybe it's not true, but sometimes even things that aren't true take hold inside, and are hard to shake off."

Like Barbara and Miriam, Abigail hadn't been baptized. Nothing was keeping her here. Her mother would heal from her surgery and not need Abigail's care any longer. Abigail's bruised heart would heal and she would head back to her clinic in Indianapolis. In short, she was transient.

But, he realized with a sinking heart, he wanted her to stay. But what could he possibly offer that could compete with the gift from *Gott* she so desired?

"Well." He tried his best to keep his voice brisk, but it came out choked. "Let's go look at the inside of the shed again and see where you want those windows."

Abigail got to her feet and dusted off her skirt. The dog also rose to his feet, then shook and wagged his tail.

"He seems much happier without those overgrown nails," she commented, patting the animal. Then she gestured. "Lead the way."

Benjamin walked around the small building with her while she pointed out the ideal placement for windows to lighten the interior and make it workable. He took measurements and marked figures in the notepad, while the dog patiently followed on their heels. He estimated the amount of time it might take to fix up the building during his off time, while in the back of his mind he wondered if she even would be around long enough to use it.

Evidently the same thought occurred to her, too. After looking over the building one last time, Abigail stepped outside, then stopped and looked at him. "Is it worth it, do you suppose?" She waved a hand at the small building. "I might leave before it gets much use."

"I don't mind." He slipped the notebook into his pocket. "This building needs work before it can be used for anything, whether it's an ad hoc vet clinic for you or something farm-related for me."

"I don't want to take advantage of you." She bit her lip. "You've done enough, including helping *Mamm* after she moved out here—"

She broke off as June Stoltzfus came running over to them. The black Labrador ran to her side, wagging furiously. June stopped, panting, and petted the dog. "Abigail, one of the bishop's grandsons just stopped by. He said Bishop Beiler wants to know if you're available for a meeting with him."

Benjamin saw her go pale. "He wants to meet with me? Now?"

"*Ja*. I don't think it's an emergency, but I thought you should know right away."

"*Danke*, June. I'll go see him. Is his grandson still here?"

"*Nein*, he went home. *Vielen Dank* for taking care of this old boy." She tousled the dog's ears.

"It was nothing." Abigail stood rooted to the spot, watching June and the dog retreat.

"Are you okay?" He touched her arm. Two bright colors burned in her cheeks.

"Why would the bishop want to see me?"

"You've been here a couple weeks now. It's normal for the bishop to keep track of what's going on in the church community."

To his surprise, he saw tears well up in her eyes. "Have I done something wrong? Have I offended anyone?" Her lip trembled.

"Of course not. What makes you think that?" He kept his voice firm to hearten her. "You've done nothing wrong. And remember, you're not a baptized member of the church. At the moment, that might be to your advantage."

She took a deep hiccuping breath and pressed a hand to her midsection. "I don't want to be sent away, at least until I'm ready."

"Is that what you think? That he would send you away?"

"Wouldn't you think the same thing in my position?"

"*Ja*, maybe I would," he conceded. "But you're here to take care of your *mamm*. He can hardly chastise you for that."

"When I left, Jeremy Kemp was still the bishop," she said. "What is Bishop Beiler like? Is he fair? Harsh? Stern? Kind?"

"All of the above. He does what is necessary. I've seen him harsh, and I've seen him kind. Stop panicking, Abigail. You're imagining the worst."

"*Ja*, I suppose you're right. It's a bad habit of mine."

But she didn't look convinced. Instead she seemed small and vulnerable. All of a sudden, he felt protective. "Would it help if I walked you to his house?"

She glanced at him. "It might," she admitted.

"Then let's go. No time like the present."

"Let me go tell *Mamm* first."

"*Ja, gut.*"

He walked with her back to Esther's cabin, feeling rather than seeing the nervousness that emanated from her. But she said nothing. He rather admired her stoicism.

She climbed the porch steps and opened the door. He stayed on the porch, but heard every word through the open window.

"*Mamm?* Did June tell you what the bishop's grandson said?"

"Ja, liebling." Esther's voice held a trace of worry. "Are you going to see him now?"

"Ja. Benjamin said he would go with me for support."

"He's a *gut* man."

"Is there anything you need before I go?"

"Nein. Go on, *liebling.* Get it over with."

Benjamin heard her draw in a breath. *"Ja,* you're right. I won't be long… I hope."

In a few moments, she reemerged on the porch. He noticed she'd dampened back a strand or two of hair under her *kapp* and changed into a clean apron. He saw her draw back her shoulders and lift her chin. "I'm ready."

Chapter Seven

Abigail kept telling herself she shouldn't be nervous to meet with the bishop. After all, what could he do? Benjamin was right—the fact that she was not a baptized member of the church was an advantage at the moment. It's not like she could be shunned.

But her palms were sweaty and her heart was racing as if she was in trouble.

"Take it easy." Benjamin, padding along at her side, touched her icy hand. "I can tell you're still imagining the worst."

"Ja." She took a deep breath and pressed a hand to her chest. "I am, and that's *schtupid*. How much further to the bishop's house?"

"Another quarter mile, perhaps. He and his wife live in a small home near their youngest son's house."

"They're not in a *daadi haus*?"

"Nein. Their son didn't move here until later, so we all got together and renovated an existing building." He pointed. "There, you can just see it through those trees."

Abigail peered and saw what looked like a made-over barn perched on a wide lawn amid the pines and firs. "It doesn't look Amish," she observed.

"It's not. When the church purchased the ranch property and then parceled out the land among those of us who moved here, Lois—that's the bishop's wife—fancied this older building and said it could be fixed up. We had the work party last year."

"When is the next work party? Eva said they're being held about once a month."

"*Ja*, the next one is a couple weeks from now, over at the Herschbergers' place."

The chatter about renovations and work parties distracted her from her nervousness, and by the time they walked up the long gravel driveway to the bishop's home, she felt more composed.

"I'll wait here." Benjamin pointed to a set of chairs under the shade of a red fir.

"*Danke*, Benjamin." Abigail inhaled, squared her shoulders, walked up to the door of the home and knocked.

The bishop's wife, Lois, answered. "*Guder nammidaag*, Abigail. Thank you for coming so quickly. My *hutband* is in his study, if you'll follow me."

Abigail followed the older woman's taller form through a comfortable living room into a small office with a window overlooking a large vegetable garden. The bishop was sitting at a desk, writing something. He stood up when she entered.

"*Guder nammidaag*." He reached over to shake her hand, and his eyes crinkled as he smiled. "We've never had a chance to formally meet as adults. You were still a *youngie* when you left the church, and I was not yet a bishop." He gestured toward a chair.

Abigail seated herself and relaxed at the bishop's

friendly mien. "I was a little surprised to get your request…" she began, but was startled when a cat suddenly jumped in her lap.

The bishop chuckled. "I'm sorry, this lady thinks she owns the place. Meet Thomasina."

"She's beautiful." The long-haired animal had calico fur, deep green eyes and a loud purr that rumbled around the room. Abigail stroked and scratched the feline, and was rewarded when the cat literally reached up and put her paws around her neck as if hugging her. Her heart melted and she snuggled the animal.

"You can see why she's my favorite pet," the bishop said, smiling. "She loves people and is very affectionate."

"How old is she?"

"Just two, so we have many happy years with her. Lois and I got her just after we moved here, and she's a blessing. The grandkids think the world of her, and they spoil her rotten."

"I can understand why." The cat loosened her embrace and settled on Abigail's lap, apparently content to remain there while she tickled under the animal's chin.

"Now." The bishop's face grew more grave. "You've been here helping Esther for a couple weeks, I understand. Is she improving?"

"*Ja*, quite fast. She's mobile with her walker and is eager to do more than she should. I have to hold her back from overdoing things."

He nodded. "She's a fighter, your mother. Lois took care of her immediately after her surgery."

"*Ja*, that's what *Mamm* said," Abigail acknowledged. "I've been meaning to thank her."

"Lois and Esther have been friends for years, so Lois

was glad to step in. But I'm sure having you home helped Esther just as much. She missed you during the years you were gone."

"I've missed her, too." Abigail felt her eyes prickle. "*Daed* passed away while I was still in school, and I've always felt guilty I wasn't with him during his last hours. It's *gut* to be with my mother again, even for a short time."

"Which leads me to why I asked you to visit today. I've heard rumors that you're planning on opening a veterinarian clinic."

She frowned. "Just to be clear, I'm not licensed in the state of Montana, so I can't legally practice here. Benjamin has offered to retrofit a small building on his property as a clinic, but it can only be a sort of triage place. I don't have the equipment to make it a proper clinic. Nor can I charge anything for my services." She stroked the cat on her lap. "I do it for the love of animals. I'm happy to help with anything I can do, but I'll have to refer more serious cases to the clinic in town."

"I see…"

Her frown deepened. "As a matter of interest, why do you ask?"

"Do you intend to remain with us?" His words were direct.

"I—I don't know. My original goal was to stay just long enough to help *Mamm* recover. But again, why do you ask?"

"Because being a veterinarian is not the normal path for an Amish woman."

"Believe me, Bishop Beiler, no one knows that more than me. I'm simply here for a short time to recover from—from some blows in the secular world, as well as to help *Mamm* recuperate. In the meantime, if I can use my gifts to help heal any animals that are brought to me, I see no harm in that."

"And that's what I'm leading to." He leaned back in his chair and steepled his fingers. "I'm concerned about the example you're giving to the church's young people. As you know all too well, the *Ordnung* discourages worldly pursuits. A professional degree—no matter how useful—is seen as prideful. If you remain with us, you would have to sacrifice your career to be baptized. If you plan to open a clinic, you're welcome to do so, but you will have to forgo becoming fully Amish."

Abigail felt a flush of anger. "So those are my choices," she stated through clenched teeth.

"*Ja*, those are your choices."

Fresh on the heels of her earlier conversation with Benjamin, Abigail felt more defensive than she might otherwise be. "Bishop Beiler, I became a veterinarian because of a calling from *Gott*, just as you followed *Gott*'s call to become the bishop. Could *you* so easily have refused His calling?"

His face hardened. "You know I couldn't. But that's hardly the same thing."

"It's *exactly* the same thing. A gift is a gift. Benjamin tells me you've been an outstanding bishop, so you've used your calling to serve others. My calling is animal medicine, which I feel I am also using to serve others."

"I understand that. But I'm concerned that you might be setting a bad example. Your education and success as a veterinarian might unintentionally encourage other young people to leave the community to follow a path into the *Englisch* world."

"You know I would never encourage anyone to do that."

"Perhaps not on purpose, but your very presence may act as an encouragement."

"How?" Her temper threatened to bubble over, and she clamped it down. "I've hardly even seen any *youngies* since I got here. Most of my time has been spent with *Mamm*."

"Everyone, including the *youngies* who were toddlers when you left, knows what path you took. That's why there's been such a buzz of interest when you returned to our community. I've overheard conversation among *youngies* expressing admiration for what you did. That concerns me."

"I know I followed an unusual path, but what would you have had me do? Refuse my calling?"

"Not at all. You're not baptized. You were free to do whatever you wished. But you have to understand there would be repercussions within the church family as a result."

"Meaning, I'm not welcome here." She glared.

"I didn't say that." The bishop's voice was patient. "But you chose a different path, one that took you away from the community. It's not reasonable to expect no fallout from that decision. This is the point I want to emphasize to the *youngies*."

"You're assuming everyone is eager to leave the church," she argued, "but that's not the case. Everyone's paths in life are different. So are their journeys with *Gott*."

"Abigail, I'll be blunt. I have my reservations about your return." He frowned.

She felt her face flush with anger. "Since you're

being blunt, then tell me what you want me to do. Do you want me to leave?"

"*Nein...*"

"*Gut*, because I'm here to take care of *Mamm* after her surgery, and I won't leave until she's better. *Mamm* is improving. Probably within four or five weeks, she won't need me any longer. Then I can turn my back on this community and you won't have to see me anymore." She scooped up the cat, placed it on his desk and stumbled out of the room.

She went outside, blinded by tears. Benjamin scrambled to her side as she began walking. She was thankful he didn't pepper her with questions, but merely handed her a folded handkerchief. She nodded and buried her face in it. Her shoulders heaved.

How dare the bishop question her gift? How dare he give her an ultimatum?

She didn't like how glibly he dismissed her calling as trivial and unimportant, as if the difficult decision to leave and train herself in the veterinary sciences was a childish whim or girlish impulse. She had answered a call, just as the bishop himself had, to serve *Gott* as best she could. Why could he not understand that?

Deep down she knew his lecture was inevitable. The choice she had been avoiding was now upon her. She had to make a decision whether she wanted to stay, give up her career and join the church community of her birth. Or if she would leave, and abandon the faith and way of life in what she now realized had been an anchor for her.

Always in the back of her mind, during all the years of her schooling and practice, she knew she wanted the opportunity to return to her church and her people.

Until now, she hadn't realized how deeply that desire was ingrained.

But she was only fooling herself. Being a veterinarian was not what Amish women did. It was as simple as that.

Her anguish broke through with a sob.

Benjamin's heart leaped into his throat when he saw Abigail's tearstained face as she came staggering out of the bishop's house. He feared the worst—that she had been asked to leave—and in that moment he realized how much he had foolishly wanted this small, spunky woman to stay.

He wanted to kick himself for his interest in yet another ineligible woman. Would he never learn? What was behind his penchant for women straddling two worlds?

But self-recrimination would come later. Right now Abigail needed him, starting with the clean handkerchief he always kept in his pocket.

After a few minutes of walking silently by her side, she took a deep shuddering breath and mopped her face. "I'm sure you're burning up with curiosity about what happened," she observed with a bitter tinge to her voice. She twisted the scrap of cloth in her hands.

"*Ja*, sure," he acknowledged. "But not until you're ready to tell me."

She hiccuped, a childish sound, then related what the bishop said during the meeting. "In some ways, the meeting went worse than I thought it would," she concluded. "I know it was wrong of me, but I lost my temper."

"I'm sure that helped your case," he observed with some sarcasm.

"*Ja*, no doubt." She sniffed and stared down the road. "So now I have to make a choice—stay or leave. That's what it comes down to."

"That's pretty much as you thought it might be," he pointed out.

"*Ja*. I have some time to make up my mind, but in the end, I have to choose between my profession and my church." Her voice rose in frustration. "Is it such a bad thing, to be a professional?"

"You knew there would be consequences…" he began.

"*Ja, ja*, I know." She swiped at her eyes with an angry gesture. "But he makes it seem like it's something shameful or dishonorable. All I want to do is help animals."

"It's a cultural conflict," he admitted. "Of course, there's nothing shameful or dishonorable in being a vet. But you must admit, how many Amish veterinarians are there?"

"Okay, not many. But here's the thing—until I came back to take care of *Mamm*, I had forgotten a lot of what I cherished while growing up Amish. I realize now how much I want to stay, how much I want to be baptized. But I didn't tell that to the bishop. That's when I lost my temper. I told him I'd leave as soon as *Mamm* could spare me. I would turn my back on the community, and he wouldn't have to see me anymore. Then I stormed out."

"Real mature," he observed dryly.

He half expected her to explode with anger at his ill-timed quip, but instead she gave a bark of laughter.

"*Ja*, I guess." She stooped down, picked up a stone from the gravel road and chucked it into the ditch, her movements clipped and angry.

"I wonder if the bishop is right," he mused. "It literally never occurred to me that your being back and fitting in so well might be a problem for *youngies*. I mean, that's kind of how you ended up becoming a vet, isn't it? Didn't you say a veterinarian made a strong impression on you when you were a *kinder*, after he cured one of your favorite cows?"

"*Ja*. But it's not like I wasn't interested in animals already by that age. It's just the first time I saw what someone could do with them."

"Then you must admit the bishop's concerns are valid. Every time you fix up an animal, you might be making some *youngie* wish they could do the same thing when they're older. And wham, they've left the church community."

"If that's the situation, they would have left the church community anyway. Like your sister. Her calling to be a nurse was a higher calling than staying with the church."

He winced and felt the familiar knife twist in his midsection at the reminder of his losses.

"Maybe it would help if we explored the bishop's concerns."

She glanced at him. "Why?"

"Because potentially he's the one that holds your future in his hands."

She blew out a breath. "*Ja*, I guess. Sure, let's do it."

"Okay then. Let's say you open your vet clinic and treat a thousand animals a week." He saw her smile at his exaggeration, and pressed forward. "Suddenly you find yourself surrounded by admiring *youngies* who think it's wonderful that you went out into the *Englisch* world and became a vet, then came back and were baptized. What would you do under those conditions?"

"Hmm." He was pleased to see she looked thoughtful. "You mean, what would it be like if it seemed my dancing off to get a veterinarian degree didn't impact my future as a member of the church community? Is that it?"

"*Ja.* In short, having your cake and eating it, too. What the bishop sees is someone who did just that—who went out and became a professional, then came back and expected to be accepted by the community as if nothing out of the ordinary had happened. He's afraid if that's what you do—stay here and expect you can be baptized—then it will have an impact on the future of other *youngies*, who expect they'll be able to do the same thing."

"But that's what a *rumspringa* is all about—a chance for *youngies* to decide if they want to stay or go. It separates the wheat from the chaff."

"But you might say you were chaff when you left—and now if you decided to stay, you would want to become wheat. See what I mean?"

"*Ja,* I see what you mean," she said crossly. "But it's not like I'm a rock star or a celebrity. I just don't think that many *youngies* have a burning desire to do what I did. It was hard work, and being so far from family and all the support I grew up with sent me into despair a few times when things seemed bleak and I wasn't sure I could hack it. In other words, I don't think I'll be an influence one way or the other—neither positive nor negative. But those who want to leave the Amish should leave. Those who want to stay should stay."

Benjamin looked at her. It pained him to ask, but he did anyway. "And which category will you choose, to leave or to stay?"

She looked away. "I still don't know."

"That's what I thought." He fell silent as they neared his house. Suddenly he was anxious to get away from her.

The silence between them continued. Abigail's strides, which had been aggressive and angry, slowed. She paused a moment, met his eyes and said, "*Danke* for coming with me to the bishop's, Benjamin. It was… comforting."

She spun on her heel and walked away. He stared after her, wondering if she was taking his heart along with her.

Chapter Eight

Two weeks after her ill-dated interview with the bishop, Abigail watched her mother hobble from the table to the sink, where evening sunlight streamed through the western window and bathed the kitchen in a golden glow.

"Soon you won't need me," she observed. "I don't know how long it normally takes someone to recover from hip-replacement surgery, but you're back on your feet far sooner than I thought you would be, *Mamm*."

"*Nee*, I'm still slow." Esther started washing dishes. She insisted on doing this chore over Abigail's objections. "But it's not in my nature to let someone else take care of me. I'm grateful you're here, *liebling*, but it irks me to have you do all the kitchen work, especially since more and more people are asking you to look after their animals."

Abigail stretched her arms over her head. "*Ja*, it was busy today. My little clinic is hardly even furnished, but word is getting around. I'm glad I thought to bring a pet scale. Half the stuff I do involves knowing how much an animal weighs. I still have to refer about half of them to the clinic in town, though. I can't really do small-animal work without an X-ray machine."

"People seem to trust you—" Esther began, then broke off as she heard a pounding on the front door.

"Abigail?" called a voice she recognized as Benjamin's.

She strode over and yanked open the door. Benjamin stood panting on the porch.

"Lydia is in labor," he said without preamble. "Can you come?"

"*Ja.* Give me a moment to gather some supplies." Calmly, she selected a basket and began filling it with what she knew she would need to assist with a complicated whelping.

Benjamin fidgeted, and she noticed his agitation with some amusement. He was as twitchy as an impending father. "How long has she been in labor?" she asked.

"I noticed it a few minutes ago."

"Well, I know from experience it will take some time before the first puppy shows up. Calm down, Benjamin."

He blew out a breath. "I know you're right. And this is her second litter. But the fact that she's going into this with both a cast on her leg and a cone around her neck makes me nervous."

"I'll get rid of that cone first thing." She picked up her basket and kissed her mother's cheek. "I don't know how late I'll be."

The evening shadows shaded most of the path between Esther's place and Benjamin's. He took the path at a fast walk, almost a jog, and she hurried to keep up with him.

"You said you noticed her a few minutes ago, but do

you know how long she has been in labor?" she asked to his back.

He slowed fractionally and allowed her to catch up. "Probably a couple of hours. I'm kicking myself because I was working in the shop and left her in the house, and it wasn't until I went in that I noticed she was pacing up and down, limping on her healing leg. I have a whelping box I made for her, so as soon as I saw her behaving that way, I put her in the whelping box."

"*Gut.* That's a start. Classic nesting behavior. Have you taken her temperature?"

"*Nein.* I don't have a thermometer."

"I have one, so it will tell me something about how far along she's progressed."

Benjamin dashed up the porch steps and into the one-story log cabin. Abigail followed, clutching her basket of supplies.

The space Benjamin had arranged for his dog to birth her puppies met with Abigail's full approval—it was a large closet that had been emptied and lined with a secondhand baby-crib bumper, with a thick padding of thrift-store towels on the floor. The only disadvantage was the darkness—beneficial to the dog, no doubt, but inconvenient to a veterinarian.

Lydia was lying awkwardly amid these comforts, her battered plastic cone preventing her from behaving as a mother dog should. Abigail kneeled down next to the panting canine. "Let's get you out of this thing," she murmured, and untied the awkward barrier.

The moment the cone was off her neck, Lydia relaxed. She even licked Abigail's hand in apparent gratitude, then leaned down to sniff at the cast she had been unable to fully explore for the past few weeks.

While she was occupied, Abigail slipped in a thermometer. The dog hardly noticed.

"You'll have to light a lamp," she told Benjamin, who was hovering just outside the closet door. "I'll need to be able to see as things progress."

"*Ja*, wait a moment, I'll get one."

He returned with a lit kerosene lamp and inserted it into a shallow box mounted on the closet wall.

"Did you put that box there just for a lamp?" she asked in amazement, looking at the convenient bracket.

"*Ja*. This is the second time Lydia has used this closet as a whelping box. I needed light, too, but it was too dangerous to have an unsecured lamp in here, so I built the box to hold it."

"Clever." Abigail withdrew the thermometer and peered at the markings. "Ninety-eight-point-five," she noted. "Just right for a dog in labor."

She patted Lydia's head and stood up. "Let me unpack my supplies, and I'll need to see what you have for newborn puppies. But first, some calcium."

She spread out her supplies on the kitchen table and immediately loaded a plunger with a calcium gel, which she inserted into the dog's mouth before the animal could object.

"Calcium?" Benjamin asked. "What's that for?"

"Oral calcium," she clarified. "It helps guard against eclampsia, or milk fever, after whelping. Eclampsia is less common in large breeds, but it's nothing to mess around with. It also helps the whelping progress quickly and smoothly. Long, drawn-out birthings can stress the last puppies."

"She doesn't seem to mind the taste." He watched as Lydia literally smacked her jowls.

"It's supposed to give a nice aftertaste. Not that I've ever tried it myself," she added.

"How long before the puppies start coming?"

"Not for a couple hours at the least." She watched as he nervously fingered some colorful ribbons meant to identify each puppy at birth. "Do you want me to stay, or come back later?"

"I—I guess you can go," he said, pleating a ribbon.

Abigail knew he wanted her to stay but was reluctant to say so. She shrugged. "I don't have anything else going on, and I want to keep giving Lydia calcium as her labor progresses, anyway. You can keep me supplied with hot tea in exchange for my veterinary expertise."

He whooshed out a breath, and grinned. "*Danke!* And you can have all the tea you want!"

The moment lingered, until she grew nervous. She turned away from his compelling blue eyes. "Well, let's get things set up for when her labor becomes more active."

Besides the collection of ribbons, Benjamin had a scale, some iodine, sterilized scissors, stacks of old clean towels, hot water bottles and a notebook and pen. He also had a separate large basket lined with soft towels. Abigail knew he had prepared it to put the newborn puppies in until the whelping was finished, since mother dogs get restless between puppies. Having a separate basket for vulnerable newborns prevented accidental injury.

From far away, she heard Elijah bark, and the moo of a cow. "Do you need to do barn chores?" she inquired. "Milking cows or feeding chickens?"

He slapped his forehead. "*Ja*, I completely forgot. It

won't take me long. I'll be back shortly." He scrambled out of the cabin.

Abigail watched him go, then bit her lip and decided to indulge in something she'd wanted to do for some time—explore his cabin. It was a charming, old-fashioned place, and she'd never seen it fully.

The kitchen was Spartan, with a wood cookstove and shelves instead of cabinets. The small living room was outfitted with comfortable furniture he no doubt had made himself. A large braided oval rag rug dominated the room, and she wondered who had made it. His mother, perhaps?

Off the kitchen was a large but mostly empty pantry. She peeked into his bedroom but did not enter. That was the whole of the cabin—kitchen, living room, pantry, bedroom. Eminently suitable for a bachelor, but she understood why other church members didn't want to live here. It would require a lot of work to expand for a growing family.

Within half an hour, Benjamin came in with two buckets of milk. "Any progress?"

"None." She watched him hoist the buckets onto the kitchen table. "Do you need help straining the milk?"

"*Nein*, I'm used to it."

He was right. Within minutes the fresh milk was poured into jars and placed in the icebox.

Outside, darkness fully descended. Crickets chirped. She heard the call of great horned owls—the deeper voice of the male at a distance, the higher-pitched call of his mate close by.

Benjamin lit another lamp, then a third, and the lighting gave the kitchen a cozy feel. Abigail felt like she was in an intimate bubble with Benjamin and the dog, separated from the outside world.

An hour went by, then two. Benjamin did indeed keep the kettle hot, and poured her a fresh mug of tea several times. He also kept a pot on the stove with hot, but not boiling, water for filling the hot-water bottles after the puppies were born. Lydia got out of the closet once or twice and took a restless turn about the room, then settled back into her nook. She shivered and panted, typical signs of a progressing labor. Abigail kept the animal well primed with calcium.

She felt the change in mood as the night progressed. Benjamin seemed very approachable, and she found herself talking with him as she'd rarely done with anyone else.

She told him about the time she'd gotten kicked by a horse, which had left a huge bruise on her leg.

In turn, Benjamin described his journey west to Montana. "I wasn't sure what to expect, but once I got here, I loved it."

Then Benjamin changed the subject to Mountain Days. "The festival liaison in town, a guy named Jonathan Turnkey, is optimistic that my demonstration will give a boost to my furniture-making business." Benjamin rubbed his chin. "I hope so. It's been something of an uphill battle for me."

Watching Benjamin's face in the lamplight, his eyes were shadowed and dark, but crinkled easily with humor. Up to this point, she'd regarded Benjamin with a reasonable amount of disinterest—as a kind and helpful neighbor, a solid member of the church—but that was it.

Now, for the first time, she reconsidered that. In the time since she'd been back with her mother, she learned everyone thought highly of him. He was a respected, trustworthy member of the community. In short, an eligible bachelor.

Yes, *he* might be eligible. The question was, was she?

Lydia's panting took on a more urgent tone. Peering close, she saw the dog was close to birthing her first pup.

"Go ahead and fill the hot-water bottles," she instructed Benjamin.

He hurriedly funneled hot water into the rubber containers, screwed the lids on tight and slipped them under the towels in the basket.

With soft groans, Lydia had the first puppy. Immediately Lydia turned and began vigorously licking the newborn, familiarizing herself with the puppy's scent. Abigail stayed vigilant so the new mother wouldn't accidentally hurt the baby with the clunky cast on her leg. The puppy made little mewing sounds. It was mostly white, with some large brown spots down its back and some pale brown markings around the eyes and ears.

It wasn't until Lydia began to birth the next puppy that Abigail carefully lifted the first baby out of the whelping box. She wiped its tiny nose and the inside of its mouth before placing it in the scale. "Fifteen-point-two ounces," she said. She peered at the baby's underside. "And a male. What ribbon color do you want for him?"

Benjamin selected a blue ribbon, which he tied around the baby's neck. Then he took the tiny animal, cuddled him for a few moments and placed him in the warmed basket. He noted the puppy's birth order, weight and ribbon color in the notebook.

Abigail turned her attention to Lydia, who had just had another puppy, which was a female.

The night wore on. Puppy after puppy arrived— eight, nine, ten, eleven...

"What an enormous litter!" she exclaimed. "I think Lydia is getting tired, poor thing." Holding a lamp close, concern gripped Abigail. "The next puppy is breech, with the tail coming first instead of the front paws," she told Benjamin. "I'm going to see if I can turn it. If I can't, we'll have to take Lydia into the vet clinic in town for an emergency C-section. I don't have the right equipment for that."

She saw his face turn pale. "Do what you can."

She had turned breech puppies before, and at least Lydia was a large breed with more room to work. Using the greatest care, she manipulated the puppy's position inside the mother, gently pushing and turning. She knew the signs of when a puppy would turn.

After a tense fifteen minutes, when she was getting cramped from bending over in such an awkward position, at last she felt the blessed movement she was hoping for—the puppy slid around nose-first. "Got it!" she breathed.

Lydia seemed to realize things were right. In a few minutes, the puppy was born.

"Boy," murmured Abigail. "And no wonder it was breech. Look how big he is."

But unlike the other puppies, who mewed and wiggled immediately after birth, this one was lying still and silent.

Abigail did what she could to help clear the puppy's nose and mouth, but the tiny body was unresponsive. "Not giving up," she muttered, and started massaging the newborn's underside. She covered the puppy's face with her mouth and blew into the lungs, and continued palpating the heart and lungs.

Lydia seemed concerned about the fate of the tiny animal in Abigail's hands. She whined and licked her hand. One minute passed, then two. Suddenly Abigail felt a twitch under her fingers. "C'mon, honey, come on…" she urged.

With a quick motion, the newborn puppy took its first breath. Abigail released her own breath, which she didn't realize she was holding. "He's all right." She grinned at Benjamin.

He grinned back, the tension whooshing out of the small whelping closet. For a moment Abigail was caught up in his eyes, made dark by the lamplight, but sparkling with gratitude…and something more.

Confused by her emotions, Abigail placed the puppy next to the mother dog's nose, and in seconds Lydia was greeting her latest newborn, licking him vigorously.

"I'm out of ribbons," commented Benjamin. "I didn't expect this many puppies."

Abigail palpated the mother's belly. "I think that's the last one, so he can be the only one without a ribbon. A dozen puppies! That's a lot for a dog this size." She gently poked the newest baby. "He's going to be a big boy, probably larger than his father. Look at his markings—three brown spots down his back and some markings on his face, like a mask."

"Badger marks, that's what they're called." Benjamin stood up and stretched after the cramped position on the floor. "Here, you must be tired." He reached down to help her up. "I can make more tea."

She put her hand in his as he assisted her to her feet.

The moment lengthened as they stood together in the dark closet lit only by kerosene lamps.

He leaned in. "Abigail," he breathed, and lightly touched her lips with his.

Abigail's heart gave a lurch in her chest as she returned the kiss. For just a moment, she gave in to temptation. She felt a completion, a rightness…and then fear. Fear of her own weakness, her own longing. She pulled back. "B-Benjamin," she stuttered. "We can't."

He locked his hands behind the small of her back. "Maybe not, but it answers a question."

"Wh-what question?"

"Whether you felt the same as I did." He grinned.

She caught the impish light in his eyes and smiled back, but felt compelled to add a warning. "It'll never work out, Benjamin. I have too much uncertainty in my future."

"I know. I'm sorry. But you can't blame me for trying." He released her.

To cover her confusion, she turned to the basket containing the mewling newborn puppies. Her hands shook. "It's time to get them with their mother. They'll need to feed."

"Let me change the bedding first." Benjamin picked up the last-born puppy and handed it to Abigail, while he encouraged Lydia out of the closet.

Abigail held the tiny scrap of puppy, newborn-blind but now gloriously alive, and felt her heart melt. She'd never had a dog of her own and wondered if she would ever be settled long enough to have that luxury. She was aware Benjamin was working, but was lost in her own little bubble with the puppy.

"Guder daag?" Benjamin waved a hand in front of her face.

"I'm sorry." Abigail snapped out of her reverie. "I'm quite taken with this little guy. What a sweetheart."

"Let's start getting the other babies with their mama. I imagine they're hungry."

One by one, they transported the puppies with the rainbow of ribbons around their necks to the now-clean bedding underneath Lydia.

A yawn split her face. "What time is it?"

Benjamin held a lamp up to the clock on the kitchen wall. "Three in the morning."

"No wonder I'm tired. Still, the whelping went better than I anticipated. I'll keep the cone off Lydia's neck, but let me know if you see her chewing at her cast."

"I'll do that. And, Abigail… *Vielen Dank* from the bottom of my heart. I was so worried about her." He gestured toward Lydia, who was lying with a canine smile on her face and a pen full of puppies getting their first meal.

She smiled. "I'll check in with them tomorrow. Or rather, later today. Meanwhile, I'm off to get some sleep. I won't need a lamp, there's plenty of moonlight to see me home. *Gude nacht*, Benjamin."

She stepped out into the cool, moonlit night and started walking home. The pair of great horned owls that lived in the area boomed back and forth to each other. Abigail took deep, cleansing breaths and tried to calm herself.

Was she falling for Benjamin? She didn't want to. She'd fallen for someone before—hard—and it had turned out disastrously. Why, oh, why had her heart leaped when Benjamin kissed her? And why had she let her guard slip to reveal her emotions?

She rubbed her eyes, which were scratchy and tired from her all-night vigil with the dog. Undoubtedly, the intimate setting had something to do with it.

Sparks had flown in that little closet setting. But she was as wrong for him as Barbara had been in his past. She was likely to return to the *Englisch* world soon enough. She didn't need to leave a trail of broken hearts behind as well—hers or Benjamin's.

She would aim to keep her interactions with him strictly professional from now on.

Benjamin watched Abigail's dim figure disappear into the moonlight. Then he wandered back in and looked at the young family in the whelping closet. The last pup born was the only one without a ribbon. He'd seen the love in Abigail's eyes as she held the tiny dog she had saved. Without Abigail's quick intervention, there would have been eleven puppies, not twelve.

He reached down and gently picked up the last pup born. It mewled and feebly pawed at being removed from the comfort of his mother and siblings. Benjamin cuddled the tiny animal, noting the faint markings around his eyes that would darken with age into a badger mask, which often characterized Great Pyrenees.

He was shaken by that moment he'd impulsively kissed her. So he wasn't the only one who had felt something between them.

He wondered if he should set himself *two* goals for the summer. The first was to organize the Mountain Days demonstration as the bishop had asked him. But he wondered if he could establish a second goal—to convince Abigail she should give up her aspirations to return to the *Englisch* world and instead stay here in Montana.

He looked down at the newborn litter. Every one of these puppies, in theory, already had a home. His waiting list for livestock guard dogs was long. But this little puppy…well, Benjamin was going to keep him.

Perhaps someday, the little puppy could be a wedding present for a bride. A bride who loved animals.

Chapter Nine

It was hard for Abigail to stay away from the litter of newborn puppies. She also knew she was using the puppies as an excuse to see Benjamin.

"I don't know what it is about this breed," she commented when the babies were three days old. She handed him his lunch hamper, then reached for the youngest puppy. "I've never spent much time around them, but they're beautiful. Aren't you?" She held aloft the still-blind animal. "I think this guy is my favorite."

"Well, you can legitimately say you saved his life. As for this lady…" He bent down and tousled Lydia's head. "She'll be mighty glad to have that cast off her leg."

"Three more weeks." Abigail cuddled the puppy to her chest. "I'm glad there were no post-whelping complications. What time are you leaving for the Herschberger farm tomorrow?"

It was the first barn-building Abigail had attended since she was a teenager, and she was looking forward to it…with the possible exception of seeing the bishop.

The church leader's ultimatum had disturbed her more than she thought. It's not as if he'd said anything she didn't anticipate. It's just that she still didn't know where her future lay. Her calling to practice animal medicine was still strong. But the longer she remained here, the stronger the pull she felt to return to her roots.

"Around seven in the morning," Benjamin replied. "Are you sure Esther is up for going? It's likely to be a long day."

"I doubt I could keep her away. This will be the first social function she's attended since her surgery, and I know every other woman there will keep her from lifting a finger. She's cooking up a storm right now. Speaking of which, I should get back and help. I don't want her overdoing it."

"I'll pick you up tomorrow at seven, then."

"*Danke.*" Abigail took her leave and started walking back to her mother's cabin.

But something caught her eye. In the pasture where Benjamin had his cows, several young calves gamboled about while their mothers rested in the shade, chewing their cud. But it wasn't the calves she noticed—it was a pair of coyotes at the far end, eyeing the babies with hunger in their eyes.

Those cows were part of Benjamin's livelihood. She had to warn him. Silently she retreated to the cabin and, without knocking, yanked open the door. "There are two coyotes in the field with your cows," she hissed.

Benjamin wasted no time. He strode out the door, grabbing his straw hat and jamming it on his head as he went. She ran after him.

But rather than approach the pasture fence, he motioned for her to hide herself behind a large tree while he did the same. "Watch," he advised.

"Watch?" she squeaked. "Those coyotes could take a calf, couldn't they?"

"Of course they could. Just watch." He gestured.

It was then that Abigail saw Lydia's mate, the Great Pyrenees dog named Elijah, silently gliding behind some trees along the fence line, straight toward the coyotes. Every previous time she'd seen the massive dog, he'd worn a goofy, happy expression. That expression was gone, and he looked grim—and dangerous—as he focused with laser intensity on the predators.

Her breath caught. She glanced at Benjamin, but he didn't seem worried. The cows chewed their cud and the calves frolicked about, oblivious to the presence of the hunters.

With a speed faster than she thought possible for a dog that size, Elijah raced full throttle at the coyotes, barking and snarling. The predators fled instantly, slipping under the fence and fleeing into the forest. The calves dashed toward their mothers. The cows snapped to their feet in alarm.

Elijah stared after the departing hunters, then turned and stalked back among his herd animals. She could almost see a smug expression on the dog's face.

She released a breath. "Impressive," she murmured.

"That's a Pyrenees for you," Benjamin replied. He stepped out from behind the trees and walked toward the fence, calling the large dog toward him. "Their first line of defense is barking, but they wouldn't hesitate for a moment to defend their herd more seriously if necessary. Their long fur protects them from teeth and claws of any predators they're fighting. That's a good boy..." he crooned, and gave the dog the accolades it deserved.

"I'm going to have to find out more about this breed,"

she commented, reaching over the top of the fence to join Benjamin in fussing over the dog. "There's just something about them I find fascinating."

"I feel the same way." He buried his hands in Elijah's fur. "They're powerful animals, and although they're perfectly capable of killing a predator, they prefer to act as a deterrent. That's why they're so barky. They're roamers, so they have to be confined to the field where their flock is, or they'll go off and patrol a much bigger territory. First thing in the morning, Elijah beats the boundary of this pasture and makes sure nothing has changed overnight."

"That's due to their independent nature, *ja*?"

"*Ja.* Above all, they're stubborn. They like to think for themselves, not blindly obey commands."

"And they're loyal." She tickled Elijah under the chin.

"Very loyal," Benjamin agreed. "They also work best in pairs. I've seen them do actual teamwork—one dog drawing a predator's attention while the other dog sneaks up from behind. But Elijah will be fine on his own until Lydia is able to join him again. Nonetheless, that's why I'm thinking on getting a second female. That way I can breed each one once a year while the other one stays teamed up with this big boy." He gave the dog a final pat on the head.

"I can see why so many church members are interested in herd guardians," she said. "There are a lot more predators out here in Montana."

"*Ja*, and all of us have livestock that's vulnerable."

"I can't wait to tell *Mamm* about this little bit of drama. She'll be impressed."

She finished her walk back to her mother's cabin. Esther was sitting at the table stirring a batch of cake batter. "I've decided to make cupcakes instead of a layer cake," she told Abigail. "Easier to handle."

"*Ja, gut. Mamm*, you'll never guess what I just saw…" Abigail described the incident with the coyotes while she started on some casseroles. "Great Pyrenees are magnificent animals," she concluded.

Abigail enjoyed afternoons cooking with her mother. It was something she'd missed after she'd left for school—the pleasant domestic bustle she'd taken for granted while growing up. She knew her mother missed her father fiercely at such times, since he was always the biggest fan of her cooking. Abigail wondered if her mother would ever remarry. Most Amish didn't remain single for long after losing a spouse.

"Benjamin said he would pick us up at seven o'clock tomorrow morning." Abigail pushed a glass-lidded casserole dish into the oven. "He asked if you were up for going, and I said I couldn't keep you away."

Esther chuckled. "I've missed seeing everyone at the Sabbath services, so this is the next best thing. Besides, I understand another couple of families have moved here from Pennsylvania. Lois said her brother-in-law will be visiting as well. I haven't met any of the new arrivals yet. Here, *liebling*, I think these are ready to bake."

It wasn't until late evening that everything was cooked and baked to Esther's satisfaction. Abigail was tired, but didn't want to admit it in the face of her mother's industry.

"That should do it," Esther concluded at last.

Abigail wiped the last dish and put it away. "I'll get up early and have everything heated."

"Then let's go to bed," her mother advised. "We'll have a long day ahead of us tomorrow."

The next morning dawned bright and sunny. Abigail rose early and had everything heated and tucked in insulated carriers by the time Benjamin rolled up in his wagon.

"Ready, Esther?" he called as the older woman came out on the porch with her walker.

"Ja!" she called back cheerfully. "Let's go!"

Abigail carried the food to the wagon and nestled it among Benjamin's tools in the wagon box. Then she and Benjamin assisted Esther up into the wagon seat. The woman grunted once or twice in pain but otherwise climbed in with a dexterity that surprised her.

"It will be *gut* to see everyone," chattered Esther with childlike glee.

Abigail exchanged a grin with Benjamin over Esther's head.

"I know everyone's anxious to see you," he told Esther.

Soon, other wagons joined them on the road toward the Herschberger farm. Esther waved as people called greetings. Within a few minutes, Benjamin guided the horse up the gravel driveway and found a place to park. He hopped out and lifted Esther down from the wagon seat, then started unhitching the horse. "Do you need help going in?" he asked Abigail.

She shook her head. "We'll be fine," she told him. "Go build a barn."

He grinned—which momentarily took her breath away—then shouldered his tool belt and picked up a large wooden box of additional tools from the back of the wagon. She watched as he headed toward a cluster of men, who were busy planning the barn-raising strategy under the supervision of a foreman.

The barn's skeletal walls were already framed and lying on the ground, ready to be lifted into place. Soon teams would lift the walls into a vertical position using ropes and poles, and the barn would begin to take shape under their skillful hands.

It was a process she'd watched dozens of times during her childhood. It wasn't until she'd left the community and entered the *Englisch* world that she realized how rare the skill of carpentry was, and how few people used it.

Everywhere she heard the babble of voices and the shriek of children as they ran around the farm.

"*Komm, Mamm*, I'll settle you on the porch and then come back for the food." She made sure her mother was steady on her walker, and hovered nearby as Esther started moving over rough ground.

"Esther!" A woman's voice rose about the chatter. "Look, Esther is here!"

The older woman smiled as half a dozen of her friends descended upon her, chattering and asking questions.

Eva Hostetler wandered over, a smile on her face. "*Gut* to see you here, Abigail," she said. "Your mother looks so much better."

"*Ja*, she is. And she was so looking forward to today." She watched as her mother, helped by solicitous hands, made her way to the house. "I think she's in *gut* hands. I'm going to grab the rest of the food."

"I'll help." Eva fell in beside Abigail as they returned to the buggy.

"Where's your *hutband* and children?" Abigail lifted a covered basket out and handed it to Eva, then reached in for the other.

"Daniel is busy with the men, of course. And Jacob and Mildred are somewhere, playing." She paused and a smile hovered on her lips. "And it seems we'll have a new *boppli* joining us in December or so."

"Oh, Eva…" Abigail stopped and stared at her friend, then threw an arm around her neck and gave her a hug. "That's wonderful!"

"*Ja.* I just pray things go well. I—I lost the last one early."

The smile dropped from Abigail's face. "I didn't know that. I'm so sorry."

"It was *Gott*'s will." The young mother sighed. "But it was harder than I thought it would be. It made me realize how precious our other two are and how much I like being a mother."

"I'll pray for you." Abigail realized how serious she was about the trite-sounding phrase. "Pray for a safe pregnancy and delivery."

"*Danke.*" Eva took a deep breath and the smile flickered back on her face as she started walking again toward the house. "Don't tell anyone yet that I'm expecting, okay? I want to get a bit further along, at least until I'm showing."

"Don't worry, I won't." Abigail reached for the basket Eva was carrying. "But meanwhile I'll carry both baskets. I don't want you stressing yourself."

Eva chuckled and held the basket out of reach. "I have two active children. I'm always running around and carrying things. I think I can carry some baked goods. Now, how is the clinic going?"

Abigail walked toward the house and told her friend about the clinic's development. Once indoors, she unpacked the hampers amid the chattering women and felt a flush of warmth to be back within the camaraderie of the community.

She and Eva worked side by side, setting up tables and chairs, and laying out food and beverages while the din of hammers and saws dominated the barn-building area. She paused to watch. Benjamin stood braced with a pole in his arms, joining the other men to keep the first wall in place while the second wall was lifted to join it. She took a moment to appreciate the muscles in his arms as he strained to hold up the pole.

Eva came to stand beside her, watching the activity. "It should be a nice large barn," she observed.

"I've missed barn raisings," Abigail replied. "It's like the Bible verse says—one body with many parts, and each part has a different function, but together it makes a unified whole. Building a barn is almost like a dance, watching it all come together." Her gaze lingered on Benjamin. His shirt was already damp with sweat, and he joked and chatted with the men nearby. "But sometimes I feel like an outsider."

"There's Daniel." Eva pointed. "He's helping lift the second wall into place. How can you feel like an outsider? That's what you're doing with your veterinarian skills, aren't you? Contributing to the unified whole. Same with Benjamin, ain't so? He's using his skills to organize the Mountain Days demonstration."

"Reluctantly, *ja*."

"Reluctant or not, he seems to be doing a *gut* job. I've heard a number of people talking about how they can make their particular demos more interesting and interactive. I think people are pretty excited about it, to be honest."

"That's *gut* to hear!"

With the second wall in place and secured, she saw Benjamin remove his pole and begin working on a cross girt. Abigail turned back to help the other woman with lunch preparations. Walking next to Eva, she noticed an *Englisch* man pull up in a car and exit the vehicle. He walked over toward where the men were working and stood, watching. He seemed very much out of place in his plaid shirt, blue jeans and cowboy hat.

"Look." She pointed. "Who's that?"

Released from bracing the pole, Benjamin fished a handkerchief out of his pocket and mopped his face. Then he slipped his favorite hammer out of the loop on his tool belt and prepared to work on the cross girts.

Then he noticed the *Englisch* visitor, looking as out of place as a petunia in an onion patch. Benjamin suppressed a sigh. The man was none other than Jonathan Turnkey, the liaison for the Mountain Days celebration in the town of Pierce. Benjamin liked the *Englisch* man well enough, but he had work to do.

Slipping his hammer back into the loop on his tool belt, Benjamin strode over and assumed a cheerful demeanor. "Good morning, Jonathan!"

"Good morning." Jonathan shook Benjamin's hand. "I heard a rumor a barn was going up and had to see if for myself."

"*Ja*, this one is for the Herschberger family. We're trying to get a barn built for everyone who needs one before winter."

"A good goal." Jonathan's eyes rested on the activity. "What a pity you couldn't demonstrate something like this for Mountain Days."

Benjamin chuckled. "It would be hard to organize. What would we do with the barn once it was built? It's not like we could leave it in the field at the fairgrounds."

"Well, actually, you probably could. But in that case it would become a public building, and if it's not built exactly to code, all the bureaucrats would have a fit."

"So bureaucrats plague you, too?"

"Oh, yeah. They plague everyone." Jonathan gestured toward the activity. "I know there's a lot to do before sunset, but can you show me around?"

For the briefest moment Benjamin thought about refusing. The man was right—they had a lot to do before sunset, and taking the time to show an *Englisch* visitor around would only slow things down. But Benjamin knew the goodwill of the church and the success of the demonstrations hinged to some degree upon Jonathan, and he changed his mind.

"*Ja*, sure," he said. "But you'll excuse me if I don't take long? Every pair of hands is needed."

Some of the men working on the structure gave Jonathan wary nods as Benjamin walked him around, but Benjamin was careful not to let him engage anyone in conversation and slow down the work. And he blessed the man for not pulling out a camera to document everything, which was increasingly common in encounters with the *Englisch* in town.

Instead he discussed the method of barn construction used by the church community. "This technique was used in pre-industrial America," he told Jonathan. "The skeletal sides you see are called 'bents.' We make them ahead of time, constructing them where they lay.

We lift them into place using ropes and poles, then use cross girts as horizontal framing members connecting the end posts beneath the roof plate."

He walked slowly with Jonathan, pointing out how the horizontal tie beams would be connected between the feet of each pair of rafters in the roof structure, and then fastened to the end posts below the roof plate. "We build temporary scaffolding and lay it across the horizontal beams so we can work at higher elevations."

"No premade trusses," observed Jonathan.

Benjamin lifted his eyebrows. "You sound like you know construction."

"Of course. My dad worked in construction all his life."

Benjamin smiled. "Then we speak the same language. You're right, we don't use premade trusses, which are often required by code. But our barns are sturdy and well-made, and will last for generations." He noticed a flurry of activity at another of the bents lying on the ground. "I'm needed to help lift the next side into place. I'm sure the bishop won't mind if you stay and watch."

Jonathan nodded. "Thank you, I will. And I promise to keep out of the way."

With a smile, Benjamin rejoined the men and prepared to help lift the third wall of the barn into place.

But he was more self-conscious than before, aware of a strange pair of eyes upon the scene. From the more subdued chatter of the men, he knew they were also more self-conscious.

He knew many townspeople were interested in how the church community did things. But the church did things the way they did because it was traditional, not because it was quaint. They didn't do it to show off. That would be *hochmut*.

Yet here, in what should have been an ordinary barn raising, he suddenly felt like they were showing off for the *Englisch* observer. It was an uncomfortable feeling, like being an exhibit in a zoo. Still, if the bishop didn't have an issue with it, neither could he.

By lunchtime, he was ready for food and a break. The women had set up tables under the shade of trees. Jonathan had fallen into conversation with some of the grandfathers whose bodies were too old to work construction, but who had come to the event for the social opportunities. The older men sat in chairs, canes clasped in front of them, and chatted amiably with the visitor. Benjamin felt grateful to the graybeards.

"Who is that?"

He glanced over and saw Abigail, a covered casserole dish in her hands. She had a sheen of sweat on her forehead from working in the hot kitchen. She jerked her head toward Jonathan.

"His name is Jonathan Turnkey," he told her. "He's my liaison with the town's Mountain Days event. He'd heard we were having a barn raising and came to see what it was all about."

"You don't like him?" Her voice held a note of surprise.

"*Nein*, I like him just fine. But it kind of changed the atmosphere among the men when he showed up. Everyone became a bit more self-conscious, I noticed."

"*Ja*, I understand that." She pushed a wisp of hair away from her eyes. "I was always being watched, especially when doing farm calls. A lot of people don't think women can make *gut* livestock vets, especially a small woman like me. I was always being judged while on the job." She placed the casserole dish on a table and wiped her hands and then her forehead with her apron. "How long is he staying? Will he be joining us for lunch?"

"I don't know…"

"Well, he's welcome if he wants to stay."

He looked at her in some amazement. "You really don't mind, do you?"

"Mind what?"

"Having an *Englischer* join us for lunch at a barn raising."

"*Nein*. Why should I?" Her expression altered a bit as she looked at him. "Benjamin, don't forget—I spent ten years living and working as an *Englisch* woman. I like them. And you said you liked this Jonathan Turnkey, *ja*? So go ask if he's staying for lunch."

"I wonder if I'll ever develop your easiness," he mused. "You're like a chameleon. Very adaptable."

She chuckled. "You might say I went through two schools when I left the community—veterinarian school, and the school of hard knocks. I had to learn to be *Englisch* in a hurry, and I found it wasn't so bad."

"And now that you're back, have you decided which world you want to live in?"

Her serene expression disappeared and a scowl took its place. "*Nein*. And don't push me, Benjamin. I'm not ready to make up my mind yet."

"As you say." He turned to look over at Jonathan, who seemed perfectly at ease among the graybeards. "Well, I suppose I'll go ask if he wants to stay for lunch."

He watched as Abigail walked back toward the chattering women, admiring her figure, then grinned to himself. He liked her spunk.

Feeling better about Jonathan's presence, he went to talk to the *Englisch* man.

Chapter Ten

When Abigail went to remove Lydia's cast three weeks later, she found Benjamin in an unusually jubilant mood.

"Guess what!" he sang as she approached his front porch, with her vet tools in hand. "I was able to convince Luke Fisher to demonstrate grain grinding at the Mountain Days demo next week!"

Abigail smiled. "You've been wanting that for a long time. What convinced him?"

"I suspect his wife, but I was too smart to ask." He gave her a triumphant grin that nearly buckled her knees. "That's the last member of the church community I'm going to ask. We have so many demos, we could practically have our own stand-alone fair."

"I like how the bishop took your idea and turned the last 'barn raising' into a 'booth raising,'" she observed. "Now it seems everyone will have a handsome place to demonstrate their skills and sell their wares. You said you're going to have a whole booth for your furniture?"

"*Ja*, and I've half built some chairs and a table so I can show people how it's done. I'm also having order forms printed up in case someone wants to place an order."

"*Mamm* has been joining the other women for the last week sewing up bunting and banners to make everything look colorful and welcoming. She mentioned she was making bunting for your booth."

"That's *gut* of her. It's like the whole church is throwing itself into this with a lot more enthusiasm now."

Abigail noticed how his dark blue eyes twinkled, and the dimples that bracketed his mouth were showing more often. She had been thinking about those dimples a great deal lately, especially after that night when the puppies were born. Their kiss still lingered in her mind.

She pulled her thoughts together. "You, too," she told him. "You seem to be enjoying yourself?"

"*Ja.*" His grin faded into a thoughtful expression. "I guess I am. It's nice to see it all coming together. Are you still interested in helping set things up next week?"

"*Ja*, of course. I wouldn't miss it for anything."

"Then I may ask if you could work in my booth. I'll be doing a chair-making demo and have some pieces for sale, as well as forms for orders. But I'll also be acting as the information booth, so having an extra person to answer visitors' questions would be helpful."

Abigail's heart leaped at the thought of spending the whole day in Benjamin's company. "Of course. In fact, I'm probably your best bet for answering questions since I have both the *Englisch* and the Amish perspective. How's business?" she added, knowing he had been concerned about his finances.

Benjamin grimaced. "Slow. That's why I'm hoping the fair will give me more exposure and bring in orders.

If it doesn't, I'll have to go to work for someone this fall. I prefer to work for myself, but…" His voice trailed off.

Abigail knew by now how much he valued his independence. "You're so skilled," she assured him. "I can't imagine you'd have a problem finding a job."

"I know you're right. I just like working at my own pace, in my own shop. Sometimes I wonder…"

"Wonder what?" she prompted as he gazed into the middle distance.

He snapped back to the present. "Sometimes I wonder if I shouldn't have migrated out here. My business was thriving in Indiana. Here, it takes time to build up customers. I'm bringing in some income by providing dairy products to the Yoders' store, but since dairy farming isn't my full-time job, the income isn't enough to keep me going. I may be pinning too much hope on how much of a jump start this demonstration may give me." He sighed. "Sometimes I think I should give up woodworking altogether and stick to cows."

"I'm not a financial expert," warned Abigail. "But diversifying your income seems smart to me. You have both the cows and the furniture business. When one is slow, you can ramp the other up, and vice versa."

"You're right." Benjamin scrubbed a hand over his face, then quirked a lopsided smile at her. "I'm sorry, I didn't mean to dump my worries on you."

"That's what friends are for, ain't so?" Abigail smiled back. "Meanwhile, let's see how Lydia's getting along."

The magnificent white dog thumped her tail when Abigail approached, and seemed only too happy to escape the closet with her litter of puppies, still all adorned with a rainbow of ribbons around their necks. The babies' eyes were open and they were moving around on their feet, comically unsteady. Abigail grinned at her favorite little animal, the youngest puppy whose life she had saved.

"Time enough to cuddle him later," she murmured, before turning her attention to the mother.

It took some time to remove the cast using the battery-powered cast saw and cast-spreader tool, and Lydia remained placid throughout. "I've never seen such a calm dog," she remarked to Benjamin, who sat on the floor with his pet's head on his lap. "It's like she knows her ordeal is over."

"They're smart, these Pyrenees," he remarked. He stroked Lydia's thick ruff. "She's never fought you during everything you've done for her."

"How easy are these dogs to train?" She worked her way through the cast.

"It depends on what you mean by 'train,'" he replied. "If you mean the usual 'sit, stay, come, roll over' that people teach their dogs, they're terrible. Pyrenees are bred for independent thinking, not mindless obedience. But they can work cooperatively and protect entire flocks of any livestock you put in their care."

"Impressive." She noticed how Lydia watched the process taking place with her leg with stoic interest but no panic. "Then maybe she *does* know her ordeal is over."

Abigail finally was able to peel back the halves of the hard casing around Lydia's leg, and she began removing the padding. "This is going to feel *so* much better," she crooned to the dog. "You've been such a *gut* girl, not chewing on your cast even without a cone on."

At last the animal's leg was free of the obstruction. Lydia leaned down and sniffed at the shaved skin that had been covered up for so many weeks. Then she rolled to her feet and took a tentative step. Then another. Then another. Then she turned, walked up to Abigail and gave her a kiss.

Abigail's heart melted at the dog's gesture. She pulled the animal toward her by her ruff and pressed her forehead to the dog's forehead. For a moment she felt a communion with the animal before the canine pulled away and returned to the closet to attend to her puppies.

"That was amazing," breathed Benjamin.

"What?" She looked over to see him staring at her.

"I've never seen her behave that way toward anyone. It's like she was thanking you."

"Well, you're the one who said they're smart dogs."

"*Ja.* Maybe I didn't realize just *how* smart."

"Time for me to see my favorite puppy." Abigail reached into the closet and fished out the ribbonless male. "Goodness, he gets cuter every time I see him."

"You should give him a name."

"Why?" With sudden dismay, Abigail put the puppy down, and he wobbled back toward his mother. "A name implies permanence, and I'm not here permanently."

Why did she see a small tug of amusement at the corners of Benjamin's mouth? "Well, regardless, I can't thank you enough for your care of Lydia. Look at her! Except for the shaved fur on her leg, you'd never know it was broken."

"*Gut.*" Abigail repacked her veterinary supplies. "Well, I'm off. *Mamm* is hosting a sewing circle again this afternoon to work on bunting, though I think that's just an excuse to have some women over to visit."

Abigail walked back to her mother's cabin, thinking about Lydia and the puppies…and their owner. Lately

Benjamin was becoming far too easy to talk to and work with. He was a comfortable man. A handsome man. Despite his financial concerns, he seemed to be more at peace lately. Maybe the bishop was right to give Benjamin this task, perhaps knowing it might help him expand his business. The bishop was a wise man.

She scowled at the ground. Wise, yes. But the church leader was still implacable when it came to her own future. She knew she had to choose: whether to remain a vet and leave her church, or abandon her career and stay.

Her mother was approaching the point where she could live independently again. Soon Abigail would have to make up her mind about whether to stay or leave.

"*Gott,* show me Your will," she prayed in what was becoming an alarmingly frequent petition. So far her prayers had not been answered.

Back in the cabin, Abigail packed away her vet supplies, gave the house a quick dusting and set out a series of folding chairs. Her *mamm* had made some blueberry cheesecake tarts, which were now chilling in the icebox.

Abigail snitched one of the treats. "Do you sell these at the Yoders' store?" she asked, her mouth filled with the sweet creamy taste.

"*Ja.* They're quite popular."

Abigail swallowed. "I can see why. You always were the best pastry chef, *Mamm.*"

Esther's face creased into a grin. "You always did have a sweet tooth, *liebling.*"

Impulsively Abigail leaned down and kissed her mother on the cheek. "For sure and certain, it's been nice spending time with you."

A knock at the door interrupted the sentimental moment. Abigail answered, and within a few minutes the house was swarming with smiling, chattering women, their arms full of colorful fabrics.

Esther held court from her favorite chair, and Abigail served iced tea and the tarts. But the women had come to sew, and after the treats were finished, they settled in with needles and thread.

"I'm going to wrap these around the booth poles," said one woman, holding up her solid green fabric. "I have yellow and blue swags as well, so that will catch the eye."

"Do you think I should wrap my poles, too?" asked another woman. "I was going to have skirting on the tables, and wrapping poles in fabric might be too much."

Listening to the discussions, Abigail smiled. Most of the women had never displayed anything. The Amish stricture against pride—*hochmut*—was so ingrained, it was challenging to step outside their comfort zone and think in terms of what would attract the eyes of visitors…especially *Englisch* visitors.

While many of the church women had their own smaller booths for demonstration and sales, a large number were participating in a demo of one of their best-known skills, quilt-making. Benjamin had recommended at least three large quilting frames, and Esther had volunteered to act as spokeswoman, explaining to visitors how hand-quilting was done as a team project and how the designs were created.

Abigail herself—having no particular skill worth demonstrating—kept her plan to work the information side of Benjamin's booth.

The Friday before the Mountain Days festival dawned warm and lovely. Benjamin rose early, full of nervous energy. Today, nearly the entire church community would join him in setting up the demonstration area. Tomorrow was the event itself. After so many months of planning, it was hard to believe the moment was finally here.

He made sure Lydia and her puppies had plenty of fresh food and water as well as outdoor access, since he would be gone most of the day. He smiled at the wobbly male puppy Abigail adored. He hoped that, someday, she would accept the gift of the puppy to have as her own.

After loading his wagon full of tools, he swung into the seat, clucked to the horse and drove toward Abigail's cabin to pick her up.

She was waiting for him, a hamper of lunch in hand. *"Guder mariye,"* she said as she climbed into the seat next to him. "Nervous?"

"How did you know?" He gave her a grin as he directed the horse toward town. "I hardly slept last night."

"It will be all over tomorrow afternoon. Meanwhile you've worked so hard, planning every last detail, I can't possibly see how it can fail."

"I hope you're right."

He was mostly silent as they clip-clopped toward the outskirts of Pierce, where the fairgrounds were located. He thought he would arrive before anyone else, but to his surprise the bishop and two other families were already there, measuring out their designated demonstration area. Additionally, a slew of *Englisch* townspeople were swarming over the fairgrounds setting up carnival rides and finalizing the display halls for photography, artwork and garden produce.

"Guder mariye!" he called to the bishop. He pulled

the horse to a stop and jumped out. "I've got stakes and ribbons for marking booth locations."

"Ja, gut," Bishop Beiler replied. *"Guder mariye,* Abigail. Are you helping set up?"

"Ja." She climbed down from the wagon and said no more.

The day passed quickly. Benjamin consulted with Jonathan Turnkey, the event coordinator, to make sure the demonstration area was being set up correctly, but after that the Amish were mostly left to themselves.

More and more families arrived, and the air soon rang with sounds of hammers and chatter. Benjamin noticed how the men concentrated on putting up the infrastructure, but it was the women who gave the spaces touches of home. Beyond bunting and banners and flagging, he saw tablecloths, baskets and other domestic props.

Small groups of townspeople setting up their own displays often wandered through to see what the Amish group was doing. Benjamin noticed a lot of intergroup chatting as both Amish and *Englisch* became acquainted with each other. He heard lots of laughter.

At noon, people broke for lunch, spreading quilts on the grass and opening hampers of cold chicken and macaroni salad. Abigail sat with Eva Hostetler and her family while he found himself seated with the bishop.

"Benjamin, this is turning out very well," the bishop said, biting into a chicken leg. "I must say, you've done an excellent job."

The rare praise made Benjamin pause. He hardly knew what to say, but finally settled on a simple response. *"Danke."* Then honesty prompted him to add, "I'll be glad when it's over."

"*Ja*, me, too. But this should establish us as strong partners with the *Englisch* in town. We took for granted the ties we had in Indiana, but here, we're starting out new. No longer will we be seen as standoffish or remote. We can be seen as neighborly and helpful. Cooperative."

"I suppose. The best part is, as always, the camaraderie of working with the whole church community on a common goal."

The bishop laid down his chicken leg. "And you, Benjamin. Has working on this project helped you overcome your aversion to the *Englisch*?"

"So that *is* the reason you gave me this assignment." He quirked a smile at his church leader.

"*Ja*, of course." The older man spoke as if the conclusion was obvious. "You were eaten up with bitterness inside over decisions made by other people. You were blaming those who were blameless. I hoped this would help."

"I won't say I'm cured, but I suppose this project helped." Never would he admit the biggest reason behind the shift in his attitude was Abigail.

Petite little Abigail, now sitting and chatting so demurely with Eva, had changed his mind about many things. He knew he was pinning hopes on a future with her, but he also knew he didn't dare tell her until such time as she had made up her mind about what she wanted to do.

Benjamin was a patient man. He would wait.

Work resumed after lunch. By the time the evening shadows loomed over the fairgrounds, the demo area was finished—booths had been set up, display areas were cordoned off and temporary corrals were enclosed.

Each stand had a sign politely asking visitors to refrain from photography, though he knew that request was likely to be ignored.

He called the group together before departing. "Those of you bringing animals will need to be here especially early," he said. "All buggies and wagons should be parked there—" He pointed toward a roped-off area. "All horses, except the draft horses, can be let loose in that field. It has plenty of shade and I'll make sure the water tubs stay full. Those bringing draft horses and milk cows already have your areas set up."

He continued giving instructions and receiving input, and within half an hour everyone seemed satisfied.

"Okay, let's go home," he concluded. "We have a long day ahead of us tomorrow."

As he hitched up his horse to the wagon, Abigail joined him. She was smiling, and it was hard to admit the leap within him at her dancing brown eyes.

"This is going to go very, very well," she said as she climbed onto the wagon seat.

"I hope so. I alternate between elation and despair. Elation, because everyone seems enthusiastic. Despair, because it's something I've never done before, and this is—to borrow a phrase from the *Englisch*—where the rubber meets the road." He climbed up beside her and clucked to the horse.

"You've been obsessing over every detail for so long that I can't imagine there's anything you've overlooked," she assured him. "Relax, Benjamin. You might be in charge, but it's very much a group project. Everyone can work at setting up his own booth space or demonstration area. And the people in town have been so kind and helpful."

"Yes they have," he admitted. "I'll admit, it was enjoyable watching the fair staff mingle with the church participants. Everyone seemed to get along."

"It will go well, Benjamin. Don't worry."

"I appreciate that you'll be helping answer questions in my booth tomorrow."

"It works out perfectly since I don't have any special skills I could demonstrate."

He laughed out loud at that. "No special skills? Except for setting broken bones on dogs or stitching up cow udders or helping a pig farrow."

She chuckled. "Maybe, but I can hardly demonstrate that to a crowd, can I? No, as far as everyone is concerned, tomorrow I'm not a vet. I'm just a church member, that's all."

Back home that evening, Abigail helped her mother wash dishes. "I think everything is packed for tomorrow," she told Esther. "You sure you don't mind if I'm in the information booth instead of with the quilters?"

"*Ja*, sure. I'll just send all the nosiest people toward you." Esther chuckled. "Unlike you, I'm not so easy with the *Englisch* that I could spend all day answering questions. But as the bishop said, I'm looking at tomorrow as an educational opportunity. Not many people in Montana know about our church."

"I think you'll be surprised how much interest there will be," Abigail replied. "Just get used to the fact that a lot of people will ignore the No Photography signs."

Esther pointed to a large duffel bag near the door. "Why are you bringing so many veterinarian supplies?"

"Just as a precaution." Abigail dried a dish. "With so many farm animals at the demo, it's wise to be ready.

I'll keep the bag in the information booth. Benjamin's nervous," she added. "I think that's half the reason he wants me in the booth to answer questions. I told him I had more experience dealing with the *Englisch* and their questions, so it might calm him down if I was there."

Esther paused in her work and looked at Abigail. "You like him, don't you?"

"Ja." Abigail knew exactly what her mother was asking. She rinsed a dish. "I suppose I do. But it makes no difference. The bishop made it clear what my choices are. I'm not ready to give up the gift *Gott* gave me, *Mamm.* The gift of working with animals. Since that means I won't be allowed to be baptized into the church, it would be cruel to toy with Benjamin's affections. I won't do it."

Esther sighed. "I was hoping to see my youngest child settled someday…"

"Mamm." Abigail allowed a ghost of a smile to cross her face. "Your youngest child hasn't been settled since she was eight years old. It's a different lifestyle I've chosen, but it's not a bad one."

"Perhaps not. But I don't see you as happy, *liebling.* I think that's what worries me. When you came back from your work as a vet in Indiana, you looked shell-shocked somehow. Maybe the work was too hard, I don't know. All I know is you've blossomed since you came here."

Abigail knew she had been troubled because of her terminated romantic interest in Robert, her boss. But Esther didn't know about that…and hopefully never would.

She handed her mother the last dish for drying. "We'd best get an early night. Benjamin is picking us up at the crack of dawn. I hope I can sleep tonight. I think I've picked up on some of Benjamin's nervous energy."

"Everything will go well," Esther predicted. "What could possibly go wrong?"

Chapter Eleven

The day of the town celebration dawned bright and clear. The weather promised to be warm, but not hot.

"What a gift," Benjamin called out as he helped Esther onto the wagon seat. "I know everyone in town was hoping that the weather would hold."

"Did you get any sleep last night at all?" teased Abigail, swinging her bag of veterinarian supplies into the back of the wagon.

"Not a whole lot," he admitted. "I kept imagining a raft of things that could go wrong."

With Esther occupying the more comfortable wagon seat, Abigail climbed into the wagon box and seated herself on a pile of feed sacks. "Just remember, the bulk of your work is done. At this point, everyone participating is responsible for his own demonstration."

"I know. It's just that I feel…" He gestured. "Accountable."

"There's no Sabbath service tomorrow," she told him. "It's an off-Sunday, so you can sleep until noon if you like."

"And I might just do that. Look." He pointed. "We're not the only ones getting an early start."

In fact, as they made their way toward town, Abigail noted quite a number of wagons heading in the same direction. She saw three separate farmers walking, leading well-brushed Jersey milk cows for the milking demonstration. She saw another two sets of men with bridles of draft horses in hand, leading the massive equines for the plowing demonstration. The animals' coats gleamed.

"Is there anyone *not* participating?" she wondered out loud. "I mean, seriously, even if a church member doesn't have a specific skill to demonstrate, it looks like everyone's showing up simply for support." Her heart swelled at the thought.

"I honestly can't think of anyone who wanted to be left behind." Benjamin lifted an arm to wave at someone. "Like you, Esther—even the older crowd is coming to join with quilting or cooking or to keep an eye on the kids or something."

"I know it's *hochmut* to admit, but it makes me proud to be part of this group." Abigail spoke quietly. "I grew up taking for granted the number of everyday skills and talents within the community. It wasn't until I left to go to school that I realized how fascinated the wider world is in those skills. I have a feeling today is going to be very popular."

By the time the fair had officially opened and the first wave of *Ensglisch* visitors strolled through, the Amish demonstration section was fully staffed and underway. Many people had wares for sale, and sales were brisk. But the skills on display—basket weaving, butter churning, quilting, leather working and endless other occupations—were popular beyond words.

As the day went on, the crowds grew thick. Very thick.

In one large field, two sets of draft horses were fully harnessed and resting in the shade of large pine trees. Once an hour, the farmers hitched them to a cultivator and showed viewers how they directed the massive teams of horses across the fields.

In another area, four placid dairy cows with doe eyes and fawn-colored fur were on display. People were invited to sit down on the stools and learn how to milk them.

Under the shade of three separate canopies, quilting frames had been set up, and a large number of women were grouped around, sewing busily, answering questions to curious onlookers. Quite a few *Englisch* women were allowed to join in, with neighboring Amish women showing them how to guide the needle through the top of the fabric with their dominant hand and redirect it from below with their nondominant hand. Meanwhile dozens of colorful quilts were displayed for sale.

Two women who were expert basket weavers showed interested visitors what kinds of materials they used and how they prepped them for working. Children and adults alike were invited to try their hand at manipulating the softened branches and other materials into the beginnings of baskets. Finished baskets sold briskly.

The leather workers had brought along hides in various stages of completion, and Eva's father, Eli, showed how he fashioned bridles and reins from the finished pieces, riveting the leather and making the ribbons supple.

In each demonstration area, a prominent sign discouraged photography, but a large number of people ignored the suggestion and recorded the church members at work. The bishop had already warned the church members of this likelihood, and advised them to gracefully ignore the actions.

Benjamin's booth featured two signs—one for his furniture, the other for visitor information. Abigail, stationed on the information side, answered questions almost nonstop. She was gratified to see a great deal of interest in Benjamin's construction techniques, and saw more than one person fill in a form for a future order.

But it wasn't until afternoon when things took a turn for Benjamin. Esther left her post with the quilters and hobbled over on the arm of an unknown Amish man of about her age, trailed by another *Englisch* man who had the look of a businessman about him.

"*Mamm*, are you okay?" asked Abigail in some alarm.

"*Ja*, I'm fine." The older woman had some high color in her cheeks. "This is Mark Beiler, the bishop's brother, who's visiting from Indiana. Mark, this is my youngest daughter, Abigail."

A bit confused, Abigail shook the older man's hand and greeted him politely.

Esther then turned to the *Englisch* man. "Mark wanted us to meet this gentleman, Greg—Greg... I'm sorry, what did you say your last name was?"

The *Englisch* man stepped forward. "Greg Anderson, ma'am." He shook Abigail's hand. "I own a large construction firm specializing in log homes. I have a branch office in Indiana, which is how I know Mark. Your mother suggested I might be interested in the furniture made by this young man." He tilted his head at

Benjamin, who was involved with a customer and barely noticed the new arrivals.

"He's busy at the moment, as you can see," Abigail replied, "but if you'll have a seat, I'm sure he'd be very interested in talking with you. In fact, you'll be able to sample how comfortable his chairs are." She gestured toward one of Benjamin's specialty rocking chairs.

Esther turned. "I'll head back to the quilters now."

With Mark Beiler solicitously at her elbow, Abigail watched in some bemusement as her mother limped away.

Her attention was diverted by several *Englisch* women, who descended *en masse* on the booth with questions, but she was aware of Benjamin behind her, greeting the newcomer. He showed the visitor the variety of furniture he made, and the man flipped through a photo catalog of the various pieces that Benjamin specialized in. But she was so occupied that she couldn't catch much of what was being said until Mr. Anderson walked away, clutching a catalog and a business card.

For a few more busy minutes, the booth was swamped with visitors. Benjamin joined her in answering questions. People were genuinely eager to know more about the Amish lifestyle, how they'd ended up in Montana and the specific skills being demonstrated.

And then, as if from some hidden signal, the crowds around the booth dissipated as people wandered in different directions, and she and Benjamin had a rare moment of peace.

"Whew." She slumped against the booth's side and gulped some water. "I never expected it to be this busy."

"Did you hear what happened with Greg Anderson?"

Benjamin's smile was broad, and he nearly quivered with happiness.

"No, what happened?"

"He wants a standing order of furniture!" he burst out. "He owns a huge log-home business with branch offices in many states, and he likes my furniture so much he wants to showcase it in many of his display homes. He said that could amount to hundreds of pieces of furniture!" Abigail gasped when he suddenly swept her up in a hug and spun her around.

She laughed from the pure joy of being in his arms before remembering they were in public. She stepped back and returned his grin. "I'm so glad for you! *Gott ist gut!*"

"*Ja,* and when..."

He broke off as screams could be heard from one of the nearby fields. He jerked around and stared. Abigail heard dog growls mingled with cries of horror.

Instinctively she reached for her duffel bag of veterinarian supplies when a teenage Amish boy ran up to the booth. "Abigail!" he gasped. "A dog—it's attacked one of the dairy cows. There's blood. Can you come?"

"*Ja.*" She jerked the duffel strap over her shoulder and raced after the teen. She feared the worst. She'd seen cows savaged by dogs before, and it would haunt her if she had to put a beautiful milk animal down, and in front of a crowd, too.

A circle of people, both *Englisch* and Amish, pressed around the milking demonstration area. One of the beautiful Jerseys stood trembling and injured. The owner, a man named Ephraim King, stood at the cow's head, holding her halter and trying to soothe the injured animal. An *Englisch* woman crouched at the edge of the demo area, weeping in remorse, her arms around the large dog that had savaged the cow.

"I'm so sorry," she gabbled. "He's never seen a cow before. He just broke away from me. I'm so sorry, I'm so sorry…"

Abigail pushed her way to the front of the crowd and kneeled before the cow. "Hold her halter tight," she told Ephraim. He nodded and regripped the lead rope.

She dropped her duffel and unzipped it until she found some antibacterial wipes, which she used to wipe the wound clean. The first thing she had to do was see how injured the animal was. The onlookers fell into a respectful silence as she worked.

She could feel the cow tremble beneath her hands. She saw teeth marks, and a rip in the cow's tough skin about four inches long.

"Quite a dog," she muttered. While she sympathized with the visitor for losing control of her animal, she would recommend a muzzle for her dog while in public. Better to have a cow savaged than a child.

"It's not as bad as I thought," she told Ephraim. "I'm going to stitch her up."

He nodded. "Do whatever you can."

Abigail worked quickly. She carefully anesthetized the cow's flank where she intended to suture. Then she rummaged in her duffel bag for sutures and a needle.

It took half an hour of careful stitching to get the cow sewn up. During that time, crowds wandered in and out, though many stayed to watch. Ephraim remained unmoving by the cow's head, stoically holding the animal's halter and keeping her calm. The woman with the dog stayed on the sideline, hiccuping once in a while, but otherwise not moving. Abigail was barely aware of her surroundings. Her entire focus was on repairing the animal in front of her.

At last Abigail felt satisfied over her handiwork. She gave the cow a shot of antibiotics as a final precaution, then stood back. As often happened when helping an injured animal, she felt a warm glow inside her, a confirmation that her skills were from *Gott* and not something to be taken lightly.

She put her supplies back in the duffel bag and turned to speak to Ephraim. However, the farmer jerked his head toward something behind her, a meaningful expression in his eyes.

Abigail whirled. She had been so involved she hardly considered the ebb and flow of people around her, but now she realized one person had been standing nearby the whole time. A man, obviously a photographer since he was armed with elaborate equipment, had clearly been taking pictures of her as she worked.

She thinned her lips. "May I help you?" she asked.

"Just wondering how an Amish woman can do what you're doing. I thought they sewed quilts, not cows."

She bit back an uncharitable retort and instead quipped, "Don't underestimate us. They're actually quite similar."

She was gratified to see a flare of uncertainty in his eyes before he gave her a vague smile. "Right," he said. He held up his camera. "I hope you don't mind that I photographed you."

Silently she thumbed toward the obvious signage over the booth requesting no photography.

"Oh." Again he looked crestfallen. "Sorry," he muttered.

She relented. "I should explain I'm a licensed veterinarian," she admitted. "I'm just here visiting."

He eyed her *kapp.* "Then you're not Amish?"

She clamped down on a quiver of uncertainty. "I was born and raised Amish."

"I've never met an Amish veterinarian before. Actually, I haven't met any Amish at all." He reached into a pocket and withdrew a business card. "My name is Charles Young. I'm a reporter from Billings. I heard there were Amish demonstrations here in Pierce and decided it was worth an article. I'd like to interview you, at your convenience."

Abigail took the card and glanced at it. The one overwhelming thought in her mind was the bishop's warning about influencing other church members to pursue a worldly degree. She was also keenly aware that an interview in a newspaper was little more than pride. *Hochmut.* It was an impossible request.

"I'm sorry, Mr. Young." She handed him back his business card. "I prefer not to be interviewed."

He blinked in what seemed like sheer surprise. "Th-that's a first," he stuttered. "Most people would jump at the chance to be in the newspaper."

"You said you've never met any Amish before?" she asked.

"That's right…"

"Then one of the first things you'll learn about us is we don't care for publicity. We agreed to this demonstration—" she waved a hand across the whole area "—merely as Amish appreciation and awareness for the town of Pierce, which is our new home. That's all."

"But—but that's what an interview would do!" the

man argued. "It would help people understand the Amish!"

"Please, Mr. Young, I have a cow to attend to." She reached down and picked up her duffel bag of supplies. "May I direct your attention to our bishop? He can address the issue of an interview. Not me."

"I see." Mr. Young pocketed his card. "Where would I find him?"

"Do you see that booth?" She started to point toward Benjamin's booth, then realized it was empty. Instead, Benjamin was lurking on the edge of the crowd, obviously listening. She nodded toward him. "This gentleman can help you find our bishop."

As if on cue, Benjamin walked forward. "*Ja*, I can. Will you come with me?"

She exhaled a deep breath as Benjamin escorted the reporter away. She turned to Ephraim, who quirked an amused eyebrow at her. "Persistent" was all he said.

"*Ja*." She looked at the cow. "She'll be fine, Ephraim. She might be off her milk for a day or two, and you might keep her inside the barn tomorrow. I'll be by in about a week to remove the stitches."

"*Vielen Dank*, Abigail. This could have been so much worse."

"I agree. Meanwhile, I'll go talk to the woman whose dog attacked. If nothing else, it needs to wear a muzzle. Can I leave my duffel bag here?"

"*Ja*, of course."

Abigail tucked the bag into a corner, then turned to find the dog's owner.

The woman had retreated to a nearby bench and was tightly gripping the leash of the dog, a large German shepherd mix. Her face was ravaged from crying.

As Abigail approached, the woman bounced to her feet, and the dog stood up as well. She began babbling apologies, but Abigail held up a hand to silence her and turned her attention to the dog, letting him sniff her. He took his time doing so, since she had traces of blood on her. But at last he permitted her to stroke his head, and even wagged his tail.

The barrier crossed, Abigail gestured to the woman. "Sit down. We need to talk." She seated herself.

The woman dropped bonelessly onto the bench. "I'll pay for all the vet bills, I can't believe he did that…"

"Ma'am, calm down. What's done is done. It's better that he attacked a cow than a child."

"Oh, he'd never attack a child…"

"But you didn't know he would attack a cow, either."

A look of hysteria crossed the woman's face. "You're not suggesting I have him put down?"

"Of course not! He's a beautiful dog." She stroked the canine's head. "But you must understand, this incident has opened you up to a lawsuit. Oh, not from us, don't worry. But any time a dog attacks, it becomes a liability issue."

"You talk like a vet."

"I *am* a vet. I work out of state and I'm just here visiting. But as a vet, I'll need to report this incident to the authorities. That's why I strongly recommend you have your dog wear a muzzle while out in public from now on. With a legal incident filed against him, a muzzle demonstrates you're taking the issue seriously."

"But I said I'd pay for everything…!"

With a touch of irritation, Abigail waved her hand. "There are no costs. I've taken care of the cow, and she'll be fine. Ma'am, please understand it's not a matter of payment, it's a matter of liability."

She'd met pet owners before who simply could not believe—notwithstanding all evidence in front of their very eyes—that their animal was capable of aggression.

Despite her earlier hysteria, anger and denial flooded the woman's features, and she jerked to her feet. "You can't file anything with the authorities if you don't know who I am," she snapped with a look of triumph. "I'm leaving and there's nothing you can do about it."

She snatched at the dog's leash and disappeared into the crowd.

Abigail heard someone come up behind her, and saw Benjamin. She exhaled in frustration. "No matter how much weeping and wailing she does, she refuses to accept responsibility for her dog's behavior. I hope he doesn't do anything worse. Did you help Mr. Young find the bishop?" she added.

"*Ja*, and happily turned the reporter over to let him deal with it. You handled him well, Abigail. Far better than I would have."

She looked at the ground, feeling a girlish quiver at the rare compliment. *"Danke."* Then she raised her eyes to meet his. "You want to know what was going through my head when he said he wanted an interview? My meeting with the bishop. He warned me about influencing *youngies* to leave and get a worldly degree, and I didn't want to be involved in something that might make that come true."

"That was wise thinking." He glanced around. "I'd better get back to my booth."

"I'll go with you. My work is finished here."

* * *

Benjamin was impressed with how Abigail handled herself with the reporter and the dog owner. But even he had to admit, those two were the low points of an otherwise fun and eventful day.

Jonathan Turnkey came by the booth toward evening. "Well, Benjamin," he boomed. "I'd say this whole day has been a rousing success." He reached over to shake his hand. "I'm sorry you won't be here tomorrow, since the fair runs the whole weekend."

Benjamin shook hands. "It's our Sabbath, of course."

"Right. I understand. Things are usually slower in the morning because most people are in church, but everyone will come pouring in afterward. Your demo area would be very popular."

"I realize that, but the bishop would never approve. Jonathan, have you met Abigail Mast? She grew up in our church back in Indiana. She's here for the summer helping her mother recuperate from surgery."

"Nice to meet you." Jonathan shook Abigail's hand, then turned back to him. "I hope you'll consider repeating this demonstration area next year."

"Well…" He hesitated. "It will be up to our bishop. I'm not in a position to make unilateral decisions for the community."

"I hope you'll present the idea to him, then." Jonathan glanced over the thinning crowds as the day wound down. "I think this has worked to your church's benefit, though. People are now aware there's an Amish population near Pierce, and that can help your businesses develop."

"*Ja*, no doubt." Benjamin smiled as Jonathan left.

Then he let out a sigh and slumped into one of his rocking chairs. "I'm so glad today is over."

"You must be pleased it went so well." She dropped into a chair beside him.

"I am. And I'm over the moon about meeting Greg Anderson. Depending on how many orders he places, I may even have to hire someone to work for me. Plus I received four orders from other visitors."

"Benjamin, that's wonderful!"

He smiled at her. "It makes my future more...secure. It's something that interests me a lot more than it used to."

He saw she understood his unspoken meaning because her face shuttered just a bit. But did he also detect a gleam of longing, or was it his imagination?

"Well." He interrupted his own thoughts with an attempt at levity. "I'm glad tomorrow is the Sabbath. I intend to fully enjoy my day off."

Her chuckle seemed a bit forced. "You've earned it. Me, I was invited over to Eva's. It's so nice rediscovering her friendship."

"Eva's a *gut* woman," he agreed. "Very well-liked. And," he added, "I have to admit the *Englisch* are much nicer than I anticipated. A little different, *ja*, but Pierce is a nice town full of nice people."

"Sounds like the place is growing on you at last."

He laughed. "I don't know if I'll ever feel totally at ease with the *Englisch*, but I understand I can't hold someone like Jonathan responsible for why Barbara left ten years ago."

"There are many things to admire in the *Englisch* world." Abigail looked out at members of the community as they began the laborious task of breaking down their displays. "But I like it here."

Benjamin didn't respond to that, though his heart leaped. Instead he looked over toward Ephraim King, whose cow Abigail had helped. Ephraim had moved the animal toward the back, away from the spot where the dog had attacked her. The cow looked more comfortable and was chewing her cud.

"I guess we should help everyone pack down," he said. "There is a lot to do to get home before dark."

Chapter Twelve

The next morning, Abigail noted her mother seemed tired. "It was a bit harder than I thought to be away from home all day," Esther admitted. "Even if I didn't do much more than sit in the quilting area."

"And feel like the proverbial fish in a fishbowl," replied Abigail, setting a cup of tea before her.

"*Ja*, very true. But you know what? I think people liked it. I met the nicest *Englisch* lady who asked if she could try her hand at quilting, and she sat next to me for a bit. She's an expert seamstress and always admired quilting, but had never tried it." The older woman's face glowed with pleasure.

"It was interesting, working at the information booth. By the end of the day, my jaw was tired from talking so much. By the way," she added in a teasing tone, "how did you meet this Mark Beiler, the bishop's brother?"

"Oh." Esther flapped a hand, and spots of color formed in her cheeks. "Lois, the bishop's wife, introduced us."

"Any particular reason?"

"*Nein*. She was introducing him to many people."

Abigail didn't push, but it amused her to see her mother blushing. "I'd best be heading for Eva's. I'm stopping at Ephraim King's place on the way to check on his cow."

"Don't forget to bring her some of those pastries—her *kinner* will enjoy them."

"*Ja*, I'll do that."

Abigail packed a basket of pastries amid some vet supplies and set out for Eva Hostetler's farm.

It was a beautiful, quiet summer morning, as befitted the Sabbath. Abigail smelled the fresh mountain air and wondered if she could ever return to her Indianapolis clinic. It was a thought she kept resolutely pushing to the back of her mind. *Gott* had not yet provided her an answer to her dilemma. She was trying to be patient.

First she made a detour to Ephraim's place. She found the older man and his wife seated in rocking chairs on their porch, reading their Bibles.

"*Guder mariye!*" they called simultaneously when they saw her.

Abigail returned their greeting and stopped at the base of the porch steps. "I'm on my way to visit Eva Hostetler and wanted to see how your cow was doing."

Ephraim rose from his chair. "She is fine, thanks to you. Come and see her."

The cow was lying down and chewing her cud, an excellent sign. Her eyes were calm and alert. She didn't even blink when Abigail looked her over.

"How did she milk this morning?" Abigail asked Ephraim.

"A bit off, as you said she might be, but not bad." He scratched the animal's forehead, and the cow closed her eyes for a moment with enjoyment. "I don't mind keeping her here in the barn for as long as you think it's necessary."

"The wounds are healing nicely. She'll have a bit of scarring, but I'm thankful the damage was to her flank and not her udder. Let me know if you see any change in her condition, including lethargy, but otherwise I think she'll be fine until it's time to remove the stitches."

"Ja, gut."

Abigail left the Kings' farm and continued on the road toward Eva's.

Her old friend sat on the porch with her husband, chatting and sipping lemonade, supervising her two young children playing in the yard. She had started wearing a maternity dress, though her middle was barely thickened. She raised an arm and waved as Abigail approached. *"Guder mariye!"* she called. "You're just in time for lemonade."

"And I've brought some pastries *Mamm* sent," replied Abigail. *"Guder mariye*, Daniel. How are you today?"

Eva's husband was a pleasant-looking man with mild blue eyes and laugh crinkles at the corner of his eyes. His chestnut-brown beard was full, and he had the contented look of a man satisfied with his life.

"I'm fine, *danke*. Glad yesterday is finished, and that today is not a church Sunday." His eyes twinkled. "In fact, if you and Eva would like to visit, I hear a hammock calling my name." He pointed toward some stout netting slung invitingly between two trees.

"Not until you have one of *Mamm*'s pastries." Abigail fished a container out of her bag.

"One of Esther's pastries? You don't have to convince me." Daniel took the delicacy, snatched a napkin off the tray with the lemonade and made his way toward the hammock.

Eva called over her children to take a pastry. The children ate, then dashed back into the yard to play.

Abigail settled into Daniel's chair with a sigh. "*Ach*, yesterday was busy. I'm so glad today is the Sabbath."

Eva chuckled. "I think many people feel that way. I imagine Benjamin is happy it's over and that it went so well."

"I think so, *ja*." Abigail glanced over at her friend. "You look so happy, Eva."

"I am." Eva's gaze rested on the grass, where her children were playing in a sandbox, and where her husband was relaxing in the hammock. "*Gott* has been *gut* to me." Her eyes sharpened. "But what an unusual comment to make out of the blue. Does this mean you're *not* happy?"

"*Nein*, I wouldn't say that. It's just that…" She sighed and left the thought unfinished.

"Are you staying in Montana?" Eva nibbled a pastry.

Abigail felt the full weight of her friend's simple inquiry. "That's the big question." She stared at her glass of lemonade. "I don't know if you heard, but the bishop more or less gave me an ultimatum. I can stay and be baptized, but give up practicing animal medicine. Or I can continue my career but forgo baptism. It's a hard decision, Eva." Without warning, she felt tears prickle her eyes. "I've been trying not to think about it, trying to take direction from *Gott*, but I don't have any clear answers yet."

"So you're in limbo."

"*Ja*, and it's an uncomfortable feeling."

"I can imagine whatever you decide is of prime interest to Benjamin, too."

Startled, Abigail snapped her head up. "What do you mean?"

"It's obvious, isn't it? He wants you to stay."

"*Ja*, but to what end? We have no future, Eva. At least not until I'm settled."

Eva cocked her head. "Is the pull from the *Englisch* world that strong? To leave here and go back to being a vet?"

"*Ja*, at times." Abigail scrubbed a hand over her face. "It's a calling, Eva. That's the only way I can describe it. But why would that put me at odds with the people I grew up with? That's what I don't understand."

"*Mamm! Mamm!*" Eva's little girl, Mildred, came running up. "Did you see the butterfly? It landed right on Jacob's head!"

Eva chuckled at her child's enthusiasm. "Do you think it was *Gott*'s way of giving him a kiss?"

The little girl's eyes grew large. "*Ja!* I'll go tell him!" She dashed down the porch steps and over to her brother.

Abigail followed the child with her eyes. "That's another thing, Eva. The Lord tells us not to covet, but I'm coveting your family. I never thought I'd be in this position, a woman my age with no *kinner*."

"It's not too late, you know. You're no *grossmammi* yet."

"I know…"

"But I must say, the contrast between our different paths in life is remarkable." Eva sipped her lemonade. "I often thought of you out in the *Englisch* world, grap-

pling with your studies. Becoming a veterinarian—
that's a lot of book learning. Do you have any regrets?"

"Sometimes." Abigail gestured toward the children.
"Like right now. But I can't imagine you have any regrets about the path you've chosen?"

"None." A look of contentment startlingly similar
to her husband's crossed Eva's face. "Daniel and I get
along so well, like bread and butter. He's everything I
could hope for in a *hutband*. I try to be everything he
could hope for in a wife."

The simple equation for marital happiness made
Abigail blink hard. The benefits of that equation went
beyond Eva and Daniel. They extended to the children playing in the yard, and the unborn baby inside
Eva. Someday those children would make similar decisions about a spouse, and the blessings would carry
on through future generations.

None of this was unfamiliar to Abigail. Her own
brothers and sisters were happily settled. Her *mamm*
had enjoyed many loving years with her *daed*. It was
only she, Abigail, who had stepped off the familiar path
into the unknown territory, following a *Gott*-given call
toward animal medicine.

But at what price?

She verbalized out loud what Benjamin had asked
her weeks ago. "Is this something I can do ten years
from now?" she wondered. "Or twenty years from now,
when it will be too late to have children?"

Eva looked at her with sympathy in her eyes. "It
comes down to how strong the pull is, I suppose," she
said. "I've never had a calling like that. I've heard they
can be great blessings, but difficult to bear. I just never
expected to see that conflict in action, so to speak."

Abigail nodded. "It's funny. Yesterday after I finished sewing up Ephraim's cow, I felt what I often feel after helping an animal—a warm glow inside me. I've always seen that as a confirmation my skills are not something to be taken lightly. Definitely not something that should be put aside. That's the hard part, Eva. The bishop told me I must put aside my gift to become baptized."

Eva winced. "An impossible decision."

"*Ja.* Out in the *Englisch* world, there is great emphasis on women having careers. But that's not what this is for me. Careers can come and go, careers can change, careers can be put aside while concentrating on something else, such as raising a family. But gifts from *Gott*? Those aren't so easy. Sure, I could put it aside, become baptized and never practice medicine again. But could *you* so easily toss a blessing back into the face of *Gott*?"

Eva shook her head. "Sounds to me this is something you need to discuss with the bishop."

"I tried." She remembered her sour conversation with the church leader. "And failed. He's a *gut* man, the bishop, but he has no understanding how strong my calling is, or why it was given to a woman."

Comprehension dawned in Eva's eyes. "I see. If this were Daniel, or even Benjamin, it wouldn't be nearly as complicated, *ja*? But because you're a woman, the bishop can't understand why you simply can't exchange one job for another—why you can't exchange being a vet with being a mother. Is that it?"

"*Ja*, that's it exactly." Abigail felt relieved Eva understood. "But he's right. Let's say for the sake of argument that I got married and had children. How could I continue being a veterinarian under those conditions?

Being a mother is a full-time job. I couldn't give the task of raising them to someone else. That's my conflict, Eva. I can't do both things at the same time."

Her friend nodded. "It would take a special kind of *hutband* to understand that conflict."

Abigail's first thought, naturally, was whether Benjamin could be that special kind of *hutband*. But it was immaterial whether or not he could accept a wife with outside commitments. The bishop had already made the church's position clear.

Benjamin paced up and down his porch, watched by a patient Lydia, who was taking a break from her puppies. Occasionally he wiped his sweaty palms on his trousers. He'd seen Abigail walk away and knew she was visiting Eva. He just didn't think she would take so long.

With a sigh of irritation—at himself—he dropped into one of the porch rockers that were his specialty to build. Of all the days he wanted to ask Abigail to be his wife, why did he have to choose a day when she would be off visiting people?

He'd thought about this, prayed about it, agitated about it. He knew it was a risky thing, since Abigail wasn't baptized and still felt conflicted about staying.

But maybe he could convince her.

It was that little issue—convincing her—that worried him. He knew she had feelings for him, but were those feelings strong enough to overcome her commitment to animal medicine?

He was seriously thinking about having a heart-to-heart talk with the bishop in hopes the church leader would loosen his strictures against Abigail's career. But he knew what the older man would say: that one exception would soon turn into multiple exceptions, and before long young people would expect to be able to leave the community, do whatever they want, then return and expect no consequences from their behavior.

He absently stroked Lydia's fur while staring blankly across the lawn in front of his cabin. In his mind's eye, he saw the space filled with children and playthings. He was ready for a family...and he knew the woman he hoped would build that family with him.

But if Abigail would not—or could not—be baptized, he couldn't marry her. It was as simple as that. He had already made a lifelong vow to remain with the church during his own baptism. It was not an option to compromise that vow in the interests of marrying an outsider.

He closed his eyes. Despite his best intentions, he'd done it again. He'd fallen in love with a woman with ties to the *Englisch* world, and he knew he risked losing Abigail to that world.

A noise from Lydia caused him to snap open his eyes. The large Pyrenees dog stood up and wagged her tail, staring through the trees at a solitary figure that walked with a basket in her hands.

Benjamin rose to his feet, wiped his hands down the sides of his trousers once more and walked toward the road to meet her.

"I have some nice fresh lemonade if you'd like to join me," he said with a guileless smile. "We can celebrate the end of the Mountain Days ordeal."

She chuckled, her brown eyes crinkling in the summer sun. "I had lemonade at Eva's, but I wouldn't mind a cup of hot tea if you were to offer."

"It seems a bit warm for hot tea, but it's easily done."

"And how's this darling girl?" Abigail dropped her basket on the ground and kneeled down to fuss over Lydia. "It looks like she's fully recovered. I'm so glad."

"She's taking a break from her puppies." Benjamin paused to admire Abigail's starched *kapp* from above and how it contrasted with the dark hair it covered. "They're getting pretty demanding."

She laughed and rose to her feet as she picked up her basket. "She seems like a *gut* mother."

"She is. Come on in." He turned and made his way to the cabin.

Abigail walked beside him, then stopped for a moment as they approached the house.

He turned. "What's wrong?"

"Nothing." She gestured toward his home. "Just admiring the cabin. I stop and admire it every time I come here. It's just so pretty."

He was surprised and gratified. "*Ja*, I feel blessed to have it. I don't know when it was built, but I'm guessing sometime in the nineteen-forties. It has a venerable feel to it."

"It just sits so well in this landscape." She gazed around at the towering pines, the snow-capped mountains behind, and the cozy log cabin before them. "Sometimes I feel like I've stepped into a postcard. It's so classically Montana, or at least my impressions of Montana long before I ever came here."

It was the perfect opening to inquire if she planned to stay here, but Benjamin chickened out. Instead he let her admire the view a moment or two longer, then reissued his offer of hot tea.

The cabin's interior was typical of any number of Amish households: uncurtained windows, an oil lamp centered on the plain kitchen table, hearty cookstove along one wall, wide pine flooring. The kitchen was contiguous with the living room, which sported a braided rag rug his mother had made him years ago nestled between several comfortable chairs he had collected or made through the years.

Abigail touched the kitchen table. "You made this, I suppose?"

"*Ja*, of course." He filled the kettle and placed it on a propane burner, since the weather was far too warm to use the wood cookstove. "I made most of the furnishings except those easy chairs in there." He pointed toward the living room. "But there were excellent thrift stores in Indiana, so I found some comfortable seating."

"It's nice. Cozy. While the water is heating, I have to fuss over my little boy." She made her way to the closet, where the puppies were sleeping in a pile. She fished out the youngest one and brought him back to the table, where she cuddled him in her lap. "Look, his badger markings are getting darker." She touched the coloration on the puppy's face.

"He's the biggest of the litter so far." Benjamin pulled together the tea things and waited for the kettle to boil. When he poured the water into the mugs, to his annoyance his hand trembled and he spilled some of the water.

Abigail looked at him sharply. "Are you okay?"

"*Ja*, I'm fine." He set down the kettle and pushed her mug across the table.

She lifted the paper tag and dipped the tea bag up and down with one hand while holding the puppy to her chest with the other. "You seem distracted."

"I am." Abruptly he sat down. "I guess I'll just blurt it out. Abigail, I want to court you."

She froze and stared at him. "Benjamin…"

He waved a hand. "I know your concerns. Believe me, Abigail, I know them very well. The whole time you've been here, I've been kicking myself for falling in love with a woman with one foot in the *Englisch* world…again. But it is what it is."

She looked down at the puppy against her chest. "This doesn't come as a surprise, Benjamin. And under any other condition, I'd welcome your courtship."

His heart leaped.

"But that doesn't mean it's wise," she continued. She lifted her head and he saw moisture in her eyes. "It's not that I have one foot in the *Englisch* world, as you put it. It's that I have both feet in the world of animal medicine. You know what the bishop told me. I have to make a choice."

"I'm willing to give you time."

"Time for what? That's not the issue I'm facing. The issue is one of choice. I have to choose which course I want to take."

"But—"

She interrupted, a thread of anger in her voice. "Benjamin, let's say for the sake of argument the bishop allows me to be baptized and still keep my career. If we got married, then children would inevitably follow. Most women in the community don't work outside the home once *bopplin* arrive. It's too difficult to juggle all those responsibilities."

"But—"

She forged ahead again. "Besides, when I was visiting with Eva this morning, she confirmed what I already know—most women in our church consider motherhood the ultimate career. But they don't have the background I do. They didn't spend eight years in school and two years in practice. That's a hard thing to give up." Her eyes filled with tears, and she clutched the puppy closer to her chest.

Something akin to anger settled across him. "Then you're throwing away a chance at love, at happiness, just for the sake of animals?"

"I don't know." Tears spilled over her eyes. She stood up so fast her chair tipped over, and she shoved the puppy at him. "As *Gott* is my witness, *I don't know*."

She fled. The screen door banged after her.

Benjamin was left with a puppy in his arms. Somehow it seemed symbolic.

Chapter Thirteen

Abigail slept poorly that night. She tossed and turned and thought about the fork in the road ahead of her.

Down one path lay the fulfillment of husband, children, family, church. The thought of marrying Benjamin gave her a deep longing. But despite the domestic draw, somehow it seemed sterile without the single-minded pursuit she had followed for ten years.

Down the other path lay the expression of her gift from *Gott*—animal medicine. That choice was not necessarily incompatible with husband, family or church. But it *was* incompatible with an Amish husband and church ties. Could she face life without Benjamin?

In some ways, life had been so simple before she left the Amish and went to college. She knew the expectations of an Amish woman: marriage, children, faith. But as a professional veterinarian, those goals became conflicts.

Living back among her community made her realize how much she ached to reembrace the faith ties and connections she'd grown up with. She hadn't realized the depth of that yearning until she had subsumed herself as an adult.

Subsume. That was an accurate word. If she came back to her church roots, she would be expected to follow the *Ordnung*, which meant subsuming her will and her pride to that of the community. It was surprisingly difficult to reconcile herself to that thought.

She dragged herself out of bed early and splashed water on her face, determined to put on a cheerful appearance for her mother. Esther didn't have to know the depth of her despair, or even the offer of courtship from Benjamin—something she knew her mother would welcome. Instead, she started coffee and pulled out ingredients to make muffins for breakfast.

Esther had barely risen and was still in her bathrobe when Abigail heard a knock at the front door.

Instinctively her mother drew the top of her bathrobe closer. "Who could that be so early in the morning?"

"Well, it's not *that* early. You just overslept." Abigail kept her voice light and teasing, but her heart jumped. At this hour, it could only be one person—Benjamin.

But when she opened the door, she was surprised to see a stranger, a middle-aged man with a neat beard and unruly hair, with a sheaf of newspapers tucked under one arm. He was dressed in scrubs.

Scrubs?

Startled, she drew herself up. "Good morning. May I help you?"

The man smiled. He had a pleasant face and cheery blue eyes. "Good morning. I'm sorry to call so early, but I'm trying to find Abigail Mast. Does she live here?"

"I'm Abigail Mast."

He stuck out a hand to shake. "How do you do? I'm Dr. John Green. I own the veterinarian clinic in town."

Automatically she shook hands. "What can I do for you, Dr. Green?"

"Do I understand you're a veterinarian?"

How did he know that? "Er, yes. Yes, I am, though I'm not licensed to practice in Montana."

He smiled wider. "Do you have a few minutes to talk?"

Baffled as to what this could mean, she nodded. "I'd invite you in for a cup of coffee, but my mother just got up. Please excuse me a moment."

She left him standing at the door and went into the kitchen. "It's a man from the vet clinic in town," she hissed at her mother. "He wants to talk to me, I don't know why. I've invited him in for coffee. Why don't you go get dressed?"

Esther, to her credit, didn't argue. She merely limped from the kitchen, through the living room, and closed her bedroom door behind her.

Abigail returned to the front door. "Please come in."

The man followed her into the kitchen and sat in the chair she indicated while she poured him a cup of coffee, then one for herself. She sank down in the chair opposite. "As a matter of interest, Dr. Green, how did you know I'm a vet?"

"Please, call me John. And I knew because of this." He spread out one of the newspapers in front of her.

Abigail glanced down and gasped in surprise. A photo of her was splashed across the front page. Her face wasn't visible, but she was crouched down in front of Ephraim King's cow, suturing the wounds from the dog attack. Her *kapp* was clearly visible, her dress and apron puddled on the ground as she kneeled before the animal.

The caption read, "Amish veterinarian treats cow injured in dog attack at Mountain Days Festival."

She groaned. "I didn't realize he was taking photos at the time. The bishop will *not* be pleased."

Dr. Green looked puzzled. "Why would he not be pleased? It's a charming picture."

Trying to explain to an *Englischer* the complexities behind the Amish stricture on photography—as well as her own tightrope she was walking—seemed futile at the moment. Instead, she changed the subject. "Is there something I can do you for, Dr. Green? I mean, John?"

He sipped his coffee. "You said you weren't licensed in Montana. Where are you licensed?"

"Indiana. I went to school there, graduated two years ago and was working at a clinic in Indianapolis. We handled both large and small animals. Having grown up on a farm, I especially like working with farm animals." She glossed over her experience with the dog she'd nearly lost. "I took a leave of absence since my widowed mother had hip-replacement surgery a couple months ago, so I came here to take care of her while she recuperated. In fact, here she is."

Esther, properly dressed, limped slowly into the kitchen.

Abigail conducted introductions. "Dr. John Green, this is my mother, Esther Mast."

John rose and shook the older woman's hand. "How do you do, ma'am? I'm sorry to call so early, but I wanted to talk with your daughter before I went to work."

"Nice to meet you," replied Esther politely. She looked at Abigail. "I'll take my coffee onto the porch.

It's such a beautiful morning." She poured herself a cup and shuffled outside.

John smiled. "That's to give us privacy in our discussion, is that it?"

"Ja." She smiled back. "But she's probably just as bewildered as I am why you're here."

"Then I'll come right to the point. Are you looking for a job?"

If he'd started tap dancing on the kitchen table, Abigail couldn't have been more shocked. She stared at him, speechless.

He continued into the silence, "Rural veterinarians are surprisingly hard to find. One of our older vets wants to retire, and we were going to advertise to find a replacement. I'd like to invite you to apply. Our pay scale will be lower than what you might be making in a comparable clinic in a more urban area, but it's not bad for this region. The clinic will even pay for your Montana certification."

She rubbed her forehead. "This comes as quite a surprise…"

"Evidently." He chuckled. "Did you have immediate plans to return to Indiana?"

"I—I'm drifting a bit at the moment." She sighed and wondered how much to tell him, then decided to be honest. "Dr. Green—John—I don't mean to sound like I'm waffling, and I appreciate your generous offer, but I don't know how to respond yet. In a nutshell, I'm facing a conflict with my church." She plucked at her apron. "I may look Amish, but I'm not baptized. I'm now facing a choice—to leave my church behind and work as a professional, or leave my calling behind and become a fully baptized church member."

To her relief, he did not dismiss the issue as insignificant. He nodded with gravity. "That is quite a conflict. I'm a man of faith myself, so I understand what it's like to stand at a spiritual crossroad. I won't pressure you to make up your mind one way or the other, of course. But in the meantime, why don't you come see our clinic and meet our staff? It's best to be fully informed, as I imagine you know."

"*Ja*, of course. I would like that."

"If you're free right now, I can drive you in, show you around and drive you back. Otherwise you're welcome to come see it at your convenience."

Her professional curiosity was piqued. "Now would be fine. Let me just make sure my mother doesn't need anything."

"I'll wait in my truck while you explain things to her and get her settled." He rose.

Abigail followed him out the front porch. "It was nice meeting you, Mrs. Mast," he said, and walked toward the pickup truck parked a short distance away.

Esther stared after him. "What was all that about?"

Abigail sank into one of the porch chairs. "*Mamm*, he wants to hire me to work in the vet clinic in town."

Esther's eyes widened. "And what did you tell him?"

"The truth—that I can't give him an answer yet. But he offered to show me around the clinic. Will you be okay if I'm gone for an hour or so?"

"*Ja*, sure, I'll be fine." Esther flapped a hand. "I'll be curious to hear all about it. But don't let him bully you into anything you don't want to do, *liebling*."

"He doesn't strike me as the bullying type, but you're right, *Mamm*. I won't be bullied into anything."

Making sure her *kapp* was neatly in place, she walked toward the pickup truck.

"It's been quite a while since I've driven in a motor vehicle," she ventured as he put the truck in gear and set off down the gravel road.

"Those of us in town have watched with interest as the Amish church settled here," he said. "I haven't talked to anyone yet who hasn't thought you've all been fine additions to the community."

"That's *gut*. Good. That's why our bishop agreed to have the church members participate in the Mountain Days event on Saturday. He wanted to make sure we are cooperative with the people in town."

"I was at the event but missed the whole incident with the dog attacking the cow. It's a good thing you were nearby and had some medical supplies with you."

"A lot of our church members have turned to me to help with their animals since I've been back," she admitted. "I can't take any payment, of course, but I've started an ad hoc clinic in a shed a neighbor helped retrofit. However, I can't do much, since it lacks both electricity and modern equipment, such as an X-ray machine."

"We're fully equipped," he replied. "I started the clinic about twenty years ago, specializing in large-animal work. There used to be a second clinic in town, mostly concentrating on small-animal work, but the vet who ran it retired, so we inherited his customer base. We brought in two of his vets, so now we offer a full range of services for both farms and small animals. We employ four vets, two vet techs and the clerical staff. We're a close-knit group."

"Sounds lovely." She hesitated. "The clinic where

I worked could be tense at times. The head vet was brilliant, but he had a volatile temper. We felt we were walking on eggshells a lot of the time."

He smiled. "We're nothing like that, but I know just the type you mean. There's a lot of ego and insecurity tied up in people who behave that way."

His simple explanation sent a shaft of understanding through Abigail. She thought back to Robert and finally recognized that, for all his brilliance, he was likely covering up a certain amount of personal self-doubt. "Interesting," she murmured.

"Here we are." John pulled up behind the modest clinic and unbuckled his seat belt. He paused and smiled at her. "I'd like to say 'welcome'...but I'll understand if that's premature. Meanwhile, let me introduce you around."

Abigail followed him into the building.

Benjamin vaguely noticed a pickup truck come and go from Esther's cabin, but he was too distracted to give it much thought. Instead, he worked on formulating his case to present to the bishop. Abigail had no idea, but he planned to plead with the church leader on her behalf.

The day promised to be hot as he set off toward Bishop Beiler's home. Back in Indiana, the bishop and his wife lived in a *daadi haus* behind their youngest son's farmhouse. Here, however, the community had renovated an old barn into a cozy little home set well off the gravel road. Lois Beiler kept a garden and chickens, and the bishop limited himself to raising a few pigs for the table.

He found them in the garden, wearing oversize straw

hats and harvesting peas. Benjamin waded in amid the flourishing vegetables. "*Guder mariye*, both of you."

They looked up. The bishop straightened and exclaimed, "Benjamin! *Welkom*. What can we do for you?"

Benjamin resisted the urge to wipe sweaty palms on his trousers. "I wonder if I could speak to you for a few minutes, Bishop?"

The older man looked at him for a moment without speaking. Then he turned to his wife. "Not too long in the sun, okay, *geliebte*?"

Lois smiled. "*Ja.* There's some lemonade in the icebox if you'd like to sit on the porch."

"*Danke.*" Carrying his basket of pea pods, the bishop inclined his head toward Benjamin. "Shall we get something cool to drink? It's warm out here."

"*Ja, danke.*"

Within a few minutes, Benjamin found himself seated opposite a small table in a comfortable rocking chair, with a glass of lemonade before him. A handsome calico cat with stunning green eyes promptly jumped onto the bishop's lap and curled his head beneath the older man's chin. The bishop chuckled and stroked the animal. "This is Thomasina, my favorite pet," he explained. "I'd be lost without her."

"I can tell." Benjamin sipped his drink, more out of nervousness than thirst.

The bishop regarded him with mild eyes. "You're as nervous as a cat, Benjamin."

"*Ja.* Maybe I am. I'm here to ask a difficult question."

"I'll do my best to answer."

"Bishop... I want to court Abigail Mast. But I can't, since she's not baptized. She said she had a conversation with you some time ago about the choice she had to make—to stay or to go. To remain a veterinarian or to be baptized. She's wrestled with it ever since."

Bishop Beiler nodded and leaned back. The cat curled up in his lap, and he absently stroked the animal's fur. "I understand your hesitation. I also believe I understand Abigail's confusion. But, Benjamin, did she tell you my concerns?"

"*Ja.* Basically, she must choose one of two options."

"That is correct. I do not believe those two options are compatible. I'm glad to hear she understood what I was trying tell her."

"But surely you don't think she would ever try to influence anyone to leave the church?"

"Have you seen the newspaper this morning?"

Baffled at the abrupt change of topic, Benjamin stared for a moment. *"Nein."*

"Since I have a cat on my lap, I'll ask if you can step inside the house and fetch the newspaper on the kitchen table."

Puzzled, Benjamin did as he was asked, bringing the folded-up paper back outside to the porch.

"Take a look at the front page," urged the bishop.

Benjamin unfolded the paper and saw a huge photograph of Abigail as she was working on the injured cow on Saturday.

"Oh, no…" he breathed, and dropped back into the rocking chair.

"As you can imagine, this didn't please me," said the bishop.

"But surely you know she had nothing to do with it?"

"Of course she didn't. But still, her photo is in the newspaper for all to see."

"But I overheard her conversation with the photographer that day," Benjamin argued. "She said she wasn't interested in any publicity and refused to be interviewed. She pointed out the signage requesting no photography. She's not responsible because some *Englischer* paid no attention."

"Regardless of how it happened, the fact remains. Her photo is in the paper. This tells other young people in our church about a glamorous possibility—that they can behave in a manner contrary to the *Ordnung*, and get rewarded for it. It smacks of *hochmut*. Pride."

Benjamin felt a sliver of annoyance run through him at the bishop's stubbornness. "Are you suggesting she should have stood by and done nothing when Ephraim's cow was attacked? The animal might have died."

"Not at all. She did the right thing. It was her choice to become a veterinarian, and she's obviously *gut* at what she does. But in making that choice, she left the church."

"Did she tell you *why* she became a veterinarian?"

The bishop waved a hand. "Something about how a vet saved one of her favorite cows when she was a child."

"It goes deeper than that. Far, far deeper. She knew the ramifications of what would happen when she left to go to school, but she went anyway—because she was called by *Gott* to study animal medicine. Each of us must follow the path *Gott* lays out before us. To stray from that path can only lead to being separated from *Gott*. Abigail desperately wants to be baptized, but she cannot lay aside the gift she was given in order to do so. Can you have no clemency toward that conflict?"

"Benjamin, I've made my position clear. Abigail knows she has to make a decision, and I won't blame her for whatever choice she makes. But she cannot have it both ways."

Abruptly, Benjamin stood up. "I'm sorry to find you so resolute. You're putting her in a difficult position."

The bishop raised his chin and looked stern and sad at the same time. "Benjamin, I don't want any bad blood between us. You're a *gut* solid member of the church, and I value your counsel. Can you not see things from my perspective? I am not a dictator. I was given the role of bishop by lot—chosen by *Gott*'s hand. I have to consider the needs of the entire community, not just the needs of a single person who chose to step outside that community to develop her gift. Now let me ask you something," he added. "Did Abigail send you here to talk to me?"

His anger faded and he sat back down, bowing his head. "*Nein*, I came here of my own volition. I asked her yesterday if I could court her. She said no, because she wasn't baptized. It's—it's like *Gott* keeps taking away the women I love, Bishop. I didn't mean to fall in love with Abigail, but it seems I have."

"At least she's aware of the barriers," said the bishop. "Despite her choice to leave us for an education, she's grown into a steady, solid young woman and a contributing member of the community."

"But you're not willing to relent on the last step she would need to take?"

"It's not in my hands, Benjamin." The bishop's voice was firm. "The decision is in her hands."

Chapter Fourteen

The Pierce Veterinary Clinic was a bright and cheerful place. Framed prints of Montana's spectacular scenery decorated the walls of the waiting room and examination rooms. Behind the receptionist's desk was a wall of client files. John Green walked her through the facility's amenities: the kennels out back, the small animal cages inside, the surgery, the X-ray machine, the paddocks in back with holding facilities for horses and cows. Her eyes sparkled at the thought of practicing here.

"It'll be quiet in here today because Mondays are usually our farm-call or house-call days," explained John. "We don't schedule in-clinic appointments. Most of us are in and out of the office on Mondays. Generally we have a vet on call for walk-ins, but even then it's not unusual to be without a vet in the office. Even our small-animal vet does house calls on Mondays. Ah, here comes Steve." Walking her around the horse paddock, John pointed to an incoming pickup truck. "That's Steve Morrison, our vet who wants to retire. Oh, and here's Lucy Gonzales. She's our small-animal expert. Come and meet them."

By the time the clinic opened its front doors, Abigail had met everyone with the exception of the on-call vet, who worked weekends and was off on Mondays and Tuesdays. She was shown the inventory of medicines, supplies and equipment. She was even given a fast tutorial of the billing system by Cara, the receptionist.

Then John Green drove her home. "I won't ask for a decision right away," he told her. "Steve wants to retire at some point, but he's not in a big rush. However, it's clear you'd fit into the clinic very well. If you have a CV, I'd love to see it, but don't feel the need to give us an immediate answer."

Abigail promised to send him her *curriculum vitae*, as her professional résumé was termed. "I'll keep you posted as to what my decision will be, but as you've gathered, I have a lot to think over."

"I understand." He pulled into Benjamin's driveway, then drove toward Esther's cabin in back. "I apologize for the unorthodox job interview, but it was a pleasure to meet you."

"Likewise." She shook his hand. "I appreciate the vote of confidence." She unstrapped her seat belt, exited the vehicle and watched him drive away.

She felt a tumultuous volcano inside her. Her professional interests warred with her spiritual needs.

She lifted her eyes skyward. "Any other surprises in store for me, *Gott*?" she murmured. It seemed almost a cruel joke to have such a job offer laid at her feet at a time when she was being tugged in so many directions already. She scrubbed a hand over her face and went inside to find her mother knitting in the living room.

Abigail collapsed onto a sofa. "Whew."

"Well…?" prompted her mother after a short silence.

"It's perfect," pronounced Abigail in the gloomiest voice possible. "The facility is clean and modern, the staff is lovely, the clientele includes a lot of farm calls and the pay is generous for this area. In short, I could be very happy there."

"Except for one thing," her mother added.

"Except for the matter of whether or not to be baptized." She covered her face with her hands. "As *Gott* is my witness, *Mamm*, I don't know what to do."

"Ach, liebling." Her mother lurched to her feet and dropped down onto the sofa next to her. Abigail leaned into her mother's shoulder and burst into tears. For a little while she was a child again, drawing comfort from a mother who had stood firm for her daughter as she faced endless difficult decisions in her life.

When the storm passed, Abigail straightened up and mopped her face with a handkerchief. Esther angled herself on the sofa to face Abigail. "I know this is difficult for you."

"It's worse than you think." Abigail twisted the fabric in her hands. "*Mamm*, you should know this. Benjamin waylaid me yesterday on my way back home from visiting Eva. He—he said he wants to court me."

She saw the flare of joy in her mother's eyes. "I didn't know that," Esther murmured.

"But he also said he knew he couldn't," continued Abigail, "because of my status in the church."

"Putting aside the obvious barriers," asked Esther, "is courtship from Benjamin something you would welcome?"

"Ja," she confessed. "It would be." She wiped her eyes with the handkerchief. "Finding someone like Ben-

jamin is the last thing I expected when I came here to take care of you, but that's what happened. If I took the job in the clinic, it would mean I'm still not a church member, but I would still be near Benjamin. I'm not sure my heart could handle that."

"You might have to move to town to avoid him…"

"*Ja*, I might." She dropped her head in her hands. "In some ways, I wish Benjamin hadn't said anything. It's made my situation even worse. I'm being pushed to stay, to give up my education and be baptized."

"But Benjamin's interest makes things more complicated?"

"*Ja*. It's not just Benjamin, it's a deeper longing. It's funny, *Mamm*. Yesterday when I was visiting with Eva, I couldn't help but notice how happy she was. Her husband is a *gut* man, her children are darling and she's expecting another *boppli*. She's a very content woman. But what do I have? I have a career I've spent ten years developing. But at what cost? If I go back to Indiana, I'll be alone. I won't have a *hutband*, I won't have children, I won't have a church."

Esther made a helpless gesture. "I can't guide you, *liebling*. I see your conflict, but since I've only experienced one side of it, I cannot advise as to the other. I never wanted anything but marriage and children."

"I know. This is my own battle. But maybe what I can't understand is why *Gott* gave me such incompatible longings. I wanted to study animal medicine since I was eight years old. But I love children. I want a family. I want to become baptized. I cannot have it both ways. That's what the bishop told me, and it's true."

"Abigail, let me ask you a serious question." Esther's calm voice pierced her confusion. "What if…? What if you gave up your career and joined the church? What if you gave up your career and married Benjamin? You'd still have your knowledge and skills. You may not be able to practice in a professional setting like the clinic in town, but you could do things informally, kind of like what you've been doing since you arrived. Could you live with that?"

Abigail took a deep breath and stared at the opposite wall. "I don't know," she finally said. "That may be what I'll have to do. There's too much here to give up and return to Indiana. I'd have the church. And I'd have Benjamin."

"And you'd have a very happy mother," added Esther with a small smile. "It's been nice having you home, *liebling*. I'm hopeful the success of the church here in Pierce will convince some of your brothers and sisters to move here, too. I miss being close to my grandchildren."

"*Gut*, more pressure," Abigail teased, but it was true. It would be hard to give up the warm and loving relationship she had rediscovered with her mother.

Most Amish young women didn't have to sever ties with their parents. They remained in close contact. When the normal milestones in life came along—courtship, marriage, babies, child-raising—the parents were there to offer guidance and advice.

But Abigail had left her parents behind when she'd reached eighteen and had entered a world her family could not and would not follow. She had missed the parental guidance that kept many young adults from blundering into mistakes. She had avoided committing too many errors in her personal life—aside from her ill-advised interest in Robert—but being around her *mamm* made her realize just how much her mother meant to her, especially since her father had passed away.

It was yet another tie she would miss if she returned to Indiana.

Benjamin sanded a chair leg smooth. His hands worked expertly, but his mind was miles away. He had received an enthusiastic follow-up letter from Greg Anderson, discussing prices and the quantity of furniture he wanted. In many ways, Benjamin's financial future was more secure than it had ever been. But the same couldn't be said for his romantic future.

He kicked himself for baring his soul to Abigail yesterday. He should have known better than to reveal his vulnerabilities.

And now the bishop knew how things stood between them. Why couldn't he have kept his mouth shut?

He thought about Barbara, the young woman he'd courted when he was eighteen. Would he have been happy with her? In retrospect, Barbara had always been somewhat flighty and light-minded. Bound within the vows of matrimony, they would have made a marriage work, of course. But now, for the first time, he felt relief that he hadn't married her.

Or perhaps that conclusion was easy to make when comparing a youthful Barbara to a mature Abigail.

One thing was certain—he didn't think he'd ever met someone as fascinating as Abigail Mast. For such a small woman—no more than two inches over five feet—she packed an astounding amount of skills, abilities, personality and intelligence into a lovely form.

As for the bishop…well, it was perhaps sinful to think dark thoughts about the church leader, but he didn't understand the older man's unaccountable stubbornness over Abigail's future. The only mark against her—even the bishop admitted this—was the conflict of her professional abilities. He insisted she had to pick one or the other—being a vet or being baptized.

Benjamin paused in his work and frowned. For the first time, he looked into the future and tried to imagine Abigail as his wife. For the sake of argument, he pretended the bishop had given permission for her to remain a working veterinarian as well as a baptized member of the church.

That would mean his wife would be working away from home, in an office setting.

Certainly there were many precedents for Amish women working. The Yoders' store in town was proof enough of that. It seemed the only objection the bishop had was Abigail's choice of profession, which had required her to get schooling in the *Englisch* world. But she had chosen to come back to the church.

If that was the bishop's sole concern—that Abigail's decisions might influence other *youngies* to follow her path—then it might be argued she was a *good* example, not a bad one.

But putting that aside, what would married life be like with a working professional? What would happen when the babies came?

He frowned and resumed sanding. It was all a moot point, anyway. The bishop had not relented, and Abigail had not changed her mind. And once again, Benjamin had fixated his affection on a woman being pulled away from the community.

And yet…and yet, he realized he no longer blamed the *Englisch* for pulling away Barbara or his sister. Nor could he blame them if Abigail chose to leave. The bishop's assignment of putting him in charge of the Mountain Days demonstrations had accomplished that much, at least.

In a moment of insight, he realized his resentment had originated in himself. Deep down he always wondered if something he had said or done had chased away Barbara or his sister. It was easier to pin the blame on the nameless, faceless wider world than to examine his own behavior.

Now that he was older, he realized he was not responsible for the decisions made by his sister, or by Barbara. Nor was he responsible if Abigail chose to leave and go back to the *Englisch* world.

He finished sanding the chair legs and noticed the mail truck just pulling away from his mailbox on the road. Ready for a break from his dark thoughts, he walked the length of the driveway to see what had come in the mail.

Two bills, a letter from his sister Miriam—he smiled at the coincidence—and several pieces of mail for Esther. He would give the older woman her letters when he next saw her.

He frowned at the mail and thought for a few moments, then went inside and checked on Lydia and the puppies. The enormous white dog was lying inside the closet with her puppies heaped in a pile beside her. She wagged her tail when he approached. He crouched down to stroke her fur, then picked up the male puppy whose life Abigail had saved. He stood up, holding the fuzzy baby to his chest. He left the house with the puppy in his arms and the letters in his pocket.

He found Abigail on her porch, rocking slowly in a

rocking chair, staring across the landscape. He found it peculiar…and worrisome.

"Abigail?" he ventured.

"What?" She snapped her head around, then pressed a hand to her chest. "I'm sorry, I didn't hear you coming."

"I brought mail for your *mamm*, and a peace offering for you." He climbed the porch steps and deposited the puppy in her lap. "Sometimes it just helps to have an animal to cuddle, *ja*?"

"Oh, Benjamin…" He saw tears start to form in her eyes as she clutched the warm bundle. She buried her face in the animal's fur. "I'm so mixed up…"

He sank down in the nearby rocker, feeling shame for adding to her confusion. "I shouldn't have spoken when I did," he said. "I made the situation worse."

"You're not the only one who has made the situation worse." She fished a handkerchief out of her apron pocket and mopped her face with one hand while clutching the puppy in the other. "I—I… Let me explain," she added. "You probably don't know about my visitor this morning."

"What visitor?"

"Actually, I'll back up a bit further. Did you know the newspaper posted a photo of me sewing up Ephraim's cow at the Mountain Days demo?"

"*Ja*, I saw it," he admitted, hoping she wouldn't ask where. He didn't want to mention his conversation with the bishop this morning.

"Well, the head veterinarian at the clinic in Pierce saw it, too. He stopped by this morning and offered me a job." She wiped her eyes again. "I'm just so torn, Benjamin. Every professional instinct in me says I should accept the position. But everything else says I shouldn't—that I should give up veterinarian work and settle in among the Amish community here." He saw fresh tears start to well up in her eyes. "I've never been so pulled apart in my life, not even when I first left home to go to school."

"And in some ways, there's the one person standing between you and your future." With some bitterness, Benjamin pointed toward the bishop's buggy as the church leader's horse clip-clopped with speed down the road. "Why doesn't he…"

He bit off his words and stared. The bishop's buggy wasn't just passing by. It made a fast turn down his driveway, past his cabin and straight up to Esther's house. The bishop, his face drawn and tense, pulled the panting horse to a stop.

Benjamin sprang to his feet. So did Abigail, clutching the puppy to her chest.

"Abigail, can you help?" croaked the bishop. "My cat was attacked by a coyote."

Abigail shoved the puppy at Benjamin and dashed toward the buggy, where a basket was nestled on the seat. She lifted a blanket and he saw her wince.

She whirled. "Benjamin, tell *Mamm* I'll be in town at the vet clinic." She climbed uninvited into the bishop's buggy, took the basket on her lap and ordered, "Get going. There's no time to lose."

The bishop wheeled the horse around and took off at a fast trot. Benjamin watched them disappear in a cloud of dust.

Chapter Fifteen

"Tell me what happened." Abigail rested her hand lightly on the blanket and felt the bloodied animal still breathing, making tiny sounds of pain. She said a prayer the cat would make it.

"A coyote came out of the forest near the barn." The bishop's words were clipped, and he concentrated on guiding his horse as quickly as possible along the increasingly busy road toward Pierce. She sensed his emotions were under tight control. "I didn't know the cat was outside until the coyote made a dash and grabbed it. I ran at them with a shovel and actually managed to beat it off, but—but she was so badly mauled." His voice caught. "I don't think I'll ever forget the noise."

Abigail knew how haunting the screams of a cat fighting for its life could be. She also remembered how fond the older man was of this particular animal. "I should warn you, I don't know how much I can do," she admitted. "But with *Gott*'s help, I'll do my best."

The older man swiped his cheek, and she discreetly ignored the sign of his grief. "I have no other option," he stated. "I was hoping you could handle this at your little clinic…"

"I'm limited in what I can do there," she told him. "Proper veterinary care involves equipment I don't have. I can't do surgery there, and I have a feeling that's what will be needed."

Faster than she thought possible, the bishop pulled up to the clinic. "I'll take the cat in," she told him. "You hitch up the horse. I don't want to waste any time."

"*Ja*, go. Go."

He held the basket while she climbed down from the buggy, then handed it down. She burst into the clinic.

Cara, the receptionist, looked up startled. "Abigail! Hello…"

"Sorry to barge in, but I have an emergency. Is the surgery room free?"

"Yes." To her credit, the receptionist didn't argue. Instead she dashed from behind her desk. "Dog or cat?"

"Cat. Mauled by a coyote." Abigail strode into the darkened operating room while Cara followed and flipped on the lights. "The owner is right behind me, attending to his horse and buggy. Is Lucy available?" Abigail had met and liked the small-animal expert.

"No, she's out on a call. All the vets are, in fact. Dr. Green should be back in an hour. But one of the techs is here. Shall I get him?"

"*Ja*, please."

Abigail placed the basket on the counter in the surgery and lifted off the blanket, fearing the cat had already died. But it was still alive. Bloodied and torn, it was making the same pathetic catches of pain in its breath.

She weighed the animal, then immediately sedated

it. If nothing else, it was a merciful act to put the animal out of pain while preparing it for whatever repairs were needed.

Thomas LaGrande, the vet tech, bustled in and peered at the animal. "Poor thing," he murmured, then turned to scrub his hands.

"Let's hope she makes it." Abigail closed her eyes and breathed another prayer. It wasn't even so much for the ravaged animal in front of her as it was for the impression she might make on the man out in the waiting room. She prayed for skill—for the skill *Gott* had given her to save injured animals.

For a tense hour, she and Thomas labored over the cat. Abigail started an intravenous drip of saline and antibiotics. Thomas constantly monitored vital statistics. The best surprise was the animal's internal organs appeared undamaged. But the coyote had left some serious bite wounds around the cat's neck, and one of her back legs was shockingly mangled.

"Can you save the leg?" asked Thomas, as the extent of the damage became clear.

Abigail gently probed the injured limb. "I think so. See? The tendon is intact." She pointed. "If the tendon still works, that's half the battle. It seems it's mostly muscular damage we have to deal with. And, of course, the broken femur."

She bent over the operating table, suturing the muscles. Her back cramped and she had to stop and stretch it out once or twice before resuming work.

"You've a good touch with stitches," observed Thomas. "As good as Lucy."

The tech's compliment helped ease the tension. Abigail gave a grim chuckle. "Thank you. I was always good at sewing and quilting when I was a child, and I like to think that early training helped when it came to sewing animals back together."

She was nearly finished repairing the lacerations in the cat's neck when John Green came in. "Cara said you brought in an emergency case. What's the status?"

Abigail finished the last knot and reached for some antibiotic powder, which she dusted liberally over the wounds. "Just finishing up. I think she'll make it." She gave a breath of relief. "It was touch and go for a while. This animal belongs to our church bishop. She's his favorite pet. No pressure there," she concluded with a hint of sarcasm.

John leaned close and examined the wounds Abigail had stitched, and the cast now over the animal's back leg. He listened to her breathing, and gently pried open an eyelid to peer at the ocular membrane. "Well, this is better than any résumé," he said. "Excellent work, Abigail. Her vitals look good and I think she'll make it."

She smiled in pure relief. *"Danke, Gott,"* she breathed to herself. She stripped off her gloves and watched as Thomas gently transferred the cat to a recovery cage. "I'll go talk to the bishop and explain the situation to him."

"Do you want me to come, too?"

"No, but thank you. I'll handle it."

She wiped a hand over her face, took a deep breath and walked out of the surgery room into the waiting area.

The bishop was hunched over in one of the chairs, his head in his hands as if he was in utter despair. Abigail walked quietly toward him. "Bishop?"

He jerked up his head and she saw moisture on his cheeks. He drew a ragged breath. "She's gone, isn't she?"

Her throat closed up at the man's obvious grief. "*Nein.* She's in bad shape, but she didn't have any damage to her internal organs. Her back leg needed a lot of work, so I cleaned it up and set it in a cast. She has some bad bite wounds around her neck, but they're cleaned and sutured now. If animals come through surgery of this scope successfully, their chances of recovery are high."

He stared at her as if he didn't believe her. Then he leaned back, covered his face with his hands and took a shuddering breath.

Abigail had witnessed the agony of people losing a beloved pet many times in her career. Here was the almost agonizing relief of reprieve.

She crouched down before the church leader and briefly touched him on the knee. "You did the right thing bringing her to me immediately. Thanks to your quick thinking and fast response, she's likely to survive."

"No, Abigail." Bishop Beiler removed his hands from his face and looked at her with reddened eyes. "It's thanks to *you* that she's likely to survive. I know it's unworthy to put so much earthly store on a pet, but I raised her from a tiny kitten and I've always loved her. I'm grateful beyond words we'll have more years with her."

"She'll have to stay here a few days," Abigail warned as she stood up.

"You're a mess," the bishop observed with wry humor. Startled, Abigail looked down at herself. Her apron and dress were indeed a mess—covered with blood, antibiotic ointment and clotting powder. She grunted. "Normally I wear scrubs. I didn't even think about what I was wearing when I took the cat into surgery."

"*Ja*, I meant to ask. How did you—"

He was interrupted when Dr. Green came into the waiting room. "Are you the bishop for the Amish church? I'm Dr. John Green."

"*Ja*. I'm Samuel Beiler." The older man stood up and shook hands. "Did you help with my cat, too?"

"No, I was out on a call. It's all thanks to Abigail's skill that it seems your pet is likely to make it. But we'll have to keep her here for a few days to monitor her recovery."

"*Ja*, sure, that's fine." The bishop fished a handkerchief out of his pocket and mopped his face. "I'm sorry to be so emotional, but she's a *gut* cat. It was hard to see her attacked."

"Coyote?"

"*Ja*."

The older vet nodded. "They're a serious concern around here."

"My mother's landlord, Benjamin Troyer, raises Great Pyrenees dogs," volunteered Abigail. "I have a feeling they're going to be even more popular after this."

"With good reason," agreed John. "Those dogs are excellent at guarding both livestock and house pets. People, too. We had a fine Pyrenees as a house dog when our children were young, and he would have died to protect our kids from any harm."

"I wonder…" Bishop Beiler hesitated. "Can I see her?"

Abigail frowned. "Your cat?"

"*Ja.*"

"Why would you want to? She's sedated, and frankly she's not a pretty sight at the moment."

"I want to see what you've done." His voice was gentle.

She glanced at John, and he gave a small nod. She sighed. "Then follow me."

She led the way to the animal's recovery cage, where the sleeping cat was lying on a soft blanket. Abigail opened the cage so he could get a better look.

"Don't touch her right now," she advised.

The bishop peered closely at his pet and swallowed hard. "Tell me what you had to do," he said. "Tell me what wounds she had."

A strange request, but Abigail accommodated him. He stared at his cat for a long time. Then he straightened up and shook his head. "Unbelievable. Miraculous."

"A gift from *Gott*," she murmured.

He shot her a look. "I think I understand that now."

Abigail closed the cage door and led the way back to the waiting room. "We should probably go back now." She was anxious to get home and change clothes. "John, we'll figure out the costs involved in the emergency surgery at a later time." She didn't want him to think she was taking advantage of the clinic's resources without compensation.

The older man nodded. "Most of the expenses are the vet's time and skills," he reminded her. "You're freelance on this."

She nodded. "Thank you."

"How long will the cat have to stay here at the clinic?" asked the bishop.

John looked at Abigail. "It's your patient," he prompted.

"I'm guessing a week," she told the church leader. "I recommend keeping her sedated for at least the next twenty-four hours, and then she'll be on pain medication for several days while recovering from the trauma. After that it's a matter of making sure no infection takes hold. When that danger is over, she can go home. She'll be in that cast for about eight weeks, so her mobility will be impaired."

"And I promise to keep her indoors," added the bishop with a small smile. "Or maybe I should get a Great Pyrenees from Benjamin."

"Ja, gut." She smiled back. It seemed, somehow, that the bishop had turned a corner in his attitude toward her. "Are you ready to go?"

"Ja." Still looking a bit dazed at the events of the last hour, the church leader nodded to John and shuffled out the clinic's glass front door.

John clapped her on the shoulder. "That was some excellent work, Abigail. You're just the kind of vet we're looking for. Please, give some serious consideration to our offer."

"I will, thank you." She looked out the glass doors at the older man unhitching his horse. "He's the one who holds my future in his hands. Maybe it was *Gott*'s will that this all happened."

"Keep me posted." The older vet smiled.

Abigail walked out of the clinic to where the bishop was unhitching his horse. She climbed into the buggy seat. After the church leader had directed the horse out of town, he glanced at her. "I have much to thank you for, but one thing puzzles me. How is it you were able to barge in and conduct surgery in the animal clinic? How is it they know you?"

So much had happened in just the last few hours, it was hard to grasp everything. The bishop didn't know about her unexpected job interview this morning. "Let me tell you about my day," she began.

After Abigail had departed with the bishop, Benjamin visited with Esther for a time while she cooed and fussed over the fuzzy puppy. Then he returned home, nestled the puppy in with his littermates and gave Lydia a pat on the head. He wondered what was transpiring in town. Just this morning he had watched the bishop's display of affection for his cat. Now the poor animal was likely to die. It was a harsh lesson on the ephemeral nature of life.

Restless, he wandered outside, toward the pasture where his cows were chewing their cud under the shade of the fir trees. Elijah, Lydia's mate, was also lying in the shade. His massive head rested on his paws, but his eyes were alert. Benjamin knew he owed his herd's security to the magnificent working dog in the field. It wasn't just coyotes that could stalk livestock. Here in the wilds of western Montana, Benjamin had seen a few wolves, several bears and even a cougar. But thanks to his Great Pyrenees, his cows were safe.

Yes, every last one of Lydia's puppies would be in high demand. But he wanted to hold one back—the youngest pup that Abigail had saved. If only...

Suddenly he heard horse's hooves clopping down the gravel road. The bishop, with Abigail at his side, was directing the buggy down Benjamin's driveway. He walked toward the cabin to meet them.

By the expression on the bishop's face, he suspected Abigail had managed to save the cat, but he waited until the church leader had pulled the buggy to a halt before asking. He walked up to assist Abigail from the buggy. "The cat is likely to make it," she told him.

He smiled in relief. "Praise *Gott*!" Then he noticed her appearance. "You're a mess," he observed.

She laughed. "*Ja*, Bishop Beiler said the same thing. I simply forgot I wasn't wearing scrubs and got right to work."

"And she saved my cat." The bishop finished tying his horse to a post and turned to face them. "Abigail, Benjamin, I want to talk with you both. Is now a *gut* time?"

Benjamin was surprised, and he noticed Abigail seemed equally so. "*Ja*," he replied with some caution. What on earth did the bishop have to say to them? "I have some lemonade in the icebox. Why don't we sit on the porch, where it's cool?"

"*Danke*." Somewhat stiffly, the older man walked toward the cabin.

Benjamin caught Abigail's eye and lifted his eyebrows in question. She shrugged her shoulders and shook her head, then followed the bishop toward the porch.

Lydia emerged from inside the house. The giant white dog wagged her tail at the sight of visitors. After greeting everyone, she curled up on the edge of the porch, facing toward the pasture, alert as always for any threats that might be detected.

Benjamin went inside to fetch glasses and a pitcher of lemonade, and came back to see Abigail sitting awkwardly across the small porch table from the church leader. He poured the drinks, then sank into a chair. "Is something the matter, Bishop?"

"*Nein.* Actually, *ja.*" If possible, the church leader looked ashamed. "I owe you an apology, Abigail."

He saw her eyes widen. "For what?"

"For judging you so harshly." The older man clasped and unclasped his hands. "I had it in my head that because you have your degree in animal medicine, you were ineligible to join the church. When Benjamin pleaded your case this morning, I remained inflexible."

Benjamin watched Abigail's head snap around to stare at him. "You pleaded my…"

"*Ja,* he pleaded your case," the bishop said with a small smile. "And I wouldn't budge from my position. I was stubborn…and, dare I say it, perhaps *hochmut.* Then my cat was nearly killed and you saved her life. That changed things. Not because you saved my cat," he added, "but because I had a revelation in the waiting room while wondering if I'd ever see my favorite pet again."

"What kind of revelation?" Benjamin kept his voice soft.

"That pride can affect anyone and everyone. There's a reason the Bible warns against it. I was too proud to admit I was wrong, Abigail. You once told me your skill in veterinary medicine was a gift from *Gott.* I didn't believe you. Or rather, I brushed it aside as unimportant. I've been forcing you to make a harsh decision, to choose between your desire to practice your gift and your desire to join the church."

"And now…?"

"Now I understand what you were saying. Your skills are indeed a gift from *Gott.* The Bible tells us we're one body in our faith, but we each have different gifts according to the grace given to us. That's why I wanted to see Thomasina while in recovery. *Gott* gave you the skill to save her life. Who am I to deny that?"

Abigail's chocolate-brown eyes welled with tears, but she kept them in check. "D-does that mean you'll allow me to be baptized?"

"*Ja,*" the bishop replied simply.

The tears spilled over. She covered her face with her hands. "*Danke, Gott, danke,*" she whispered between heaving breaths. His throat closed at the intensity of her emotion.

Then it struck him. Abigail could be baptized. That meant…

Benjamin looked over at the bishop, who was watching him as if reading his thoughts. The older man smiled, then nodded.

Benjamin's own breath caught. Suddenly, urgently, he wanted the bishop to leave. He had some things to discuss with the woman sitting across from him, the woman he hoped would be around forever.

"So I wanted to ask you both to forgive this old man," concluded the bishop. "I was a fool, and I'm sorry for it."

Abigail continued to weep. Benjamin fished a clean handkerchief from his pocket and handed it to her. She nodded blindly and buried her face in it.

But when she raised her head at last, her eyes were red and her cheeks were blotchy, but her face shone with a radiant joy he had never seen before. "All is forgiven," she choked.

"*Ja,*" croaked Benjamin. "All is forgiven."

Bishop Beiler pushed away his untouched glass of lemonade and rose from the table. "Then I'll go home now," he said. "Lois will be anxious to know what happened to Thomasina, and I have a lot to tell her. And I think," he added with a twinkle in his eyes, "you two have much to talk about."

Chapter Sixteen

The sounds of the horse's hooves faded in the distance as Abigail wiped her eyes. "I can be baptized," she murmured. It still seemed too good to be true.

"Abigail." Benjamin, sitting across the small porch table from her, laid both his hands palm up on the table. "If you can be baptized, you know what this means."

The full realization came over her like a thunderclap. "Oh, Benjamin…" She laid her hands in his. "Is it true? Can this happen?"

"I will ask you again. Will you let me court you?" His face was solemn.

She managed a chuckle through her tears. "Let's just say you've been doing that since the day I arrived. Ask me something else."

"All right." He smiled, and the glint in his dark blue eyes held a promise of the future. "Here's my next question. Will you marry me?"

"*Ja.*" Though she smiled, she couldn't prevent another tear from trickling down her cheek. "*Ja,* I will marry you, as *Gott* is my witness."

He closed his eyes as if in prayer. "As *Gott* is my witness," he breathed.

"But it can't be right away," she warned. "I have to go through the usual five months of instruction before baptism. But, conveniently, that puts my baptism in November, just in time for wedding season."

"And if you're baptized on a Sabbath, then we can have the wedding the following Tuesday or Thursday." He grinned.

"In a hurry, are you?" she teased.

"Let's just say I'd marry you tomorrow, if I could get away with it."

But despite the unsteady golden happiness she felt—and she knew Benjamin felt—she knew she had some serious issues to bring up.

"Benjamin…" She paused and bit her lip. "Before we go any further, you need to be aware of something. You're not asking a normal Amish woman to be your wife. I'll be working. Will that be all right?"

"*Ja*, sure…"

She waved a hand. "Don't answer so quickly. It's worth thinking through. You once mentioned you weren't much of a cook. If I'm working full-time, I won't be much of a cook, either. And it's not just kitchen duties, it's everything. Are you sure you can accept that?"

"*Ja.*" He smiled, apparently not put off in the slightest by her litany of warnings. "Believe me, Abigail, I've thought everything through from one side to the other, from beginning to end, from left to right, up and down, in and out, and every other direction you can think of. Nothing you can say can deter me from marrying you."

She shook her head. "You're giddy, Benjamin. So am

I. But we have to be realistic." She drew a deep breath. "*Mamm* asked me this morning to imagine a situation. She asked if I could be happy scaling back to part-time work, or even volunteer work, when babies started coming. I—I think I can. Obviously there will be times I won't be able to work at all. Other times I might be able to work part-time…"

"I think you're overthinking this," he interrupted, still smiling. "I may not be much of a cook, but you know what? I'm great with kids. *Ja*, there may be times you'll have a new baby when you may not be able to work. But it's a stage of life, Abigail. However many *bopplin Gott* gives us remains to be seen, but *Gott* willing, you and I will have many, many years ahead of us. When the *kinner* are older, I can take care of them full-time."

"You would do that for me?"

"*Ja.* I would do that for you." His eyes glinted. "I might even put that in our wedding vows."

She felt like laughing and crying at the same time. The laughter spilled out, and he joined her. For a moment she was dazzled at the prospect of laughing with this wonderful man for the rest of her life.

"And when the *kinner* are grown and no longer live with us, then you can take care of animals full-time, if you want," Benjamin said.

She grew sober. "I'll have to see if John Green, the vet, can accept my application under those conditions. There are times I may need to reduce my hours to an emergency basis only. He may not want to hire me if those are my conditions."

"And if not, then what?"

She sniffed and smiled at him. "Then it's what

Mamm suggested. I may simply have to be an independent freelancer working just within the Amish community, doing what I can. Anything I can't do without the right equipment, I'll refer to the clinic. Oh, Benjamin, I think this might work!"

"You're right. We may not live a typical Amish life, but we'll *make* it work." He held out his arms. "Come here."

"I'm filthy." She indicated her stained apron and dress.

"What does it matter? Soon you'll be wearing a brand-new clean dress for our wedding. Come here."

Suddenly shy, she rose and walked around the table and perched herself on his lap. He touched his forehead to hers. "I never thought this day would come," he murmured, and kissed her.

She returned the kiss and tasted the promise of a long and happy future with her soon-to-be husband.

A few minutes later she pulled back. "Now, what's this about you pleading my case with the bishop? I didn't know that."

She felt the rumble of laughter start deep in his chest. "Call it an act of desperation. I went and talked with him this morning, asking if he could find clemency in his heart for your situation. And for mine, too. I told him I wanted to court you, but he said the decision was up to you—about whether you could give up being a veterinarian. I must admit, I went away a little huffy."

"What a difference a few hours makes." She sighed with happiness, then a thought struck her. "If you have a puppy to spare, perhaps you should offer one to the bishop. It seems his farm could use a livestock guard dog."

"*Ja*, perhaps. I'll ask if he's interested. This litter is spoken for, but perhaps next year."

"Next year," she breathed. Tucked against Benjamin's chest, she could see the view from the porch—green lawn, dark conifers, distant mountains. "Next year, we'll both be living in this lovely little cabin. Perhaps we'll have a *boppli* by then. Oh, Benjamin, I love you."

His arms tightened around her fractionally. Then abruptly he sat up, nearly unseating her from his lap. "I think now would be a *gut* time to give you your wedding present."

"My what?"

He lifted her off his lap and stood up. "Stay here a moment."

"What are you talking about? How could you possibly have a wedding present for me?"

He grinned. "Let's just say I was hopeful." He gently pushed her down into the porch rocker. "Close your eyes. I'll be back in a moment."

She closed her eyes. The day had been such an emotional seesaw that somehow Benjamin's silly announcement of a present was just another part of that.

She heard him come back onto the porch. "Hold out your hands. Both hands," he instructed.

She did so, and a moment later felt the soft, warm body of a puppy fill her arms. Instinctively she embraced it while her eyes popped open. "Benjamin! The puppy!"

"*Ja*." With a grin as wide as the porch, he sat back down. "He's yours. Literally from the moment he was born, when you brought him back to life, I earmarked him for you. I was hoping to give him to you as a wedding gift. *Gott* granted me that wish."

She sniffed back more tears and hugged the animal against her chest. "*Danke*, Benjamin. He's beautiful. I'll have to think of a name for him."

"Goliath, perhaps? He's likely to be huge."

"I like it." She held the puppy up at eye level. "Hello, Goliath. How would you like to stay here with us?" The baby responded by touching her nose with his tongue. "Will he be a field guardian or a house dog?" she wondered.

"Whichever you prefer," Benjamin replied. "If you want him as a house dog, we'll have to put a fence around the yard or he'll roam. All Pyrenees need space—they're not meant to be confined—so I can make it a good-size yard."

"He can guard our *kinner*!" She hugged the dog to her chest.

Benjamin nodded with more gravity than she anticipated. "And believe me, he will. Pyrenees take their job seriously." He glanced upward at the porch roof. "I'll have to expand this house," he said thoughtfully. "It's fine for two people, but I suspect we won't be two people for very long."

"It's such a beautiful, classic log cabin," she replied. "Hopefully you can make whatever additions we'll need without changing the look too much."

"I have some ideas." He grinned at her. "I've had ideas ever since you arrived just in time to set Lydia's leg. I think I started falling in love with you from that moment on."

"It didn't take me long to return the notice," she admitted. "I was just so tied up in knots. Now it seems everything is simple and easy, even though, as I said before, we're bound to have an unconventional lifestyle." She put the wiggly puppy down on the porch. "And we won't ever have to separate Goliath from his mother…" She jerked upright. "Mother! Benjamin, *Mamm* has no idea what's happened! She doesn't know that the bishop's cat survived, or that the bishop changed his mind about my baptism, or that we'll be courting."

He smiled. "What do you say we go see her and drop all the bombshells on her at once? Won't that be fun?"

"Ja!" Giggling, she scooped up Goliath and redeposited him back among his siblings. Then she grabbed Benjamin's hand. "Race you!"

Epilogue

November in the Rockies, Abigail realized, was very different than November in Indiana. The season's first snow had capped the distant mountains and dusted the nearby conifers with what looked like powdered sugar. The air was crisp and clean, and smelled of pine.

"I'm so glad the weather held," observed Esther from the back of the buggy.

Abigail, attired in her newly made blue dress with clean black apron, turned to look at her mother. "Is this the first wedding to take place here in Pierce?"

"*Nein*, it's the third," her mother answered. "No one has a house big enough to host a wedding, so the Millers' bed-and-breakfast has become the preferred spot."

"And all of Abigail's coworkers will attend as well, even though this is a Thursday," added Benjamin, guiding the horse onto the paved road.

Many Amish buggies were heading into town, causing heads to turn. John Green, her boss, had said the community was welcome to park as many buggies as could fit into the vet clinic's parking lot, located only a block away from the Millers' bed-and-breakfast. John had closed the office for the day so the entire veterinary staff could attend her wedding. She had warned him in advance the service would be in German.

She hugged herself, then glanced over at the man who would be her husband within a few hours. As if feeling her gaze, he looked over at her, winked and smiled. His dark blue eyes were warm with love.

Trying not to become overwhelmed with emotion, she thought back over the last week. On Sunday she had been baptized, and she was now a full-fledged member of the church. Esther had wept with joy that her youngest child had returned to the fold, just as she had wept with joy five months before, when Abigail had told her she and Benjamin were to be married.

The bishop's cat, Thomasina, had actually been present at the baptismal ceremony at Abigail's request. The feline had completely recuperated and was extremely fond of her, and had taken the unorthodox approach of sleeping in Abigail's lap during the subsequent sermon. It was not a common sight to see a cat at a Sabbath service, but the bishop had been indulgent.

And Goliath. She smiled at the thought of her gigantic puppy, now nearly six months old and already seventy pounds. He was likely to top out at a massive 150 pounds at full maturity, like his sire. She made sure he was well socialized both with other dogs, as well as people. He adored her as much as she adored him.

But most of all, there was Benjamin. Her soon-to-be husband had changed over the last five months. Whereas before he had been something of a loner, and had times of bitterness or recrimination—an "odd duck," as Esther once described him—he had transformed into a calm and cheerful man, one whose smile seemed never to leave his face. His furniture business and the constant orders from the log-cabin builder had stabilized into steady work that Benjamin could handle by himself.

She remembered Eva's words when describing her marriage with Daniel: "He's everything I could hope for in a *hutband*. I try to be everything he could hope for in a wife."

That's what Abigail wanted to be—everything Benjamin could hope for in a wife.

Benjamin guided the horse to the front of the Millers' B and B, then alighted to assist his bride and his future mother-in-law from the buggy. "I'll be back in a moment," he told her, then swung back into the seat of the vehicle to park it behind the vet clinic.

John Green, her boss, stood near the door of the building. Near him was the clinic staff—the vets, the techs, the administrators. Abigail had become close to her coworkers in the last few months.

"Your big day!" John exclaimed, clasping her hands.

"Ja." She smiled at her boss. "And I couldn't be happier."

She entered the building and seated herself in the front row as the bridal party began assembling. Benjamin came in, flanked by his groomsmen, and sat next to her. He snuck his hand around hers. She twined her fingers with his.

The service started with traditional wedding hymns, and Bishop Beiler's sermon on the importance of marriage as a covenant before *Gott.*

And when at last the bishop asked her and Benjamin to rise and stand before him, Benjamin refused to let go of her hand.

"You're stuck with me now," he whispered.

She quirked a smile at him. "We're stuck with each other," she whispered back. *"Gott ist gut."*

* * * * *